The Tunnel Hoard

The Tunnel Hoard

Paul Rutherford

Whitston Publishing Company, Inc.
Albany, New York
2005

Library of Congress Control Number 2005921944

ISBN 0-87875-558-6

Printed in the United States of America

To my grandmother

Acknowledgements

I would like to thank my family, friends and co-workers for their generous time spent reading various drafts and offering their continuous encouragement. Without their feedback, this undertaking would have been more arduous and much less enjoyable.

I would like to offer a special thanks to my friend, *Times Union* coloumnist Fred LeBrun. He took an unsoliciated interest in a new writer, just for his love of the written word. His attention was a source of great motivation and inspiration for me.

Finally, I would like to thank William Greenleaf. He handed me the final keys to unlock the manuscript I was capable of producing.

It has been said that it takes a village to raise a child, sometimes that's true for writing a book. To those of you that supported me, I am forever grateful and I hope you are as proud of this offering as I am. Enjoy.

Chapter 1

World War II, Philippines 1944—Somewhere in the jungle near the mountain village of Malaybalay, Island of Mindanao, Jacob Thomas peered out from behind bamboo bars at his keepers. Morning approached as it had for the last sixteen months he'd been held captive. He pushed his long straggly hair to one side and watched Japanese soldiers scurrying about as the sun rose over the mountain. Sunlight broke through thick, jungle vines casting morning shadows over their stronghold. His nightly mental escape had come to an end and his daily living nightmare was about to begin—again.

The foul stench of rotting flesh that filled his nostrils caused him pause from the thought of another day in hell. He looked down at his ankles and the leg irons that had chaffed them raw. An aborted escape attempt by two Filipino prisoners had cost him a fierce beating and the leg irons. It had cost the Filipinos their lives. His ankles had open sores that had begun to fester. The pain was bearable—for now. He knew nothing healed here on its own. The heat and humidity were an incubator for infection. The clock was ticking on his mortality in this place of no hope and no mercy.

Turning to see if the other prisoners were starting to stir, he noticed Jesse Hamilton sleeping a few feet away. Now just a shell of the man he knew, his face was drawn and his eyes were sunken. When they first met he weighed at least two hundred pounds; today he might weigh one-fifty. He'd been struck in the head with rifle butts so many times, that he frequently lost his balance and fell down a lot. Jacob considered himself lucky he had no mirror to assess his failing condition as he began to stagger to his feet using the wall for balance. His muscles were constantly stiff and his infected ankles caused him to bristle from the shackles rubbing against his raw skin.

Suddenly, the bamboo bars were flung open and two Japanese soldiers stormed the cave, kicking and yelling at those prisoners who were still not moving. Jacob's internal clock had awakened him in time to escape this early morning chaos. He watched as his fellow captives were shocked back to their senses. In the early days of their capture, some of the prisoners would wake the others when they saw the guards approaching. Now the extra few minutes of peace that sleep brought seemed more important than an early warning.

The soldiers led them into a clearing at the foot of the mountain. There they sat in a circle, in the middle of the four-thatched roof huts and half-dozen tents that made up the camp, and fed breakfast, a bowl of fish stew-like gruel and a hand full of rice. Just the smell still turned Jacob's stomach, but he knew if he didn't eat there would be no chance of ever getting out alive. He wolfed down the food, devouring every morsel, knowing it would be all he'd see until the next morning.

After watching Jesse Hamilton, seated next to him, finish his meager meal, he turned his attention to the entrance of the large cave they had been digging for the last sixteen months. It had become his home ever since it was big enough for the two Americans and fourteen Filipino captives to lie side by side. There were now only nine Filipino prisoners left, two died from malaria, two others were shot trying to escape and one was buried in a cave-in. The cavern was now twelve-feet wide at the entrance and widened out to over twenty-feet inside. It was over a hundred and fifty-feet deep with a ten-foot clearance. The walls and ceiling were reinforced with thick bamboo logs harvested from the surrounding jungle.

Jacob inspected his leg shackles and the deteriorating condition of his infected ankles as he observed several Japanese soldiers carrying explosives. It was necessary to set

2

charges in order to loosen the hard rock enough for them to dig. A loud blast followed the soldiers from the cave. That was the signal that a long days' work was about to begin.

The guards motioned the prisoners toward the entrance, where they grabbed picks and sledgehammers. Dust from the explosion poured out as they entered, having to push aside the thick jungle foliage that had grown down over the opening. This was the most dangerous time. The severity of the blast could have easily weakened the reinforced walls and brought thousands of tons of earth down on top of them. Lately, Jacob thought that might not be such a bad thing.

He could barely see; his eyes burning from the rock dust. He held what little shirt he had left over his mouth and nose while making his way toward the rear of the tunnel. Two soldiers wearing dust masks lit torches that lined the walls, revealing a pile of fresh rock that had been excavated from the explosion. Jacob and Jesse headed to the back wall to start digging. Several of the other prisoners lined up next to them and began swinging their assorted tools. The remaining captives loaded sacks and carried them from the cave. Jacob worked at a slow deliberate pace that the heat, lack of air and his deteriorating physical condition demanded—any harder would be suicide.

"Jake, how do I look?" Jesse asked.

"You look fine," he lied.

"I'm not feelin' so good today."

"Me either Jesse, must be the heat."

"Yeah, that's probably it," Jesse replied, managing a slight grin. "Why you think we're still digging this godforsaken cave anyway?"

"I don't know; it doesn't make any sense. The Japs like tunnels, but not something this big. It's in the middle of this bug-infested jungle at the foot of this mountain. I would think they'd want to be on higher ground, not down here."

"I think they're gonna hide something, Jake. Do you think?"

"I don't know, but if it gets any bigger, they could hide the whole damn Japanese army here."

"I'm just not feelin' too good."

"I know, Jesse, I know," Jacob consoled him, knowing that he was easily confused and frequently lost track of their conversations.

"You think were ever gonna git outta here?" Jesse asked.

Before Jacob could answer, a hard, rifle butt strike to the kidneys caused Jesse to groan as he fell to his knees. The deliverer was yelling something in Japanese. Jacob had reached down to help when a sharp blow between his shoulder blades caused him to lose his grip, knocking them both to the ground. He struggled to his feet while he watched Jesse try and regain his senses. He knew he couldn't help. The soldier stood over Jesse and readied to strike again. He continued to shout while gesturing him to rise.

Jacob wanted to save him, but knew that would be signing his death warrant—still, he felt compelled to do something. He reached down for his pick in anticipation of the soldier delivering what Jacob was sure to be a deathblow. The other guard was following the rock carrying prisoners toward the entrance, not able to see Jacob slowly position the tool to attack. The scene seemed to stun the Filipinos working on the wall; Jacob knew once he struck their fates were sealed.

His mind was tormented; was it better to end this misery like a man or waste away at the hands of these devils? Taking one of them out with him would have to be enough to justify ending his life and that of his fellow prisoners. His promise to Sarah momentarily delayed his actions, but every man had a breaking point and he had reached his.

He was about to strike when a loud yell caused him to hesitate. The soldier standing over Jesse lowered his rifle, quickly spinning toward the sound and bellowing his response, as Jacob lowered his pick. He could see the relieved look of the other prisoners. He helped Jesse to his feet, while the conversation continued to hold their guard's attention. Jesse held his back and steadied himself; his eyes conveyed his gratitude.

The soldier finally turned to the prisoners on the wall and motioned them to exit the cave. Jesse leaned against Jacob as they headed toward the entrance. Once outside, they were directed to leave their tools and assume a seated position in the middle of the camp.

"What's going on Jake?" Jesse whispered, rubbing his back.

"I don't know; this is the first time we ever stopped digging without having to blast more rock."

"Something is goin' on. Look at the way they are all scrambling around to straighten up the camp."

"Yeah, it seems a little more hectic than usual."

From the far end of the camp a high-ranking Japanese officer, surrounded by a half-dozen heavily armed soldiers, emerged. He was a big man, with a large bull-like neck and short, closely cropped, hair. One thick hand rested on his revolver and the other on the carved ivory handle of his long sword, as he walked toward the prisoners. Jacob watched his barrel chest heave from the heat and exertion. Carried closer by two thick legs, a small figure hidden by his hulk appeared at his side. It was a young boy, no more than eight years old; he looked Filipino to Jacob, but could have been half-Japanese.

"What the hell's a kid doing in the middle of the jungle?" Jesse asked, watching the entourage get closer.

"Shhhhh, keep quiet."

"Man, he looks like a mean one."

"Quiet." Jacob warned him again, as a soldier standing at attention caught his eye.

Jesse quieted himself, as the group reached the prisoners. The dozen soldiers that made up the jungle encampment stood at attention; their eyes locked on the approaching visitors. Jacob watched from down cast eyes while the soldier in-charge of the camp stepped forward to greet his guest. They exchanged the standard salutes and bows followed by an order from the officer. The commander turned and repeated the directive and quickly several soldiers moved to hustle the prisoners to their feet. Jacob struggled to rise before he and the others were positioned in a straight line. The Americans stood out among the Filipinos; they were at least six-inches taller and much broader, although what was left of their threadbare clothes hung on their emaciated frames.

The Japanese officer approached the line of prisoners and slowly eyed each one he passed. The rest of his group followed behind while the young boy clutched his waistband. The prisoners kept their eyes pointed toward the ground; they knew not to make eye contact with any of their keepers. Jacob looked the officer in the chest. The officer stopped and carefully inspected him from the head to toe. Placing a thick hand under Jacob's chin, he slowly lifted his head until they were eye to eye. His touch was firm but gentle, not exactly what Jacob had been used to from this cruel enemy. Removing his hand, he turned and headed toward the cave.

The prisoners were motioned to the ground while the small entourage, accompanied by the commander of the camp, followed him toward the labor of their misery. The group disappeared through the opening, leaving the remaining guards to stand watch over the prisoners. It was obvious to Jacob that this was a man of great importance. No one was talking, not even his keepers as the minutes ticked by.

Finally emerging, the Japanese officer was very animated, directing the camp commander's attention to the rocky slope leading up to entrance and the overgrown jungle road that connected the camp to the mountain passage and civilization. The commander nodded and bowed in response to the verbal barrage being heaped upon him.

The young child stood quietly, not seeming to Jacob to be the least bit intimidated by the situation or his surroundings. The officer looked toward him and the rest of the prisoners, becoming more vocal as he waved his arm and pointed a stubby finger, while shouting at the camp leader. He punctuated his directions with a hard stab of his thick digit into the chest of the much smaller man. The force of the blow caused him to stumble back, while still acknowledging his superior's directives.

Having issued his instructions, the large officer quickly turned and headed back toward a hut at the far end of the camp while the commander relayed orders to the soldiers guarding the prisoners. Jacob and the others were rousted to their feet as the officer, with the boy clinging to his side, and his personal guards passed by them. The sound of clanging leg irons caused the officer to pause. He then offered more direction to the bewildered camp commander, who obediently nodded in agreement. He then directed an order to one of the soldiers closest to the prisoners, who quickly reached for a rusty key hanging from his belt. The guard moved toward Jacob, where he knelt and unlocked the metal leg restraints. The relief was unexplainable. For the first time in months he could walk without the friction of metal against his raw skin. The other prisoners had their chains removed and were hustled back to work. Jacob realized that the arrival of the officer had instilled a sense of urgency. Whatever was going to happen to him was now not far off.

~ ~ ~

Chapter 2

Present Day—It was late fall in upstate New York. The leaves were all but gone and a clear sky ushered in a brisk wind. Connor Mason, sleeping face down on his bed, was startled by a sudden jolt to his back. He didn't move, feeling two small hands dig into his tight muscles and two bare legs lock their knees tightly against his sides. The hands moved from his neck to his bare shoulders. They were strong, causing him to flinch. Finally he opened one eye as he turned his head until he heard his neck crack.

"Are we having fun?" he asked, his morning voice more muffled by the sheet that surrounded his face and the weight of the hands pressing him into the mattress.

"I thought you might be a little stiff after yesterday's work out," said a chipper-sounding woman's voice.

"Well, I am a little, thank you very much." A slight smile appeared on his face. "What time is it and what are you doing here?"

"It's 7:00 a.m. and I had this uncontrollable urge to watch *Sports Center*. Sooo, since I know you never lock your door and your TV is on twenty-four hours a day, I figured I wouldn't wake you."

"So why did you wake me?" He pushed up from the bed.

"Your TV was off and since I was here anyway, I thought you might like to fuck me," she replied playfully, rolling off next to him.

"What would ever make you think that, Maggie?" He

was not able to hide his widening grin when he turned over to the view of her naked body.

"Well, if you're not interested, I guess I can go find someone who is." She started a mock escape, slowly sliding down toward the foot of his king-size bed.

"I didn't say I wasn't interested. I was just inquiring as to your mental state when you said you thought I might like to fuck you," he returned, pulling her towards him.

Gazing at her five-foot nothing figure, she was the perfect little hard body, one hundred and five pounds of shredded muscle, with all the right curves. Her short blonde hair and soft brown eyes were in flawless contrast to her tanned skin and large pearl white teeth. As he kissed her full pouty lips, Maggie Andrews seemed to him like the complete package— almost.

Connor had met Maggie six months ago at Pauley Simms' Boxing Club. Pauley's was a yuppie boxing gym where housewives, businessmen, novices, wannabes, and professional fighters came to train. Pauley Simms was an ex-professional fighter, who after an 11-1 pro record, decided that it was safer to manage than get his own brains scrambled in the ring. Unfortunately, most boxers had little money to pay a trainer, so Pauley developed a non-contact program in order to pay the bills while waiting for the next Champion to walk through the door.

Connor's father, Guy, had been taking him to Pauley's since he was ten years old. Guy Mason and Pauley were friends and he frequently invested in some of his more promising fighters. Connor loved the place and he loved to box, but his Dad and Pauley kept him from going any further than the Novice Heavyweight Golden Gloves Championship he had won six years ago.

He was working out on the heavy bag and talking to other fighters the first day Maggie walked through the door. She was dressed in black short shorts, her exquisitely rounded bottom just slightly exposed, and a tight fitting white crop top. She turned every head in the place as she glided across the floor toward Pauley. After speaking a few minutes, she nodded, and he took out some cloth wraps from the large gray metal cabinet behind his desk and started wrapping her small hands. He fitted her with a pair of boxing gloves, fastening them with a Velcro strap. She then bounced over to join a non-contact class that was about to begin.

Connor watched her the entire 45-minute session. She was a focused bundle of energy attacking every station as if she was fighting for her life. Speed bag, heavy bag, shadow box, jump rope, pads; she worked the full three minutes at each discipline, drank some water, toweled off during the one-minute break and at the sound of the buzzer was back at it. Her intensity never dropped.   He couldn't help but be impressed.

At the end of class, Maggie climbed into the ring with the other participants to do some abdominal work. She placed her towel on the floor and lay on top of it. Connor climbed in from the other side and settled next to her. She turned and gave him a smile. He wasn't sure, but he had to imagine she noticed him earlier. At six-foot two with light red hair and intense blue eyes, he definitely stood out among the shorter ethnic fighters in the gym. When they started doing crunches, he couldn't take his eyes off her ripped mid-section.

He asked how she liked the class and she said she liked it fine, even more now that he was talking to her. Although anything but shy, that gave him the courage to suggest they get something to eat after they showered. She said she'd love to. They went to the diner down the street and hit it off immediately. She went home with him that night and they had sex on his living room floor. Maggie didn't make love—she had sex. Making love was too personal, too confining, she had told him, and she wasn't interested in a relationship. She liked her freedom, the freedom to choose her lovers or leave them when it wasn't right. It felt right to Connor—for now. That was six months ago; he sensed a connection with her and subconsciously he needed to know why.

Lifting the sheet, he invited her naked body next to his. He drew her closer. Her small frame seemed to disappear in his arms. She rolled on her back and pulled him on top as her legs parted allowing him to enter. Morning sex with Maggie didn't require much foreplay; she always seemed ready. Connor could sense her arousal when he reached down to guide himself inside. He loved hearing the sigh she gasped. Except for her hands, that barely reached the top of his wide shoulders and her legs that wrapped tightly behind his knees, she was invisible under his large frame. He totally engulfed her and he liked making her feel warm and safe. For the next several minutes the outside world ceased to exist; his demons were held at bay while they shared this peaceful bliss.

As their bodies melted together, Connor could feel Maggie's back begin to arch, alerting him to her impending climax. He placed both hands under her to angle her closer while he quickened his pace. Her body convulsed under him hastening his own surrender. He squeezed her tightly, rocked by an intense wave of orgasm. He lay on top of her not moving for over a minute, and then rolled off, feeling completely spent. She quickly curled up next to him and buried her head in his chest. They wrapped their arms around each other and drifted off to sleep.

Almost three hours later, a loud knock awakened him to the reality of the day. Connor slowly started to get up, still sore from yesterday's workout, when Maggie bounced to her feet and bounded off the end of the bed.

"I'll get it," she yelled.

"Maggie, how about some clothes or at least a towel," he shouted, watching her naked behind disappear. "Not that anyone would mind that outfit." He smiled, knowing she was too far down the hall to hear.

"Don't worry," she called back, "I'll grab a towel. I wouldn't want to scare any of your neighbors."

~ ~ ~

The man at the door paced impatiently while he knocked again and yelled out Connor's name, hoping his familiar voice would encourage a more rapid response. Before he could knock again, the door flew open and a tanned,

11

blonde, naked pixie with a towel draped around her neck greeted him.

"Hi, Alex," she said, as he stood stunned. "Connor's in the bedroom, go on in."

He watched her turn and head down the hallway, before following her inside. No longer reeling from his reception; he admired the view as she veered into the bathroom.

"Connor, you there?" he announced, walking toward the open bedroom door.

"Yeah, I'm here," replied the raspy morning voice.

~ ~ ~

Connor, having won the struggle to get to his feet, was searching for underwear in his dresser. As he pulled on a pair of black boxers, he couldn't help notice his changing physique in the mirror. His stomach, that had always carried a few extra pounds, was actually starting to show signs of a six-pack. His weight lifting and diet were starting to pay off thanks to Maggie's influence. He felt stronger and was starting to look pretty good. Some consolation, he thought for what he'd been going through the past year.

"Hey, did you forget we had an appointment with the bank this morning?" Alex scolded. Alex Litowski was Connor's best friend and business partner. They had been friends since grade school and almost inseparable—except for the last six months.

"God, Alex, I completely forgot." He shook his head as he slowly turned. "What the fuck happened to your nose?" he blurted out, spying the white bandage and his slightly black eyes.

"Bumped into a door knob," Alex returned, casting his eyes away.

"Yeah, you bumped into a doorknob named who?" Connor inquired, concerned for his friend's welfare.

Before Alex could answer, Maggie came swaggering back into the bedroom. She had a towel wrapped around her waist displaying all her wares from her pierced navel up. The room fell silent while both men watched her gather up her t-shirt and sweats from the floor near the foot of the bed. She pulled the t-shirt over her head and dropping the towel, pulled on her navy sweat pants. She then slipped her small bare feet into a pair of unlaced running shoes.

"Gotta go," she said, walking over to Connor, and grabbing the back of his neck, planted a long kiss on his lips. "See you later, Alex." She released Connor and headed toward the front door where she donned a short denim jacket that was lying on a chair.

"Am I going to see you later?" Connor shouted, hearing the front door unlock.

"We'll see what the day brings, hon," she yelled back, as he listened to the door shut behind her.

"Connor!" Alex said loudly. "We are in a world of hurt my friend and we've got to do something real soon."

"I know, I know." He searched for socks in the second drawer.

"Well, I don't think you do, or you just don't want to face it," Alex railed. "Let me recap the situation for you. We've got four properties under contract we need to close on by Friday, not to mention material and payroll money. The crews are finishing up the last two houses and we need projects for them or they'll be working for our competitors by next week.

"The bank appointment you decided to blow off this morning was to increase our line of credit. Without it we might as well shut the door. We need a hundred thousand dollars to cover our obligations this month and we only have around twenty! All our money is tied up in inventory we can't seem to sell. If the renovation business in downtown gets any more crowded, it may not matter.

"Couple that with the fact that you've had your head up your ass, or should I say up her ass, for the last six months hasn't helped. Man, you've got to wake up and smell the coffee," he pleaded. "I know not knowing about your Dad has got you messed up, but life goes on. We. . . ."

"Okay!" Connor snapped, cutting him off. "I get the

13

picture." He turned to face Alex and leaned back against the dresser. He ran his hands through his red hair and behind his neck while he contemplated a solution. "How many houses in inventory do we have completed and ready for sale?"

"Twelve."

"How many of them are under contract for sale?"

"Two."

"What's our monthly cost of carrying the inventory?"

"It's around six thousand a month."

"What's our equity position in the properties not under contract?"

"Maybe three-hundred thousand across the whole lot."

"Alright, let's get the other ten rented out and stop the bleeding," Connor suggested; his mind now focused. "Once they're rented, we'll refinance them and pull out some cash. That should keep us going for at least ninety days. I'll start pulling the paperwork together this afternoon."

"That's a good medium term solution. But we need the money now! It'll take at least sixty days or more to refinance those properties."

"I know. I'll get the short term money to keep us going till the refinances are complete," Connor reassured him.

"Where?"

"Don't ask."

That ended the discussion and he knew Alex was not one to press. Connor observed him breathe a sigh of relief. The problem appeared to have a satisfactory solution—for now.

Connor handled the financing and money issues. Alex took care of the day-to-day operations and construction. They had been purchasing and renovating houses in downtown for just over two years. Connor's background in finance and his time spent working in the family mortgage business coupled with Alex's real estate and construction skills seemed a perfect match. They started buying in tougher downtown neighbor-hoods, where most wouldn't invest.

Connor had asked his father to back their first few ren-

14

ovations. They had approached him with the project and asked his advice on whether to venture into fringe neighborhoods, not far from drug and crime war zones, or stay in suburban areas where it was a more competitive, but safer market. He said it was their decision, but he was once told, in order to make money—"You must be daring when others are afraid and smart when others are greedy." They took this passed down advice to heart and began buying rundown urban properties, refurbishing them and marketing to black inner-city renters through urban radio, flyers and house signs.

In the first year they sold over twenty houses, carving out a nice little niche business in an untapped area. The next year competition followed them in. People who wanted a piece of the profitable market they pioneered were driving up property prices. The second year of operation found higher acquisition costs and an already limited purchaser base being diluted. Profit margins were shrinking and qualified buyers were getting harder to find, resulting in higher carrying costs due to longer time on market. That, coupled with having to use their first year's profit and payroll tax withholdings to keep the business afloat, left them staring in the face of a potential IRS problem. They had the daring part down he thought; it was the smart part they were having trouble with.

Connor knew mortgaging the inventory was only a band-aid. It bought them time—time for what he wondered. Having settled the crisis for now, he redirected his original question back at Alex.

"So what happened to the nose? No bullshit, Alex."

"I was boxing down at Pauley's and I got popped and it broke. No big deal."

"Alex, you do non-contact boxing, now what happened?" Connor shot back.

"Why does it matter?"

"Maybe it doesn't. So just tell me who did it and I'll decide?"

"Don't you have enough to do without worrying about my nose? You've got to find a hundred thousand dollars by the end of the week," Alex countered. "Not to mention your own personal problems."

"My own personal problems," Connor mocked, his irritation mounting.

"Yeah, your Dad's missing and you've been sleeping with a whack job, who has you so turned around that you can't concentrate on anything important for more than a few minutes. She just pops in and out whenever she wants. No calls, no notice. You don't date; you just fuck—when she feels like it!"

"And why is that different than any other woman?"

"Let me finish, please. How about Susan? Your fiancée—remember her? Who's due back from England—when—next month? How are you going to handle it when Maggie comes waltzing in and tells her not to worry, it's not serious, we just sleep together."

"I'll jump off that bridge when I get to it, Alex. It's my problem."

"Well, the nose is my problem," Alex blurted out. He turned and headed toward the living room.

"What problem?" Connor said, seizing the opening and following him. "I thought you said it was no big deal, now it's a problem."

"Yes, it's my problem. You don't need to deal with this; you've got enough on your plate already. We're not in high school. You don't have to fight my battles."

"You're right, Alex, we're not in high school anymore, so quit acting like it and tell me how you got your nose broke," he snapped, totally focused on getting an answer.

~ ~ ~

Alex sat on the living room couch with his head in his hands. He knew Connor was like a pit bull, when he got hold of something, he wouldn't let go. He was tired of fending him off; if he told, he still might be able to talk some sense into him. The business was in trouble and this was no time to get sidetracked.

16

"Sid Vicious," he said, his eyes directed toward the floor.

"Sid Who?"

"Sid Vicious."

"Who the hell is Sid Vicious?"

"I forgot that you haven't been to Pauley's in the last few months," Alex remembered, straightening up. "His real name is Chris Duggan, one of Frank Handrahan's Australian imports. Frank's been bringing him up here to spar with some of Pauley's fighters. They call him Sid because he's from Sidney. Some of the guys named him 'Sid Vicious' because he's a nasty, bad ass, S.O.B. This guy is bad news Connor; we don't need him in our lives. Let it go, the nose will heal, it's over," Alex pleaded.

"How'd you end up tangling with this guy?" His voice was suddenly calm and his deep blue eyes glared at Alex like he could see right through him.

Alex knew that look and the measured tone. It unnerved him now, like it did others when they were in high school. Connor hated bullies; they were both sophomores when a senior on the football team thought it would be funny to trip Alex in the cafeteria. He put out his foot when Alex walked by and he went flying, tray and all. Everyone was laughing while he lay on the floor covered with food. He remembered being so embarrassed that he just wanted to cry.

He watched from the cafeteria floor as Connor got up and slowly walked over to the senior, who immediately · jumped up from the table. He was at least five inches taller and twenty-five pounds heavier than Connor, who seemed locked in on the aggressor's eyes. He approached to within six inches of the larger boy's nose, insisting that he apologize and help clean up the mess. He was calm, very calm, scary calm. The whole cafeteria fell silent as all eyes were frozen on them.

The senior, obviously deciding he was not going to be "faced" by an under-classman, stepped back and threw a right hand toward Connor's chest. Connor slipped under the punch to his left, a maneuver Alex knew he'd practiced a thousand times at Pauley's. Popping up, he fired a left hand to the exposed rib cage of the larger boy, who grimaced with pain, while Connor recoiled and threw a hard-left hook that connected to the temple, followed by a straight right hand to the chin. It had started and ended before anyone could move. A lighting-fast three-punch combination had the upper-classman on the seat of his pants in a daze. That was the first and last high school fight Connor ever had.

Alex knew the look, and it made him scared, not for himself but for his friend. This wasn't high school and it wasn't a clumsy football player they were dealing with. This was a professional fighter, with a real bad attitude. He also knew that all he could do was tell the story and what happened—happened.

"Alright, Con," Alex conceded. "I stopped into Pauley's to grab a workout and I see Karen and Jill talking to this character. You know them, they're realtors, Jill's a small brunette, kinda cute—Karen's taller with long black hair."

Connor nodded, seeming to hang on his every word.

"Well, they spy me and Karen hurries over. She asks if I can get this asshole away from Jill. I guess he's hitting on her and being real crude. So I go over, excuse myself and say I need to talk to her about a real estate transaction before class. The guy tells me to bugger off; he's talking to the Sheila. I bust on him a little, telling him her name's not Sheila and I really need to speak with her. He tells me to get lost and he's not going to tell me again. Jill tries to walk away and he grabs her by the arm.

"I can see that she's really scared. So I step in between them and tell the guy to let her go. He lets go of her arm and turns his shoulder like he's going to walk away. I look over at Jill and he winds up and sucker punches me in the nose.

"The next thing I know I'm flat on my back, blood all over my face, with Pauley and the girls standing over me. The girls drive me to the emergency room, where they tell me my nose is broken. They bandage the nose, give me some painkillers and send me home."

"That's it?" Connor questioned.

"That's it."

"What the hell did Pauley say?"

"You know Pauley, Con. He doesn't want any trouble and I don't want to cause him any. He asked me what happened and if I was all right. I told him that it was a misunderstanding and I'd be fine. I could see him laying into Handrahan and that animal while the girls helped me out of the gym. But we both know it's not going anywhere. Pauley can't afford bad publicity; he's just hanging on as it is. Shit happens. I'll just stay away from Pauley's when that idiot is there. We have to forget about it, we've got more important things to deal with right now."

"You're right," Connor agreed. "We have got important things to take care of."

Alex was surprised and relieved that Connor seemed willing to let this go. Maybe he was wrong about Maggie and she was having a positive effect on him.

"I'll meet you at the office later, Alex. I'm going to finish getting dressed and start getting the paperwork for the refinances in order."

"All right, Con. I'm going to check on the crew on Third Street—by the way don't forget the money, we'll need it by the end of the week for the closings," he said, as he made his way toward the door.

"I got it covered, Bud," Connor replied, watching him leave.

Connor went back into the bedroom and donned a black t-shirt and jeans. He threw on a pair of blue and white cross trainers, grabbed his leather jacket and baseball cap and headed out the door. Climbing into his black Ford Explorer, he picked up his cell phone and dialed Capital Rehab. Nancy Dorsey, his office manager answered.

"Hi, Nance, it's Connor. Do me a favor and pull the deeds together for all completed rehabs in downtown that are not under contract and order full residential appraisals on them. Thanks a lot. By the way, if anyone's looking for me I'll be on the cell. I've got something important to take care of."

19

He placed the phone back in its cradle and drove off in the direction of Pauley's Gym.

~ ~ ~

Chapter 3

The arrival of the large officer and his entourage had created quite a stir. Jacob noticed his captors were much more intent on getting the maximum labor out of the prisoners. It was apparent from the camp commander's actions they were behind schedule, and that had the entire camp on edge.

As the workday ended and the prisoners were led back to the cave, Jacob was still feeling the euphoria of no longer wearing his leg shackles. He settled in next to Jesse Hamilton, who had already surrendered to a coma-like sleep. He rested his head against the rock wall and allowed his mind to drift back to how this horror began.

It was March 1942; he was a corporal and head communications officer for Major General Jonathan Wainwright, field commander of the allied forces, now fighting for their lives in Bataan on the island of Luzon. He had just gotten word that Supreme Commander General Douglas MacArthur was indeed abandoning the fight in the Philippines. MacArthur, it was rumored, was now preoccupied with a personal venture that had erased his love of duty and replaced it with one of self-preservation. Twenty thousand fighting men were about to be left to the mercy of the Japanese army. Surrender was inevitable. The December 1941 surprise attack on Pearl Harbor had left the American air force in ruins, leaving no hope for air support or reinforcements as the Japanese moved quickly on the Philippine capital of Manila.

General Wainwright had originally planned to delay the invasion at the beach and then fall back toward Bataan, where he would await help. But the rapid advancement of the enemy had taken the allied forces by surprise and left them ill prepared to blunt their arrival on Philippine soil. On Christmas Eve 1941, they landed to token resistance on the beachhead and nine days later took control of Manila.

Wainwright, under direction from MacArthur, who was safely tucked away on the fortified island of Corregidor, ordered the troops to fall back to Bataan. They were not prepared for an early retreat and had to leave most of their supplies behind. After the first week they were reduced to half-rations. By the third, the front line troops were receiving less than one-third their normal allotment. The 26th Cavalry was forced to shoot and eat their horses. The allied army was starving; food, not fighting became their number one priority. Chaos reigned as the troops realized their leaders had abandoned them and there would be no reinforcements and no escape.

Jacob knew they were in a hopeless situation and a POW camp was not the place to wait out the war. The reports he relayed to Wainwright from the Philippine underground depicting the cruelty and inhumanity of the Japanese in Manila reinforced his resolve to not fall into the hands of this merciless enemy. He had reasons, desperate reasons to escape that fate.

The only son of an Indiana wheat farmer, he had a young wife, Sarah, who was pregnant with their second child when he left. His aging parents were depending on him to take over the farm that had been in the Thomas family for four generations. He had responsibilities beyond those to his country. How would they survive if he didn't make it back? He thought back to holding Sarah the day he left and how small she felt. He could still remember the faint smell of her perfume, as he looked into those emerald green eyes that had melted his heart so many times. He told her he'd come back. Wiping the tears from her cheek, he smiled when she made him promise. He stood beside her at the train station while his father took their picture, him in uniform and her in a pale yellow sundress. He could still recall the cotton fabric of that dress and the soft touch of her skin. He hadn't felt anything soft in a very long time. The breeze lifted the dark hair from her face while she waved when the train carried him out of sight. He had to get back to her. He had a promise to keep.

By April 1942, General Wainwright was preparing to leave for the island of Corregidor and seemed to be paying little attention to his immediate surroundings. The fate of the men under his command was sealed and there was little else he could do but evade his own capture. By late spring of 1942 the word came down from MacArthur to surrender to the Japanese.

Jacob knew surrender was not an option. He and several enlisted men joined Colonel Russell Volckman, who had decided to ignore MacArthur's orders and led the men into the mountains north of Bataan. Once there, they made contact with the Philippine underground and began organizing an anti-Japanese guerilla army. They became the eyes and ears of the allied forces, tracking enemy movements and relaying that information to MacArthur, who had left Corregidor and was now stationed in Australia.

In less than six months, Colonel Volckman had established a large underground army in the mountains of Luzon. Realizing the Philippines was a large archipelago with hundreds of islands, he relayed to Jacob and the others that an appropriate strategy would be to form resistance groups on several of the larger islands. With the majority of the Japanese army concentrated in Luzon, it was doubtful these areas would command little more than token forces. A well-organized militia could prove vital to the liberation of the entire Philippines, not just the main island.

Jacob and a dozen guerillas, among them two Americans, Privates Joseph Merducci and Jesse Hamilton, were dispatched to Mindanao, the southern most and largest island. Their mission was to establish a camp, set up a line of communications and prepare a local fighting force to assist in taking back the country upon MacArthur's return. Jacob had a different objective, a simple one, get as far away from the enemy as possible and someday get home to Sarah and his family.

They had left the Japanese infested island of Luzon by boat late at night. Jose Santiago, a Filipino fisherman, captained the small boat. Jose was originally from the port city of Davo in Mindanao and had extensive knowledge of the surrounding waters and safe harbors. He was a trusted member of the underground and was familiar with the patrol patterns of the Japanese.

They traveled close to shore and avoided open seas. It would take them almost three weeks to reach their destination. The first week was tense, but the further they traveled the more it seemed to Jacob like they were escaping the war. The water was turquoise blue and the land a beautiful backdrop of beaches and palm trees. The fishing they did on route helped to push the conflict further from reality. Finally with their island destination in sight, he was able to relax. So far there was no sign of the enemy.

Privates Merducci and Hamilton were acting like there was no war at all. Jacob knew that compared to where they were from, the Philippines wasn't all that bad. Merducci had grown up in the Hell's Kitchen section of New York City. The son of an Italian immigrant, he had worked with his father hauling block ice up long flights of stairs to high-rise tenements. He watched his father suffer a heart attack and die in his arms. He swore never to haul ice again. When the war broke out he enlisted. Jesse Hamilton was a black man who worked in a slaughterhouse on the south side of Chicago. Cows were led into his pen where their heads were locked in place. He would stand over them, straddling the enclosure, and deliver a deathblow with his sledgehammer. He had found it far easier to kill a human enemy than a defenseless animal. Unlike Jacob, they seemed in no hurry to get back home.

As the small boat rounded the point and entered the Bay of Macajalar, near the port city of Cagayan De Oro, Jacob came face to face with a harsh reminder of his situation. A heavily armed Japanese patrol boat was bearing down on them. The three Americans quickly headed for the cover of the small wheelhouse. They knelt down below the open windows and prayed the Japanese vessel would pass. Jose started to angle the boat toward land. Jacob knew they'd need to be closer than the two hundred yards that separated them from the shoreline in order to have a fighting chance for survival. As he peered out of the small window of the wheelhouse he saw the remaining Filipino guerillas acting like they were just out for a days fishing. They waved and smiled, while the Japanese patrol sped past, no more than thirty yards away.

For the moment he thought the danger had passed, but the moment was all too brief. The boat suddenly came about and started quickly closing on them. Jose turned and headed straight for shore. Jacob doubted the Japanese would take prisoners this far south. Chances were they'd be executed if they stopped. If they opened fire, they'd be sitting ducks for her big deck gun. Reaching shore appeared their only option and it was still seventy-five yards away.

Suddenly a warning shot sailed over the bow and exploded in the water. A voice over a loud speaker yelled instructions in Japanese. He didn't have to speak the language to know they were being ordered to stop. Two panicked guerillas jumped in the water and started swimming for shore. Jacob watched the commotion outside as he sensed his companions were beginning to get restless. Another round from the large deck gun landed less than 10 yards in front of the boat. The chase was over; Jacob knew there would be no more warnings and no escape. He heard Jose cut the engine and they all would now have to await their fate.

Without warning Merducci bolted from the wheelhouse and dove over the side, swimming franticly toward shore. Jacob watched stunned when the Japanese vessel roared past the boat and Merducci, leaving both rocking in her wake. The patrol boat was bearing down on the two Filipino guerillas, who had just gotten close enough to land to now be running out of the water. A loud blast of machine gun fire left their bodies surrounded by a pool of red washing up on the shoreline.

Merducci, having witnessed the fate of the Filipinos, turned and headed back toward the boat. He was almost there when the Japanese came up behind him. Jacob was sure that from the sound of her engines, Merducci knew they were right on top of him when he turned and put his hands in the air. They maneuvered up along side and two Japanese soldiers pulled him from the water. Once on board, he was struck in the face with a rifle butt. He fell to his knees where he was forced to his stomach and his hands were tied behind his back.

Jacob had to plead with Jesse to not start firing; knowing if he did, there would be no chance. If they didn't resist, they might survive and he still might get home. The guerillas were sitting on the deck with their hands on their heads as the patrol boat pulled along side.

Jacob and Jesse walked out of the wheelhouse with their hands in the air and joined the others. Two Japanese soldiers boarded, while the big deck gun and two large machine guns were manned and pointed at the sitting prisoners. Another half-dozen soldiers in clear view kept their rifles ready. The two soldiers searched the small boat and quickly rounded up a cache of weapons. The arms were transferred to the patrol boat and the rest of the invaders came aboard. With silent precision they knocked the guerillas to their sides and rolled them on their stomachs. Their hands were tied behind their backs and they were searched for weapons. They then lifted the frightened prisoners into a seated position facing the hostile vessel.

The Japanese captain appeared on deck. He uttered a command and two soldiers lifted Merducci to his feet while another forced a thick piece of bamboo into his mouth and tied it on either side around his head. Jacob could see the terror in his eyes, as his teeth bit down on the bamboo bridle and blood from the rifle blow streamed from his forehead. The two soldiers brought him forward to the side of the boat and pinned him against it so hard that it looked like he might fall overboard.

The captain walked toward him and drew a razor sharp sword from his waistband. A third soldier stood behind Merducci and fastened a bayonet to his rifle and placed it on his back. A nod from his superior and he began to slowly drive the blade into Merducci's kidney. The pain was so intense that he couldn't scream or cry; all he could do was bite down on the bamboo stick. Jacob and the others watched in horror as he lifted his head and arched his back trying to escape the excruciating intrusion. At that moment, the captain with one clean surgical motion separated Merducci from his body. His head fell into the water and the soldiers tossed his remaining torso over the side.

Jacob instantly felt himself retreating into a state of shock. It was an event all too horrible for him to deal with. The lesson, however, was not yet over. The captain motioned for his soldiers to bring the prisoners on board. He then gave another command and Jose was separated from the others. He began shaking and his legs got unsteady. He fell to his knees, but was quickly lifted to his feet by soldiers on either side of him. A soldier on board the Japanese boat handed a gasoline container over the side to another on the fishing boat, who quickly poured the combustible liquid over entire deck.

Aboard the patrol boat, Jacob heard Jose starting to cry. He knew his fate was sealed, for this was an enemy without compassion. The captain barked another order and the prisoners were lined up so they would have a clear view. Jacob tried to look away, but a Japanese soldier righted his head. It didn't matter, because his brain no longer seemed to be processing this inhumanity.

The two soldiers holding Jose tore the shirt from his body. The third soldier put down the gasoline container and withdrew a knife from his belt. One of the men holding Jose's arms grabbed him by the hair and pulled his head back. The soldier with the knife looked up at the patrol boat commander who gave him a quick nod. He then placed the knife on Jose's stomach about six inches left of and one inch below his navel. With one violent stroke he opened his belly and watched Jose's insides came falling out. The captors released their grip and he fell to the deck. Horrible moans could be heard, as he lay sprawled, writhing in pain.

The soldiers climbed back aboard the patrol boat while another pointed a flare gun toward the gasoline soaked vessel.

He fired and the boat burst into flames. Screams were the last sounds heard as they sped away from the watery bonfire and headed to port. The lesson was clear; try to escape, you die; disobey an order; you die.

From that point on everything in Jacob's mind was unclear. The shock of seeing such violent treatment of men he knew left him in a self-induced daze. He remembered bits and pieces of being taken off the boat and spending several days in a makeshift stockade. He recalled being interrogated and struck, but remembered no pain or anything he said. He and other prisoners were loaded into the back of a covered truck that seemed to drive up and down mountain roads forever. When they came to a stop, they were led several miles into the jungle until finally reaching a Japanese encampment at the base of a mountain whose jutting rock face resembled the head of a tiger. He and the other prisoners were placed in bamboo cages and left for the night.

That was sixteen months ago, although he had no way of knowing exactly what date it was. There were no seasons in his jungle hell; monsoon rains followed by a steamy heat that choked off every breath of air marked the only change. Jacob and his fellow captives had spent the long days since their captivity digging a large tunnel into the base of the mountain. As he finally escaped consciousness and lapsed into a restless sleep, his last thoughts were of his wife and family and the agonizing realization that he would probably never lay eyes on them again.

~ ~ ~

Chapter 4

Traffic was brisk when Connor wheeled his SUV up Washington Avenue toward Fuller and on to Wolf Road. The mall on his right was busy with early holiday shoppers as he turned and continued down the four-lane street. Wolf Road was a long stretch of strip centers, office buildings, hotels and restaurants, surrounded by middle class neighborhoods, branching off from the main thoroughfare. There was no longer any residential housing. The expanse was one of the hottest commercial locations in the entire Capital District. A large mall anchored one end and the airport the other, with easy access from three major highways. Connor barely gave notice to the heavy activity. His mind was engaged, drifting between his business, Maggie and the confrontation he was about to initiate.

Just past a small shopping plaza on his right, Connor spied the sign for the Fitness Factory, home of Pauley's Boxing Gym. He put on his directional and turned into the narrow driveway nestled between the Fitness Factory building and a car dealership. The way opened up into a spacious parking lot, almost a quarter full. Fairly busy for late morning he thought, as he looked for a spot near the entrance, located at the rear of the building. He parked and headed down the covered walkway toward the double glass doors. He entered and was greeted at the front desk by a fit redheaded girl. He didn't remember her name, but had seen her working before and quickly located the gold nameplate pinned to her warm-up jacket.

"Hi Judy," he said, walking toward the metal door that separated him and access into the main facility. She gave him a warm smile and nodded, buzzing him in.

As he entered, the noise of an aerobics class organizing on the suspended floor to his right soon gave way to the clanging of free weights and Nautilus machines that lined the left side of the room. The separation of the two formed a natural walkway, leading to an interior glass door. He opened it and walked down a short hallway, past entrances to the men's and women's locker rooms and a drinking fountain located between them. He was ushered into the main room by the sound of heavy bags being hit and trainers shouting encouragement to their pugilists.

Pauley's gym housed a full-size boxing ring, twenty hanging heavy bags, some outdated weight lifting machines, a half-dozen speed bags and various other boxing station equipment. The ring had red and white satin covered ropes with a red apron and stretched white canvas floor, displaying Pauley's Gym logo. The large circular design consisted of two red boxing gloves, straddled by the words "Pauley's" on the top and "Boxing" on the bottom. Past boxing heroes hung on the walls, along with their various quotes of encouragement. The room was bright, due mainly to the huge glass windows along the front. The walls were freshly painted and the floors were mopped spotless daily. With the exception of Pauley's beat up wooden desk and large gray metal supply cabinet, located in the far right corner, it was nothing like the dingy gyms he'd seen in the movies. It was brass, glass and ass, as Pauley would say. It was meant to attract the paying fitness customer, not motivate the struggling professional wannabes. Someone had to pay the bills.

Connor quickly surveyed the room to see who was who. He noticed a couple of local trainers working with their boxers, along with a few fitness participants warming up for the next non-contact class scheduled to begin in fifteen minutes. A couple of amateur boxers jumped rope and a short, young Hispanic man that Connor didn't recognize, was shadow boxing in the mirror to right of Pauley. He was sitting at his desk with his head down. His pencil moved franticly on the pad in front of him, while his other hand pounded a calculator.

Pauley Simms was around five-nine, one hundred and sixty pounds; his slightly crooked nose stood out on a long rugged face highlighted by light green eyes. Premature hair loss belied his mid-forties age; he was lean, fit and appeared to Connor as though he could step back in the ring at any time. He had known Pauley for sixteen years, since he was ten. He loved and trusted him and certainly didn't want to cause him any trouble.

As he looked toward the ring, he recognized Frank Handrahan standing on the far apron talking to a fighter bent over in front of him. At the near end, Leon Harris, a black heavyweight was sitting on a stool covered in sweat and breathing hard while another boxer, acting as trainer, stood above him in the corner. No instructions were exchanged and none were needed. Harris was a seasoned pro who was once 13 and 0 before tearing a rotator cuff. He never totally recovered. Lack of money had forced him to come back long before he was ready. The final result was a 3-3 record over his next six fights, a right arm that he could barely lift above his shoulder and a chronic injury that he didn't have the medical coverage to repair. He was now thirty-five pounds over his fighting weight of two-twenty-five. He helped Pauley part-time with fitness classes and took sparring jobs whenever he could find them. Connor felt bad to see a promising career and a nice man relegated to an obscure existence as an underpaid punching bag. He had heard rumors that an old drug habit was sneaking back into Harris's life. He hoped it wasn't true, but in his heart he knew it was a distinct possibility.

Pauley was still calculating away, appearing not to notice the next round was about to begin. Harris slowly got up from the stool, as the fighter facing Handrahan finally turned around. Connor knew instantly that this was his man—"Sid Vicious." He was five-ten, heavily muscled with short blonde hair combed straight down on his forehead. He had a large round head with small dark eyes, a wide nose and a large

31

mouth outlined by a pencil-line thick goatee. Both biceps were adorned with barbwire tattoos that wrapped completely around his large arms. His legs and calves were thick, but not particularly defined. He was so white it looked to Connor like he hadn't been outside in months.

He charged forward, as Harris raised his gloves and lowered his over-weight body to withstand the onslaught. Connor watched intently while Sid began to go to work on his out of shape foe. He threw several hard body punches, causing Harris to lower his hands. He then went immediately upstairs to the head. Harris picked and slipped several head punches, which forced Sid to go back to the body. Connor could see Harris wince, as the body blows echoed a re-sounding thud. Finally, a horrific punch to the rib cage caused Harris to drop his hands, leaving him open to a hard left hook to the temple that sent him staggering back to the ropes. Sid followed recklessly to put the finishing touches on his work.

As he bore in, Harris threw a sharp left jab that caught Sid on the end of the nose, stopping his charge. Harris bounded off the ropes and landed two hard left hooks to the body, the second catching the short-rib causing Sid to back off. It was obvious to Connor that Frank Handrahan, who was watching from the ring apron, didn't like what he was seeing. Paid punching bags were not there to steal confidence from a fighter, they were there to take a beating and make that man feel invincible. Connor watched Harris glance over at Handrahan and knew the look was telling the fighter he was only a couple of punches away from losing a badly needed payday.

Sid cautiously came forward to mount his assault. His punches were wide and hard. As Harris continued to turtle up and not throw anything of substance in return, Sid appeared more confident. One hard body punch and Harris dropped his guard allowing his daunting opponent to connect with a vicious right uppercut to the jaw. Harris crumpled to the canvas; Sid looking delighted, raised his hands and shouted while making his way back to a smiling Handrahan. The corner man jumped in the ring and helped Harris back to the stool.

Pauley, hearing the commotion, finally looked up from his papers, he stood and made eye contact with Harris sitting on a stool in the corner of the ring. The weary fighter slowly raised a tired arm to let him know he was all right. Pauley started to sit down, when he made eye contact with Connor watching him from the front of the ring. A half-smile came to his face as he left the desk and headed toward him.

"Hello, C. Mason."

"Hi, Pauley," Connor replied, his eyes returning to the ring.

"Hear anything about your Dad?"

"Nothing yet, but we're still hopeful."

"Yeah, me too—What's up? Haven't seen you in a while. Are you looking for a workout?"

Connor sensed that Pauley knew full well what was on his mind. "You might say that," Connor returned, finally turning to look at Pauley. "I want you to set a little sparring session with Frank's boy over there."

"You don't want that, Con." A pained look crossed his face.

"Yeah, I do, Pauley."

"Connor, that guy's a handful. You haven't been boxing or even training lately. Even if I could set it up, Handrahan is never going to let it happen. He wants big, slow sparring partners. He's not going to risk his psyche by pitting him with a mover like you."

"Handrahan will have nothing to do with the decision."

"No games, Connor. I feel sorry about Alex, but please believe me, you don't want to get in the ring with this one. He's nasty and he's a hitter," Pauley pleaded.

"Pauley!" Connor said firmly. "I can do this guy; I have to do this guy."

~ ~ ~

Pauley Simms had been around confident men all his life and he knew Connor was all of that. Every one of them was going to win, until they didn't. Connor was one of the best technicians he had ever coached. He was big, quick feet, good power and most of all an excellent thinker in the ring. He had a good amateur career, but, not including some supervised sparring sessions, hadn't boxed competitively in over five years. He was like a son to Pauley, and he didn't want to see him hurt, especially when it was unnecessary. He also knew Connor, and once his mind was made up, that was it. At least in a controlled environment he could minimize the damage—he hoped.

"O.K., C. Mason, you make the match and we'll do it Saturday morning, but I'm telling you Handrahan is not going to let it happen."

"Thanks, Pauley," Connor said, as he turned and headed toward the ring.

"Don't thank me for saying it's all right to get brain damaged," Pauley replied.

Connor walked toward the far ring apron where Handrahan, having removed Sid's gloves, was busy cutting the tape from his thick hands. Pauley followed a short distance behind, not wanting a repeat of what happened the other day, especially when he noticed the twenty or so people that had just filed in for the non-contact class, including Maggie.

~ ~ ~

"Hey Frank, who's your new boy?" Connor asked, making his way closer.

"Well, well if it isn't the golden boy," replied Handrahan. Connor recognized Handrahan's nickname for him during his amateur boxing days. "How are you these days?" he offered, his tone making it obvious that he couldn't care less about his response.

Connor knew Frank Handrahan well; he had spent a lifetime in the fight business. At fifty, he was six-feet tall, barrel chested, with two buggy whips for legs and a large red nose, courtesy of three decades of heavy drinking. He had been fortunate enough to have discovered and trained a flash in the pan boxer, who ten years ago, on one lucky night, won the vacant WBO Heavyweight Championship in a box off with the number one contender. The rematch was worth about five million, which Frank's fighter lost on a first round knock-out.

Connor had heard Frank was still a big winner, pocketing thirty percent, about one and a half million. The money should have taken care of a comfortable retirement. However, after taxes, a bad divorce and risky investments, he was down to less than a hundred thousand within a year. The experience seemed to have left him more ill tempered and bitter than he already was, but it did get him quite connected in the fight business. This was a game of not always what you know, but who you know. Pauley was a much better trainer and Connor represented a nagging reminder, as he used to regularly whip up on Frank's bigger, stronger protégées when he brought them up to train.

"I'm fine, Frank," said Connor, who then directed his attention toward his future adversary. "You looked pretty good in there."

"Thanks, Mate," came a guarded reply.

"You know my Mom really likes a good fight."

"Your mum?" said Sid, sounding slightly confused.

"Yeah she loves it, she's an animal," Connor continued.

"Well, maybe Frank here can get the old girl a good seat for my next fight," Sid said smugly, seeming to be tiring rapidly of his new fan.

"Oh, I'm sorry. You don't understand. I mean my Mom likes to fight. I go out and find opponents for her. After watching you, I think you could give her a pretty good tussle. She has a walker, but I expect it would still be competitive. She not real good on the movement side, but then again, neither are you."

"You want me to fight your mum?" Sid barked, obviously not finding the same humor that the twenty or so onlookers appeared to be in Connor's remarks.

"Yeah, frankly I think she'll kick your ass all the way back to Australia, but Frank obviously brought you here to fight the best, so what do you think kangaroo breath? Want to go waltzing Matilda with Mom?" Connor chided, totally focused; oblivious to the entertainment he was bestowing on the partisan crowd that now surrounded the ring.

"Get lost Golden boy, we're not wasting any time with the likes of you," retorted Handrahan, placing his arm on Sid to keep him from charging after Connor.

"Don't interrupt, Frank. This is between me and your walking meat sack. Mom needs a match and I think 'he da man.'" He punctuated his message by pointing his finger at Sid.

"What is it with this bloke? You must be daft to want some of me," screamed Sid, his face reddening.

Connor could see that Sid's anger was getting the best of him and it was about to deteriorate into something beyond Handrahan's control. He knew another incident would wear out this pair's already thin welcome. Suddenly Handrahan leaned toward Sid and grabbing him firmly whispered in his ear. Sid seemed to calm down for the moment as he nodded in agreement.

"I get it, you're a little off kilter cause I popped your mate on his snout. Is he your Sheila? You 'ere to fight for your little girl's honor, are ya?"

"Actually, I'm here to find out if you could actually win a fight without sucker punching someone. The display I just saw tells me that the only way you have a career, is if Handrahan has enough dough to pay your opponents to lay down or look the other way while you hit them," said Connor, his voice just as even as when the exchange started.

"You wouldn't have to turn away for me to beat your arse."

"Sounds like a challenge. What say we throw a couple of shrimp on the barbie and I take you dancing?"

"I'll be waiting for ya," replied Sid, much to the obvious dismay of his manager, who let out a loud moan.

"Forget about it, Mason. He's not fighting or sparring

with anyone unless I say so," snapped Handrahan.

"Come on Frank, it'll be like old times, you bring'em in and I'll beat'em up. Everyone knows that you couldn't train seals. If this guy had any real talent, you'd need Pauley for him to have a chance to get out of his own way."

"Don't let this bloke talk to you like that Frank," Sid pleaded. "I'll squash him like a bug."

"Alright golden boy, Saturday morning, we'll see who can train," surrendered Handrahan, finally succumbing to his apparent dislike for Connor.

"Thanks, Frank. I'd say you won't be sorry, but you will." He turned and headed for the exit.

"Hey, Golden boy," Sid called from the ring. "Bring your mum and I'll kick both your arses."

"Mom's busy, how about I just bring a body bag, so you'll have something to wear on the plane back home," Connor retorted, continuing out of the gym. "See you Saturday, Pauley."

"Yes—you will." He scratched his head as he returned to his desk and his calculating.

Connor opened the connecting door to enter the Fitness Factory, when he felt a tug on his jacket. He quickly whirled around to see Maggie standing in front of him. He hadn't noticed her in the gym with the rest of the non-contact boxing participants.

"Hey, Maggie," he said, in a subdued voice, the adrenaline rush caused by the confrontation having subsided.

"What was that all about, Con?" Maggie inquired, her concern obvious.

"It was the start of the game."

"Start of what game?"

"It's a mind game, Maggie. I want to get Mr. Down Under in there as agitated as I can get him prior to Saturday."

"Why would you want that guy any madder than he already seemed to be?"

"Because, when he steps in the ring, I want him so wild that all he wants to do is kill me. Anger is a funny emotion in boxing. It can cause you to make mistakes, expend energy you normally can conserve; it can suck you dry in the first couple of rounds. It's just part of the game."

"Connor, why do you want to fight with this guy?"

"He's a bully, Mag. He likes to take advantage of people weaker than him. He broke Alex's nose and he needs a lesson."

"So this is about Alex?"

"It's not just about Alex. The way this guy behaves is wrong. He's a predator and he's in my house. I grew up at this gym and he makes people I know and care about scared to be here. It's not right and something needs to be done."

"This is not what you're supposed to do."

"What are you talking about? How do you know what I'm supposed to do?"

"I don't, someone else does. It won't take you where you need to go, it's a detour."

"I'm sorry Maggie, I don't have a clue what you're talking about."

Maggie reached out and took his hand. He could feel the hair on the back of his neck stand up when she touched him. "I'll see you tonight and explain it to you," she said softly, releasing his hand and heading back to class.

Connor stood a little stunned and a more than a little confused. He knew Maggie was different and he liked that. But this was weird, and he had no time for weird.

Connor turned and continued out of Pauley's, through the Fitness Factory and into the reception area. He raised his hand to acknowledge Judy as he walked quickly by the front desk and out of the building. He got in his truck and checked his cell phone. His preprogrammed voice mail alerted him to a message. He punched in his password and listened.

"Hi, Connor, it's Mom. I need you to come to the house as soon as you can. No need to call, I'll be here all day."

He chuckled to himself, wondering how his mother would react to him setting up boxing matches for her. Suddenly his heart started to race, hoping for some word about his Dad, the anticipation leaving a sick feeling in the pit of his stomach.

He drove out of the lot in the direction of I-87, heading north toward Clifton Park and home. He needed to speak with her about other matters, so her message came at an opportune time. He resisted the urge to call back, afraid she had news he didn't want to hear over the phone. He resigned himself to the fact he was going to take the longest twenty-minute ride of his life.

~ ~ ~

Chapter 5

It had been three weeks since the large Japanese officer and his entourage, including the young boy, first made their appearance. Work on the interior of the cave had ceased a few days after their arrival. The Japanese were now concentrating the prisoner's efforts on the ramp leading to the cave opening and on widening the jungle path that connected the mountain road to camp. Jacob and the others labored to secure the slope by building a base of rock and dirt and clearing jungle foliage that seemed to grow back overnight. The heat and humidity were even less bearable, now that the long days had the added burden of a relentless sun.

Jesse's condition seemed to be worsening as a fever had set in. Jacob wasn't sure if it was malaria, snakebite or just a general failing of his abused body. At this point it really didn't matter, time was their new enemy and they were running out of it. The one saving grace was he was still free of the leg irons, and that alone was a relief. He could at least move around without the constant friction of metal rubbing his raw skin. The infection in his ankles continued to spread, but not at the accelerated pace he expected.

The visit of the Japanese officer had instilled a sense of tolerance and urgency in his keepers. There were fewer beatings, more food and more work. They were definitely on a timetable and the need to keep every prisoner functioning had become a priority. Jacob could tell that time was running short, even the soldiers had begun to participate in the workload over the last week, something they had never done before.

The long day's work ended as Jacob helped Jesse up the newly reinforced dirt and stone ramp to the cave. They settled against the wall not far from the other prisoners. Two guards were posted outside the entrance while the makeshift bamboo door was closed and tied. The door and the guards were hardly necessary anymore, Jacob thought. This was a group that seemed to no longer possess the inclination or energy for escape.

"I feel really bad, Jake," said Jesse weakly.

"I know Jess, get some sleep. You'll feel better tomorrow."

"Not this time. I don't think I'll see the light of morning."

"Don't talk like that. We're going to get out of here and get home. You've got to hold on," Jacob said, not even half-believing his own words.

"I'm going to get out, but not the way you want to. You know something; it's okay. My body is just wore out and I can't take it anymore. Don't worry 'bout me, I got nothin' to go home to, not like you, Jake. You keep going and you get home to that lady of yours and your kids, keep your promise to her," Jesse replied, his voice tailing off. He shut his eyes and seemed to pass out against the wall.

"Jesse, Jesse," Jacob repeated. There was no answer. Jacob reached over to feel Jesse's neck. After detecting a weak pulse, he settled in, not sure if his friend would make it till morning. He didn't want to be alone and he didn't want to die. He wanted to be home with the ones he loved, the ones he wanted to protect, the ones he wanted to grow old with. He had to hang on; he couldn't just give up, he thought, as exhaustion caused him to sink into a deep sleep.

Sunlight had just begun to peek over the mountaintop, when Jacob was awakened from his coma-like sleep by the morning rousting. This was the first time in a long while that he failed to wake before their entrance. A hard kick initiated his senses and he started the slow tedious process of getting to his feet. He looked over at Jesse, who lay motionless a few feet away, wondering if his long time companion in captivity had

41

abandoned him. He laid no blame; he envied him. To have such a clear conscious, free of responsibility seemed like a blessing. He wanted to be free of this place, his pain and his terminal existence. His promise had kept him alive, but also kept him trapped; what started as his light to survival had begun to deteriorate to his burden of misery. If Jesse chose to escape this torture, why couldn't he?

Jacob watched intently while a guard hustled over to Jesse and gave him a hard kick followed by a familiar sounding command. A soft groan was heard as his eyes slowly opened. He looked disappointed, seeming to realize that even when the mind gave up, the body, no matter what the condition, still failed on its own timetable. Jesse was given a few extra moments to struggle to his feet; a month ago he would have never been afforded that luxury. He looked over at Jacob, but made no gesture; his eyes were lifeless.

They filed out of the cave with the other prisoners toward the middle of the camp to consume the morning meal. Jacob tried to get Jesse to speak, but he remained unresponsive. He left his food untouched, as the prisoners were motioned to their feet to begin another day of hard labor. Two Filipino's devoured the sparse meal he left behind, quickly scraping the wooden bowl clean with their fingers. Jacob was now sure the man he had shared his tortured existence with was gone. His body remained, but sometime during the night his spirit departed.

The prisoners were directed toward a long bamboo table shaded by a thatched roof. It was lined with tools needed to continue clearing jungle growth from the road leading to camp. They picked up machetes, picks and hoes and headed down the road accompanied by a half-dozen guards. They had already cleared almost two miles of heavy foliage in the previous weeks.

The early morning mist rising from the jungle floor formed an eerie cloud that escorted them to the end of the previous day's effort and the beginning of the new day's labor. The sun was already hot when they began clearing vines and small trees. Several of the soldiers joined the effort, knowing the camp commander monitored their progress closely. Jacob knew they didn't want to disappoint him, but especially feared disappointing the large officer upon his return.

Jesse was chopping through thick jungle leaves with a machete when Jacob tried to get his attention. He noticed a soldier watching them closely. His duty was to maximize the prisoner's workflow with as little disruption as possible. Three of the guards had relinquished their weapons in favor of sharp tools to assist in the task at hand. One of the captors oversaw their stacked rifles, while the other kept an eye on the remaining charges.

"Jesse, Jesse," Jacob pleaded, trying to evoke a response.

He finally turned to acknowledge Jacob. "It's time for me to go, Jake," Jesse responded, in a quiet monotone voice.

"What do you mean time to go? Go where?"

"You take care now, stay strong. I got to do what's best for me."

Jacob stood facing Jesse, feeling helpless, when he heard a guard coming up behind him, turning just in time to see his coiled rifle. Jacob knew immediately he was about to bear the brunt of his message; no work stoppage would be tolerated; there was a schedule to keep.

Before the soldier could strike, Jesse reached out and grabbed Jacob by the shoulder, pulling him to the ground and out of harm's way. The soldier, not prepared for the removal of his target, stumbled forward from his lunge, while Jesse raised his machete and delivered a lethal blow across the neck and shoulder of his enemy. The strike was so fierce that it almost decapitated him. The other soldiers standing nearby were caught totally surprised by this sudden deadly aggression. Jesse charged towards them with his weapon raised.

The guards, who had joined the work force, scrambled to get back to their rifles, while the soldier watching them, fumbled to get his weapon in firing position. Before a shot could be fired, Jesse was close enough to strike out at the next closest guard who in his terror was unable to shoulder his gun in time to protect himself. He fell to his knees screaming; his hands shielded his head as he awaited a death-blow from this

43

prisoner seemingly locked in a violent rage.

Jesse appeared to have used the little energy he possessed to quickly close on his quarry, leaving him defenseless for the split second needed to take his life. He prepared to strike, but at the last second halted his motion and stood over his would be victim, his arms pointed straight out at the shoulders and his weapon dangling in his right hand. He threw back his head and started to laugh, a loud boisterous laugh, while the remaining guards, having regained their senses took aim. His strange actions left the soldiers looking stunned as they hesitated with their target at point blank range—but only for a moment. A volley of bullets completed Jesse's plan and ended his miserable captivity.

Jacob remained on the ground. The whole terrifying scene took only seconds to play out. Crawling over to his fallen friend, he knew he was gone. As the other prisoners crouched with their tools in hand, waiting to see how Jesse's actions would affect their longevity, Jacob wondered why Jesse failed to strike out at this cruel enemy who had orchestrated his last seventeen months of horror. He then realized it was not about revenge; it was about tolerance for pain and measured response. He had experienced so much suffering that it was only necessary to deliver enough in return to evoke the action required to set him free. The first guard he killed accomplished that task, a second killing, no matter how warranted, was not required.

Jesse had nothing to hang on for, nothing to go back to, nothing to push him to endure any more of this inhuman existence. He had found his peace, and Jacob took solace in that. Jacob carefully removed the dog tags from Jesse's neck and gripped them tightly while he kept one eye on the guards, who now seemed less disoriented. He then placed the tags around his neck, next to his own.

The soldiers, having regained control, herded the prisoners together and motioned them to the ground. They talked among themselves for a few minutes, and then led four Filipinos to dig graves just off the path. They were gone less than thirty minutes when they returned for the bodies. Jacob said a silent good-bye to his friend. He was sorry that his final resting place was a shallow grave in this strange land, but at least in the end it was on his own terms.

Jacob knew that finishing the road was more important to his keepers than leaving to report the incident to the camp commander. They now had two less bodies and much more to accomplish before they completed their required task. The prisoners were hustled to their feet and back to work. The guards, who were laboring on the road, did not rejoin the effort; they remained alert. Jacob noticed them keeping a close watch on him.

The next twelve hours were marked by steady progress with Jacob and the other prisoners continuing to transform a narrow path into an eight-foot wide road. The shock of the early morning's events seemed to have produced an adrenaline rush that blocked out the usual fatigue caused by toiling in this blast furnace of heat and humidity. Jacob was surprised they were all still alive after Jesse's revolt. As the light started to fade, he could make out, through the thick jungle foliage, the mountain road that brought him to his prison almost seventeen months ago. Their burden was almost complete.

~ ~ ~

Chapter 6

Headed North on I-87—Connor was not paying much attention to traffic or anything else. He was distracted by the anticipation of finally getting some information on the disappearance of his father. He and his best friend and business partner, Dan Illeron, had left for a few weeks of fishing in Mexico. He would usually call, but hadn't since the second week, and that was ten months ago. He wanted to phone ahead and speak to his mother, but was still paralyzed by the thought of getting bad news. He just had to get there and hear what she had to tell him.

He got off at exit 10 and headed west toward Route 146A, passing the development where he and his two older brothers had grown up. A few years after he left home, his father sold the house and bought an old horse farm on twelve acres and refurbished it. Guy Mason had little interest in horses, and Connor knew he liked his privacy. He put in a tennis court, a swimming pool and renovated the old horse barn into his office. He liked to keep to himself and kept most of his business dealings very private. Connor wasn't even sure what his father did for a living before he went to work in the family mortgage business. All he remembered was his Mom telling him about an import company.

When he was young, he recalled his father spent a lot of time overseas. Sometimes he was gone for months at a time. Connor always knew when he was returning because his Mom would get a fax, and all it would say was "Come Join the Adventure." He smiled at how happy getting that message made her. She would take him and his brothers and they would fly to Grand Cayman and check in at the Hyatt Regency. They always spent at least a week; Dad would meet them there, usually with Dan Illeron and sometimes their attorney, Wes Adams. They all enjoyed the beach and sun. His Dad and Dan would spend the week drinking Coronas, telling stories, laughing and scuba diving. His father really hadn't traveled much in the last fifteen years or so. He had helped him and his brothers get settled in their lives and careers. Connor often felt he missed the travel and the part of his life he lived before making the decision to spend more time with his family, although he never remembered hearing him complain. Connor missed him—now, more than ever.

He pulled into the long driveway leading up to a modest white Victorian with a large porch that wrapped around the entire house. The circular drive branched out in several directions. One led to a large gazebo and small outbuilding by the tennis court and pool, the other to his father's office in the renovated horse barn, and the third to a newly built four-car garage. Manicured lawns, ringed by bright white fencing that once separated the land into pastures when the property was a working horse farm, marked the grounds.

He parked in front and got out of his truck. As he walked up the stairs toward the double oak doors, two large yellow labs bolted out of the doggie door to greet him.

"Hi, girls," he said, petting the excited animals. "Is Mom home? Is she in there?" he asked enthusiastically, entering to the smell of fresh brewed coffee.

"Mom, you in here?" he yelled, stepping onto the stone floor foyer.

"In the back, Connor," came a faint reply.

Connor made his way down a short hallway, past the stairway to his immediate right, the dinning room to his left and the small sitting room to his far right. He entered into a large open kitchen that made up the majority of the first floor. The large countertop in front of him separated the kitchen area from a spacious family room containing two large leather couches, a wooden apothecary table, a stone fireplace to the left and a large wood table ringed with eight, heavy wooden, high backed chairs to the right.

The room was bright, with high wood beam ceilings and three-quarter length glass windows. The walls were decorated with highly glossed wooden skis, snowshoes and tennis rackets that his Mom had bought at a flea market and refinished, along with pictures purchased from New England artisans. Various pieces of stone craft and woodcarvings that Connor's father had brought back as a reminder of his travels shared space with black rod iron lamps on several wooden end tables. The room was earthy and comfortable. Although he had never actually lived there, it still felt like home.

Stepping off the stone floor of the hallway on to the kitchen's wide plank wood covering, he followed the countertop around into the open family room, continuing toward a glass four-season room. He could see his mother through the door, sitting on a brightly cushioned rattan love seat, as the dogs ushered him toward her. Ellen Mason was around five-feet five-inches tall, one hundred and twenty pounds with short dirty blonde hair. Wearing a black and white warm up suit and white sneakers, she appeared much younger to him than her mid-fifties age. She was tanned from working in her garden and smiled when she saw her youngest son walking toward her.

As he got closer, he noticed several photo albums resting on the glass coffee table in front of her. One of the books was open in her lap. It displayed several pictures of the family in Grand Cayman fifteen years ago.

"Hi, Mom," he said, sitting next to her.

"Hi, Connor, I guess you got my message."

"I did, did you hear from Dad?" he asked, holding his breath.

"I'm sorry, honey. I got a message for Dad, not from him."

"What do you mean a message for Dad?"

"Everyday I check his fax machine and e-mail. Most of the messages don't amount to much, just things I can handle on my own. But last night a fax came through on letterhead with this message." She reached into her pocket and handed him the folded paper.

"The eagle has landed signed GF," Connor read out loud. "What's that supposed to mean?"

"I don't know," she replied. "Your father left me specific instructions to let him know immediately if this message ever came for him. It got to be kind of a joke; he's asked me to watch for it for years, whenever he was away for more than a few days. Now it comes and I can't reach him," her eyes welling up and her voice starting to crack.

"What do you want me to do?" Connor asked softly, as he took her hand and squeezed it gently.

"I'm not sure," she replied, seeming to regain her composure. "I think we should call Wes Adams."

"Alright, I'll give Wes a call at his office."

Connor got up and headed into the family room, stepping over the dogs sleeping next to each other in the warm sun shining through the glass. He walked over to the end table by the leather couches, and picked up the portable phone. He read the pre-programmed list on the handle, hit star-2 and the speed dial connected him with Wes Adam's direct line.

"Hello, this is Wes Adams. I'm not available to take your call, but if you would leave your name, number, and a brief message, I'll return your call as soon as I can— BEEEEEEEEP."

"Wes, this is Connor Mason. I need you to call me as soon as you get this message, it's important. Use the cell number; I know you have it. Thanks."

He hung up and headed back into the sunroom where he noticed his mother flipping through the pages of her photo album.

"Wes isn't in right now, Mom. I left a message. I'm sure he'll get back to me sometime in the next 24 hours."

"Thanks, honey," she said not looking up. "I like going back through the old albums. We had fun back then, didn't we?" Her voice tailed off as she spoke.

"Yeah, we did," he said. He sat back down as one of the dogs moved closer, settling at his feet.

"Mom, I need a favor," he asked, rubbing the dog's head.

"What is it, honey?" she returned, looking up from the album.

"I need to borrow some money."

"How much do you need, Connor?"

"I need a hundred thousand dollars for around ninety days," he returned, immediately sensing her apprehension. His father had always made all the financial decisions since they'd been together. She had immersed herself in family, friends, her garden, crafts and social responsibilities. They were comfortable, but not wealthy by any means. The house was paid for, but with Guy missing, their modest savings and investments would probably not support her for the duration of retirement. It was a slap of reality he was sure she'd avoided—till now.

"Of course, honey. I don't have that kind of cash available, so I'll have to write you a check from the home equity line," she said, her hesitation punctuating an unspoken concern. "I'm not sure what the monthly payments are or even what the interest rate would be."

"Don't worry about it, Mom," he reassured her. "I've got some temporary cash flow problems in the business. We're refinancing some properties and I'll pay you back as soon as they've been completed. Just send the monthly payments to the office and I'll take care of it."

"That's fine," she returned. "You know I trust you Connor, it's just that your father usually took care of these things."

"I know, Mom. I wish he was here, too."

"How's Susan?" she asked, changing the subject. "Is she still in London?"

"She's well. I expect her home any day now."

"Make sure you bring her by when she gets in," she said, as she got up from the chair and headed toward the kitchen. Connor and both dogs followed her. She walked around the countertop toward a small desk area, nestled between ceiling high cabinets that lined the kitchen wall. She opened the top drawer and removed a checkbook, then wrote the check and handed it to him.

"Thanks, Mom. Don't worry, I'll get it back to you," he said, reaching over to give her a hug.

"You're welcome, hon. I'm not worried about the money," she reassured him, burying her head in his chest while she held him tightly.

He released her and turned to leave, when he suddenly stopped and whirled to face her.

"Mom?"

"What honey?"

"Dad wasn't on a fishing trip in Mexico, was he?"

"Not exactly."

"What exactly was he doing there?"

"Wes will explain it to you when you see him. I really didn't get involved in those things."

"What things, Mom?"

"Things that made your father happy."

"Dad was involved in things that you really don't care about."

"I care about him, Connor. I trust him and I care about him."

"That was why you were looking at the Cayman Island pictures—'Come Join the Adventure.' I need more information, Mom." He was starting to feel a little frantic. "If you tell me what was going on, maybe I can figure out a way to find him. I need to know why he was in Mexico?"

She walked over to him and reaching out placed two soft fingers on his lips to calm him. "You can't find your father, dear. Wes will explain it to you when you see him. Just give him the fax and he'll answer your questions." She turned and headed back toward the sunroom with the two dogs following close behind.

Connor stood and watched as she left him. He wanted more answers—he needed them. But he knew his mother was in no frame of mind to give him the satisfaction he desired. He chastised himself for being so self-absorbed that he never noticed the clues to his father's secret activities, now slamming him head on. He left the house knowing he would have to wait for Wes Adams to fill in the details of his father's life for him.

~ ~ ~

Chapter 7

Connor had spent the rest of the morning and early afternoon placing rental ads for the properties that they planned to refinance. He caught up with Alex and the crew working on 3rd Street toward the end of the day. Alex was happy to hear that he had secured the short term financing they needed, although he never asked about the source. He was also unaware of what had taken place at Pauley's gym and Connor's scheduled Saturday morning rendezvous with Sid. He decided that Alex would find out soon enough and nothing constructive would be accomplished by discussing it at that moment.

Darkness was just beginning to creep in, a little after six o'clock, when Connor pulled up in front of his Manning Avenue home. He got out of the car and headed for the front door, too preoccupied with the events of the day to recognize the small figure coming up the sidewalk. As he climbed the porch stairs, his concentration was broken by the familiar creak of the first step he had just heard two steps ago. He whirled around to see who was behind him.

"Jesus, Maggie. Do you want me to have a heart attack?" he said, startled by her sudden appearance.

"Baby, I know how to give you a heart attack and its got nothing to do with sneaking up on you."

"Touché."

"Connor, we need to talk about some things."

"Our relationship has suddenly disintegrated to just talking. I don't think I'm ready for such a drastic change."

"Very funny, smart ass. If that's what you want, it can be arranged, you know." An impish smirk crossed her face.

"That's okay, I kind of like it just the way it is. As a matter of fact, considering the day I've had, it would be nice to have someone to talk to," he said, reaching out and taking her hand.

He opened the front door and led her through the foyer and into the living room, where they found a seat on his tan leather couch. Maggie took off the baseball cap she was wearing and shook out her short blonde hair which fell perfectly in place. Connor folded his hands and leaned forward, resting on his elbows while he waited for her to get situated.

"Con, what's up with this fight on Saturday?" she blurted out.

"What do you mean what's up with the fight?"

"I mean, besides what you told me at the club about him being a bully and all, why do you feel compelled to put yourself in harm's way with that guy?"

"I don't know, Mag. I don't feel like that when I'm fighting. In fact, I feel a strange sense of calm. It's just my opponent and me, no distractions—just the business at hand. I know it sounds weird to be calm when all hell's about to break loose, but I can't explain it. It just kind of comes over me. Why are you so uptight about this anyway? In the six months we've known each other, you've never said anything about the things I do."

"I have this feeling about you. I've had it since we met."

"I know, Maggie. I have this feeling about you too, and I think I'm starting to get it again right now." He leaned over to pull her closer.

"Stop, that's not what I mean," she said, pushing him away. "We need to talk about this, there are issues you need to deal with and I think I can help you."

"Maggie, what are you talking about?" he said, suddenly confused.

"It's something I can't explain. I get feelings about people. You're supposed to do something and I'm supposed to help you. The fight is just a distraction. You have habits, addictions that keep you from focusing on what you need to get done."

"What habits? What addictions? What the hell needs to be done and how do you know about it, if I don't even know what it is?"

"You like to fight because it allows you take all your energy and focus on one thing. You don't have to feel what's going on around you. It's like sex; you like it because it allows you to escape. It takes your focus and gives you a sense of peace—but it's only for a short time. The sex and fighting help you cope with the uneasiness you feel, they're your drug, your addiction."

"Mag, don't go mental on me, please. You're not making any sense. I'm not addicted to fighting or sex or anything else."

Maggie got up from the couch and started to pace in front of him. She took off her denim jacket and tossed it on the leather ottoman. Connor watched intently, not sure how this little drama was going to play out. She faced him with both eyes shut as she rubbed her temples.

"Maggie, we don't need to. . . ."

"Wait," she shouted. "Look Connor there are things about me that I need to tell you. I need you not to judge me, I need you to listen."

"Okay—Okay, come sit down."

"I can't sit down right now."

"Fine, stand up then."

"Fine."

"Fine—go ahead, I'm listening."

"Alright." She took a deep breath. "Five years ago I was engaged and living in Lansing, Michigan. One weekend my brother and nephews were visiting and we went to the local pond to go ice-skating. I went out to check the thickness when I fell through. It took almost thirty-five minutes for rescue workers to get me out of the water. They had to use electric paddles to shock my heart. Later in the hospital the doctors told me that I was clinically dead for over twenty minutes.

55

It was a miracle I survived. Ever since then things have been different.

"And what has that got to do with me and my addictions?"

She sat down next to him and placing his hands in hers, peered directly into his deep blue eyes. Her gaze began to make him feel a little uneasy, as she just continued to stare. He suddenly felt the hair on his arms and the back of his neck start to rise, like a low electric current was running through his body. He pulled away from her and jumped up, breaking the connection, and causing the sensation to cease.

"What the hell was that Maggie?"

"Do you know what happens to us when we die, Connor?" Her voice and face went suddenly deadpan.

"No, I don't, Mag, but I have to tell you that you're freaking me out, more than just a little."

"I do."

"How did you make the hair on my arm stand up?"

"I didn't."

"What do you mean you didn't? If you didn't, what did?"

"Maybe not what, but who."

"Maggie, I've had a tough day so far. I don't have the energy or inclination for games. Tell me what you need to tell me."

"What I need to tell you is there are things that tell me— or give me feelings, that you're being driven to complete a task that will give someone the peace they desire."

"What makes you feel like I'm being driven? And who is this someone?"

"You don't sleep much, you're always searching for a meaning to your life, your existence. You want to take care of the people around you, but that's only because it keeps you from focusing on taking care of yourself. The boxing, the sex, help you escape, but it doesn't last—it's just your fix. You want more and more of it, because you haven't finished what needs to be done."

"WOW. That's some real insight, Mag. How did you

come up with all that after just six months? I sure sound like one hopeless case," he mocked, not able to keep the sarcasm out of his tone.

"No, you're a hopeful case. I can help you, it's what I'm suppose to do, it's my own vindication."

"Vindication for what?"

"For being alive, when for all practical purposes, I shouldn't be," she said, her voice tailing off.

"Alright, Maggie, let's get to it. Give it to me in plain English, so I know if I'm crazy or you are. What has you being clinically dead and the fact that you can plug me in like a light bulb got to do with anything in my life right now?"

"Come sit by me," she said, patting the cushion next to her.

Connor sat down. Sid, his father, the business and countless other issues were running through his head. He had no time for this babble, but he cared for her—maybe too much. He wanted to keep an open mind, although her mental stability was now a real issue to him. Maybe Alex was right, she was a whack job. "Mag, I've got a lot going on right now, give it to me straight up."

"That's the only way I know how—so here goes. When I was trapped under the ice I. . . ."

The sound of a ringing phone interrupted her.

"Hold on a second, Mag. I'm expecting an important call, I'll be just a second." He got up and walked over to a portable phone nestled on a wooden end table next to a matching leather recliner. He answered and continued down the hallway toward the kitchen.

"Hello."

"Hello Connor, Wes Adams," came a measured voice.

"Wes, how are you? Thanks for getting back to me."

"Well, I got your three messages, so I figured it was important enough to call you at home when I couldn't reach you on your cell phone. What can I do for you?"

"I went to see my Mom and she had a message for Dad. She said that you would know what it meant."

"What was the message?"

"It was a fax. All it said was 'The Eagle has landed signed GF.' Do you know what it means?"

"Jesus Christ, I can't believe it," he mumbled. "Is it on letterhead?"

"Yes."

"What's the address on the letterhead?"

"The letterhead is from the Pryce Plaza, Cagayan De Oro, Mindanao."

"Jesus Christ, that's it."

"What's it? What's going on?" Connor asked, sensing the excitement in his voice.

"I can't talk about it over the phone, Connor. Come down to my office," he returned, now sounding a little calmer.

"I'm a little busy right now, Wes. How about I come down first thing in the morning?"

"You need to come down here right now," came the stern reply.

"Okay, I'll see you in twenty minutes."

"I'll be waiting for you."

Connor clicked the phone and headed back toward the living room where Maggie was waiting patiently, now looking totally composed and ready to tell her story.

"Maggie, that was Wes Adams, my father's attorney. He needs me to go to his office right now. He has information about a message that was sent to my father. We'll have to talk later."

"Let me go with you, Con. This may have something to do with what's going on."

"How could it possibly? I don't have a clue what this is about or what you think is going on."

"Something is going on, Connor. I feel it."

"I haven't got time for psycho analysis or women's intuition or any of that right now. I've got to go Mag. I'm sorry, I'll call you when I get back and we'll sort this all out."

"Connor. . . ."

"Maggie, please! I've got to. . . ."

A loud knock on his front door stopped him in mid-sentence. He looked at Maggie, shaking his head as a bewildering sensation engulfed him. He turned and went to answer the door.

"This is like a three fucking ring circus today," he muttered to himself, straining to see out a small window. He could barely make out the figure of a tall, slender brunette wearing a long raincoat. Her back was to him when he opened the door.

"Can I help you?" he asked hurriedly, knowing he had no time for more distractions.

"Yes, you sure can," she said, still not turning around.

It only took a brief second to register, but Connor recognized the voice immediately. He could feel his heart in his throat and his palms begin to get moist.

"Susan?"

"Hi, sweetheart." She spun around and hurried toward him. "Surprised to see me?"

"More than you could ever imagine," he sheepishly returned, as she hugged him tightly.

"Let's go in, I've got another surprise for you," she said, releasing her grip from around his neck.

"I've got one for you too," he returned, half-smiling in disbelief at the predicament he was now faced with.

~ ~ ~

Chapter 8

It had been three days since Jesse passed. The long days were marked by even lonelier nights for Jacob. As he rested his head against the cave wall, he missed him, not realizing how much until these last few nights. His captivity was even less bearable now that he was forced to face it without the familiar voice he had heard for the last year and a half.

As the exhaustion of working in the jungle heat carried him off to sleep, he thought about Sarah and the family he would probably never see again. It made his heart hurt to believe that he wouldn't be there to grow old with them. Before, the pain of separation was relieved by the soothing presence of his friend, now he had to rely on a restless sleep to quell the suffering—till the next night, when he would be alone again.

Jacob and the other prisoners were suddenly woken from their sleep trances by the loud sound of trucks heading toward the camp. The bright beams of headlights danced inside the cave walls, the uneven terrain causing them to bounce up and down in the night. Jacob moved closer to the cave opening to improve his view.

As he cautiously peered out from between the bamboo bars, he could make out a line of vehicles moving slowly down the path that he and the other prisoners had spent their long days widening. At least one hundred heavily armed foot soldiers, with lanterns and torches in hand, intermingled with what looked like at least twenty canvas-covered troop carriers.

Why the heavily armed escort and what's in those trucks, he pondered.

He had begun to creep closer when a rifle butt whacked against the bamboo bars startling him. One of the guards had noticed his advance and motioned him to back away. The guard showed no interest in enforcing any additional discipline. Jacob figured the magnitude of the invading convey, would continue to garner his attention, and probably that of remaining camp occupants as well.

He crawled back several feet to avoid any further confrontation. From his new vantage he could still see the camp clearly. The truck headlights had lit up the black jungle night like it was midday. Emerging from one of the vehicles, he could make out the large officer that had visited the camp weeks before along with the young boy who had clung silently to his side. The boy grabbed onto his waistband as both appeared to back up to survey the situation. The trucks continued toward the center of the encampment, as the foot soldiers were deployed to form a heavily armed perimeter. Torches, lanterns and headlights continued to light the area, their bright glow attracting hordes of flying insects. Jacob watched the large officer with the young boy intercept the camp commander.

Jacob fixated on their interaction, while the officer intermittently swatted mosquitoes and other bugs from his face. His underling was afforded no such luxury. He stood frozen at attention; seeming to hang on his superior's every word. The boy stood quietly by the officer's side, like he had during his visit weeks before. Upon completion of his communication, the officer abruptly turned from the commander, allowing him to break his rigid posture. The camp leader then hurried toward the cave opening and the men standing guard. Seeing him approach, Jacob moved further back, not wanting to attract his attention.

Upon reaching the entrance, the commander motioned to one of the guards, who sped off in the direction of the tents housing the remaining camp regulars. They had been woken by the commotion and were watching the intrusion. In a matter of moments, the camp guards came scurrying toward the tunnel. One of the soldiers was weighted down with something that didn't allow him to move with the same urgency. As he neared, Jacob felt his heart sink. The guard carried the one thing that had plagued his existence in this inhuman place— leg irons.

Just the thought of hard metal rubbing against his sore ridden ankles made his stomach turn. He retreated toward the rear of the tunnel, curling up in a fetal position and closing his eyes, hoping somehow that his continued torment would not include this additional torture. He had just begun to drift off, when the answer to his concerns rushed him in a flurry.

The guards, led by the camp commander, stormed the cave. Jacob and the remaining prisoners were rousted to their feet. Jacob found himself in a daze. The commotion having had startled him just early enough to avoid a painful kick or riffle-butt strike. He could see two of the guards removing the makeshift bamboo door from the entrance. Two others lit torches that lined the stonewall. The prisoners were then led deeper into the tunnel, almost one hundred and fifty-feet from the entrance. The opening remained illuminated from the truck headlights, combined with the torches and lanterns carried by the invading force. The captives were motioned to the ground, while the guard with the leg irons dropped his heavy load. A resounding thud echoed the reality of Jacob's situation. He was about to be reunited with a long time nemesis—pain.

The seated prisoners were fitted with the shackles. Jacob winced when the hard steel meet his raw skin. After a day, he knew what little tolerance he had would be gone and he would be left to the mercy of an increasing misery. Once the restraints were administered, the soldiers turned their attention to the commotion outside.

The guards appeared increasingly restless as they watched the trucks and soldiers continue to pour in. One of them came to the rear every few minutes to report the increasing numbers to the camp commander. Even in his diminished capacity, it was obvious to Jacob that their leader and his small command were outsiders in this event. He could read the worry in their faces and their actions. Huddled against the rear wall in shadows of the torch-lit bowels of this stone world, Jacob watched the camp commander pace, anxiously awaiting his next piece of news. For the first time since entering the tunnel, he wondered if he would ever see the sun again. Something big was happening out there beyond his senses; if it was going to contribute to his demise—he wanted to know— he needed to know what it was.

Suddenly the guard assigned to the entrance came running, going directly to his superior, who, upon hearing his animated message, broke into a full sprint toward the light. As Jacob watched, he could see in the headlight lit entrance, two silhouettes that waited to greet him. Even at a distance, because of the disparity in size, he knew it was the large officer with the small boy. He observed the commander slow his pace when he saw them. The large officer stepped forward to intercept his slowing underling, barely giving the camp leader a chance to perform his traditional bowing and groveling, before a barrage of orders dispatched him rapidly back to his station.

The commander looked particularly uneasy as he shouted at his men. The guards quickly rousted the prisoners to their feet and directed them to stand against the near right-hand wall. His metal bracelets abruptly reminded Jacob of the pain to come, rubbing raw what remained of his scabbed skin. In his malnourished condition, he knew the sores would no longer heal to a point of allowing him any relief—but then again maybe it wouldn't matter.

Jacob kept an eye toward the entrance, as he and the other captives, intermingled with the guards, leaned against the stone wall. It had become apparent that the fine line between prisoner and keeper had been erased. They were now just men, awaiting their fate. He couldn't help wondering why the urgent need to move them a few yards, when the answer came heading straight for them. The large officer moved to the side, while the first truck slowly made its way up the man-made embankment and into the tunnel. The headlight beams highlighted his girth, projecting a large shadow on the walls and ceiling.

Jacob watched anxiously as the first truck tried to enter, only to have the canvas top get snagged on the rock ceiling. It was three to four inches too low to fit the troop carrier inside. The guards and their commander looked horrified when the truck failed to maneuver under the ten-foot barrier. Jacob shuddered to imagine the repercussion of this missed calculation. A loud scream of frustration from the large officer triggered the bewildered appearing commander to again head rapidly toward the front of the tunnel. His gait slowed when he saw his superior had withdrawn his ivory handled sword, waiting to dole out the required punishment for a failure of this magnitude. It was clear, this was a major setback and someone had to pay.

Upon reaching his superior, the camp commander dropped to his knees. Jacob was witness to his pleading, as the hulking figure raised his sword. He was squirming and yelling, frantically pointing toward the wedged vehicle. The officer seemed to hesitate for a moment, but then, grabbing the weapon with both hands, raised it high above him before rapidly descending it in the direction of the terrified commander's exposed head. Jacob wanted to turn away, not wanting to see the decapitation, but he couldn't. What he did see was the sword just above his prey, the razor sharp blade just nicking his bare-neck enough to bring forth a small flow of blood.

The commander sat on the back of his legs with his head hung, quietly sobbing. The heat and humidity caused the small cut to steadily flow bright red, darkening the collar and back of his sweat-ridden shirt. He was quickly snapped out of this self-indulgence by a swift kick from the large officer standing over him. The blow seemed to jolt him back into focus and the gravity of his situation. He turned and called weakly to his shocked men at the rear of the cave and four of them headed rapidly toward their embattled leader.

He rose to his feet, ignoring the heavier blood flow now running down his back. When the soldiers arrived, he gave them their orders and they quickly dispersed, encircling the captive vehicle. The large officer had backed away, while the young boy who had been standing quietly against the tunnel wall joined him. The child placed his hand on the large officer's waistband, taking his customary place, seemingly oblivious to the events that had just transpired. The soldiers used their bayonets to puncture the tires, causing the trapped vehicle to drop six inches, freeing it from the rocky grasp of the cave ceiling.

The truck rocked back and forth on the uneven floor, making its way to the rear of the cave on its rims. The camp commander and his charges looked relieved when the truck pulled up tight to the rear wall, so close to the left sidewall that the driver had to exit out of the passenger door. One by one, the vehicles entered while the soldiers punctured the tires, enabling them to continue. The drivers parked two abreast, starting at the rear and lining up from left to right.

The prisoners and the remaining guards were forced to adjust their position, having less than four feet between the wall and the vehicles parked side by side. It was obvious to Jacob that whatever was in the vehicles, would not leave anytime soon—if ever. With the tires destroyed, and the way the trucks were sandwiched in, it would be next to impossible to move them with any great expediency.

The prisoners sat with their backs against the cave wall, facing the trucks, while the camp guards hovered nearby. Some leaned against the wall and others on the parked carriers, keeping one eye on their charges and the other on the convoy entering the cave. The torches that lined the walls, providing a shadowy light, burned low, causing an eerie reflective glow against the metal of the now disabled vehicles. Jacob leaned his head against the rocky wall as he felt himself drift off to the grinding of gears and creaking of tireless rims. Maybe morning, not far off, would answer his questions—for now he escaped in his dreams—maybe for the last time.

~ ~ ~

65

Chapter 9

Connor stood momentarily stunned, before Susan took his hand and led him into the house. He tried to think, but his usually sharp brain would not engage. He had been on overload all day, and this was something he found himself totally unprepared for. He decided he had no choice but to come clean. After all, what other option was there? He ran scenarios over and over in his mind in the brief milliseconds it would take for the two women to come face to face.

He had never mentioned Susan to Maggie, although he now wished he had, and then maybe this situation could have been avoided. How would they take it, what would he say, and how the hell could he get to Wes Adams' office on time?

Maggie, this is Susan my fiancée, Susan this is Maggie the woman I've been sleeping with since you left. Maybe you two could work things out, because I need to go to my attorney's office to find out what my father was doing in Mexico and what the secret message meant. Just leave me a note with the outcome. Anything you decide will be all right with me. Oh God, what a mess, he thought when he and Susan entered the living room.

As he slowly raised his eyes from the floor, a sense of relief crossed his face. Maggie was not where he left her. That feeling suddenly turned to panic, when the thought of her walking out of the bedroom—naked, leapt into his head. *She wouldn't do that*—and then he thought, *yeah—she would.*

"Connor," Susan said. "Did you miss me?"

"Of course I did, Susan."

"You seem a little distracted, is everything all right?"

"Not exactly," he said, half-listening for Maggie's expected entrance.

"What's wrong? Is there something I can do?"

"I really don't think there's anything you can do to help with this Susan."

"Maybe my surprise will help take your mind off what's bothering you."

"Maybe," he replied, still distracted.

Susan led him over to the couch and sat him down. As she stood in front of him, Connor was preoccupied with the possibility of Maggie coming down the hall behind her.

"Susan, I don't have time to sit right now," he said nervously, attempting to peer around her.

"You have time for this," she returned, a smile starting to cross her face.

Connor knew Susan James was not used to taking "no" for an answer. She was a true Capital District Blue Blood, if ever there was such an animal. Her mother came from old money, and her father was a well-known local litigator for the firm started by her mother's grandfather. Ten years ago, her father won a huge settlement in a class action lawsuit against a large chemical company, propelling him into public prominence. Connor had heard that he quickly embraced his success by celebrating in every bar and with every strange woman he could get into his bed.

Just before Susan entered Cornell Law School, he flipped his Porsche while heading up the Northway to his summerhouse on Lake George. He and his personal secretary of two weeks were killed instantly. It was booked as a terrible accident and tragic loss of life. No autopsy or toxicology reports were ever made public. Money buys influence that sometimes saves those that are left the embarrassment of the whole truth being revealed, he remembered thinking.

Susan had worshipped her father, even though not blind to his overt abuses. It was no secret that she felt her mother's family had him so far under their thumb, that when he finally tasted his own personal success, he rebelled against the conformity he had been obligated to live with for so many years. Her father's death drove her away from her mother and her mother's family. She had told Connor she was determined to be the best attorney she could be and not bound for the family practice—she would do whatever it took to have her own career and more importantly, her independence.

They had met at a political fundraiser three years earlier. It was a black tie affair and Susan was the only person close to his age. He watched her from across the room while he stood at the bar, balancing a beer bottle between two fingers, fidgeting with his bowtie and generally noticing he was the only person in the place not there to impress anyone. She later told him that his devil may care demeanor made him all the more attractive, coupled with the fact that she was sure her family would never approve of someone with such a blatant disregard for social strata. He introduced himself and found her charming, funny and articulate, as well as beautiful. It was not love at first sight, but he soon realized that he was able to do something most men had failed to—hold her interest.

She asked him to lunch under the guise of soliciting real estate closing business. They met the next day and one thing led to another and that to a ski weekend in Vermont. They dated on and off for the next year. Both were busy with new careers, and had little time or interest in a commitment.

Susan worked long hours and that was fine with Connor. He liked her, but he also liked not having to be with her all the time. Her work schedule and ambition did not intimidate him, as it had her other suitors. He gave her the space she needed and that was very important to Susan. About eight months ago, they decided to get engaged and move in together. It was more of a business decision than a romance, but the relationship worked for them.

Just after the engagement, Connor had heard inklings that Susan had a one-night stand with a married partner of the Albany law firm where she was working. He had never pressed her on it, and he wasn't sure why. Maybe he was a little apathetic about their relationship, knowing in his heart that, despite their outward appearance, it wouldn't be long-term. Whatever his reasons, that guilty knowledge had opened the emotional door for his ardent feelings for Maggie. Connor imagined that she was probably hoping her indiscretion might give her an advantage climbing the partnership ladder. Susan viewed her mind, her connections and, he now guessed, even her body, as assets to take her where she wanted to go—it wasn't personal, it was just business.

He figured that something had to have happened when, after a very brief employment, she was able to leverage a brilliant personal recommendation from her old company that landed her a new job with a prestigious New York City law firm. After two months, she was offered an opportunity to work in their London office. The chance to work in Europe with the concern's largest commodity clients was the fast track she was looking for. It was something he knew she had to pursue—it was her career. So their engagement went from living together, to a weekend New York City commute, to an overseas relationship a little over six months ago.

Susan stood in front of him and began to unbutton the long raincoat she was wearing. Connor watched impatiently, while she slowly exposed a pair of bare shoulders, opening her coat just above her breasts. She then abruptly let it drop to the floor, revealing a white lace bra that featured her erect nipples, thong panties, white, thigh high, garter stockings with lace tops and black high heels. At five- foot ten with long auburn hair, large brown eyes and full sensuous lips, she was quite the sight. Any other time this would have been an exquisite welcome home present—but not today. Connor could only sit back and manage a beleaguered grin.

Susan posed for just a moment, before she walked over and straddled him. She put one arm behind his head, leaned forward and kissed his neck. Sliding her other hand down his chest, she began rubbing his crotch. He shut his eyes and wondered how this could get any worse, until he opened them to the sight of Maggie standing in the hallway. He couldn't imagine how she felt seeing this half-naked Amazon, of whom she was totally unaware five minutes ago, all over him. She stood and watched for what seemed like an eternity. He hoped she could see the apology in his eyes, as he watched her turn and head for the back door. He listened till he heard the door quietly shut and the faint sound of her car starting. His heart ached as he envisioned her pain.

Susan continued her advance and he knew that resisting would just cause more questions and take more time he didn't have. Still, he felt obligated to try.

"Susan, I have to go. I have an important meeting that I'm really late for."

"We haven't seen each other in six months and you can't take a few more minutes to get to a meeting that you're already late for anyway," she returned, unzipping his pants.

"I need to leave right now."

"What you need to do is be quiet and enjoy your surprise," she returned, having found what she was looking for in his boxers. "I see at least part of you is not in a hurry to get to a meeting."

He realized it was no use to resist. It wasn't a horrible physical punishment or anything; after all she was his fiancée. He tried to rationalize his relationship with Maggie, they had no commitment, words were never exchanged—there was no formal understanding in place. He really didn't even know that much about her. It was not his fault, they never talked about other people, for all he knew she had other lovers. Why then did he feel so guilty?

Having freed him from the confines of his jeans and boxers, Susan adjusted her thong panties to one side and guided him inside her. She let out a loud gasp as she slid down on top of him. Connor felt overwhelmed by an increasing emptiness. She continued to make love to him, her soft moans becoming louder as she increased her pace. After a few minutes, he could feel his physical self override his absent mental state. His mind started to drift while his body surrendered to her favors. When she felt his release, she held him tightly and planted a long, wet kiss on his lips.

"See honey, that only took a few minutes and now you can go to your meeting with a clear head, if you get my meaning," she said smiling, obviously enjoying her conquest and clever innuendo.

70

"Very funny, Susan," he returned, with an unmistakable hint of sarcasm.

"I thought so," she replied, smirking a little.

"I need to go, Susan. I'm going to be very late."

"Where is it you have to go that's so damn important you can't enjoy a few minutes with me after six months?" she blurted out.

Connor removed her hands from around his neck and taking her knee, he gently, but firmly rolled her off of him. He got up, pulled up his jeans and tucked in his shirt. Susan remained on the couch just watching him. He took a minute to collect himself, as the image of Maggie watching them continued to swirl through his mind. He hated how weak and vulnerable it made him feel. He didn't want the distraction—not now—he had no time for it.

Finally his attention turned back to Susan. She wasn't saying a word; she just sat and stared, with her big brown eyes that highlighted the quizzical look on her face. For a brief moment he admired how physically lovely she was. She was every man's dream—every man, but him. He prided himself on how mentally tough he was, how he could control his emotions—he finally had to come to grips with the fact that the mind cannot always control the heart.

"Connor what is it, what's going on with you?" she questioned, breaking the silence.

"I'm sorry, Susan. Wes Adams has some information about my father and I was supposed to be at his office twenty minutes ago."

"Is that all it is? It seems like a lot more than just that."

"That's it," he lied.

"Well, let's go then, I'll dress in the car," she said, as she got up and grabbed her raincoat.

Why not, he thought, picking up his leather jacket and following her out the door.

~ ~ ~

Chapter 10

Connor was very familiar with the office of Adams, Lock, Gold and Associates located on the tenth floor of the Tower Building in downtown Albany. The concern employed twelve senior partners and over fifty associates. Including support staff, they totaled over two hundred employees; easily the largest firm in the Capital District. Wes Adams was one of his father's best friends. He founded the enterprise over twenty-five years ago, after a ten-year career working for a large New York law firm. When he left, he was able to entice several large corporate clients to follow him. The ready customer base enabled him to jump-start his new practice and attract local, as well as out-of-area talent. Wes often said the better the people you surrounded yourself with, the less real work you'd have to do.

From what Connor had observed he was not an attorney who loved the law, in fact, there were other things he seemed like he would much rather be doing. But, he was well respected in the profession and that enabled him to travel in circles and assess opportunities that would normally be unavailable. He often said his favorite clients were entrepreneurs, the movers and shakers of the business world. Connor's father had told him that Wes often talked about starting a "real business" as he called it.

According to Guy Mason, the problem was, he was unable to mentally accept the all or nothing risk associated with start-up companies that either make millions or send the founder into bankruptcy. He needed a safety net, and while that allowed him to dabble in several ventures, it would never produce the big winner—the one that would allow him to escape the albatross that was the day-to-day running of a large firm. The law was a means to an end—and he always seemed to be searching for the end.

It was 7:30 p.m., when Connor, glancing at his watch, pulled his SUV into the underground parking lot. The attendant motioned him up to the window, barely getting the parking coupon into his hand before he bolted from his truck. He headed through the glass doors toward the elevator with Susan, now clad in tight designer jeans and a simple white silk top, in hot pursuit. They entered the elevator and pushed the button for the tenth floor. His mind was whirling, as well as his stomach. He couldn't tell if it was anxiety or the after effect of the incident with Maggie. No matter, it was like he was riding the elevator alone. He didn't want to ignore her, he just didn't know what to say—at least not yet.

The elevator opened outside the lobby to the law office. Two large etched glass doors with big gold handles marked the entrance. They entered, where a tired looking receptionist sitting behind a large oval counter directed them to Wes Adam's office.

Connor quickly made his way down the long hallway lined with offices, leaving Susan scurrying behind. He noticed several associates settling in for a long night when he passed by their open doors. Susan, picking up the pace, finally caught him, grabbing his arm as they continued toward the corner suite. The door to the office was ajar when they reached the end of the corridor. Connor didn't break stride. He pushed open the door and walked in to see Wes sitting behind a large mahogany desk, piled high with client files on either side.

Almost sixty years old, Wes Adams was around five-feet ten with a slender frame, making him always seem to Connor to appear taller than he was. He had thick, dark brown hair graying on the sides, brown eyes and a slightly oversized nose and mouth. Overall he was a pleasant man, with pleasant features. Connor had heard that he had a passion for young women and was currently on his third wife who was around twenty years his junior. Rumor had it that although he had money and the firm afforded him a nice living, with three households to support, he was always looking for more.

"Hello, Connor," Wes said, looking up and then glancing at his watch.

"Hi, Wes," Connor returned. "Sorry I'm late. Susan just got back from London and surprised me just as I was leaving."

"Must have been quite a surprise."

"You have no idea," Connor replied, managing a slight smile, still in a bit of disbelief of the evening's happenings so far.

"How are you Miss James?" Wes asked.

"I'm fine Mr. Adams, it's good to see you again."

"It's nice to see you, too. How are things going with your London assignment?"

"It's great. I love London. The firm I'm working for has been very gracious in letting me get settled, and I really like my job," she answered enthusiastically.

"Really. That's a very refreshing attitude," he said, his inflection revealing hardly the same tenor of excitement.

"Wes," Connor interrupted. "Can I ask you some questions, please?"

"Of course you can," Wes replied. "I'm sorry to have kept you waiting with my small talk." He punctuated his sarcasm by again looking at his watch.

"Sorry, sorry. I get it. I'm just a little anxious."

"I understand, Connor. We're all a little anxious about your father," his tone turning serious.

"Thanks for your concern."

"It's a lot more than just concern. Your father was one of my friends and I don't have many people that I put in that category."

"What was going on with him, Wes? I feel like he had this secret life that I didn't know anything about."

"Why don't you take a seat," he said, pointing to the two large chairs situated in front of his desk. "Can I see the fax you received?"

"Sure," Connor said, as he and Susan settled into the

seats. He reached into his pocket and pulled out the folded paper.

"Thanks," he returned, taking the paper and unfolding it. "I really can't believe after all these years, I'm actually holding this."

"Wes, can you give me a clue?" he pleaded, feeling Susan squeeze his hand in an attempt to quell his impatience. "My stomach is one big knot. I need some answers."

"Your father was involved in some very interesting projects that he was kind enough to include me in. He assisted his clients in facilitating transactions that they couldn't accomplish on their own. It often involved a degree of risk and a foreign location that most wouldn't deal with. He loved the adventure that life offered him, and reveled in the uncertainty. Few people could do what he did."

"What were these transactions, Wes? It almost sounds like he was a hit-man or something."

"Nothing like that, the transactions were of a financial nature," he smiled.

"Alright, Wes. Could we get a little more specific? Why don't we start with the fax; what's that all about?"

"I think I would rather have your father tell you himself."

"Is that a fact," Connor replied, not sure where he was going with this. "How are we going to accomplish that?"

"Come with me," he said, as he got up and headed for a door located on the far wall.

Connor gave Susan a puzzled look before they both rose from their seats and followed him.

~ ~ ~

Chapter 11

As morning's natural light bathed the cave opening, Jacob was awakened by the loud whine of a distressed truck. Its engine was clearly laboring to assist its spinning tires in gripping the crumbling earth it was losing contact with. The soldiers, guarding the prisoners in the rear of the tunnel, sprang to their feet, blocking Jacob's view and the origin of this new commotion. He didn't, however, have to see what his ears already told him. The loud crash of falling metal and a rapidly revolving beam from the tumbling vehicle's headlights revealed that the manmade ramp had given way under it's weight.

Over a dozen trucks, with tires slashed to the rims, had found their way into the stone tomb. From the sounds emanating outside, it was immediately apparent to Jacob that no other vehicle would make its way to this final resting place. The camp regulars stood frozen, not only physically pinned by the disabled vehicles, which forced them to huddle tightly against the stone wall, but now mentally pinned by yet another failure. They were rustling nervously while they waited to take their cue from the camp commander, who had been supervising the truck's entrance.

Jacob watched his captor's body slump in response to this latest catastrophe. Even at a distance the morning sun, which dimly illuminated their rock prison, disclosed a man under extreme duress. The camp soldiers observed their leader, cowering away from the large officer, who had immediately turned his attention to the activity outside. The officer, with the small boy gripping tightly to his waistband, hurried toward the light, disappearing through the opening. His booming voice was unmistakable as it momentarily quieted the chaos. He could be heard barking orders that grew more faint as he moved further from the entrance.

The commander, having seen that he was not the immediate concern, turned and began walking slowly toward Jacob and his other charges. He moved trance-like, only breaking gait when he bumped into the last vehicle to make it into the tunnel. The guards, who had been slashing tires, followed silently behind. Jacob knew their fate, like the vehicle lying outside, had tumbled completely out of their control.

Upon reaching the rear of the tunnel, the camp commander stopped and leaned against the stone wall before sliding down to a seated position; his knees up with his head hanging between them. The guards following him settled in, keeping a respectable distance from their leader. No one spoke as soldiers and prisoners sat together—the only sound was their labored breathing—a consequence of the dense dead air surrounding them and the inanimate objects they shared space with. Jacob looked over at the broken leader, now slouched even lower against the wall. Even in the shadows, he could see the color had drained from his face, leaving him with an ashen white complexion. For a moment, he almost felt a kinship toward him. They were both condemned men waiting for their sentence to be carried out.

The commotion seemed to have subsided, with the noise emanating from outside having decreased to a low steady rumble. Jacob sat quietly, wondering what cargo was carried in the crippled vehicles, which now occupied a majority of the space they had carved out of this jungle mountain. His thoughts were interrupted when a prisoner handed him a canteen filled with water. One of the guards had passed it, an act of unexpected humanity. Jacob was sure that the destiny of the guards and prisoners were now intertwined, as he accepted the container. He took a few small sips, then reached down and lifted his shackles, revealing the infected sores on his ankles. He winced when the metal rubbed over the inflamed area. He poured a small amount of water on each ankle, before carefully easing the leg irons back into place. He then passed the canteen while he enjoyed the cooling reprieve the water offered from the friction of his restraints.

Several hours later, there had still been no communication from the invading hoard. They just sat and waited. The camp commander had hardly moved since he silently abdicated his authority, maintaining his defeated posture against the wall. Jacob watched, as the dust stirred up by the invading vehicles remained suspended in the thick air, accentuating the melancholy image of the embattled leader. He figured he was making his final peace, as maybe they all should be.

Without warning, a huge shadow grabbed Jacob's attention. The large officer had entered the cave with the small boy still clinging to his side. One of the camp soldiers uttered a quiet word, which caused the camp commander to break his stillness and slowly look up. He then lowered his head and took a long deep breath, before seeming to muster the courage to rise to his feet. He brushed himself off and started to walk slowly, but deliberately, toward his hulking superior. Jacob imagined that he had accepted his fate and just wanted to get it over with. Despite the cruelty he'd endured, he still felt some empathy toward his captor.

The large officer looked toward the rear of the cave, before turning his attention to a single file of soldiers entering the tunnel. Jacob watched as the commander made his way toward him, while the soldiers quickly formed an assembly line and began passing something hand to hand and stacking it. As the commander neared, he stopped dead upon seeing the mysterious cargo being piled behind the last truck. The officer turned to see the surprised camp leader standing, statue like, near enough to identify the contraband. He raised a thick hand and shouted, causing the beset commander to spin around and withdraw.

After making his way back, all eyes looked to him for direction. It appeared that he wanted to speak, but seemed to catch himself before uttering a word, seeming to realize the futility of anything he could possibly relay. He retreated to the position he had been keeping for several hours prior to this most recent invasion. The guards, seeing his reaction, started a quiet murmur between them. The commander suddenly raised his head and barked a sharp word that silenced them. He made it clear he was still in charge and wanted what little time he had left to be as peaceful as possible. Jacob settled back against the wall, in concert with the guards and other prisoners. The only sounds were the shuffling of feet and the grunting of the soldiers stacking their cargo near the front of the cave.

Hours passed and day became night; fresh torches were lit, revealing how the assembly line had expanded, as the contraband was stacked in three distinct piles. Jacob's back was killing him, having been in the same position for over twenty-four hours. He wanted to stand up, but weighing the misery that the leg irons were likely to inflict, he decided to stay put. He was thirsty, hungry and curious. The stacks had gotten large enough to be visible, even from his hindered position. He couldn't help but wonder what it was, as he felt his head drop, taking leave of consciousness and lapsing into his usual sleep coma.

Waking to the sound of silence, Jacob noticed that the prisoners and guards were still sleeping. He allowed his foggy mind to clear. The torches had burned down, casting flickering shadows over the chiseled walls and metal vehicles that surrounded him. He was not sure of the time, but the sun was shinning brightly through the entrance. He figured early morning, considering he was the first one to wake and the lack of noise coming from the outside. Still, it was strange not to hear something with that many people and vehicles in the camp.

As his eyes focused, he honed in on the large rows that had been formed. They were at least thirty-feet long and six-feet high. He couldn't tell from his vantage point how wide they might be. The cave was dead silent except for some heavy snoring of the men around him. In his mind, they were all prisoners; the invaders that had taken control of their world erased any distinction between them.

His mouth was dry, as he felt his parched lips. He hadn't eaten for close to two days, although his hunger didn't produce the same physical response it did when he first arrived. It was just a deeper, empty pit-like feeling in his gut. He placed his hand on his stomach and pressed hard to lessen the sensation. His loss of body mass was apparent; his ribs were now the most prominent part of a once muscular torso. It was the first time since Jesse passed that he had considered his overall physical condition, usually just dwelling on one or two deteriorating body parts. Despite his dramatic weight loss and ankle infection, he felt he was still holding up—or at least that's what he kept telling himself.

As he continued to take inventory of his condition, he heard his fellow captives starting to stir. The guards looked particularly disoriented since they were not used to sleeping in such cramped conditions. The camp commander showed no emotion when he raised his head to survey what took place during the night. Jacob focused his attention on the commander, as he watched him rise. He seemed to have regained his composure since the events of the previous day, and directed a command to one of the guards. The surprised underling quickly rose and headed for the entrance. The commander turned and watched him proceed. He continued his steady gait until he reached the last truck, abruptly turning his attention to the three large stacks. He stopped and looked back toward his superior, appearing confused. The commander yelled out and motioned for him to advance. The soldier turned and continued, not taking his eyes off the newly placed contraband.

Before reaching his destination he was met head on by the large officer, accompanied by a dozen armed guards. The young boy was missing from his customary spot, as the group moved swiftly. The startled soldier seemed swallowed up by the fast moving unit, as he blended with them and was ushered back to the rear of the tunnel. Their movement was deliberate, evoking a sense of urgency and purpose that visibly unnerved those waiting for their arrival. The camp commander stood at attention while his men scrambled to their feet.

Jacob and the other prisoners remained seated, partially hidden behind their keepers.

As he faced the original camp unit, the large officer barked an order and the camp soldier was separated and returned. Jacob sensed a confrontation; he doubted that the camp commander and his men would offer much resistance, regardless of the peril they faced. The officer walked up to the commander and leaning closely whispered something to him. The embattled leader's erect posture wilted as he nodded his compliance. He took a deep breath, turned and gave an order to his men that seemed to leave them stunned. He repeated the directive, with even less conviction than the original issue. The soldiers hesitated momentarily, than placed their weapons against the cave wall. Being ordered to disarm had them all looking very uncomfortable.

Having had his instructions complied with; the large officer started to back away, creating some distance. Once separated, he gave a loud order to his men and they quickly shouldered their weapons, pointing them in the direction of the defenseless unit and the prisoners they unintentionally shielded. Jacob could sense the panic surge through the group, as he watched the officer raise his hand above his head. He knew it was going to end someday, but nothing had prepared him for this.

He closed his eyes tightly while thoughts of Sarah and home flashed through his mind. Everything seemed in slow motion, as he felt the terrified captives rustling around him. He had been surrounded by death for almost two years, but now it was staring him directly in the face. He didn't want to die, not like this, in a strange land where no one would ever know what happened to him. Why would an enemy treat their own with such disdain and what was in those trucks that would dictate such unpredictable behavior? His thoughts were suddenly interrupted by the deafening sound of gunfire.

~ ~ ~

81

Chapter 12

Connor and Susan followed Wes through the door and into a room annexed to his office. It was less than half the size, but seemed larger due to the lack of files and other clutter. The room contained a half-dozen dark, oversized leather chairs that encircled a highly glossed, oval conference table. To the right of the table, built into the wall, was a wet bar with matching cabinets that hung above it. Directly across the room sat a large monitor suspended on a movable black metal stand that also housed other electronic equipment. There were no windows, and the walls were adorned with tasteful but nondescript artwork. A half-empty crystal tumbler, sitting on top of a rumpled napkin, was the only sign to Connor that the room had recently been used.

"Please take a seat," Wes offered, motioning toward the table while he headed to the bar.

Connor and Susan each settled into one of the large leather chairs. Susan leaned back, as she swiveled the chair bottom to the comfortable position she was seeking. Connor remained upright; barely touching the chair back, his eyes never leaving Wes, who was now searching his pockets. He pulled out a set of keys and attempted to unlock the cabinet above the wet bar.

"Would you like something to drink?" Wes asked, while continuing to fumble with the lock.

"Nothing for me," Connor replied sharply, feeling a spike in the anxiety he'd been trying to control.

"How about you Ms. James?"

"What have you got, Wes?" Susan returned; appearing to ignore the look Connor was giving her for delaying the information process.

"Soda, water, juice whatever you like."

"Got anything stronger?"

"How about Scotch?"

"Single Malt?"

"It's all I drink," he returned, opening the cabinet and pulling out a bottle of Glen Livet and two heavy crystal tumblers.

"How do you like it?"

"Neat would be fine."

Wes opened the bottle and poured three fingers into each glass. Connor was now squirming, but determined to wait for everyone to get settled. Wes returned to the table, placed the tumbler in front of Susan and then took a seat across from them.

"Are you sure I can't get you anything, Connor?" Wes asked, as he raised the glass and took a large swallow.

"Just information, Wes. That's all I'd like right now."

"Of course."

"You said in your office that you wanted my father to tell me about the fax himself. Are we going to call him or have a séance or what?" he asked, his impatience mounting.

"None of the above. Your father anticipated that in the event he was unavailable when the fax came, it would be necessary to explain its origin and direct us as to what course of action to take or not take."

"So do you have a letter or instructions regarding the fax?" Connor interrupted.

"Could I finish?" Wes retorted, taking another swallow.

"Please."

"Thank you. He did not leave a letter, but he did leave instructions on video."

"Video?"

"Yes, before he left he handed me a package to keep in case the message came in his absence. He said in the event that the fax was received and he was deemed to be unreachable in the foreseeable future, we should view the video for further instructions."

"You haven't seen the video, Wes?" Susan asked.

"I have not."

"Okay then," Connor contributed. "Let's light this candle and find out what's what."

"Let's do just that," Wes replied, as he rose, gulping down his last bit of scotch. He then turned and walked toward the picture hanging on the wall directly behind him. Connor watched while he slid his hand along the mahogany frame until he found the release button he was searching for. He pushed the button and the picture opened forward on a hinge, revealing a small safe. He quickly dialed in the combination and opened the safe door, reaching in and pulling out a videotape marked "GM." He then shut the safe and returned the picture to its original position, before walking over and placing the tape in the VCR. He grabbed the remote and headed back to the wet bar, where he took the Glen Livet and returned to the table.

"Would you like me to freshen that for you Ms. James?" he said, pointing to her glass.

"Please," she replied, as she slid the tumbler toward him.

He filled her glass and then his own. Connor sat patiently, knowing he was finally close to getting some answers. Wes was about to start the video, when a ringing cell phone distracted him.

"Let's get this thing started," Connor suggested.

"Are you going to answer your phone?" Wes inquired.

"If it's important they'll call back."

"I know, so why don't you deal with it now instead of when we're in the middle of this."

"How about if I just shut it off?" Connor returned sharply, while he removed the ringing phone from his jacket.

"Just answer it Con," Susan chimed in. "It will be one less thing for you to deal with when we leave."

Connor just shook his head as he flipped open his phone.

"Hello."

"Connor, it's Alex."

"Alex, let me call you back. I'm in a meeting."

"We need to talk right now."

"If it's not life or death, it's going to have to wait."

"It is life or death."

"Who's?"

"Yours, if you don't talk to me right now."

"Alright, alright, just a second," Connor returned, rising from the table. "Excuse me for just a moment, there's one more important thing that can't wait I need to deal with," his frustration peaking.

Wes raised his hand and eyebrows in acknowledgement, and then his scotch glass. Susan, now well into her second drink, seemed quite content to wait. Connor walked over to the corner of the room to continue his conversation.

"Alex, what the fuck couldn't wait?"

"Are you completely out of your mind?"

"What are you talking about?"

"I'm talking about you fighting that Neanderthal in two days."

"You went to Pauley's tonight," he deducted.

"Yeah, I went to Pauley's and that was the hot topic of the entire club. I'm surprised Pauley's not selling tickets, considering the number of people who know about it—except me of course."

"Look, I'm sorry I didn't tell you, but it's been one hell of a day and I just didn't want to deal with it."

"Connor, I'm your partner and your best friend. You should have dealt with it, because I look like an ass not knowing what's going on."

"Is that what we're talking about here, me making you look bad?"

"No, you told me you were going to let this go."

"I lied."

"I know. That's what I'm talking about."

Before Connor could answer, he was disconnected. He stood quietly for over a minute. He wanted to call Alex back

85

and explain, but it would have to wait. He had to have his own questions answered. He turned and headed back to the table, where Susan and Wes were patiently waiting, sipping their scotch and talking quietly.

"Ready?" Wes asked, while Connor settled into his seat.

"Let's go," Connor replied, shutting off his phone and placing it on the table in front of him.

Wes pointed the remote toward the large screen, clicking the appropriate buttons to activate the monitor and VCR. The image of a man began to come into focus. It was Guy Mason, appearing lean and fit, but looking all of his mid-fifty years Connor thought, as he watched him recline in a stuffed leather chair. He was wearing a dark blue shirt rolled up to his forearms, and blue jeans, highlighted by a wide, light colored leather belt. His large brown eyes seemed to sparkle while he waited. He suddenly sat up, as if finally getting a cue to begin. He folded his hands and looked directly into the camera. A quizzical smile crossed his tanned face and he began to speak.

"Hi, Connor."

As he heard his name, Connor could feel his body tingle. He felt a little weak and his eyes started to well up. Seeing his father for the first time since his disappearance brought him face-to-face with the reality of his loss. A sensation of emptiness engulfed him while he fought back tears and waited for the mystery to unravel.

~ ~ ~

Chapter 13

When Jacob opened his eyes, he could see the fallen guards. In the confined space, the gunfire had been so loud that he couldn't distinguish their screams from the sound of shots being fired. They were all dead, with the exception of the camp commander, who sat terrified, cowering against the cave wall. They had been cruelly executed and what remained was a bullet ridden, bloody heap of humanity—despite the fact that they were the enemy, he felt an unexplainable feeling of loss. While he took inventory of himself, he detected the moans of some of his fellow prisoners who had been hit by ricocheting bullets. Finally he realized he hadn't been shot, at least not yet.

Jacob watched the large officer beginning to make his way toward the camp commander, who was clearly in a state of shock. Jacob was sure this was not the ending he had pictured for his men or himself, killed at the hands of their countryman for no apparent reason. He wasn't sure however, if any of the events of the last few moments were even registering in the brain of the disorientated leader.

The officer waded through several bodies finally reaching his underling. He grabbed him by the collar and yanked him to his feet, continuing to grasp his shirt while he shouted in the face of the listless man. It was obvious to Jacob he was not getting the desired reaction, as the camp commander's face remained blank and unresponsive. The large officer continued his assault, violently shaking the smaller man. His seemingly lifeless body was like a rag doll in the powerful, stubby hands of his much bigger superior. Jacob couldn't imagine what he hoped to accomplish by his actions, feeling if he released his grip, the commander would simply collapse to the cave floor.

Mercifully, he gave up and stopped the verbal battering of his catatonic prey. With one thick hand around his neck, he pinned the commander against the cave wall, holding him at arm's length. With his free hand he withdrew a revolver from his waistband and placed it against his temple. His captive's only reaction was to close his eyes, signaling a silent surrender to his fate. Jacob turned his head and heard the shot echo off the stone walls. When he looked back, the lifeless corpse of the camp leader was lying at the feet of the large officer, his barrel chest heaving from the adrenaline rushing through his body. Even in the dimly lit cave, he could see the blood spattered over the face and arm of this intimidating hulk, as he turned his attention to the prisoners.

The officer directed his soldiers to once again shoulder their weapons. Jacob closed his eyes and awaited the inevitable. Another order and Jacob could hear someone rustling near him. When he opened his eyes, two guards lifted him to his feet and quickly dragged him over the bodies in the direction of his new master. Being the only American, maybe his new keeper thought he was deserving of the same fate as the commander. Jacob could see the revolver still dangling in his thick hand while the guards ushered him closer.

Upon reaching his captor, Jacob no longer felt any benefit could be gained by looking away. He locked in on the menacing eyes that appeared even more demonic, highlighted by the drying blood on his large round face. When the large officer moved forward, Jacob was determined not to fold in his final moments. He remained steadfast, while he stood nose to nose with his enemy. The officer stared directly into his defiant eyes, when with one quick violent motion he reached up and tore the dog tags from his neck. He paused for a moment to inspect the tags, before tossing them into one of the disabled vehicles. He motioned to the guards on either side and they began ushering him toward the entrance of the tunnel.

Jacob figured he must have decided it would serve a greater purpose to execute him in front of the hundreds of invading troops, instead of deep inside the dark reaches of the tunnel, where no example would be made. As he neared the front of the cave and the contraband, he took solace in the fact that at least he would have the benefit of knowing what the Japanese were hiding in this jungle hell-hole and what could possibly justify the high price of human life.

He winced when the chain connecting his shackles caught on the uneven terrain of the tunnel floor. His pain quickly became an after thought, as he was almost close enough to make out the mysterious stacks. As he neared, it became apparent that his ultimate question would remain unanswered. Several guards were covering the contraband with canvas; probably remnants from the carrier tops of the trucks that had been unable to enter the cave. At this point it didn't matter. An order from the large officer caused the deafening sound of gunfire to again echo thru the tunnel. Jacob felt his body go limp as the remaining prisoners were executed. The guards never broke stride, continuing to drag him toward the cave entrance.

Escorted into the bright daylight, it took a few moments for his eyes to adjust. His last forty-eight hours had been a nocturnal existence. He fought to focus. The sunlight had temporarily blinded him, leaving him to fill in the blanks around the large dark spots. While he rubbed his eyes, he was sure that this was the end, execution of the infidel in front of the invaders. When the spots subsided, he was astonished to see the camp had been abandoned with the exception of one troop carrier. All signs had been completely removed, the tents, the make shift grass huts, the trucks, the soldiers and equipment, all gone. Once the troop carrier departed, there would be no evidence that a camp even existed here, he thought. Except of course for the tunnel and its mysterious contents.

Nearing the carrier, in the middle of what had been the jungle encampment, Jacob was able to make out someone in the truck cab. He had no doubt that the smallish figure was the young boy. When he reached the vehicle, the two guards released him and he fell to the jungle floor. They then each took a position on either side of him, refocusing their attention toward the cave entrance.

It was only a few minutes before the large officer, followed by his soldiers, exited the tunnel. They made their way toward the lone vehicle and Jacob, who remained on the ground. He didn't try to stand, having had little water and less food for the last two days made him uncertain he could, even if he had to. However, his hunger and dehydrated condition were second thoughts, as he was now measuring his future in moments. The officer stopped short of the truck and gave an order while he pointed toward the entrance of the tunnel. Two of his men moved quickly and retrieved two long wires hanging from above the opening. The soldiers brought the wires back to the troop carrier, where they fastened them to a detonator. Jacob's eyes followed the source of the wires as they rose high above the entrance and were attached just below the tiger-head rock face.

The officer gave another order and Jacob was again lifted to his feet. A guard started the truck and began driving it slowly away from the mountain. The remaining guards, with Jacob in tow and the large officer, followed. When they reached the edge of what was the encampment, the officer turned and gave instructions to the lone remaining soldier manning the detonator. Jacob watched while he ignited an explosion that brought down an avalanche of rock, burying the cave entrance.

When the dust cleared, he could see that the jutting stone face had been erased from the mountainside. It had been reduced to a huge pile of rock and dirt that now shrouded almost two years of back breaking labor and over two dozen lost lives. The concealment was almost complete, he thought. Anyone not present would never know what had happened or what was entombed in the tunnel. Even those that had been here had now lost the most prominent landmark that could have been used to identify the cave location in this ever changing, mountainous jungle terrain.

Jacob now realized he was the last loose end. As he looked toward his hulking captor, now seemingly more menacing, his face and uniform still covered with the dried blood of the former camp commander, his attention turned from his mortality to that of his family. He put them in his head and decided that his last thoughts, before leaving this horrible existence, would be of the ones he loved.

With the tunnel and its contents secured, the large officer had just turned toward Jacob, when his focus was suddenly interrupted by a high-pitched voice. He answered in a firm, but non-threatening tone and stood waiting—his attention now on the young boy. The child bolted from the truck and headed for the large officer who had assumed a kneeling position. When the boy arrived he lifted him into his arms. He leaned forward and whispered something in his guardian's ear while Jacob watched this truly odd scene, given the surreal events of the last forty-eight hours.

The officer, with the boy still cradled in his arms, gave an order to one of the guards who disappeared around the back of the truck. He returned with a white sack and handed it to his superior. The officer placed the boy at his feet and began searching in the bag. He removed a white cloth and placed it in front of the youngster. He then pulled out several pieces of fruit, bread, dried fish and other food items and spread them on the cloth. Jacob watched and wondered how after such cruel acts, this man could prepare a picnic for a young child with the loving care of a parent. He did not however, despite this show of affection, harbor any illusions about the fact that his survival was still very much in doubt.

The young boy reached for a piece of fruit and started to raise it to his mouth, as he looked at Jacob sitting a few yards away. He stopped just before biting into the fruit, got up and walked toward the longhaired, straggly bearded prisoner. When he neared, one of the soldiers stepped forward to intercept the small visitor. The guard reached out for the boy, as he simultaneously caught the eye of the large officer sitting in the area where the child had just vacated. He shook his head slightly at the soldier, who immediately backed off and allowed the young boy access to his prisoner. The boy took a few more steps toward Jacob and reaching out a small hand, offered him the fruit. Jacob hesitated for a moment. He glanced at his guards and the officer—no one moved when he took the fruit. Once it was apparent there would be no repercussion, he nodded his thanks. The child took a few steps back and watched as Jacob devoured the offering. It had been the only thing he had eaten in two days, and compared to his usual diet, this was a feast.

After observing him eat, the boy returned to his jungle picnic. He knelt down and took two pieces of dried fish and a piece of bread and returned to his new friend. This time no one even acknowledged his actions. The guards stood at attention while the large officer, sitting by the white cloth continued to eat. The child handed the food to Jacob who eagerly accepted. While he ate, the youth backed away and bowed toward him, touching his forehead with his right hand, blessing him. In between bites, Jacob managed a slight smile at his young benefactor. Once he started, it was like he couldn't eat fast enough. He never imagined that such simple fare could taste so good.

The young boy returned to his food and began quietly eating. The officer sat near him and continued his nibbling. The other guards, with the exception of the ones stationed near the prisoner, all had taken the opportunity to find their own source of sustenance. Jacob sat and watched as he crunched on dried fish bones. The frantic sense of urgency that had engulfed the camp for the last several days had disappeared. The mission was complete, and his enemy was no longer in the same heightened state—even though the fate of the last prisoner was still to be determined.

~ ~ ~

Chapter 14

Connor, Susan and Wes sat glued to the video screen. Connor now wished he'd been drinking like his companions—feeling he could have used a little artificial reality buffer. Once his father spoke, a flood of emotion took over. He wasn't sure he could control himself, but was determined not to break down as the tape continued.

"Surprised, son? You shouldn't be. I paid more attention to you and your brothers than I think you gave me credit for. I figured you would be viewing this video along with Wes. Your personality and interests were always closest to my own."

Guy paused and Connor noticed him shifting in his seat. It was obvious that this was not the most comfortable medium in which to communicate the information he wanted to relay.

"If you are viewing this video, I am not reachable or dead. I'm usually available, so chances are I'm no longer with you. I'd like to be a little more solemn, but it's kind of hard when you're still alive. And let me assure you, I was alive when we made this video. If you haven't figured it out by now, Dan is manning the camera, so I can't attest to the final quality of the production."

Suddenly the picture started to move about like it was in the middle of an earthquake.

"Very funny, Dan."

"You know, Guy," came an off screen voice. "If you're dead, then I'm probably dead too."

"There are those that may argue that you were dead long before we made this video Dan," Guy answered, rather tongue in cheek.

"You're probably right, Guy. I just wish it was my ex-wives who thought that."

"They did, but only when you were in bed with them."

The comment caused Wes and Susan to chuckle, along with the on screen participants. It made Connor smile to remember this playful banter he grew up with. His father had a quick wit and a wonderful sense of humor. One of the joys of being around him was that he never took himself or any situation too seriously. He could always find the bright side in almost anything he thought—even his death.

"Let me apologize for getting side tracked," said Guy, sporting a playful smirk. "I would hope you will allow us some indiscretion because we are dead, you know."

"Could we move this along before we run out of tape?" said Dan, heckling from off screen.

"We most certainly can," he replied, his voice turning deliberate and much more serious. "Connor, Wes and whoever else maybe present. I'm truly sorry. This has to be a tough time for both of you and our family. No matter what the venture, I tried to be as careful as the situation would allow. This time I guess we were not as lucky. I assume you are playing this in order to get some answers regarding the fax and our activities that have left us . . . let's say, incapacitated for now."

Connor felt his throat start to tighten and stomach churn. This was the most uneasy he had been since his Dad disappeared. Wes and Susan were locked on the screen. The alcohol had obviously buffered them from the emotions he was feeling.

"Let me start with our current undertaking and then I'll backtrack and fill you in on the fax. By now, you have probably surmised we were not on a fishing trip. Dan and I left to verify a shipwreck in shallow water off the coast of Mexico. It was a project brought to us by an associate that I had worked with before, usually behind the scenes in the financial arena.

This was the first one that we've actually had an opportunity to be hands on, and after being on the shelf for sometime, I just couldn't pass it up.

"The ship was the S.S. San Francisco, an early 1900s steamer used for transport from San Francisco to Mexico. This was before the Panama Canal, so there was no direct coast-to-coast shipping lane. Once on Mexico's west shore, passengers and cargo would be transported over land to the coast, where they would board another steamer to complete their trip east, usually to New York. The major cargo was gold, originated from the Alaskan mines during the Gold Rush of 1897. Once fortunes were made, many would use this form of travel to return to their families. According to the manifest, the S.S. San Francisco was carrying just over one and a half tons, hence our interest in the project. Excuse me just a moment."

Guy paused, as he reached out of camera range and retrieved a bottle of water that must have been sitting nearby. He raised the bottle and took several long swallows. Connor sat stunned. It was hard for him to believe that the man talking was his father. He felt confused—and excited.

"Could you put the video on hold?" Connor asked, running a hand nervously through his red hair.

"Certainly," Wes returned, pointing the remote and freezing the picture.

"Wes, am I hearing this right? My father was a treasure hunter?"

"Kind of, I guess. He was involved in various projects relating to precious metals, antiquities and financial instruments."

"Yeah, I'm sure. But am I hearing correctly? He was in Mexico looking for a sunken ship with gold onboard."

"Yes, but why don't you wait, by the end of the video you'll have a better feel for what he did and after, if you still have questions, I'll do my best to fill in the blanks for you."

"Answer this one first, Wes. How does someone in upstate New York become involved in treasure hunting?"

"I once asked your father the very same question," Wes returned, leaning back in his chair and a slight smile appearing on his face. "He told me that people make things happen, not places. Why don't we continue?"

"Fine," Connor resigned. Wes reactivated the tape and Guy continued his explanation.

"I was personally interested, because the ship went down in around fifty-feet of water, making the cost of recovery probably less than half a million. As you know Dan and I are certified divers, so checking out the area didn't pose much of a problem, unlike deepwater wrecks. Like any activity of this nature, there were several obstacles to deal with. They included a third world government, bandits, drug runners and natural accidents.

"There is really no need to go into detail because, with the exception of my personal circumstances, that is not the reason for this video. Let me just say, if it has been at least six months and no witnesses have come forward and no bodies have been found, it is unlikely we had a run in with the government or an accident. The chances are it was drug runners or bandits. If that's the case, please do not attempt to find us. This is a very dangerous area and you have a much better chance of getting dead, than you do of finding out what happened. We are most likely gone, but if we are alive, we'll find a way to contact you.

"Please Connor, stay put. Your mother needs you. You can't do anything for me now. Having said that, let's focus on the reason you're here—the fax message."

"Stop the video again, Wes," Connor asked, sensing his rising anxiety.

Wes obliged and halted the tape.

"Connor you need to get through this. Then, ask your questions once you've had the time and information to properly evaluate the situation," Susan suggested.

"Susan, it's my father and I'll do this my way. I know you're only trying to help, but you're not helping.

"Fine, I'm sorry."

"Don't be sorry, be quiet."

Susan didn't answer; she just folded her arms and threw him the best attorney dirty look she could muster.

At this point, he didn't care how or what she was feeling. He needed answers and didn't want to wait. He was coping the best he could. What she didn't know was, if he didn't stop the video with his questions, he wouldn't get through it. "Wes, did you know about Mexico?"

"Of course I did."

"Have you heard anything or have any idea what happened to him?"

"No, I just know what you know."

"Have you tried to do anything to find him?"

"Yes, as I'm sure your mother has told you, I made all the standard inquires about six months ago. I contacted a law firm in Mexico City and had them follow up on tourist accidents, unidentified bodies and any government detainments. Nothing fit your father's or Dan's description."

"I think I should go down there and see what I can find out."

"Connor, you haven't been listening. You can't find him. I wouldn't know where to tell you to start, or even if he entered the country legally. Your father is a whole lot smarter than we are when it comes to these types of operations. Let's do what he would want us to—stay put."

"Maybe you should be quiet and listen," Susan chimed in, her bravado obviously bolstered by her second scotch.

Connor barely gave her a sideways glance, choosing to ignore her unsolicited contribution.

"Do you think he's dead, Wes?" Connor asked solemnly.

"What I think is not important. What is—is, and we have to deal with that. Right now, you and I need to finish watching and follow his wishes. Anything else in my opinion would be futile at this time."

Connor hesitated. He looked down at his hands resting on the table. The day had been a roller coaster of emotions. There was lots to sort out, and more to take care of in the days to come. Maggie, Alex, Sid, his father, Susan and God knows what else. He felt like he was in vapor lock, not sure what direction to take. Susan was right; take in the information and then make an informed decision as to the proper course of action. It was just so much easier said than done. "Okay Wes, let's continue."

Wes nodded and restarted the tape.

~ ~ ~

Chapter 15

Jacob sat quietly waiting and watching. The jungle hell-hole he remembered was now almost non-existent. The whole area had been completely cleansed. Once the dense vegetation overgrew the path leading to the camp, there would be no trace. The entrance to the cave and its contents would remain hidden, under its new blanket of rock and dirt, until someone returned to unearth it. He figured that the rapid plant growth would reclaim the area in less than a year. Once he was dealt with, there would be nothing left to mark his existence for the past eighteen months—not that he wanted a monument to his misery. He was just trying to grasp onto something that would give him comfort. At the moment, all that was there was a feeling as empty as the encampment.

The large officer sat and waited while the young boy finished eating. He then gathered up the white cloth and remaining food items, placing them in the sack. As he stood up with the sack in hand, he motioned for his young charge to come closer. The boy rose and walked slowly over to him. He leaned over and whispered something in his ear and the boy nodded his approval. The child then turned and headed in the direction of the lone remaining truck. When he passed Jacob, he caught his eye and gave him a wide smile. Jacob managed to nod, and half-heartedly returned the gesture. He then climbed into the cab and out of sight.

The officer gave an order and one of the guards walked over to Jacob and pulling out a set of keys, knelt down and removed his shackles. Jacob wondered where the keys had come from, finally surmising that they must have been taken from one of the fallen camp soldiers. Why would they bother to remove the leg irons? Obviously, they didn't intend to take him with them, or they would have left the restraints. But if they were going to kill him, why didn't they just leave them in place as they had the other prisoners? Then it struck him; the other prisoners were buried out of sight and his body would be left in the open. If anyone happened on him, the shackles could make them decide that something here might be worth further investigation. But just a body, or a skeleton in the jungle, would probably not ignite the same curiosity in the unlikely event that it was stumbled across at all.

Jacob's mind was now filling rapidly with scenes of his demise. The large officer started walking toward him, still holding the sack. Jacob's eyes never left him; he knew he was the keeper of his fate, as he had been for the camp guards and his fellow prisoners. He could feel his heart start to race as he watched him remove a revolver from his waistband, while directing an order to the two guards standing watch over their prisoner. The soldiers lifted Jacob to his feet and the officer grabbed him by the arm. He then directed him toward the jungle and away from the truck. He gave another order and the remaining guards loaded into the troop carrier.

He looked back toward the large officer now walking behind him. His keeper motioned for him to continue, with a wave of his thick hand that clutched tightly to his pistol. Jacob wanted to do something, not just go out like the camp commander did, without a whimper. He realized in his weakened state that he had few options, running or turning to attack would only hasten the inevitable. Still, he felt desperate to try something.

When they neared the edge of encampment, Jacob stopped. He started to slowly turn when a push to the back ushered him out of the clearing. They made their way though various growths leading deeper into the bush. Jacob knew that this was a journey he would not be returning from. Taking a couple of quick steps, he whirled to face his enemy. The officer barely reacted, making it obvious that he knew his debilitated charge could hardly pose a physical threat. Jacob felt obligated to at least speak his piece, even if was going to fall on deaf ears.

"My name is Jacob—Jacob Thomas. I have a wife and two children, one I've never seen. I was a farmer; my family has a farm where we grow wheat. I don't pretend to know what was going on here or what's in the tunnel we dug, all I know is that I don't want to die in this place. The only thing that kept me alive was the hope of getting back to my family. I know you probably don't understand a word I'm saying and I'm not going to beg for my life, but if you have any decency at all, it can't make any sense for you to kill me. What threat could I possibly be? Can't you just leave me? I promise, if by some miracle, I actually make it out of here alive—I will never tell anyone about this place or the tunnel. For Christ's sake it's not suppose to end like this. I'm from Indiana."

Jacob stopped talking and stared at his adversary, hoping for some sort of reply. The officer showed no emotion, as he returned the stare. Jacob let out a loud sigh and shook his head, resigned to the fate he expected. "You didn't understand a word I said, did you—you monster?"

"The monster understand," replied the large officer.

Jacob was so startled, that he was momentarily tongue-tied. He felt a sudden sense of hope. At least he could communicate with his would-be executioner.

"You speak English?"

"Ai."

"Then you understood everything I said to you?"

"Ai."

"You know I won't cause any trouble. I've only made one promise that I haven't kept yet and that's the one I made to my wife, when I told her I'd come home. I will never disclose this location to anyone and what took place here. That's a promise I make to you—I won't break it."

"I know," the officer replied, as he raised his revolver and fired.

~ ~ ~

Chapter 16

Connor sat attentive, as well as intent on getting through the video while Wes poured Susan her third scotch. She was already acting a little tipsy, but he didn't feel it was his place to comment on her future condition. Nor did he really care, other than the fact he would have to navigate her back to the vehicle when they left. Despite the alcohol Wes ingested, Connor noticed no marked change in his demeanor, most likely a result of ritual drinking brought on by the pressure of his chosen profession. All three watched, in their own various stages of mental debilitation, while Guy continued his explanation.

"The fax received was a coded message from George Fall, a friend I have known for over twenty years now. Unfortunately, fifteen of those years have been spent in the Philippines and not at home, where he would have liked. Let me give you a little background on how we met, before I tie in the message. Please bear with me Wes; I know you've heard this all before."

"I never mind hearing it again from you, my friend," Wes replied softly, lifting his glass in mock toast.

"I was consulting a client who was creating a rattan furniture prototype store for a franchise model, and was interested in direct purchasing. He hired me to investigate a new source of product since his original manufacturer in Taiwan, was about to close down their operation. My research found that rattan was a vine that grows mainly in the jungles of Indonesia and the Philippines. Several large commercial exporters had factories there. I decided the best place to start my search was at the national furniture show in North Carolina. Manufacturers, wholesalers and representatives converge there twice a year to fill orders with retail sellers. Factories from all over the world were in attendance. It was one big party, with booths and booze filling the entire town. If you knew George, you'd understand it was the perfect venue for him.

"After visiting several displays, I came across George representing a factory located on the island of Cebu. He was from the mid-west and had been in the furniture importing business with his father for over fifteen years. He had a wide variety of product styles, finishes and price ranges. I was impressed with his knowledge of the Philippines and the product line. He had been going over there at least four or five times a year with his father, before he retired. I also liked the fact that a German engineer, who happened to be the husband of the Filipino factory owner, ran the overseas operation. I spent the week with George picking his brain. When I returned, I introduced him to my client and they did quite a bit of business together. Whenever George was in town, we'd get together, and that's how the friendship began."

"Could you cut to the chase, Guy. I've heard this one before too," came a familiar off-screen voice.

"Hang in there, Dan," Guy replied with a smile. "We're almost to the good part."

"Thank God."

"As I was saying," he continued. "We became friends, and around three years after our initial meeting, he contacted me about getting involved in a venture to import stone craft from the Philippines. Stone craft is a process where colorful rocks, found only in Asia, are cut very thin and hand glued on wooden frames. It is very labor intensive, so you could only afford to manufacture in third world countries. The finished product was outstanding and because of low manpower costs, the margins were high. He wanted to import tables, chairs and other accessories, like small boxes, birds, animals, etc. He had a direct factory contact, where we could buy containers of the stuff at a very good price. He had the network for buying and selling, and needed a partner to help with the financing. I got involved and we started the business. We did very well—for a while.

"Like I said, George is a friend of mine, but as we worked together, there were things I was less than thrilled about. He had good intentions, but tended to trust people he shouldn't, drink too much and, for lack of a better description, whore a lot too much. He would often take someone's word, without doing the necessary due diligence. That led to promises we couldn't keep, with regard to orders coming from the factories."

Guy paused for a moment, while he shifted in his seat. He then took a drink from the water bottle. After a couple of swallows he continued.

"With things in disarray, George returned from one of his factory visits with a project I was less than enthusiastic about. One of the workers approached him with a story about his uncle who had witnessed gold bars being hidden in a secret tunnel by the Japanese army, in the mountains on the island of Mindanao. He was a young boy at the time and was either the son or concubine of a Japanese general known as Yamashita. George wanted us to finance a dig for the gold on the property that the uncle owned, but had been unable to unearth for the last forty years. As you can probably imagine, this sounded as insane to me, as it must to all of you—with the exception of Wes."

"And like I said before, I never mind hearing it again," Wes chimed in.

"George insisted, and because of the low cost, I reluctantly agreed to indulge his fantasy. Workers in the Philippines are paid roughly two dollars a day. We hired twenty men from the village and started the excavation. We made the factory worker who brought us the story, Lido, the foreman, and under direction of the uncle, he and his men went to work. The whole operation was costing us around two thousand a month, and at the time, I just chalked it up to George's mental therapy.

"He was going through his second divorce due to the amount of time he was spending overseas, and was so far behind on alimony payments to his first wife that he was in danger of being arrested. In addition, he had another family started in the Philippines and was financially spread so thin that he needed lightning in a bottle, and this was his, as far-fetched as it seemed.

"I did some preliminary research on the chances there actually was Japanese gold in the Philippines. What I found was you could buy a treasure map on every corner. It was the most active con game in the country, used to separate foreigners from their money. They relied on greed and desperation. I never thought of George as a greedy man. He was probably generous to a fault, but he was desperate and that is a bad ingredient for using good judgment. Despite that, I did find evidence that the Japanese had hidden gold. There were many documented accounts of the president of the Philippines at the time, Ferdinand Marcos, selling more gold bullion in a single transaction than was available in the country's vaults.

"In addition, we had an eyewitness, although anyone could have conjured up the story. I must admit, I really didn't expect anything to come of it, other than to give false hope to a friend."

There was a pause. Connor sensed his father collecting his thoughts. This was not a scripted presentation. There were no notes and that allowed him to keep constant eye contact, making his explanation seem even more plausible. Wes and Susan remained totally engulfed; their only movement was to intermittently raise the liquor filled tumblers to their lips. As he continued, Connor thought his father's life was more unbelievable than he ever could have imagined. Unbelievable, and at the same time—enviable.

"As you have probably surmised, we found the gold. Otherwise, you wouldn't be viewing this video. George was right, a cave did exist and we unearthed it. The source was what I determined after the operation came to an unexpected end. What was it doing in the middle of the jungle? Where did it come from? Why hadn't someone come for it before? These were just some of the questions I'm sure you're asking yourself, as I did.

"First of all, it is important to understand that the Japanese were a great warring nation that conquered most of East and Southeast Asia, prior to the outbreak of World War II. With their conquests came riches beyond any of our wildest dreams. Gold and precious gems came from the churches, temples, monasteries, banks, corporations and fallen govern-ments, as well as the gangster syndicates and black market economies of countries including Korea, Manchuria, China, Indochina, Thailand, Burma, Malaya, Borneo, Singapore, the Philippines and the Dutch East Indies. Various estimates put the total of this war loot at four to six thousand tons of gold bullion alone. In the 1940's it would have been worth over three billion dollars. Today, that same amount would have a value in excess of a hundred billion.

"The Philippines was a pre-war transshipment point, where the gold was staged and prepared for transport to Tokyo; the majority of this ill gotten gain never reached Japan. The outbreak of the war forced them to hide most of it on the islands. General Yamashita, known as the Tiger of Malaya, for his rapid conquest of that nation, was put in charge of hiding the vast fortune. Hence the loot became known as Yamashita's Gold. General Yamashita concealed the majority of the gold on the island of Luzon, in the mountains north of Manila. There were over a hundred locations. Yamashita was in charge of mapping and booby trapping the sites in order to deter anyone searching for the treasure.

"Based on our research and the story the uncle gave us, it seems Yamashita decided to make sure that he had a very significant stash of his own. This was not unusual, it had been unofficially reported that General MacArthur had gold bullion given to him by Ferdinand Marcos, along with some very desirable oceanfront land rights. When he made his famous quote, "I shall return," I think he meant he would comeback to get his money and stay in his beachside condo complex. Some of his actions, just prior to the Japanese invasion of the Philippines, may have been prompted by his personal financial ambition. At any rate, Yamashita was seeing to his own interests when he took a huge amount of bullion and transferred it to a southern island. It seems he selected a site in the mountains, just south of the port city of Cagayan De Oro on the island of Mindanao. He had a very small group of guards and prisoners of war dig a tunnel in the mountainside in order to hide his fortune.

"What happens next is probably the most mind boggling of any wartime activity. Yamashita ordered somewhere between five hundred to two thousand tons of gold loaded on the Japanese warship, the Nachi. He then had some two hundred men along with his personal guards; transfer the gold from Luzon to his mountain hideaway in Mindanao. After his troops hid the gold, according to the uncle, all prisoners and the POW camp guards were executed and the entrance to the tunnel was sealed by a dynamite blast. The remaining troops were sent to the carrier and shipped back to Luzon.

"Now the first question that comes to mind is, with so many men knowing the location, how did it stay a secret for so long? This is where you have to take measure of the value of a human life; Yamashita did not board the Nachi for the return trip with his troops. He left orders, that upon return of the ship to the Bay of Manila, one of the two Japanese subs that patrolled the bay was to sink her. The reason was to keep the treasure, that unbeknownst to anyone but those on board she was no longer carrying, out of the hands of the allies. The ship was sunk and there were confirmed reports that the sub, upon surfacing, machine-gunned down survivors in the water. Yamashita had accomplished his ruse, getting the Japanese army to help him hide his own personal fortune, and covering up the theft, by making his superiors believe that the balance of the treasure was at the bottom of Manila bay. The price of wealth that he never retrieved was over three hundred lives. More have died for less I suppose, but it hardly seemed justified."

Connor noticed his father's voice had shifted to a more somber tone as he told the tale, knowing he would never put wealth above human life—anyone's life, especially his own. It was obvious that something had happened to make him feel personally involved. This was much more than just a history lesson; it had the feel of a eulogy. He watched the screen as the story continued to unfold.

"That's how we believe the gold ended up on the island. It really doesn't matter how it got there, because I personally know that it's there. Our initial attempt to remove it was enthusiastic, but amateurish at best. There was so much we didn't know then, that we do now. We were forced to abandon the project fifteen years ago. We all left to regroup; knowing it would be quite sometime before we would be able to revisit this adventure. I won't go into all the details; it's not relevant anymore. It took close to two years to complete the dig and gain access to the cave, mostly because of delays due to army troops and rebels in the area.

"During that time, George fell deeper into debt and further behind in alimony payments. He couldn't go back empty handed, so he never left; he took refuge on the island of Cebu. I've supported him for the last fifteen years he has lived overseas; it has been by no means an opulent existence. About five years ago, he returned to Mindanao and was waiting for the appropriate time to restart the dig. 'The eagle has landed,' meant that he had reconstituted the site and was within a week of gaining access.

"The plan was to meet him on the island of Cebu at the Princess Hotel, exactly one week from the date the fax was received. No one was to enter the treasure chamber, until I arrived. The bottom line is that I am not going to be there. What you need to do Connor, is go to my office and in the top middle drawer of my desk is an address book. There is a fax number for the Pryce Plaza Hotel in Cagayan De Oro. Send a fax with the following message 'The eagle has passed'; sign it son of GM. That will alert George to the fact that I'm not coming—ever. He's a resourceful guy, I hope for his sake he can make something happen. Please don't get any crazy ideas about going over there. There are lots of adventures in life, son. Some get you t-shirts and some get you killed, this is definitely the latter.

"Please do as I ask as soon as possible. George is not the best businessman, but he has a good heart. Once he breaks through that chamber and the workers know what's down there, he will be hard pressed to control the situation. He needs to be advised that he'll be on his own. Thanks for taking care of this for me. Wes will probably be able to answer any other questions you may have.

"The only thing I liked about this video was the chance to tell you, your brothers and your mother that I love you all very much. I'm sorry I'm not able to be there for all of you. I can't really explain why I left on this adventure to Mexico, but the experience in the Philippines changed me. I was drawn closer to the edge than I'd ever been before—and I liked it. I was able to pull myself back while you boys were growing up, but with everything settled, the old feelings took over and I ventured back. I won't ask you to forgive me; just try and understand. That's it, Dan shut us down," he said, raising his hand to the camera.

And with that the screen went as blank as their expressions. The three of them sat and stared at the dark monitor. No one seemed to know what to say. Finally the silence was broken.

"Holy shit, that was one fucking amazing story," Susan blurted out, leaving Wes looking a little taken back by her colorful language.

"No more scotch for her, Wes," Connor returned smartly.

"As you wish."

"Very funny, guys. But really, is that fucking true or what? I mean it is the most unfucking believable thing I've ever heard. I don't know anyone who ever found anything, much less a cave full of fucking gold—God I'm drunk."

"No kidding."

"It's getting late, Connor. Do you have any other questions?" Wes asked, sounding a bit drained.

"Just a few, Wes. My Dad was involved in the Philippine venture and this Mexico thing that were roughly fifteen years apart. What went on in the middle? I don't recall him being away for more than a couple a weeks at a time the last fifteen years," Connor noted, looking over at Susan, whose head was on the table and her eyes closed.

"The Philippine adventure, as your father liked to call it, as financially unsuccessful as it was, led us into many ancillary opportunities. I assisted your father in setting up offshore accounts and bearer share corporations that were to be used to shelter any gold funds that were realized. Your father traveled to set up bank accounts in tax havens, like Isle of Man, off the coast of England, Liechtenstein, The Seychelles, off the coast of Africa, Turks and Caicos Islands, and of course our favorite, Grand Cayman. He made lots of contacts; they were necessary in order to find ways to dispose of large quantities of bullion.

"The treasure community is very small, so people became aware of his special expertise. Over the years many adventurers, who have had some success finding treasure or in business, have enlisted his assistance in . . . let's say spiriting away some of their assets, so governments, ex-wives and others would not get the opportunity to take all or part of it from them."

"What exactly are you trying to say, Wes? We're not in court here; just give it to me straight."

"Your father helped people hide their money. He started out in Florida with shallow water gold hunters that brought up small, daily finds, from the remnants of the many Spanish vessels that were lost there. These were monitored closely by the state government in order assure their share. Eventually, he became involved in some larger discoveries. The ones that are usually tied up in court for years, while insurance companies, governments and others lay claim to the fruits of the treasure hunter's labor. Usually, because of the litigation, many companies and individuals would go bankrupt, while waiting and hoping for a favorable ruling. He would assist them in transferring and liquidating part of the find, without anyone being able to trace it. After a while we assisted others not involved in treasure, but who had funds they wanted offshore. Two rules, no stolen funds and no drug money."

"Thank God you had rules," Connor returned, trying

110

unsuccessfully to keep the sarcasm out of his voice.

"In that business you don't survive without rules, Connor."

"If he was moving cash for people, why wasn't he wealthy? It would seem to me that it would be a rather lucrative service."

"You don't know your father as well as I thought you did."

"Based on what transpired here tonight, it looks like I didn't know him at all."

"We made good money, but it wasn't just about the money, it was the action. The money was the destination; he loved the journey. The activity kept him close to something he longed for, but at the time, he felt because of his family and the inherent danger, that it was a selfish indulgence."

"Until Mexico."

"Yes, until Mexico."

"What exactly is a bearer share corporation, Wes?"

"That's a company set up with no registered owner. Whoever walks in the door with the stock shares has the rights to the assets of the corporation: inventory, bank accounts, etc., hence the name, 'Bearer Corporation.'"

"Tough to trace ownership and easy to transfer."

"Precisely."

"Did he handle these transactions through a company?"

"Yes, he started a company known as GS Enterprises."

"GS Enterprises? Did the GS stand for something?"

"It did," Wes replied, a smile coming to his face. "It stands for Ghost Ship."

"Ghost Ship Enterprises?" Connor questioned.

"Exactly, Ghost Ship Enterprises, you put your money on board and it disappears."

"Let me guess, a bearer corporation."

"Of course."

"Was everything a big joke to him, Wes? Did he take anything seriously?"

"He took everything seriously, Connor. He just knew how to have fun, too. It's a lesson we all could benefit from."

"Maybe you're right, Wes. We could all use a little more fun," Connor conceded.

"I'll fucking second that," Susan chimed in, still not raising her head.

"What now?" Connor questioned, not about to make any decision this evening.

"Do what your father requested and forget about it. This was his game to play, not yours or mine."

"He must have left you more information, Wes. There are too many holes. What if I decided to go to the Philippines and take his place, could you help me?"

"That's not what your father would have wanted."

"That's not what I asked."

"I know. Why don't you sleep on it? I would just offer that your father felt it was much too dangerous to pursue, and I whole-heartedly agree. I think your mother would too."

"I'm sure you're right, Wes," Connor returned, as he got up from the table. "Are you sure my father left no other information?"

"I'm sure," Wes replied, following his lead and rising from his seat.

"Come on Susan, time to go," Connor said, helping her up.

"Can you show yourself out, Connor?"

"No problem, Wes. I'll talk to you tomorrow," he returned, leading Susan through the conference room door and out of the office.

~ ~ ~

Wes collected the tumblers and after pouring the excess down the drain, placed them in the sink. He then walked over to the VCR and removed the tape. Taking the video he returned it to its original location in the wall safe, placing it next to a second tape marked "GM-2."

~ ~ ~

Chapter 17

Connor was awakened by the sound of his bathroom shower. He glanced over at the clock that read 7:30 a.m. He hadn't slept well, between Susan tossing and turning, and his own mental exercises wondering how he would handle one of the toughest days he'd ever faced. The last time he checked it was 4:00 a.m. He must have dropped off into a deep sleep, explaining why, as light a sleeper as he was, he didn't hear her get up.

As he dragged himself out of bed, his mind was swimming with the revelations he had been exposed to about his father's life, and the realization that he would probably never see him again. Once he got a handle on that, he still had to deal with Alex, Susan, Sid, Maggie, and the shaky financial position of his business—not to mention a cave full of gold. He never felt so bound up; he had always been decisive, knowing exactly what direction to take. Lately, that wasn't the case. He just wasn't sure what to do next and that made him feel like not doing anything. As he sat back down on the foot of the bed, Susan made her entrance clothed in a towel, with another wrapped around her head.

"Hi," she said. "Did I wake you?"

"Not really, I had kind of a restless night."

"Me, too, I guess. My head sure feels like it," she returned, removing the towel and drying her long auburn hair.

"I was surprised that you got up as early as you did."

"Whenever I drink, it always makes me wake up early. Did I make an ass of myself with Wes last night?"

"No, just the usual colorful language, and then you passed out on the table."

"God, that's embarrassing. I guess I shouldn't drink. But what about that whole thing with your father, do you believe all that? I mean it's really out there."

"I know."

"I have commodity clients back in Europe that would love to be privy to that information, if it were true."

"I don't know if it's true or not. I probably never will, and it really doesn't matter. I'm going to go send the fax today and George will be on his own—with whatever is going on over there."

"That's your best choice, Con. Your father wouldn't have wanted you mixed up in this thing. It sounds way too dangerous."

"You're right. I don't have the time or the energy for it."

"I would have hoped you said you had too many brains for it."

"I guess we all have our shortcomings," he returned, as he got up. "I'm going to grab a shower and then I'm on the run. What are you up to?"

"I'm going to get dressed and catch the Amtrak to the Manhattan office. I'll probably stay down there for the weekend, why don't you come along?"

"I can't, Susan. I've got too much to do," he said, stopping at the bedroom door.

"Why am I not surprised," she returned.

"Sorry," he replied half-heartedly, having no intention of offering a more detailed explanation.

"I'll be gone by the time you get out of the shower," she said, walking over to him. "I'll call you tonight." She leaned forward and gave him a kiss.

"I'll talk to you later," Connor replied, as he headed down the hall.

Entering the bathroom, he could sense his stress level start to rise, feeling tightness in his neck and shoulders. At least with Susan heading to the city, he wouldn't have to worry about juggling his schedule to accommodate her, not that he would have anyway. He had planned to confront her about her alleged infidelity: but given his own situation, he felt like a hypocrite. He wasn't sure how he felt about her, or even what he was feeling anymore. Was he still in love with her? Did he ever love her? Did he miss his father or—did he miss Maggie?

He never thought about missing Maggie before; the last six months she was always there for him. Now that she might be gone, he was being bombarded by emotions that he hadn't experienced and hadn't expected too. There was an uneasiness that he couldn't seem to shake. He stepped into the shower and let the hot water pour over him, hoping to wash away those sensations. He stayed there for at least twenty minutes, relaxing his mind and body; he was definitely on information overload. He just needed to form a plan and put it in action.

Getting out of the shower, he headed back to the bedroom to get dressed, finding his jeans and a blue oxford shirt in his closet. Susan was gone, but her smell still lingered. If she hadn't made the bed he probably would have crawled back in. He hated how apathetic he was feeling. He picked up the phone on the bed stand and dialed the office.

"Good morning, Capital Rehab," came a familiar, pleasant sounding, woman's voice.

"Hi, Nancy, it's Connor. Do you know where Alex was going this morning?"

"Hi, Boss. He said he would be at the gun club first thing, and then he was going to check on the crews working on First and Third Street."

"Going shooting this early, he must really be pissed."

"That may be an understatement, if you're going to find him, you may want to wait till he's not holding a gun."

"Thanks for the advice, Nance. How are the appraisals coming on the properties?"

"I spoke to the appraisers late yesterday afternoon and we expect to have soft copies faxed to us later today or Monday."

"Great, let me know. I'll be on the cell if you need me. See you later."

"I hope so, bye."

Connor pulled on his cross trainers and jacket and left to find Alex. He got in his truck for the short ride up Washington Avenue to Route 155. It was a little overcast, but unseasonably warm for late October. Taking a right on 155, he watched for the left-hand turn on Rifle Range Road, the entrance to the Watervliet Gun Club. As he pulled off the main road, he was glad he had a truck, failing to dodge the multitude of ruts and potholes on the loose gravel surface. He knew exactly where to look for Alex. He parked by his pick-up and walked up the hill toward the long distance shooting range.

Alex loved to target shoot, especially from long range. Connor knew placing five shots in a pattern the size of a small apple from over a half-mile away was his idea of relaxation. His father was a sportsman who introduced him to the club as soon as he was old enough to shoulder a 28-gauge. He became proficient; honing his skills on skeet, trap and sporting clays, but long-range target was his first love. He never formally competed, but Connor had heard he was generally acknowledged by the membership as the best all around shooter in the club. Alex had introduced him to the sport, and while Connor enjoyed the shotgun disciplines, he never got into the long range shooting. It was just too "Zen" for him.

Reaching the top of the small knoll, he spied Alex setting up. No other shooters were around, as eight-thirty on Friday morning was not exactly prime time. Alex's elite status afforded him some flexibility when he wanted to shoot during off-hours. Connor watched his kneeling five-ten, slender, one hundred and seventy pound body unpack his Remington 700 rifle and scope. He had straight dark hair, brown eyes and a pleasant, but plain round face, temporarily highlighted by the bandage across his nose and slightly black eyes, remnants of his confrontation with "Sid Vicious." He looked totally focused, not noticing Connor approaching.

"Hey, Alex."

"Morning," he returned, not looking up to acknowledge his friend.

"What are you doing?"

"What does it look like?"

116

"Come on, you're not still mad?"

"Furious, you asshole," he answered. He finally looked up, not able to hide a slight grin.

"I knew you couldn't stay mad at me," said Connor smiling.

"Shut up and spot for me."

Connor settled down next to him and removed a small telescope from his bag. Alex readied himself, taking a prone position. Connor watched the target while Alex prepared to fire at the plate size bull's-eye around 1,000 yards away. Alex calmed himself and drew a long steady breath. Connor could almost feel him slow his heart rate; putting his body in a total state of relaxation—it was almost a spiritual thing for him. He needed to attain that state, because at this distance the slightest jerk or motion would cause a complete miss of the target—and Connor knew that was totally unacceptable.

Alex took a breath and held it, as he squeezed off the first round. Connor watched the bullet rip through the target, about five inches high and right of the center ring—a great shot, but hardly the best Alex could achieve or would settle for.

"High right in the six ring," Connor calculated, with the center being a ten, and each concentric circle decreasing by two, the further removed from the middle of the bull's-eye.

Alex took another breath, made his adjustment, and fired.

"Dead right in the eight ring," Connor reported, knowing now that he had honed in, but was just right of a perfect strike.

Another breath and Alex let fire three consecutive shots.

"Three hits in the ten spot. You are Andy Fucking Oakley!" Connor yelled, not able to control his enthusiasm.

"You know Mason, if we lived a hundred and fifty years ago, you'd be my bitch," Alex returned now sporting a wide grin.

"You're right Obi Wan, the force is strong within you," Connor returned laughing. "When it comes to firearms, I am your bitch."

"Yeah, but when it comes to fighting my own battles, I guess I'm still yours," Alex replied, his voice echoing his concern.

"It's not like that."

"I know. It just feels that way sometimes."

"I look at it this way, Alex," he said, resting a hand on his friend's shoulder. "It's comforting to know, if Sid kicks my ass tomorrow, we can get in the truck, drive a mile or so, and you can shoot him coming out of the club."

"It is a tempting thought, isn't it," he agreed, nodding at Connor. "But—I don't think I could do the jail time."

"You know, there's always something that ruins a perfectly good idea. I guess I'll just have to kick his ass."

"I guess you'll just have to," Alex concurred. "Look, I'm sorry about the call and hanging up on you last night, but I'm worried about the business."

"I know you are, I am too."

"That's why this thing with Sid is totally unnecessary, and it couldn't come at a worse time."

"There's no good time for something like this, it just has to be done, and by noon tomorrow it will be over, one way or another."

"You know I don't agree, Connor. This doesn't have to take place. That guy is not normal, he's an animal, and I don't want to see you get hurt."

"God, you sound like Maggie, Alex," Connor replied, the feeling of uneasiness returning.

"She's right, Con. If you won't listen to me, listen to her."

"I'd like to, but I'm not sure that's going to be possible for awhile."

"Alright, what happened?"

Connor explained the incident with Maggie and Susan. Alex just stood looking at him and shaking his head while he described what took place.

"Let me understand this, you're on the couch and Susan is on top of you, wearing just barely more than a smile, while Maggie is standing in the hallway taking this whole scene in."

"That's about the size of it."

"Holy shit, Con. I can't imagine things getting more interesting than that," Alex returned, not able to keep from laughing.

"Thanks for your support, buddy," Connor replied, hard pressed to find the same humor.

"Come on. If I just told you something like that happened to me, you'd be laughing your ass off."

"Maybe, but that's not the half of it."

"Please, don't tell me there's more. My stomach can't take it," Alex replied, doubling over in mock laughter.

"I don't think you'll find this quite as humorous, but definitely more interesting."

"What is it?"

Connor then recounted his meeting with Wes and the videotape of his father. Alex listened, looking totally mesmerized. When Connor finished, he just stood there with his mouth open.

"Aren't you going to say anything?" Connor inquired, trying to elicit a response.

"You are kidding—aren't you?"

"Nope."

"Do you believe it?"

"I had an incredible day yesterday. I'm not sure what I believe, or what to do about it if I did. What do you think?"

"I think that if I heard it from anyone but you, and the source was anyone but your Dad, I'd say you're full of shit and have a nice day. So, what are you going to do?"

"Do what my Dad wanted and send the fax to his friend, and be done with it."

"That's probably a good idea, but then again, we're talking a lot of gold here."

"Yeah, on the other side of the world and I have no clue where, or how to get it out if I did."

"You know how to get to your Dad's friend."

"What I know is where to meet him, but I have no idea what he looks like or if he'd even approach someone he doesn't recognize."

"You've got his fax number."

"Alex, I can't send him any message other than what my father instructed. The wrong contact could have catastrophic consequences for this guy. I don't want that responsibility."

"Answer me this question then, why does your Dad go to all the trouble of explaining this on video if he expects you to just forget about it?"

"He wants me to send the reply back to this George guy, so he knows he's not coming."

"That's bullshit, Con. He could have just told his attorney to do it. He's baiting you."

"Alex, what are you talking about? It's my Dad; he's not going to bait me."

"Sure he is. He doesn't want you to go unless you want to, so he gives you just enough information to spark your interest and a gracious way out. But if you decide you want to go, you know he's going to help you."

"How is he going to help me? He's not here, and chances are he's never going to be," Connor returned, the words making him cringe.

"Man, you are thick."

"Okay, I'm thick, enlighten me."

"Your Dad is probably one of the smartest guys I ever met—he's street smart. He had an unbelievable experience, and he felt the need to share it with you. He knows you; he thought somewhere in his heart you'd go for this. He knows when you get locked onto something you just can't let it go, so just in case, he would have left a way to help you. It's kinda like his legacy."

"His legacy?"

"Yeah, you know, something of himself that defines his life. Like my Dad is going to leave me his secret tree stand location where he gets a buck every deer season, yours left you a cave of gold. Same thing."

"It's a Dad thing."

"Definitely a Dad thing."

"Okaaaaay, even if that's all true, and I think you're

stretching here. Where would I start looking for this mysterious information?"

"The attorney. He's one of your Dad's closest friends."

"That's right, Sherlock. But I asked him last night if he had any other information."

"And he said no, right?"

"Right."

"Ask him again. If he thinks you're serious, he'll help you."

"Why would he? I don't even think he really likes me all that much."

"Because grasshopper, that's what your Dad would want him to do."

"Alex, I don't think you know shit," Connor said, smiling and shaking his head.

"You're probably right. But what if—I'm right?"

"Let me get this straight, you don't want me to fight, but you think I should travel half-way around the world and chase this treasure."

"Fuck no. I agree with your Dad; it's way too dangerous and most likely a big waste of time. But, we're talking a lot of gold here."

"Yeah, we are talking a lot of gold."

They both smiled, as Alex packed up his rifle and they headed down the small knoll.

"I'm going over to the club," Connor said, reaching the vehicles.

"I thought you might be going to look for Maggie."

"I hope she's there, but I'm not sure I'd know what to say to her after yesterday."

"Why don't you just tell her how you feel about her—be original, something good may come of it."

"I'd like to, but I'm not sure how I feel about her."

"Sure you are."

"What do you mean?"

"You figure it out. I haven't got time to pull out my couch. Personally, I think she's not dealing with a full deck, but obviously you feel otherwise. Anyway, one of us has to get some work done. I'll talk to you later," Alex returned, pulling away.

He sat and watched Alex's truck bounce up and down on the pothole filled road. He was a lot less cautious leaving, than Connor was when he drove in. Connor was feeling even more cautious when he thought about the remaining tasks that would make up his day, but at least Alex was back on track. The uneasiness was still weighing heavily as he pulled out and headed toward Pauley's.

~ ~ ~

Chapter 18

Traffic was light when he turned onto Wolf Road and headed in the direction of Pauley's gym. At this time on Friday morning, Connor knew he would be behind the work crowd and just in front of the early holiday shoppers. He pulled into the lot, parking among the small smattering of vehicles. He looked around, but didn't see Maggie's car, deciding to go in anyway, and talk to Pauley about tomorrow morning's scheduled activity with Sid.

Walking in the front door, he noticed the familiar red head at the counter. She was on the phone, but flashed him a big smile and quickly ended her conversation.

"Back again?" she inquired.

"Yeah, I'm here to see Pauley," he returned, stopping at the counter. "How are you today, Judy?" remembering her name.

"I'm fine, and you?"

"I'm well—could you tell me, have you seen Maggie Andrews here today?"

"She was here early this morning. She taught a six-thirty aerobics class, but then she left."

"Thanks," he returned, heading toward the entrance.

"Anytime," she replied, buzzing him in.

Connor walked briskly through the weight lifting area toward Pauley's. He entered and headed down the short corridor and into the main gym. There were only two boxers working out, one on heavy bag and one on speed bag. He quickly spied Pauley sitting behind his desk, his head down writing on a yellow legal pad. He was almost on top of him before he looked up from his paper work.

"Hi, Pauley."

"Good morning, C. Mason. Did you come to antagonize your boy a little more?" Pauley returned, with a slight smile.

"No. Just thought I'd stop in to see how you're doing, and if you had another match for me once I get done with Frank's tomato can tomorrow."

"Let's just get past this one and then we'll see who's next," he replied, the lightness abandoning his tone.

"Whatever you say. You're the boss."

"Maybe today, but certainly not yesterday," he returned, getting up and walking out from behind his desk.

"Sorry about that."

"You're not, but I appreciate the gesture."

"Are you going to work my corner tomorrow, Pauley?" Connor asked, holding his breath. Like any competitor, Connor was confident—as long as things were going his way. What he worried about was what to do if things were not. Doubt is not something he wanted to carry into the ring; he knew it could topple him faster than any opponent. But having Pauley in his corner, with all his experience, would erase any worry about what he would do if the fight turned against him. The only problem was that Frank Handrahan was a profit center, in a business that needed every dollar. Connor would understand if he didn't want to cross his revenue source.

Pauley looked Connor straight in the eyes, hesitating momentarily before answering. "Where else did you think I'd be?"

"I don't know," Connor returned, breathing a sigh of relief. "I thought you might have laundry to do or something."

"I'll do it tonight."

"Thanks, Pauley. You just made me feel a whole lot better. Not that I was worried."

"Well Connor, I don't feel any better, and I'm definitely worried."

"I know Pauley, but that's your job. Mine is kicking this guy's ass."

"Let's hope we can both do our job then. God knows, I've already started mine."

"We're on at ten, I'll see you at nine, Pauley," Connor said, turning to leave.

"See you at nine." He sat back down and continued his writing.

Connor walked out of Pauley's and through the weight room of the Fitness Factory, heading toward the exit. He was relieved that Pauley was going to be in his corner, but with everything going on, he was feeling distracted by the event. Given that, in some perverse way, he was looking forward to the test, despite his underdog status. He paused to survey the floor before leaving, looking to see if Maggie had come in. He didn't see her as he turned and entered the reception area. Judy was sitting behind the counter sipping coffee. He waved and walked past. She smiled, saying nothing as he left.

Upon leaving the building Connor looked again for Maggie's car. He was feeling anxious and wanted to settle things with her—it was a loose end that was eating at him and he needed to put it to rest, one way or another.

Unfortunately, she was nowhere to be found and he didn't have a lot of time to spend searching for her. He decided to go to the bank and deposit the check from his mother and then drive by Maggie's apartment on his way to the office.

~ ~ ~

Chapter 19

Traveling south on Route 370, just outside Albany, near Loudonville, Connor located the entrance to Maggie's apartment building. The Hilltop Apartment Complex was a collection of a dozen or so older brick buildings, each housing five separate apartments on three floors plus basement laundry facilities. It sat on a hilltop overlooking the nondescript village of Menands, hence the name.

The new owners had renovated all the dwellings when they took over three years ago. Maggie lived on the top floor in a spacious two-bedroom, boasting a majestic view of Vermont's Green Mountains, visible from her kitchen window. It was her little escape, she often told him, when looking out on them. It was safe and comfortable, but other than the view it really offered nothing out of the ordinary, he thought.

Connor pulled into the complex and followed the signs to building nine; he had only been to Maggie's one other time. It seemed they always met at the club or his house. He turned into the parking area, not expecting her to be home, when he spied her car. He wasn't sure if he was glad or if she'd be alone. The way he felt about her, coupled with the fine emotional line he'd been walking, made him extremely vulnerable. He knew he couldn't tolerate much more trauma right now—but he also felt compelled to see her.

He parked and walked up the three concrete stairs to the building entrance, a heavy wooden hunter green door, with four windowpanes. He found Maggie's name next to the top button. He rang the bell and waited for a response over the intercom.

"Hello."

"Hi Maggie, it's me."

"What do you want?"

"I need to speak with you."

"About what, Connor? What do we have to talk about?"

"Come on Mag. Give me a chance to explain things."

"Why should I? You always want to explain things—I need you to listen and not always do all the talking."

"Listen? Listen to what?"

"That's what I mean. Do you remember before you got pulled away yesterday, I was trying to explain things to you, and you just kept putting me off? Now you want to come up here and talk, with you doing all the talking. I don't think so."

"Look, I just need you to know how I feel about you."

"I know more about how you feel than you could ever imagine, but you don't know anything about how I feel."

"Maggie, please let me come up."

There was a long moment of silence, followed by a buzzing sound that unlocked the front door. Connor opened it and raced up the three flights to Maggie's apartment. Noticing her door was cracked open he walked in. He turned to the right, walked past the small kitchen and into the living room where she was sitting on her couch, with her back to him. Connor maneuvered around the end of the sofa and sat down on the love seat that was kitty corner to her. She was looking rather disheveled, wearing shorts and an oversize sweatshirt; her eyes were red and her hair was matted as if she just woke up. It never mattered what she was wearing or what she looked like, she always looked good to him.

"Thanks for letting me come up," he said, catching his breath.

"You're welcome."

"Look Mag, about what happened yesterday, I'm really sorry."

"What are you sorry about?"

"You know what I'm sorry about, the thing with Susan."

"That's her name. What are you sorry about—the fact that it happened or that you got caught?"

"I just feel bad about it," he returned.

"What makes you think I care anything about what happened between you and her?"

"Do you?"

"No."

"Then what are you so upset about?"

"What I'm upset about, is the fact that you always think you have all the answers and you never listen long enough to recognize the real problem."

"So Susan is not the problem?"

"Hardly."

"Let me get this straight. You don't care if I'm involved with another woman. So, from that I have to surmise that you really don't care about us. Is there even an us?"

"You always bring everything back to you. What about everyone else, do they count? Not everyone thinks like you do."

"Look, I just came to apologize, not have a philosophical debate."

"I know you did. You just don't know what to apologize for."

"I thought I did, but you've shown me the light. You're right, I have no fucking idea what I'm apologizing for."

"What you need to apologize for is not letting me communicate with you. I can help you; I need to help you and you won't let me. I really don't care who that woman is or anything about her. That's just a physical thing; I don't have the time or inclination to deal with that type of stuff anymore. There are other things, more important to deal with."

"I just left Alex and he said something that sounded like you, and now you sound like him."

"Well, if that's the case I wish you would listen to one of us, the optimum word here being listen."

Connor stopped, deciding to collect his thoughts before

continuing. This was the most upset and blunt he had seen her during the six months of their relationship. She had him confused about what she wanted, and while this wasn't the first time, nothing before carried the same gravity. He cared about her and really wanted her in his life, but at this point she was making him a little crazy.

"Alright, Maggie. Why don't you talk and I'll listen—really listen, and maybe when you're done I'll have some vague idea about what's going on. Because right at this moment, my life is in a bit of an upheaval, and I'm not really sure what I need to do to square things with us, assuming there is an us."

"You need to square things with yourself, before you can even think about us."

"Fine. Could you give me a hint? What do I have to do?"

"Come over and sit on the couch by me," she said, suddenly softening her tone.

Connor got up from the love seat and walked around her over-sized wood coffee table, and sat down next to her. He was surprised by her sudden change of mood, but decided not to question anything and just go wherever the flow took him.

"Take my hand, Connor."

"We're not going to do the electric eel thing again are we?" he asked, reaching out to take her hand and remembering their encounter at his house.

"Don't worry. I just need to know how close we are."

"How close to what?"

"Shhhhhhh," she said, raising a finger to her lips.

Connor sat quietly. Maggie squeezed his hand, staring into his deep blue eyes. He could feel a familiar current start to pulse through his body. It was stronger than the one he felt yesterday, but unlike then, he didn't pull away. The hair on his neck and arms began to rise. A low humming sound started in his head and the muscle in his left eye contracted, like a twitch was developing. The sound grew louder, as he became unnerved and pulled his hand from her, breaking the connection. He just sat there feeling drained, but at the same time, more relaxed than he'd been all day. Maggie was still not speaking; she just sat looking at him.

"Maggie, Maggie," he said loudly, trying to get her attention.

"Sorry," she replied, seeming to reorient herself. "That was stronger than I expected."

"What was stronger? Maggie, what's going on? I've been exposed to some really weird things the last twenty-four hours. If you're trying to get my attention, you've got it. So could you please give me the science behind this?"

"What do you mean, the science?" she returned.

"I mean—did you scuff your feet on the carpet or are you wired up to a car battery. I guess to put in plain English, what the fuck is with this current thing?"

"I needed to expose you to it. Without having done that, I doubt you'd take what I'm about to tell you seriously."

"Believe me, I've been though this exercise already."

"What are you talking about?"

"I'll explain it to you later, it happened at the meeting with my father's attorney last night."

"That's must be why the presence was so strong."

"The presence, what is the presence?"

"I guess, I really do have your attention. No distractions please, I need to start and finish this. Listen and try to keep an open mind."

"I'm all ears."

"When I was interrupted yesterday, I was trying to explain to you what happened to me and how we came to fit together, so to speak."

"Maybe we could come to fit together again?"

"Not if you keep interrupting me."

"Sorry, go ahead."

"As I was saying, I want to explain what's going on and why we connected, but to be honest I don't entirely understand it all myself. I told you about the accident when I fell through the ice. What I didn't tell you was what happened, when I was clinically dead for over twenty minutes. The cold

130

water slowed my metabolism down to a point, that even though I was oxygen deprived, there was no permanent brain damage.

"Don't even think about saying what you're thinking right now, or you won't get out of here with all your body parts," she said, seeming to realize the opening she left for one of his snappy comebacks.

"I'm not even thinking of going there, Mag. Go on," he answered sincerely.

"Thanks. Something happened to me—to my soul. I think I traveled to the other side and was sent back."

"Lots of people who've had near death experiences feel that way," he interrupted. "Doctors think it's a chemical that's released when we're close to death. It helps us get through it. You know the bright light and the tunnel; it's all a coping mechanism within our psyche."

"With all due respect, I'm the one who this happened to and what happened to me then, and since then, has nothing to do with a chemical release. What chemical do you think made your hair stand up when I touched you?"

"I was just trying to help you make some sense of what you think happened to you."

"Not everything has a logical explanation. Some things have spiritual properties, not physical. Science can't account for everything out of the ordinary—there are things you just have to believe, even when you don't understand."

"Alright, I'm still with you, but I've got to ask one question. Do you see dead people?"

"No, I don't see dead people."

"Thank God," he said, in mock relief.

"I feel them, though," she returned, with a deadpan look that gave him a chill.

"What do you mean you feel them?" He was no longer sure if he wanted the answer.

"I pick up these sensations of energy around people. It's one of the things that attracted me to you. I felt this force when I was near you. Sometimes it's nothing, but other times it gets stronger. Like it has with you."

"What do you mean sometimes it's stronger? Have you done this before?"

"Yes."

"What happened with the others?"

"Nothing, it started out like it did with you, but the energy never got as strong. Eventually it just went away and so did my contact with that person."

"Maggie are you telling me that what you feel about me is because of a strange energy field that you're sensitive to, and once it's gone, you're gone too," he said, suddenly feeling distressed.

"I don't know."

"But that's how it happened before?"

"Yes."

"Has this feeling always been with men?"

"No."

"Did you have a relationship with all of these people you felt this energy around?"

"Not all."

"But some?"

"Yes."

"Jesus Christ, Maggie. I don't think I can take any more of this, not now," he said, getting up.

"You said you'd let me finish and keep an open mind," she returned calmly.

He paced for a minute or so while he tried to collect himself. It had been an emotional roller coaster. He liked Maggie a lot, maybe he was even in love with her, but everything in his life was in such disarray, he didn't know if he could handle a relationship. The baggage she was saddled with seemed too heavy. "Alright, Maggie," he said, sitting back down next to her. "I'm sorry, but everything is so out of control right now, I just don't know how much more I can fit on my plate."

"I understand, but I need you to let me finish, and then give me some information, so I can try and piece things together."

"Okay. Tell me what you think is happening to you."

132

"I think that I'm some sort of conduit for the dead to communicate with the living. When I was under the ice, I saw the bright light and the tunnel, I was drawn to it; I felt like I was moving toward it. I remember seeing these shadowy figures. I wanted to stay, but something pushed me back. Ever since then I've been searching for what it all means. I get these feelings about people when I'm near them; it tears at me, calls to me. It's like I'm being pulled in a hundred directions at once.

"When I first had these feelings, shortly after the accident, I thought it was some kind of depression to do with having cheated death. I needed to find a meaning for my life, a reason why I was chosen to come back. It continued until I started focusing on one person, who I sensed this energy with. Once my attention was focused, the feelings stopped. It's like you're on one side of a fence with hundreds of people on the other, calling to be picked, once you pick one, the rest stop calling you. That's what happens. When I get involved with someone, I feel like I'm moving toward getting some answers, but when it doesn't happen, the feelings come back until I start again. It's like I need to help someone, but I don't know how or why."

"How am I involved in all this?"

"I feel the energy with you. If I can find a way to help you, it may help me."

"What is this energy, what do you think causes it?"

"I think it's a signature from the other side, it's a way to mark someone here, as the one that can help someone who has passed. . . ."

"You mean died?" he interrupted.

"Yes, died. I call it passed, because people who claim to communicate with spirits refer to when you die, as you pass over to somewhere else. Those that have passed are said to be on the other side."

"Got it."

"So what I think is that when I get close to someone here that someone on the other side wants to communicate with, they get marked with this energy. It may also mean that the person who's passed is actually with that person, or near them. That's what I mean by the presence."

"Are we talking ghosts here?"

"Maybe, I don't know for sure. But it's something."

"Why is it when I've touched you before, or you've touched me, I never got the electric shock treatment?"

"It doesn't happen with casual contact."

"Maggie, the contact we've had has hardly been casual, if you get my meaning."

"I get your meaning. I told you, I'm a kind of conduit; I need to channel the energy. It doesn't just happen by itself. You can't feel it, unless I want you to, but I sense it whenever I'm near you, it's just different. I never know how strong it is till I make physical contact."

"Okay, I think I'm pretty calm considering what you're throwing at me. Don't take offense, but are you all there?" he asked, trying his best to lighten things up a bit.

"Sometimes I wonder, but to the best of my knowledge, I'm not a nut case—really. Of course you'll have to judge that for yourself."

"As long as you think you're okay, I'll go along with that—for now. Let's say everything you're telling me has some validity. How do I fit into the picture?"

"I think that someone is trying to contact you. You're close to something that someone on the other side wants you to do. The energy I feel around you is stronger than I've ever experienced with anyone. Remember when you told me you were going to fight and I told you that it's not what you're supposed to be doing, it was a distraction?"

"Yes."

"I could sense the energy drop off when you told me, I felt, from that, it was not the direction we were suppose to pursue, it would take you away from your goal."

"My goal?" he questioned.

"Someone's goal."

"So where do we go from here?"

"Tell me every thing that's happened in the last twenty-four hours and maybe we can sort this out. You've been exposed to something that may give us a clue."

Connor hesitated, knowing he wasn't going to tell her everything that took place. He then recounted the story, focusing on his father and the meeting with Wes Adams. Maggie listened, interrupting from time to time to get clarification. She told him she needed to have as much detail as he could give her, along with an acute understanding of the situation. "What do you think?"

"I think that maybe the answer sits in a cave of gold."

"That may be true, but unless we know what the question is, it would be like looking for a needle in a haystack."

"Did your father say that anyone died as a direct result of the event?"

"Yes, he estimated that over 300 men died."

"What nationality?"

"Mostly Japanese, but he did mention prisoners of war—could be some Americans I guess. Why?"

"I don't know. It's probably not that important right now."

"Maggie, why do people on the other side reach out for the living?" he asked, his macabre curiosity driving him.

"From what I understand, it's because they had unfinished business when they died. They left something important unresolved, made a promise to someone close to them they couldn't keep, or they sense something happening to a family member or friend and feel compelled to help."

"How do you know these things?"

"I don't for sure. Mostly it's from the research I've done, while I searched for my own answers. Some people say they're contacted in their dreams, by a passed friend or loved one, or when they're in a dreamlike state. They actually see the spirit and it seems so real they can't differentiate between actual contact or fantasy. That's not the way it works for me, but remember it's not science; it's theory."

"I gotta tell you, Mag. This whole paranormal thing is a bit much for me to believe."

"I understand. But you believe there's a cave full of gold in a jungle, thirteen thousand miles from here," she stated, raising an eyebrow. "Who's asking who to stretch their imagination here?"

"Good point," he conceded.

"Look Connor, I didn't ask for this. It's just the way it is. I can't get on with whatever life I have, until I know the reason why I'm still here. Sometimes I wish I wasn't—it gets so hard. . . ," she said, her voice tailing off.

"I'm glad you're here, Maggie," he consoled, reaching out and taking her hand. "What do you need me to do?"

"How do you feel about exploring this further?"

"I'm not sure what you mean."

"I think that your father's story has something to do with this. Are you thinking about going over there?"

"Thinking about it—yes. But according to my Dad and everyone that knows about this, it is a dangerous and impossible task."

"An impossible task, what's impossible?"

"How about removing a hundred tons of gold?"

"Who says you have to?"

"Isn't that the point?"

"I think the point is going to find out, what the point is. It may not have anything to do with the gold. Going over may help get you the question, and me the answer, but you have to be a lot more open to what's around you."

"I don't know, Mag. I need some time."

"I understand."

"Are we okay?" he asked, staring into her dark brown eyes.

"Are you fighting tomorrow?"

"I haven't decided yet."

"Me neither."

"Fair enough. Can I see you later?"

"Call me tomorrow."

"Fine," he returned, leaning over and giving her a kiss on the check. He got up and headed for the door.

As he was about to leave he looked back at Maggie. She hadn't turned to watch him depart like he had hoped. He was glad to see her, but was still feeling very uneasy. His mind

136

was cluttered with ghost stories and treasure hunts. Things so far from his everyday reality, the thought of them didn't even register as a possibility two days ago. Now they were as real as his opponent for the morning's boxing match. None of which offered the expectation of a pleasant outcome.

Exiting her building, he headed off in the direction of his office. He needed to make a decision as soon as possible; his father's friend would need to know.

~ ~ ~

Chapter 20

Connor pulled up in front of Capital Rehab, housed in a corner brownstone on Clinton Avenue in downtown Albany, not far from the Arbor Hill neighborhood where he and Alex bought most of the houses they renovated. Being in a mostly black inner-city area he thought might have created some issues, but after almost two years of operation, despite his lack of color, he was well known and an accepted part of the community.

The original building had two floors, a storefront and a converted upstairs apartment. They had purchased the property at auction for three thousand dollars, rehabbing it from top to bottom; it had an urban feel, with an open office floor plan. It featured two fireplaces, exposed brick walls, wide plank wood flooring and large overstuffed furniture in the common areas. He liked the look, it was professional, homey and overall an excellent representation of their work as well as a comfortable business environment.

He entered to the sound of his office manager dealing with a former customer over the phone. As he caught her eye, she raised a finger motioning him to wait. Nancy Dorsey was a slender five-foot eight thirty five-year old, with brown eyes and dirty blonde hair, that was so teased, she looked like a sixties sitcom Mom. She was wearing her usual; a short leather skirt and skintight blouse, the kind that highlighted the boob job she bragged about having ten years earlier. When Connor hired her, he was impressed by her drive and intelligence, which more than compensated for her heavy makeup and lack of professional dress. Overall, she had been a tremendous employee, despite the fact there were times, she looked a little like a hooker. He plopped down on an oversized chair in the small lobby area and laying his head back, closed his eyes while he waited for her to finish.

"Hi boss," she said hanging up.

"Who was on the phone, Nance?"

"That was Annie Wright, she bought the property on Livingston last month. She was having some problems with her hot water."

"Have we got someone going over?"

"I was just about to call Alex and have him send one of the guys. He called just before you came in and said he was on his way to the office. He didn't sound as upset as this morning, did you kiss and make up?"

"A big wet one."

"Stop, you're turning me on."

"Yeah, I'm sure. Did you stop me for a reason?"

"We have a problem."

"Can it wait till next year?"

"I don't think so. I got a fax from the appraisers; the values on the properties we're refinancing are coming in a lot lower than we expected."

"How low?" he asked, trying to keep the concern out of his voice.

"Here's the fax, see for yourself," she returned, handing him the sheet.

Connor took the sheet and reviewed the list of properties and their corresponding values. He was stunned by what he was seeing.

"Are these right?"

"I called and double checked," she replied, sounding worried. "Are we in trouble?"

"I need to make a phone call. If Alex comes in, send him up to my office, but don't tell him about this."

"We are in trouble."

"Don't hit the panic button, I'll take care of it," he returned, regaining his composure.

"That's why you're the boss."

"This week anyway," he said, turning and heading for the stairway.

His office was on the second floor. He liked the layout with his workspace on one side, Alex's on the other and a sitting room in between, featuring soft leather furniture, oriental carpeting and a large fireplace. He sat at his desk and placed the fax in front of him, as he dialed the number for Updyke Appraisals, asking for the owner, John Updyke.

"Good morning Connor, how's it going?"

"Not too well after getting these values, John. Are they correct?"

"I'm afraid they are."

"What the hell is going on?"

"I can't get any comps to support the prices you're looking for."

"What happened? We were fine six months ago, when you did the reviews before we bought them."

"I know, but your competition is selling houses around twenty thousand dollars less than your company is."

"How can they afford to do that?"

"They basically do a cob job renovation. They just patch and paint and don't do half the job you guys do, but then, they can afford to undersell you. Until their houses start to fall apart in a year or two, they look like a better buy. Unfortunately, they are artificially depressing the values by selling at such low prices."

"Tell me about it. Can you do anything to get me some higher appraisals?"

"Not and have them hold up under bank scrutiny, not to mention jeopardizing my license. I'm sorry."

"Not half as sorry as I am. Thanks John, I'll get back to you," he returned, hanging up the phone.

Connor just sat staring around his office. He liked the business, the people and the low-key, intimate climate that he and Alex had created. The information he received from the appraiser would all but knock them from their shaky perch. It was not something he would choose to deal with on a Friday, especially after the events of the last twenty-four hours, but it needed to be addressed.

His mind was racing, trying to solve this unsolvable problem, before he would have to explain to Alex. Leaning back in his leather desk chair, he fixated on the ceiling tiles, looking for some inspiration. Suddenly, the sound of his partner, coming up the stairs, interrupted his contemplation.

"Hey Connor, how'd it go over at Pauley's?"

"Fine, we were just getting squared away for tomorrow."

"You're determined to do this thing, aren't you?"

"Obligated is more like it."

"The only one obligating you is you. Did you run into Maggie?" he asked, a mischievous smile crossing his face.

"I caught up with her at the apartment."

"How did that go?"

"It was—strange."

"What do you mean? Was she pissed or wild or what?"

"It was strange. It was a totally unexpected reaction and a fairly unbelievable story on top of it."

"Stranger than the gold thing and the couch episode? You gotta tell me."

Connor relayed the story in detail. Alex listened and was reacting much the same as he had when Connor recounted the gold tale. When he finished, Alex just sat across from him shaking his head and staring down at the desk.

"Well, what do you think now?" Connor asked.

"Man, Con," he said, lifting his head and looking him in the eye. "I told you that chick was a nut case. I mean sensing a strange energy and talking to dead people."

"She doesn't talk to dead people."

"Sorry, I mean feeling dead people around her," he returned, emphasizing his point by raising both hands and wiggling his fingers. "What the fuck is the difference. Don't tell me you actually believe all that bullshit."

"I'm not sure what I believe anymore. I've got a missing father that I discover I know almost nothing about. He says that there's a cave full of Japanese gold on the other side

141

of the world, I believe that, why couldn't this be true?"

"Because your Dad is not crazy and she is."

"She's not crazy, Alex. She has some issues that she needs resolved. It's no different than a lot of us. She thinks I can help her get some answers—I want to help her."

"What do you really know about her anyway? What's her background? Did she escape from some asylum?

"All I know is that she's from Michigan where she was engaged to some deadbeat from high school who liked playing pool and drinking with his buddies more than spending time with her. She told me she was a lot heavier then, but about five years ago she just left her job at the power company and up and moved to Florida where she got into the fitness industry. From what I can now piece together it must have been the accident that precipitated her move."

"So how did she end up here?"

"She answered an ad for a fitness manager and liked the area and decided to stay, I guess. I don't know for sure, I just know I don't want to lose her."

"What is it with you? Why does she turn your head like this? You haven't been yourself since you met. I just don't understand. Help me will you?"

"I think I'm in love with her."

"Connor, you're kidding me. I'm your best friend; you've got to believe she's a couple of fries short of a happy meal. The story she told you is so far from sanity, you can't be serious about her."

"I don't know, Alex. When I see her, my heart leaps from my chest. I feel a comfort with her, like I've known her forever. No matter how many times we make love—it always feels, like it's the first time. I've never felt that way with anyone."

"You tell this stuff to women. No wonder you get laid so much."

"Alex, you're an asshole."

"I may be an asshole, but I'm not hung up on a girl who's gonna be taken away in a white jacket. When did you start feeling this way? I knew you liked her, but not seriously.

I thought when Susan came back it would be over."

"I didn't know I felt this way, until I was in danger of losing her."

"Alright, Con. I'm not the one to burst your love bubble, but are you willing to travel half-way round the world and put your life in danger to help her get her head on straight—maybe."

"I don't know. I'm just trying to sort this out."

"Let me ask you this, what did she say about your little activity with Sid tomorrow morning?"

"She didn't say anything specific, but I know she's against it."

"Well, there's a hint of sanity after all."

"That's enough, Alex. I'm not in the mood for anymore of your sarcasm."

"I'm sorry, but let's face facts. You've gotten yourself involved in some pretty wacky things lately. I know some of it's out of your control, and the fight with Sid is for my benefit, but I didn't ask for it. You probably think your relationship with Maggie is none of my business, but what it's doing to you, affects me. We're partners; we've got a business to run here."

"Maybe not."

"What do you mean, maybe not?"

"Take a look at this," he said, handing him the fax from the appraisers.

Alex took the paper and began to study it. Connor watched his expression change when he became all too aware of the deflated values.

"Are these right?" he asked, his exasperation evident.

"I called John. They're right."

"What happened? We were fine six months ago?"

"To put it in a nutshell, we do too good a job on our rehabs. The guys doing the cheap half-assed work have devalued the market."

"We have no profit in these values, we can't even breakeven."

"I know, Alex."

"What are we going to do? Is there anything we can do?"

"I've been thinking about it since I came in. We don't have too many choices. We need to stop the bleeding and try and minimize our losses."

"Losses! We can't afford any losses."

"I know. But we've got them, and a not too pretty picture is going to get a whole lot worse unless we do something. You've got to face facts now, we're in trouble."

"What do you think we should do?"

"A couple of things. First, cancel the sales contracts we have, the properties won't appraise anyway. Let's change them into rent to own. Second, we have to shift from sales to a management company. We need to get the houses we have rented ASAP and create cash flow. Third, we need to complete whatever rehabs we have left as cheaply as possible, and then convert them to rentals. The toughest thing we have to do is cut the crews loose."

"We don't have enough cash. By the time we finish and get them rented, we'll be too broke to get these properties refinanced. Once the banks get wind that we have no cash flow, they'll never give us mortgages. We'll be out of business, Con."

"You may be right, but we need to try and protect what we have."

"I agree, but we're going to need income from somewhere to pull this off."

"I have an idea."

"Great, we need an idea—wait a minute." He stopped in mid-sentence. "You're not thinking what I think you're thinking?"

"Why not? Come on, let's go see Wes Adams and check out your theory."

~ ~ ~

Chapter 21

***Present Day, Philippines, City of Cagayan De
Oro, Island of Mindanao***—George Fall made his way up
the winding, rocky road toward the Pryce Plaza Hotel. He had
the accelerator to the floor, as his rusted 1980 Toyota Celica
barely crawled up the steep incline. In the distance he spied
his destination, a monument of idealism, situated high above
the southern port city. It was a sparkling white, castle-like
structure, featuring large rounded domes for peaks and private
balconies off its more expensive rooms. By virtue of its lofty
location and design, it was by far the most majestic building on
the whole island, in stark contrast to the makeshift shelters and
poverty that most of the residents below had to endure, including himself.

As George pulled up to the entrance, he remembered
all too long ago, when he was a guest and not the infrequent
visitor he was now. While the hundred and fifty-dollar a night
price tag was more than twenty-five percent of his monthly living allowance, and a luxury he could no longer afford, it represented more than two and a half months pay for most
Filipinos. Only on rare occasions were more than fifteen of the
hundred plus rooms in use. Regardless of the low occupancy,
he was well aware it served as a pillar of civilization to foreigners exposed to the riggers of a third world country, and
that the government deemed it necessary in order to continue
attracting international commerce to the area.

As he opened his rusted, creaky car door, a familiar face
hurried to his assistance.

"Good morning, Sir George."

"Good morning, Fernando. How's the family?"

"They are well, sir. And yours?"

"Which ones?"

"I am not sure of your meaning, sir?"

"It's just an inside joke, Fernando. I'm sure they're all well."

"Good to hear that, sir," he returned, opening the large glass door.

"Be extra careful where you park my car, Fernando. She's one of a kind."

"I will be most careful, sir."

I'm sure you will, he thought, smiling to himself as he entered the large lobby.

He felt a momentary chill, as the rush of air conditioning assaulted his sweaty body. The temperature was a comfortable seventy-two; a sharp contrast to ninety plus steam bath he had just exited. Over his rotund, five-foot seven build, he wore his usual attire; a colored t-shirt hanging over a pair of baggy kaki shorts with well-worn sneakers and no socks. He wiped back some remaining perspiration on his balding head with his right hand, which was missing half of his index finger, courtesy of a lawn mowing accident when he was a teenager growing up in Ohio. He sported a close-cropped beard whose gray accents were even more evident by virtue of his deep tan. He had been in the Philippines fifteen years, the last five splitting his time between a low rent house in Cagayan De Oro that he shared with his girlfriend and their four children, and a thatched roof hut in the jungle mountains north of the small village of Malaybalay. He was well known to most of the locals that mattered, being one of the few foreign faces that never seemed to disappear for long.

He walked up to the marble counter where another familiar face greeted him.

"Hello, Mr. Fall. How are you on this beautiful morning?"

"I'm well as can be expected, Amy."

Amy Mendez was a pretty twenty-five year old that

had been working at the hotel for the last seven years. She had long black hair, perfect olive skin and large dark eyes. Her five-foot three-inch frame carried a shapely hundred and five pounds, highlighted by slender hips and full breasts. George often thought if she was a few inches taller, and not stuck in this third world toilet, she could be a model somewhere. She was definitely a looker, and one of the few women who worked at the hotel he couldn't seem to lure into his bed. It didn't really matter. She was smart, pleasant and there were lots of other women more easily available to him.

"What can we do for you this morning?"

"Could you check and see if there's a fax for me?"

"I'll check right away," she returned, leaving for a room located behind the counter.

"Thank you."

George leaned against the cool marble and waited for her return. Waiting was not a problem; he had spent what seemed like a lifetime waiting for his big score that was now finally within his grasp. He was daydreaming of his triumphant return home, when he could square away his enormous debts and everyone that doubted him, including two ex-wives, would have to eat their words. Money would solve all his problems and deliver him to the life he longed for; spread around enough of it and all would be forgiven. All he needed was Guy Mason to return and help him complete his dream.

While he anticipated Amy's voice ending his sweet distraction, another, that ran his blood cold, stunned him back to the reality of his precarious existence.

"Good morning, Mr. Fall. I've been looking for you."

"Good morning, Colonel Vadula," he returned, recognizing the unmistakable raspy signature tone even before turning around. Colonel Marquez Vadula was the army commander of Bukidnon Province. He imagined his five-foot four-inch, one hundred and thirty-five pound frame, with jet-black hair, as he could almost feel his close-set dark eyes burning a hole in the back of his head.

Turning to face the Colonel, he couldn't help notice the two-inch scar on his throat, the result of an attack by a local prostitute trying to fend off his advances. That accounted for the damaged vocal cords that had left him with his distinctive voice quality. George had heard that it left the woman begging for her life, which he ended by placing his revolver in her ear and blowing her brains all over the backseat of his car. He was an expert marksman, with a highly developed short man's complex and overall cruel nature, especially when dealing with anyone that defied him. Generally, from George's experience, he was the best-known and most feared man on the island.

"How have you been, my friend?"

"Just dandy," he returned trying to control his mounting anxiety.

"Are you waiting for someone?"

"No, just came to see if there were any messages for me."

"Well, here comes your answer," he returned, observing Amy returning. "Good morning, Amy, any messages for Mr. Fall?"

"No, sir," she answered sheepishly.

"Good, then I guess you're free to have a drink."

"It's ten o'clock in the morning, Colonel. A little early for me."

"It's the Philippines, Mr. Fall. I think you can make an exception. I give you the permission," he said, his dark eyes fixating on George as his upper lip quivered slightly.

"Fine, Colonel. By all means let's have a drink."

"Thank you, Mr. Fall," he returned, turning to head for the bar.

George followed the Colonel to the piano bar situated just off the lobby. It was a medium size, open room that housed a dozen or so tables with large brightly cushioned rattan chairs on each of two levels. There was a full mahogany bar, grand piano and floor to ceiling tinted windows that overlooked the pool and the city.

When they entered, George observed the bartender alert the waitress to the identity of her new customers and he imagined the peril that the colonel represented. Following the

Colonel to a seat by the window, George couldn't help but notice the two pearl handled pistols with tie down holsters that accented his picture perfect tan uniform. As they sat, an anxious looking waitress stood by the table and awaited their order.

"What will you have Mr. Fall?" the Colonel inquired.

"Give me a San Miguel," George directed to the waitress.

"No beer this morning," interrupted the Colonel. "Join me in a—Chevas Regal."

"Fine, give me a Chevas on the rocks," George surrendered.

"I'll have a Chevas Regal straight up," the colonel returned, as the waitress scurried off to fill the order.

"So, Mr. Fall, I understand that you are mining again up in the mountains near Malaybalay."

"Where did you hear that, Colonel?" George returned, trying to hide his surprise.

"I have my sources, Mr. Fall. Nothing goes on in this Province that I don't know or find out about."

"Imagine that. Yes, we started to do some test mines. We're looking for a vein of low grade ore, so I can solidify my funding source and start full operation."

"I understand that some time ago you had another mining operation here that you abandoned. What caused you to leave and why are you back mining again, after so long?"

"Last time the company I worked for ran out of money. I got tired of the mining business and left, but I guess it's just in my blood, so I decided to give it another try."

"I see," he paused. "You have not been very forthcoming about your activities in my jurisdiction, Mr. Fall. The last time we spoke, about six months ago, you never mentioned anything about your mine and then you drop out of sight. I was worried that some harm may have come to you."

Before he could answer, the waitress returned with two glasses of scotch. She was clearly nervous when she reached over to serve the Colonel and his guest. Her hands were shaking so badly that the smoky liquid was spilling over the sides of the glass. As her trembling increased, the Colonel suddenly reached out and grabbed her wrist to steady her. She looked very upset while he guided the glass to the table.

"Don't be afraid," he said, releasing her arm. "I haven't killed anyone for spilling drinks—today."

"I'm sorry, sir," she returned, placing the other glass in front of George. "Anything else?"

"Yes," returned the Colonel, raising the glass to his lips and downing the entire contents. "Bring two more and try not to spill them—try very hard."

The terrified girl backed away, almost in tears as she hurried over to give the bartender the order. George noticed the hotel manager starting toward the table; when he got closer, George caught the look the Colonel shot him causing him to stop dead in his tracks. He watched the manager turn and cower back to his original station, most likely deciding for his own safety, this was not the time to inquire about the service.

"Where were we, Mr. Fall? I remember, you were going to explain your reluctance to cooperate with my authority."

George raised his glass and took a big gulp, hoping it would slow down his racing pulse. This was a dangerous man and not just in terms of his life. He could jeopardize the entire operation and the grandiose future he imagined for himself. "I'm sorry, Colonel. You know me, I'm only too happy to cooperate. The last time I saw you, I wasn't sure what I was going to do. I'd be happy to give you any information you want."

"I'm glad to hear that, Mr. Fall," he returned, watching the waitress approach.

Before she could remove the drinks from her tray, he reached out and snatched both glasses. She seemed startled at first, but looked relieved that she was not required to go through the previous stressful exercise as before.

"Anything else, sir?" Her jittery voice cracking.

"No."

She hurried off, while the Colonel gulped down his scotch and placed the one meant for his guest in front of him.

"One more question. You sent a fax from here a few

days ago with a message 'The eagle has landed.' Who in the United States did you send that to and what does it mean?"

"That's two questions, Colonel," George replied nervously.

"Before you think about being less than truthful with me," he returned, appearing to ignore George's attempted humor. "Let me assure you, that I think of you as my friend— for now. I can be of great assistance to you. My men and I can offer you protection from the rebels and other services you may desire."

"Other services?"

"Yes, you may want someone—let us say—removed from your world. I can facilitate that for you. You may want other things, like for instance, the girl, Amy, who works at the desk. She is very pretty, wouldn't you agree?"

"Yes."

"If you want her in your bed, I can arrange that for you. Whatever is in my power, I will do for you—if you will do for me."

"What is it that you want me to do for you?" he returned, knowing full well he'd been led to the question, but saw no way out, other than to ask it.

"I'm glad you asked, Mr. Fall, I have more power in this region than even our President. I have men, weapons, vehicles, helicopters, everything except money. My position is most enviable because of what I can do for others, but it is limited because there is not much on this island of value. I am therefore faced with the grim prospect of doing my job, and retiring on a Colonel's pension. This is not something that I am looking forward to, so what you can do is allow me to assist you for a small fee, reflective of the level of service I can provide. This will allow me a future when I am old."

"I think I understand what you want, Colonel."

"I hope so, Mr. Fall," he said raising the glass to his lips and drinking down the liquor. "My future and your future depend on it."

"About your question regarding the fax. . . ."

"No need to explain," he interrupted, getting up from

151

his seat and extending his hand. "I trust that now that you know my position, you will keep me informed of anything I should be aware of."

"I will," he replied, wiping the nervous perspiration on his pants before accepting the Colonel's hand.

"Thank you for your understanding of my situation. One more small favor I would ask. Would you mind picking up the bill for our drinks? They are more than I can afford on my military pay."

"Of course, Colonel."

The Colonel nodded as he turned and headed out of the bar. George was relieved to see him leave, but knew he would have to be dealt with sooner or later. He reached in his pocket and pulled out five hundred pesos to cover the bill. He left the money on the table and started for the exit. He was glad there was no fax from Guy Mason. He would check in at the hotel for two more days, and if there was still no message, he would head to the island of Cebu to meet his friend.

~ ~ ~

Chapter 22

After leaving his truck in the parking garage, Connor and Alex boarded the elevator and headed up to Wes Adam's office.

"Stop pouting, Alex."

"I'm not pouting, I'm contemplating my bankruptcy."

"It could be worse you know."

"How's that?"

"You could be me."

"Thanks, I feel a whole lot better now."

"No really, Alex. Your problems can all be solved with more money. Mine are a lot more complex. I would relish a straight forward solution, at least then I'd know what direction to head in."

"I tell you what, let's just pretend that my problems are your problems. I know it's a stretch, but work with me here. Let's work on solving my problem, and then we'll tackle your issues."

"That's why we're here," he returned, as the elevator stopped on the floor for Adams, Lock, Gold and Associates.

They entered the office area, where a familiar looking receptionist directed them to Wes's office. Connor, already knowing the way, whirled and headed down the hall.

Alex caught up halfway down the long corridor. "I can't believe we're even thinking of doing this."

"Can't believe we're thinking of doing what?"

"Going to look for gold, that's what."

"Look, Alex. We're just here to get some information, so we can make an educated decision."

"Yeah, blow me. I know you Connor, we're here to get just enough for you to justify us heading off to some Asian jungle and probably get us decapitated or worse."

"You don't have to go anywhere, Alex," he said, stopping to look at him in order to punctuate his point before resuming his course.

"What do you mean I don't have to go anywhere?" Alex returned, now hurrying again to catch him. "You don't think you're going without me, do you?"

"Precisely," he returned, as he knocked and opened the door.

"That's such bullshit, Connor."

"What's bullshit?" Wes asked.

"Nothing," Connor answered.

"Very well. How are you Connor?"

"I'm fine, Wes. This is my partner, Alex Litowski. I don't think you've met before."

"No, we haven't," Wes replied, rising his slender body from his desk to greet him. "But I have heard about him from your father. From what I remember, he told me you are quite the expert with firearms."

"I'm a pretty fair shooter."

"Better than pretty fair from what I recall Guy saying about you."

"Thanks."

"What can I do for you?" Wes asked.

"We're here to test out a theory that Alex has, Wes."

"And that would be what?"

"The theory is that you know more about the gold than you let on last night. Alex speculated that if I convinced you I was going to pursue this, you would reveal other information to assist me. In fact, you would be compelled to, because my father left you instructions to do so."

"Is that so?"

"I don't know, but that's why we're here. So tell me, Wes. Are you holding out on me?"

"I wouldn't call it holding out—protecting you would be more accurate."

"I knew I was right," Alex chimed in.

"So you do have more information?"

"Yes."

"Let's get to it then."

"Just one moment, gentlemen. What exactly are your intentions regarding this matter?"

"I'm not sure yet, Wes," Connor replied. "I just want the whole story. But, I'm leaning toward taking my father's place and meeting George Fall in the Philippines."

"I see. And you Mr. Litowski, what is your involvement?"

"Right now, I'm a passenger on this train wreck. I just want to see if I can get out of this alive," he returned, flashing a smile and brushing the brown hair from his forehead.

"That may be closer to reality than you think if you choose to pursue this."

"We'll make that choice, Wes. What else did my father leave you?"

"Come with me," Wes returned, shrugging his shoulders and releasing a loud sigh.

Wes walked from his desk to the small conference room he had led Connor and Susan into the night before. They followed him, each taking a seat in one of the high back leather chairs. They watched while Wes opened the wall safe and removed a video marked "GM-2."

"He gave you a second tape?" Connor observed.

"Yes."

"Why didn't we just deal with this last night?"

"Because that's not what I was instructed to do," he returned, placing the videotape in the VCR.

"What exactly were your instructions?"

"I was instructed by your father to show you the original tape and monitor your reaction. If you showed an inclination to pursue a course of action that may put you in danger, I was to use any and all means to dissuade you. After doing so, if you still chose to participate, despite my objections, I was to assist you in anyway possible."

"So are you going to try and talk me out of this?"

"No."

"No?" Connor questioned.

"No, I recognize the futility of trying to talk you out of anything. I'll give you the information and hope that you're bright enough to figure out that this is not a good idea."

"Fair enough."

Wes pointed the remote and Guy Mason appeared. He was wearing a faded jean shirt and kaki pants. He sat in an overstuffed chair that Connor recognized as being in his home office. It was obvious that this second tape was an after thought. He looked a little disheveled and hadn't shaved for at least a day, maybe two. Connor was glued to his image while he quickly glanced at some notes, before beginning to address them.

"Hello Connor, Wes and anyone else who may be viewing this. Please forgive my appearance as we're getting ready to leave for Mexico and I've been hurrying to complete preparations the last few days at the expense of some personal hygiene. After giving the original tape some thought and talking it over with Dan, we decided that a follow up might be necessary. I have left the decision to Wes as to whether or not to disclose its existence, I can only assume he used his best judgment.

"Connor, I know you've convinced Wes that you're going after the gold and he feels he can't change your mind. I won't waste any of our time trying to talk you out of it; it's your call. Just be aware that there are some real obstacles that you're going to need to deal with. I can only give you so much advice—the rest is up to you.

"First of all, you're dealing in a third world country with some civil unrest. The army is very powerful, the island and the province are a feudal state, it's 'he who has the most guns wins.' If they get wind of what's going on, get out of there. Once they know the location and have access to the cave, you, George and anyone else involved are expendable. Hopefully, they have not paid much attention to George's return; make sure you address that issue with him.

"Secondly, there are Muslim rebel forces in the area.

156

When I was there fifteen years ago, they didn't seem as dangerous as they do now. They are called the Abu Sayyaf and have been responsible for a raft of kidnappings, targeting mainly foreigners. They are a dominant force and pose much the same problem as the military. The only good thing about having both in the vicinity is that one tends to offset the other in terms of occupying each other's attention. With proper lookouts a confrontation can be avoided. If either are spotted, shut down and get out until it's clear."

Guy paused for a moment and leafed through his notes. Connor could only imagine what was going through his mind. He probably knew that one day he would be faced with the prospect of dealing with this scenario, but never thought he wouldn't be around to do it himself. Can you really pass on all the information necessary to do this successfully, when you don't believe it would ever be used he wondered. His concerns were interrupted as his father continued.

"The next issue is removing the gold; this is going to be a little tricky. Once you begin the process, whomever you have assisting you cannot be allowed to leave the dig—no exceptions. Use as few men as possible, and be prepared to keep them there several weeks if necessary. My advice to you would be to forget about getting it all out. The longer you are involved, the more dangerous it becomes. Take out what you can and leave satisfied—be smart, not greedy. Having seen it first hand, it is an overwhelming amount, and impossible to sell all of it on the open market. I'll have more to say about that later.

"The most expedient and safest way to get it out of the country is by air. I have an associate in Atlanta that was involved in the original operation. His name is Billy Hilliard and his number will be made available to you. The biggest hurdle you'll face is transporting the gold from the jungle to the landing strip. It is a heavy dense metal, so space won't be a problem, but weight will. We had originally planned to move the product by jeepney. A jeepney is a converted jeep taxi, with an open back that is very common to the Philippines, it is a rugged vehicle that can handle the load and tough terrain and not garner undue attention. You may have another transport option after talking with George, but that was our plan. Once you reach the landing strip, Billy and his people should be able to take over from there.

"I have a buyer who will purchase the gold, as is, at 99% of market price. He is a Saudi Prince, but the product will have to be delivered to Saudi Arabia. Billy knows the location and the drill; we've sold to the prince on other occasions. If for some reason he is not in the market, you will need to address another issue. Most gold bars are hallmarked to identify the owner. This is a brand that was in the original mold when it was poured. You will need to smelt down the bars and put our hallmark on them.

"We had formed a mining company, called Bukidnon Mines, Ltd., and created a mold that the gold could be poured in. If you choose not to, and are intercepted outside of the Philippines, chances are you will not be able to prove ownership and the gold will be held until the hallmarked owner is contacted. That would only be the beginning of your problems. We had portable smelters on site, I don't know what condition they are in and it may be a luxury that you have to forego. If so, it will raise the danger level and lower the price, because it will have to be sold on the black market, or to another private buyer. I'll supply a list of potential purchasers and the pros and cons of dealing with each. Excuse me one moment."

The three of them watched while Guy returned to his notes. Connor could feel his father's angst when he watched him run his hand through his salt and pepper hair, obviously under some time constraint as he attempted to distill the most prudent information regarding this activity.

"Wes, could you please pause the video?" Connor interrupted.

"Certainly," he returned, freezing the screen.

"Are you familiar with what he's talking about here?"

"Yes."

"What is this Bukidnon Mines, Ltd.?"

"Bukidnon is the Province in the Philippines where the

mine is located. We had originally planned to set up a long-term mining operation in order to remove the gold under our own hallmark. The uncle, who was the living witness, owned the site, so we established the company and transferred ownership of the property to Bukidnon Mines, Ltd."

"Bukidnon Mines, Ltd. is—let me guess, a bearer share corporation."

"You're a quick study, Connor," he returned, flashing a patronizing grin.

"Thank you. Where are the bearer shares located?"

"They're in a safety deposit box in Grand Cayman."

"Where in Grand Cayman?"

"First National Bank of Grand Cayman in Georgetown."

"Are they accessible?"

"They are, but you need two of three signatures in order to gain access."

"Whose signatures?"

"Your father's, George's and mine, and one of us has to be there in person."

"What's your read on the buyer, this Saudi Prince?"

"If he's in the market, he's solid. We've done some other transactions with him. He can buy up to a billion dollars worth, in today's market that would be around one hundred tons. I think that would suit any of your needs."

"How do we contact him and the other guy my father mentioned, Billy Hilliard?"

"Your father left a package, in addition to the videos, I'm sure you'll find everything he mentioned in it."

"Can I have the package?"

"My instructions were to give it to you after you had viewed the tape."

"I understand, let's continue then."

Wes nodded and restarted the video. Guy was still reviewing his notes as the freeze frame released him to motion. All three participants directed their undivided attention when he began to speak. It was obvious to Connor that his message carried a new heightened sense of importance to all of them.

The instructions and dialogue were technical, but the underlying theme was of gold and adventure—the things that dreams were made of.

"I think it's important at this point to discuss the magnitude of the gold sitting in this tunnel," Guy continued, looking up from his notes. "There is possibly up to two thousand or more tons. To put that number in perspective, it is almost one quarter of the entire U.S. gold reserve sitting in Fort Knox. With the exception of Germany, France and Switzerland, it is more bullion than most countries have in their national vaults. This staggering amount makes the discovery all the more dangerous.

"Gold is the most highly sought after commodity in the world. If there is any questionable fluctuation in a country's paper money or economy, gold is the only accepted medium for international trade. It is the American Express of foreign currency; it's accepted anywhere. Absent a long-term plan and a lot of luck, it would be impossible to remove and sell all of it, without catastrophic repercussions. There are governments that would not want this kind of wealth to fall in the wrong hands, especially a corrupt leader of a third world country. It could have a tremendous negative effect on price if it was dumped on the open market.

"There is a real danger from a company called Morgan Gold International, headquartered in London. They are to gold what Debeer's is to diamonds. The company controls seventy percent of production in the free world. Rumor has it that they are deeply vested in gold mines in communist countries as well. Gold is the one thing that will supersede borders and politics. A company like Morgan Gold would never want this unearthed unless they controlled it. I dealt with them briefly fifteen years ago and when it comes to their interests, they're ruthless. I have little doubt that had we been successful and refused to deal with them . . ." he paused. "They would have killed us. If their name surfaces anywhere, drop everything and leave. They are the most dangerous obstacle in your path; they have money, contacts and power. Have no doubt they can reach you anywhere, and they will know about any significant open market transactions that take place.

"The safest buyer is one who has no intention of reselling. The Saudi prince I mentioned stocks gold. He is not interested in appreciation as much as in assets that will maintain their buying power. He has great wealth and having gold bullion will enable him to secure what he already has. None of that gold will likely ever be sold; helping him will help safeguard your identity and maybe your life. If what I'm telling you is making you a little nervous, it should. Be nervous, be scared and most of all, be smart."

"Wes, hold the video again please," Connor requested.

"Certainly."

"I take it that you're familiar with Morgan Gold?"

"I am. They're the OPEC of gold traders. They control so much of the world's production that they literally set the market price. When you consider worldwide production being ten to twelve million ounces a year, which roughly equates to 312 tons, and the contents of the tunnel being six or seven times that amount, you can see how the market could be affected."

"I'm just a layman, Wes. I'm still not sure I understand all of this," interrupted Alex. "Why do they care about what we could sell, when they have so much of it and control market price?"

"Availability dictates the market. Let me put it in simpler terms. Let's say you're a crack dealer in the city," he said, as Connor and Alex managed a smile at his choice of analogy. "You sell your product for ten dollars a bag. Now some Jamaican drug dealers come into town and they offer the product at the same price, market value. Are you with me?"

"I'm following you, Mon," Alex returned, in his best accent.

"In order to meet financial obligations you need to sell your current inventory because more is on the way. Now there are two sellers in the same market and double the amount of product. You need to sell more to move your excess and capture more of the market, so what do you do? You're forced to drop the price, given the same demand and an increased supply. This increases your sales, but you have a reduced profit margin. Now the Jamaicans need to keep pace, so they drop their price, etc., etc. You no longer control market price or margins. A glut has forced the price down. What are your options? Keep lowering the price—or terminate the Jamaicans. Do you follow that?"

"Supply and demand, I follow your economics."

"Good, now consider the globe being the marketplace. Slip up with these guys and there's no escape without a rocket ship."

"We're toast, in other words."

"They're from London; we're more like English muffins," Connor injected.

"Oh, that's funny, Con," returned Alex sarcastically.

"Look, if we've got a private buyer those guys shouldn't even be in the picture."

"Don't presume to underestimate these people, Connor. This is serious business to them. If they find out and believe for one minute you could successfully get that much gold to market, they would do whatever they could to ensure their domain—whatever necessary."

"Alright, Wes. You made your point, let's get on with this."

"I'm concerned, you're being a little too flippant."

"Sorry, Wes. But in my mind, we're light years away from them being an issue. I need to take in the rest of this and then decide what's next. By the end of day, this could all be a moot point."

"I'm relieved to hear that."

"I thought you might be. Can we continue?"

Wes nodded and with the press of a button Guy continued his briefing.

"I have included a package that will give you most of the background information you'll need. It includes contact phone numbers, addresses, a list of suggested equipment, pictures, etc. You can get current updates from George on the political and military climate. Keep in mind that you're dealing with an extraordinary amount of wealth. Trust no one. George is my friend, but he is also desperate. That is not good. When your personal financial situation is an issue, it can cloud your judgment, make you take risks you normally wouldn't. George has these problems, and that is a problem. This is not a cure all. If you are financially at risk, forget about this project. You have to be in a position to walk away at a moment's notice; your life may depend on it."

Hearing those words, Alex caught Connor's eye, reinforcing what Connor already knew; they were poster boys for when not to get involved. He shook his head ever so slightly to signal this was not to be discussed in front of Wes, while his father continued.

"The last item is money. You can't accomplish this without at least a half-million dollars available. You'll need to prepay for planes, equipment, pilots, transport, bribes and God knows what else. If I was there I could raise it, but not being present, you'll need to come up with it yourselves. Find an investor who is willing to lose it, tell them they probably will lose it. The information in the package may help you. The only other option is to do a small move with ten to fifteen bars to finance the operation. I don't suggest that however, time is important. Once you start, the clock is ticking; every minute the cave is open is one minute closer to something going wrong. Use the most important piece of equipment you'll bring—your brains.

"Now I need to spout a little philosophy," he said, seeming to relax for a moment. "Connor, if you choose to pursue this, please remember that your success is not measured by how much gold you get out. It's measured by if you get out. This is something you do for yourself, not to get rich, although that is a potential by product, but regardless, you will be enriched. You may not understand that all right now, but if you undertake this, monetarily successful or not, it will change you. If you do get the gold out, do what's right with the money, you'll know what I mean after you've spent some time over there. Someone once wrote, 'a rich man may have a chest filled with gold, but a richer man has a life filled with adventure.' My wish is for you to have both, but if you have to choose, take the latter, the money will be long spent before the memory ever fades—Welcome to the Adventure, son. Take care of yourself; we're heading off to ours."

The last thing Connor saw was his father lean back in his seat, a satisfied smile crossing his face as he nodded and the video faded to black. The three of them just sat there and starred at the blank screen.

"Questions?" Wes asked, breaking the silence.

"Got the package?" Connor returned.

"In the safe. I'll get it for you," he said, getting up to retrieve the information.

"Wes, do you know who wrote that quotation?" Alex asked.

"He did," Wes replied, returning to the table with a thick manila folder.

"Why didn't he just say it was his?" Connor questioned.

"Because," Wes said, hesitating as he sat back in his seat. "It had nothing to do with the message."

"I get it," Connor said, after a brief pause.

"I hoped you would. It's important."

"I know," Connor returned. "Can we take a look at the package?"

"Sure," Wes said, sliding the folder toward him.

Connor opened it, revealing an eight by ten photograph of his father standing in front of three huge stacks of gold bullion. It was obvious from the dark edges; the picture was shot in a place where no natural light could penetrate. Connor was speechless when he slid the photo over to Alex and awaited his reaction.

"Holy shit," Alex exclaimed. "I can't believe what I'm looking at. Is this for real, Wes?"

"It's not only real, it's legendary," Wes remarked, with a look of insider satisfaction.

"What do you mean? What's legendary about it?"

"What you're looking at is the 'Tunnel Hoard.' It is as famous as the 'Lost Dutchman Mine,' 'The City of Gold' or any other tale of misplaced riches. Yamashita's gold is well-known

Filipino and Japanese lore. The fact is; he did hide his government's ill-gotten gain, but legend has it, there was one place that he buried more than in all the other sites combined. It was identifiable by three distinct stacks of gold bars. Ask anyone in the gold trade that knows about Asian legends and they'll know the 'Tunnel Hoard.' You can bet your last breath, Morgan Gold is well aware of the story, if not the actual existence."

"Why didn't my father mention it?" Connor asked, leafing through the rest of the file.

"I really don't know why. Maybe he thought it was enough to deal with without making it out to be the monster it is. Or maybe he just felt it wasn't relevant to the operation. To him it was just a commodity that offered a unique business challenge—it was the challenge more than the gold that interested him. To the best of my knowledge, he was the only person to have seen it since it was entombed and he was always down playing that fact. It was a very personal thing, but he knew what he was dealing with. He just never had the need to feed his own ego by exposing it to everyone he met. Also, his own personal safety may have played a part in his humility."

"I don't know how you could see all that gold and not be motivated to remove it at all costs," Alex contributed.

"I think, Mr. Litowski, that you and Mr. Mason had better be able to separate the two, the price of not doing so may be higher than you can afford," Wes returned. "You need to internalize the ability to walk away from this. It is your one safety valve, and even that's not a sure thing."

"What do you mean; even that's not a sure thing?" Connor questioned, a sense of concern engulfing him.

"For the same reason your father may have not been compelled to make his exploits public knowledge. If the wrong people find out that you know it exists and the location, they may be inclined to think of you as a threat regardless of the fact you were unable to mount a successful operation."

"Kind of sounds like we're damned if we do or damned if we don't, Mr. Adams," Alex interjected.

"That, my boy, is a distinct possibility."

"Well, I guess we have a lot to think about," Connor

replied, gathering up the contents of the folder, as Wes and Alex nodded in agreement. "I need to go over this information and then make a decision."

"You need to do it quickly as well. There is another party who is awaiting your decision, and he doesn't even know it."

"George Fall."

"Yes, George Fall."

"I'll let you know by noon tomorrow, Wes."

"Yeah, if you have any teeth left so he can understand you," Alex retorted, referring to his Saturday rendezvous with Sid.

"Funny, Alex."

"It's not funny, it's tragic."

"What are you two talking about?" asked Wes, sounding slightly confused.

"Nothing important, Wes," Connor returned, as he stood up and prepared to leave.

"That's for sure," Alex contributed, following suit.

"Fine then. I'll expect to hear from you by noon," Wes said, leading them out of the small conference room and into his office.

Connor nodded, and he and Alex headed for the exit. They left the reception area and entered the elevator, still not speaking. Connor was lost in his own contemplation as to what course of action to undertake. The issues surrounding the removal of a cave full of gold were overwhelming to say the least—overwhelming and tempting beyond anything he could have ever imagined.

As they entered the garage and handed the attendant the parking ticket, Connor could sense Alex's concern.

"We're basically fucked here, aren't we, Con?"

"What are you talking about?" he replied, accepting his keys from the attendant and getting in the truck.

"You know you're going for it," Alex returned. "And we're not equipped to do this."

"Well, if we do this, and I'm not saying we are, it's your fault."

"How is it my fault?"

"You're the one who said go see the attorney, he'll help you. I was going to just let it go," he returned, rolling his eyes.

"Sure you were; nice try. I had nothing to do with this. You always do what you're going to do and that's the truth."

"You're right, Alex. But as I said before, you don't have to go," Connor said, pulling out and heading toward the office.

"What am I supposed to do, sit here and watch the business crumble while you're a half-a-world away having all the fun?"

"I don't get the feeling it's going to be a lot of fun."

"I know, but I can fantasize, can't I?"

"Be my guest, it's your fantasy."

"Thanks. But really, how do you see us pulling this off? Your Dad basically spelled out all the problems, not to mention our own financial situation. Everything he outlined fits us to a 'T.' We are desperate and we don't have the half-million he says we need to get it out."

"Desperation is only a frame of mind, Alex. Our financial dilemma is not going to change regardless of what we do. It is what it is. It could however, get substantially brighter if we were successful. All we're doing is trying to make a bad situation better."

"That's all well and good from the desperation side, but what about the little matter of the money to make this happen?"

"I don't think we need as much as my father suggested."

"Well, we don't have any and I'm sure we need some."

"I have the hundred thousand I deposited this morning plus I can tap my credit card cash advances for another fifty thousand."

"You got to be kidding. You'd take borrowed money and invest it in this white elephant?"

"Maybe, how much can you come up with?"

"Forget it."

"I'll tell you what. Let me make some calls and then

we'll piece together a plan and see if this has a chance of being feasible."

"Who are you going to call?" Alex asked, as they pulled up in front of the Capital Rehab office.

"The first call I'm going to make is to Billy Hilliard to see what the going rate is for smuggling gold out of a foreign country," he answered, hurrying toward the office door.

~ ~ ~

Alex followed just shaking his head. Connor was the unquestioned leader and he hadn't steered him wrong yet. The unfortunate thing was the circumstances surrounding this venture made it a clear-cut prescription for disaster. Alex wanted to talk him out of it, but couldn't even talk himself out of it. The idea of it was taking him over, as it seemed to have taken Connor. He and his best friend were heading into a freefall without a safety net and the thing that scared him most—he was starting to like it.

~ ~ ~

Chapter 23

High in the mountains, in a private hospital overlooking Geneva, Switzerland—Charles Morgan sat hooked up to a blood transfusion machine that replaced his tired life fluid with a fresher and more youthful source. It was a procedure afforded the super rich he had performed every six months, allowing him the illusion of increased vigor necessary to maintain an iron hand over his domain. At seventy-nine years of age, he had no intention of vacating his seat of power for many years and long ago made the decision to do whatever necessary to maintain his authority. No matter how many corporations shielded the identity, if you go high enough up the ladder you always come to one man. In the gold industry he knew he was that man.

Morgan Gold International, the mother company to hundreds of corporate subsidiaries world wide, controlled over seventy percent of the planet's gold production, including unreported mining in communist countries. The nature of the commodity allowed him to transcend boarders and politics; next to food, water and shelter, it was the worlds most sought after necessity. Presidents, kings, rulers, heads of state as well as less scrupulous sorts were at his beck and call and that level of influence he would never relinquish, it was as important as the air he breathed—maybe more so.

His temporary headquarters was a spacious private suite that, in addition to the required medical equipment, also housed state of the art communication and computer hookups. While he waited for his next scheduled contact, Jonathan

Ames, his personal assistant, entered to give him an update on his empire.

The families of Morgan and Ames had been inter-twined in the gold trade for over one hundred years. It was an embezzlement scandal in the early 1900s that threatened the company and relegated the Ames family from its lofty position as partner to silent associate. Since that time, a member of the family had served as a behind the scenes second in command. There was no love lost between him and his charge, but there was a job to do, a very important one and that took precedence over any personal differences they had.

His associate was nineteen years his junior and although he carried no official title, those brave enough to venture into his netherworld of highest finance, knew he was an irreplaceable fixture in the hierarchy. His skills were beyond balance sheets and production reports; he was a gatekeeper of the dynasty. Anyone or anything that threatened the position of the company was his to deal with, sparing no expense and showing no mercy. His job was to keep a pulse on world markets through financial reporting agencies and a wide web of international informants. He would apprise his superior of impending situations, and after being informed as to a course of action, carry out the response, allowing for plausible deniability of any activity deemed publicly inappropriate. It was a tradition that had been in place for the last seventy-plus years.

At just over six-foot tall, one hundred and eighty pounds with a full head of gray hair, he was a portrait of British demeanor, in stark contrast to the much shorter, balding curmudgeon, Morgan imagined Ames saw him as. Despite their physical differences, he knew the one thing they shared equally was their passion for power and control. Together, they were a most formidable team.

Carrying a thick folder under one arm, Jonathan Ames ventured closer in order to be heard over the hum of medical machinery.

"Good afternoon, Mr. Morgan."

"Good afternoon, Jonathan. Have you got the reports?"

"Yes, sir. They are right here," he returned, motioning to the folder.

"It's about bloody time. What was the hold up?" he said, reaching out his one free limb not bound by a transferring tube.

"The usual, sir. It just takes time to complete the compilation," he replied, handing him the information.

"Well, we are going to have to find a way to speed it up a bit."

"Yes, sir."

Taking the reports, he began carefully sifting through the distilled data. It was a daily synopsis of the company's financial position, highlighting major changes, good and bad, along with a detailed summary of the cause, political climate of the region, major players and projected long term effect. It allowed him to get a timely overview of his financial juggernaut. After over thirty years of reviewing this intelligence, it was easy to focus in on the material numbers, especially those he couldn't control. The ones that reflected projections of non-Morgan Gold controlled mines and what their expected production could do to the market price of gold. This was of constant concern and irritation to him.

"Nothing here out of the ordinary, would you agree, Jonathan?"

"Yes, sir, quite ordinary."

"What have our contacts reported? Anything of concern?"

"There are unconfirmed rumors of several mines in Indonesia that have hit major veins of high grade ore. Nothing that would cause a real ripple in our immediate future, but given our lack of presence, the situation could escalate beyond our influence if we fail to address it."

"What was the source of this information?"

"One of the associates at an Australian law firm that represents the company."

"Damn Aussies, never seem to get the facts right the first time. Let's keep an eye on it and try to get confirmation from a field operative."

"Yes, sir."

"What else?"

"We're having some issues in our Ukraine mines, the Russian mafia is giving our people fits with transport out of the country. They are threatening to expose our exit routes if we do not double their protection fee."

"I see. Who is in charge of that sector for them?"

"One moment," he returned, walking over to a one of a half-dozen, computer terminals. "Based on our latest information, a Boris Chernov is in charge of the operation there."

"What would be his expected disposition regarding negotiating this matter?"

"He is a most unreasonable sort, I've been informed."

"I think," he returned, pausing for a moment. Mr. Chernov should meet with a most unfortunate accident in the near future—the very near future. Then we'll renegotiate in good faith with his replacement. At that time we can make it clear that failure to be reasonable could result in the same circumstance that befell his predecessor."

"I'll make the required arrangements."

"Very good. Anything else worthy of our attention?"

"How deep in the rumor mire do you wish to explore?"

"Let's see," he returned, peering at the clock located by his bedside. "We have seventeen minutes before the next scheduled contact. Let us muddle on into the depths."

"As you wish. We have a report from the Philippines that there is activity in the southern sector, near Malaybalay, Mindanao."

"What type of activity?"

"Mining activity, sir

"How large?" he returned, dismissivly.

"Tiny, sir."

"Why then are we entertaining this subject?"

"A familiar name was associated with the information—George Fall."

"Now that's a name I haven't heard in quite some time. Refresh me, Jonathan. Who is he?"

"If you recall sir, it was some fifteen years ago that he

was associated with the Yamashita Gold legend."

"Now I remember, the Tunnel Hoard. Didn't we dismiss him as a bit of a dolt? Couldn't get out of his own way as I recall. But, there was another man involved that we felt was quite capable."

"Yes, sir. Guy Mason was his name. We had some dialogue with him."

"I remember. Is he associated with the mining operation there?"

"We don't know as of yet, but we'll find out."

"I don't know if the legend exists, but Mr. Mason was quite convincing when he approached us as I recollect. If it does in fact, resurface, we wouldn't want it to fall into the wrong hands, would we Jonathan?"

"Of course not, sir."

"I really don't have the time or inclination to watch this play out. Are there radical factions in the area?"

"They are in Cobato, the next province over. A Muslim rebel group known as the Abu Sayyaf."

"Let's see if we can entice them to become more active in the vicinity of the mine. That may nip their whole venture in the bud."

"We're not sure of the exact location, as of yet, sir. But I will put our field operatives to work on it."

"Good. Inquire as to the whereabouts of Mr. Mason. Should he decide to enter the picture, he should be permanently dissuaded from participating. No sense taking any chances."

"I understand."

"Do you? I mean permanently."

"It will be done. I'll keep you informed."

"Put this issue on our itinerary, Jonathan. We can't afford to take it lightly; no matter how far beyond the realm of reality it currently seems. I want no surprises."

"There will be no surprises, sir."

"Very good," he replied, turning his attention back to the financial statements scattered on the bed.

That signaled the end of their daily update. As

Jonathan Ames left to begin to put in motion the required events to protect and enhance the empire, Charles Morgan contemplated his required tasks; there was information to collect, palms to grease, bribes to pay, and men, who had been deemed a threat to their financial kingdom, to eliminate.

~ ~ ~

Chapter 24

Connor bolted through the Capital Rehab door with the information he received from Wes Adams tucked neatly under one arm. Nancy Dorsey appeared to be caught completely by surprise by the abrupt entrance as he proceeded up the stairs toward his office.

"Do I still have a job?" she yelled to her fast moving employer.

"At least until six o'clock," Alex answered, while he followed Connor at a much less accelerated pace.

"Good God Alex, what's going on?"

"Nan, as soon as I have a clue, I'll let you know," he returned, continuing toward the staircase.

"Time to polish up the resume," she said, watching both men disappear out of earshot.

When Alex reached the top of the stairs, Connor was already sitting with the folder opened to a list of names and phone numbers. He motioned for him to shut the door while he finished dialing and pressed the speaker button.

"Asian Airlines, may I help you-all," answered a female voice with a distinct southern accent. Alex shot Connor a look of disbelief as he settled into a chair next to his desk.

"Billy Hilliard, please."

"Who may I say is callin'?"

"Tell him Mr. Mason is calling."

"One moment, sugar."

He could tell they were placed on hold by the country music now blearing through the speaker. Connor smiled at

Alex. At the very least he was expecting an oriental sounding voice, certainly not a southern belle or the accompanying music selection. He was feeling somewhat amused, when a man with a strong southern twang answered the line.

"Billy here."

"Hello, Mr. Hilliard?"

"You sure don't sound like Guy, who am I talkin to?"

"This is Connor Mason, I'm his son."

"Is that a fact? Where's your daddy, Connor?"

The question caught him off guard causing him to hesitate for a moment before answering. "He disappeared in Mexico a little under ten months ago."

"You just passed the first test, son. Now, there can only be one reason why you-all are callin'. So what I need to hear from you is four words before I hang up. Take your time, you got ten seconds."

Connor sat stunned while Alex just shook his head. The conversation hadn't even started and it was about to end and with it, all hope for their involvement. Connor could feel the mounting pressure. The dead air made the seconds seem like minutes. Suddenly the words popped into his head, it was the only thing that made sense.

"The eagle has landed," Connor returned, holding his breath while he waited for the voice on the other end to reply.

"That's good. Where you at, boy?"

"I'm in Albany, New York, but I've got some questions. . . ."

"Not over the phone. Gimme a minute," he interrupted.

"Fine" Connor replied, realizing he was never going to get control of the conversation.

"You got an airport near you in Schenectady where I used to meet your daddy. I can be there in five hours."

"I'll meet you there, but how will I know you?"

"You'll know me. You ain't ever seen the likes of me in your parts. See ya in five, son," he returned hanging up the phone.

"You think we might be getting in a little over our heads

here, Connor?" Alex asked.

"I'll let you know in about five and a half hours."

"Appreciate that. What now?"

"Here's a list of equipment my father suggested we have available," he said, handing him a typed page. "Have Nancy call around and price it all out. We'll also need two tickets to the Philippines."

"Would those be round trip or one way?"

"You're just full of it today, aren't you? Anything else you'd like add?"

"One more thing. I'll do whatever you want regarding this whole crazy situation. But you've got to do something for me."

"And what might that be, bud?"

"I want you to forget about the fight with Sid tomorrow."

"Are we back to that again?"

"Yeah, we're back to that again and we're gonna keep going back until you give up this insanity. No, I take it back. We're gonna trade insanities; I'll trade you the insanity with Sid for this bigger insanity of going after the gold. Consider it a negotiation, maybe then you'll be able to stomach it."

Connor thought for a moment. The incident with Sid seemed like light years ago, considering the events of the last forty-eight hours. He had decisions to make—important decisions. This altercation was no longer high on his priority list. Maggie was right; it was a distraction, one that he no longer needed or felt as compelled to participate in. Maybe by letting it go, it might help him square things up with her.

"Alright, brother. You win, I'll call off the fight."

"Thank you, God," he returned, looking up at the ceiling in mock prayer.

"You better save those thank you's. I've got a feeling we're going to need them."

"Amen."

"Now let's get to work. It's two o'clock, I'm going to run some numbers and get an exact picture of our financial situation, so once we meet with our southern fried flyboy, we can

177

see where we stand. You get started on the list and the tickets. We'll leave here at six-thirty and head to the airport."

"What should we do about the crew, Con?"

"Cut them loose, Alex. No sense in denying the inevitable. Keep one guy on to cover maintenance issues and let the rest go."

"What about Nancy?"

"What about her?"

"Are we going to let her go?"

"Let's keep her for now. Who the hell would hire her anyway, especially if she interviewed in the outfit she has on today?"

"What's the matter, you don't like tight tops and short skirts anymore?"

"Not as much as you do, Alex." He flashed a mischievous smile at him.

"What's that supposed to mean?"

"You know what it means, closet stud."

"What are you talking about?" he returned, sounding a little defensive.

"Let's just say I'm pretty sure if we did a comparison, I would venture a hefty bet that the make-up on your briefs would match the stuff she has on her face."

"How did you know?" he surrendered.

"I didn't till now, I only suspected. Thanks for confirming it for me."

"You bastard."

"Guess I'm not the only one with girl trouble, huh bud. At least mine don't have a husband in the picture."

"It's nothing serious, it's only fun. Besides, that guy is worthless.

"It's fine, Alex. I'm just busting your chops a little. As long as you're having a good time and no one gets hurt, it's fine by me. I like her, she's a good lady."

"And a very classy dresser, you might have added."

"No doubt, brother, no doubt. Alright, that's enough for now; let's take care of business. On your way out you can let Nancy know she's still employed."

"I'm on it. I'll hook up with you at six-thirty," he said, getting up to head downstairs to give Nancy the required assignment and inform her she still had a job.

"See you then," Connor returned, pulling out a pen, paper and calculator from his desk drawer.

~ ~ ~

Chapter 25

The day had already surrendered its last bit of daylight, a little after seven, when Connor and Alex pulled up to the entrance of the Schenectady County Airport. It was a small facility where Connor remembered attending the yearly air show in his youth. However, its most recent notoriety came from the fact that it was the home of the air national guard, whose recent trip to Antarctica on a humanitarian mission had garnered national attention. To the best of his knowledge, most of the air traffic was the non-commercial type, consisting of private planes, local businesses and charter companies. The six-dollar an hour security guard waved them through and they headed toward the small terminal.

As they pulled up to the brightly lit boarding area located just outside the doors, a private silver twin engine jet came roaring towards them. As it entered the light Connor could make out the company name written in bold black letters across the tail—Asian Airlines.

"Whatta you think Alex?"

"I think that's our boy, Con."

"What is that plane? Is it a Lear jet?"

"No, it's a Citation."

"Really?"

"Yeah, really."

"Whats one of those babies go for?" Connor asked, as he opened the truck door and got out."

"New, almost four mill," Alex returned, following him slowly toward the aircraft.

"No shit?"

"Word."

They stood near the building while the plane came to a stop about twenty feet away. The roar of her engines was still winding down when the door near the cockpit opened and Billy Hilliard came swaggering down the attached portable stairway. As he deplaned, Connor knew there would be no mistaking him. He was a sight not often, if ever, seen in upstate New York. At six foot six and at least 280 pounds, he looked like a giant walking towards them. He was big all over, from his curly brown hair, hanging out from under a huge black Stetson, to his size fifteen lizard-skin cowboy boots. He was wearing an expensive dark gray suit made out of some kind of shiny material with a white shirt and black Texas string tie. At fifty something with a big head, large brown eyes high-lighted by bushy eyebrows, large mouth with a thick brown mustache and wide flat nose, he looked to Connor like a cow-boy bar room brawler who had just hit the lottery. He flashed a big toothy smile and reached out a huge paw of a hand to greet them.

"Evenin' boys, Billy Hilliard," he said, taking Connor's hand and shaking it firmly.

"Hello, Mr. Hilliard," he returned, not able to help but notice the disparity in the size of their hands. "I'm Connor Mason; this is my associate, Alex Litowski."

"Howdy partner," Alex replied, extending his hand and at the same time appearing to wince at how stupid he just sounded.

"You-all not making fun of me, are ya boy?" he said in a stern voice taking Alex's hand and holding it in his vice-like grip.

"No sir," Alex returned, suddenly looking very uncom-fortable.

"It's ok, son. I'm just funnin' ya a little," he said, releas-ing Alex from his grip and winking at Connor. "Come on boys, let's get on the plane and out of this cold so we can talk."

Connor, with Alex in tow, followed Billy when he turned and headed back toward the plane. He flashed Alex a look that said keep quiet and let me do the talking. After his initial foot-in-mouth experience, he was sure he'd be more than happy to oblige.

Entering the tight fuselage, they maneuvered into one of four high back tan leather chairs that faced each other separated by a small table. As Connor settled in, the inside seemed even smaller when Billy Hilliard folded his hulking frame into a seat opposite them.

"Ok, boys. What can old Billy here do for ya?"

"I'm looking for your going price to fly a plane full of gold out of the Philippines, Mr. Hilliard," Connor asked.

"You can call me Billy, son. Only people who owe me money call me Mr. Hilliard, and you ain't one of those—yet."

"My question still stands," Connor returned, pausing for just a moment. "Billy."

"Well, as you probably can imagine, it's a site more complicated calculation than meets the eye."

"Excuse my ignorance. Maybe you could educate us," Connor replied, starting to feel an edge coming on as he had no interest in beating around the bush.

"I'm not trying to be smart here. But we need to get down to the nitty gritty, so to speak. I know your daddy, Connor. We've done quite a bit of business together over the years. He always had a plan; do you have a plan? Do you have any idea what you might be getting yourself into?"

"I need some more information, Mr. Hilliard, in order to form a plan. That's why we're having this conversation. I have to assume that you have an interest in this project—a real interest or you wouldn't have got in your expensive aircraft here and flown five hours to meet with us. As far as having an idea about what I might be getting myself into, I'll admit it's vague, but I'm a quick study."

"I asked you-all to call me Billy."

"Fine."

"When did George Fall contact you-all with the message?"

"Two days ago."

"I guess the clocks a tickin then."

182

"That it is. So what do you need to know in order to give me a price? My father told me that you could transport the gold to a Saudi prince who would make the buy."

"How do you know George Fall?" Alex interrupted.

"I met George during his first attempt to move the gold."

"Did you know my father then?" Connor asked.

"No, I met your daddy, later. George had an investor that he partnered with that was familiar with my services. I was contacted to arrange transport."

"George had outside investors?"

"Oh yeah, old George was in a bit of financial trouble, so he sold part of his share to an ex-attorney general of Ohio, who was big in the building business as well as illegal arms sales. He took this picture he had of your daddy surrounded by all these gold bars and used it to convince the old gent to invest. I don't think Guy knew anything about that till later. At that time George needed around fifty thousand to catch up on back alimony and taxes. He contacted me to move a bit to sell in Hong Kong, in order to jumpstart the mining operation and pay back his investor. I met your daddy just before that move."

"What happened?"

"There was a problem and they couldn't get the gold to the plane."

"What kind of problem?"

"Son, it doesn't matter. It was just one of a thousand things that can go wrong with this type of operation."

"Is that so?"

"That son, is just not so, it's gospel."

"Why are you so interested then?"

"Truthfully, it's three reasons. I like money, action and pussy; not necessarily in that order. This deal will guarantee me at least two out of three," he returned, sporting a wide grin while he leaned back in the chair. "You see, I got this pretty wife back home in hot 'lanta. She spends too much and doesn't screw anywhere near enough. I get bored real easy, so I go to Asia. Lots of pussy, and with a little luck, lots

183

of action."

"What about the money?" Alex asked.

"I'm a businessman, son. I don't do a deal unless I'm going to make money."

"Which segues us nicely back to my original question, Billy. What's it going to cost?"

"Alright, son. My suggestion is that you-all have three planes available. Move as much as you-all can in one trip and forget about the rest."

"Go on," Connor returned.

"I know the area. Y'all are going to have to make sure that I have at least a thousand yards of clear runway available. There are only a couple of places in those mountains where that would be possible. The closest is near the Del Monte compound, on their private golf course."

"What are you going to fly in there?" Alex asked.

"DC-3's I imagine."

"DC-3's don't require that much room to land, they could get down in half that."

"It's not the landing I'm concerned with, boy. It's gettin airborne again with all that weight. I'd hate to come up short carrying your gold, not to mention what it'd do to my airplane."

"Why can't we just take the gold to the airport? You're a transport company, couldn't you just fly in there?" Connor inquired, his mind whirling.

"I could fly in there, but you-all never be able to get the gold to me. There are too many checkpoints."

"Checkpoints?"

"The military sets them up trying to intercept rebel supplies and weapons. Mostly it's just to scare foreigners, so they can extort protection money. The real problem is when you run into rebels, posing as military. If you're a foreigner, be prepared to spend some jungle time."

"What do you mean?"

"I mean you-all are a valuable commodity that is going to be kidnapped and held for ransom. They have held some hostages for years."

184

"Oh, that's just great," Alex blurted out.

"Don't worry, Alex. Nobody would pay much for us. Go on, Billy."

"This is no joke, son."

"Do I look like I'm joking?" Connor returned, staring directly at him with his piercing blue eyes.

"No, I don't believe you are."

"Can we continue then?"

"As I was sayin', I can land the planes, thirty minutes apart. You-all have time to get on about two tons in each plane. That's about sixty to seventy-million dollars worth, depending on market."

"How much will it cost?"

"Well, we're goin' to need three pilots, planes, fuel and at least a dozen mercs. . . ."

"Mercs? What the hell are mercs?" Alex asked; surprising Connor that the thought of being kidnapped didn't keep him occupied longer.

"Mercenaries, son. Soldiers of fortune."

"I know what mercenaries are. Why do we need them?"

"Just in case."

"In case of what?"

"In case we're loading the gold and someone decides to try to stop us from leavin'."

"We talking a fire fight here, Billy?"

"Just maybe, boy. This ain't no Disneyland attraction, this is serious business. Maybe you and your partner better think this over."

"That's what we're trying to do," Connor interrupted. "How much, Billy?"

"Three hundred thousand up front and ten percent of the take. The first five million guaranteed."

Connor and Alex looked at each other. The fee was substantially more than they imagined or could possibly come up with. There was an awkward period of silence while Connor's mind searched for options. He hadn't decided on a course of action, but wasn't prepared to throw in the towel just yet. His thought process was suddenly halted when Alex broke into a fit of nervous laughter.

"You got to be fucking kidding me," Alex said, still laughing. "Three hundred thousand and five million guaranteed! We don't have that kind of money."

"Let me explain how this works."

"Please, please—explain. Not that it will make one damn bit of difference."

"Shut up, Alex," Connor snapped.

"Shut up, what are you saying shut up. This is over," Alex returned, getting up from his seat.

"It's not over for me. If you want to leave, leave. If you're going to stay, be quiet," he replied. Alex shrugged his shoulders and shaking his head settled back in his seat."

"Go ahead, Billy."

"As I started to explain. Only the three hundred thousand is at risk. The five million guarantee is based on the first load that gets out. If only one plane with two tons onboard gets out, I would get my five million out of that load. If none of it gets out, I don't get anything."

"Except three hundred thousand," Alex chimed in.

"Alex!"

"Sorry Con, but this is ridiculous, we don't know anything about this guy and you're seriously considering giving him three hundred grand. Even if we had it, how do we know he can do what he says?"

"Good question," Connor surrendered, still trying to figure the finances needed in order to make this happen. "I actually have another question in addition to Alex's, Billy. At what point in the transaction do you take responsibility for delivering the gold, and what are your qualifications to do this? I know my father recommended you, but he always taught me to do my own due diligence and since he's not around, I'd like you to—give us some background."

"Fair enough, boys. First, I take responsibility at point of delivery to the buyer. When the old prince has the product at his doorstep, that's when it shifts to me. With this kind of cargo, I take no financial risk during transit. Too many things

186

can go wrong."

"How do we know that once you fly off with the gold, you won't just tell us something went wrong?" Alex challenged.

"Because you'll know if that happens."

"How would we know?"

"Cause one of you is going with me."

"Really," Alex returned sheepishly, suddenly appearing very worried at the possibility of flying anywhere with Billy and a plane full of smuggled gold.

"Truth, son."

"Well, that takes care of the first question. How about the second?" Connor interjected.

"Did you ever hear of Air America?"

"No."

"That was the code name for top secret ops ran by the CIA during the Vietnam War. I used to fly for them. Running guns, supplies, troops and lord knows what else in and out of Laos, Cambodia and China. We were the part of the war that no one back home was supposed to know about. It was strictly off the books and totally deniable by politicians and the military.

"When the war ended, we were no longer needed, so I started Asian Airlines. I had the contacts, the pilots, and I liked the life style. There was lots of business in selling arms and supplying mercenaries in that part of the world, and there was a need to transport both. That's how I got into the business. We operate mainly in Asia, but I can move almost anything or anyone, anyplace on the planet, if the money is right."

"Did you ever move drugs?"

"Years ago I moved a lot of things. I wasn't as particular as I am now. When I flew for the CIA, I wouldn't have been surprised if some of the cargo contained drugs. I didn't ask questions then, but I do now. The bottom line is, son, I can do what you-all need done. I know it, your daddy knew it, and you-all can depend on it. That's a fact. The other fact is, without me or someone like me, you amateurs would never get a god damn thing off that island," he returned, sounding annoyed by the questioning and disdain for his obvious experience.

"I'd have to agree with that, Billy," Connor replied attempting to defuse his aggravation. "You are definitely a lynch pin to the operation. But there is no way we can come up with three hundred thousand—do we have any room for negotiation?"

Connor watched while Billy sat back in his seat and rolled his big head from side to side until his thick neck cracked. He adjusted his cowboy hat back on his forehead and folded his large hands in front of him. There was a moment of silence as he stared at his young guests.

"Connor, if I didn't respect your daddy as much as I do, the answer would be no. But I'll tell you what I'm gonna do. You get me one hundred and fifty thousand and sign a personal note for the rest and I'll get the planes for you."

"Anything else?" Alex contributed sarcastically.

"One other thing? I need you-all to bring me some provenance, son."

"Providence—you want a city in Rhode Island?" Alex blurted.

"No, provenance. I want some down home concrete proof the gold is actually where you-all say it is."

"You were there before, you saw the picture with my father."

"I saw the picture, but I never did see no gold."

"What if I go there and verify the gold is where George says it is. That was obviously good enough when my father did it."

"You ain't your daddy, boy. Not by a long shot."

"I know that, but I still got some growing to do. How about giving me the chance?"

"This is your chance, son."

"Maybe it is; what kind of—provenance do you require?"

"In the picture of your daddy in the cave, lower right hand corner is a stack of tiny gold bars. They were poured in

Burma, they are the size of your index finger and weigh 'bout a kilo. Bring me one of those and we're on. If you-all can't get it, I'll forget about the note, but you forfeit the hundred and fifty thousand."

"You're telling us if we can't get you this bar, no deal and we lose our money?" Alex interrupted.

"If you-all can't get me that bar, there is no way this side of Memphis you can get six tons out of there and delivered to the planes. So, if you-all can't get out two pounds and you-all are paying someone to risk their life to move a shit load more than that, you-all are stupid and deserve to lose your money."

"What is so tough about getting it out? You walk in and haul it out, just like any other mine."

"You never been in a mine like this before."

"What do you mean? A mine like what?"

"A Filipino mine, boy. It ain't nothing like you could ever imagine in your wildest dreams."

"What exactly are you talking about?"

"Ask old George when you get there, he'll fill you in."

"Fine, Billy," Connor conceded, growing tired of the sparring. "How's it all supposed to play out?"

"You-all have to be in the Philippines by next Wednesday. Wire the money to my offshore account on Monday and I will meet you at the hotel in Cebu, where you-all are meeting George, a week from Wednesday. Bring me the bar, sign the note and we'll set the time and place to fly it out. You have my number and here's the wire instructions to my account in Thailand," he returned handing him a folded piece of paper from his inside jacket pocket.

"What if we need to move fast?" Connor asked, reaching for the information.

"I'll have everything ready to go at a moment's notice."

"You know, Billy, you could just go to George directly with the deal," Alex added.

"Son, the only thing I would deal directly with George for is going drinkin' or whorin', other than that he is pretty useless. That's information I would take seriously if I were in your shoes."

Connor paused for a moment, mentally trying to determine if he could muster enough resources to make this financially feasible. He glanced over at Alex, who to his surprise, had not stormed out when he had the chance. He felt he was hooked; just as hooked as he was. All reason had deserted him; all that was left was to find a way to make it happen.

"Thanks for your time, Billy," Connor said, getting up from his seat and extending his hand. "We'll be in touch."

"You're welcome, boy. I sure hope you get some news 'bout your daddy soon," he returned, shaking his hand.

Connor nodded as he and Alex followed Billy when he rose to open the door. They deplaned and watched while her engines started and she began to taxi toward the runway. Connor waited in silence as Billy Hilliard and his expensive jet disappeared into the crisp, cool, evening sky. He knew in his heart that he would be seeing him again soon—very soon.

~ ~ ~

Chapter 26

It was after nine o'clock when Connor dropped Alex off and headed home. He was tired, hungry and in no frame of mind to discuss their situation any further this evening. They had decided to get together in the morning, after he informed Pauley that the fight with Sid was off. On the one hand, Connor was relieved at the thought of not having to expend much needed energy, but on the other, the reality of backing down was weighing heavily when he pulled up in front of his Madison Avenue home.

He got out and headed for the front door, stopping momentarily to stare up into the clear starlit night, wondering if that's what it would look like on the other side of the planet—and would he ever find out. His mind was clearly engaged. He didn't bother to turn on a single light, letting his subconscious guide him through the pitch black and into the kitchen. Opening the refrigerator door, the light revealed a small silhouette sitting at the table to his left. He felt numb, not reacting to this nighttime intruder whom he recognized almost immediately.

"Hi Mag," he said quietly, realizing he wasn't startled, seeing how this wasn't the first time she had made an unannounced visit.

"Hi, Con. How are you doing?"

"Tough day," he returned, walking over and hitting the light switch on the wall. "What brings you out? I didn't expect to speak with you till tomorrow."

"I was thinking about what we talked about."

"And?"

"I want to be fair and it's not fair to involve you in my problems."

"A little late now, don't you think?"

"Not really. I just needed to tell you not to take that trip overseas. I don't want anything to happen to you because of me."

"What else, Maggie? You spent some time thinking on this, that can't be all."

"You want the truth?" she returned, sounding a little uncomfortable.

"Yes."

"I don't believe you're equipped emotionally to understand what to look for."

"How so?" he replied, too drained to disagree.

"You're linear in your thinking. You attack everything straight on, almost like you're wearing blinders. Your focus makes you effective in your business, but this is different, much different. You need to take in things around you and not just rush to completion."

"You honestly feel that I'd miss the point?"

"I do. Your entire focus seems to be on getting this treasure out. If that's all you're about, you'll never get the real answer you're looking for."

"Maybe the gold is the answer."

"It may have something to do with it, but it's not the answer."

"How do you know it's not? We don't even know the question."

"I know that both are over there, somewhere. Probably a clue lies in that cave. But I believe if you're preoccupied with only getting the gold, you probably won't recognize it."

Connor didn't answer right away; he pulled out a chair from the kitchen table and faced her. She looked good and he was glad she was there, despite how tired he felt. He took both of her hands in his and looked into her liquid brown eyes.

"Mag, do you really believe that someone on the other side wants my help?"

"I do."

"Do you think that it's your job to help me, help, who-ever is making contact?"

"Yes."

"Well then, have some faith. They did, they chose me," he said, inching his chair closer. "I can get the job done, trust me."

"I want to believe that, I really do."

"Then just believe it," he said, leaning over and hugging her tightly.

"You decided. You're going," she returned, burying her head in his chest as a tear ran down her cheek.

"If we can pull the financing together, we're going."

"Who's we?" she asked, looking up at him.

"Alex and I, unless he changes his mind."

"Let me go with you."

"Forget about it," he returned releasing her.

"Why not, Con?"

"It's way too dangerous Mag. I can't be thinking about you and get this done. I'll be thinking about you enough as it is."

"I can help you if I'm there."

"I have no doubt, but you're not going. I'll keep you informed. Besides, I need someone here I can trust to ramrod anything we may need done."

"I can do that, but if something is confusing over there, I can be on a plane at a moment's notice."

"If I need that, I won't hesitate to ask," he returned, feel-ing that there would be no circumstances he could ever imag-ine that would allow him to put her in harm's way.

"Okay, I have to go," she said, rising from her chair.

Watching her get up, he hesitated for a moment, but just a moment. "Stay."

"I can't."

"Why?"

"You'll need all your energy for your fight tomorrow and for what lies ahead of you over there."

"I'm not fighting. I'm going to Pauley's in the morning to call it off."

"I'm glad," she returned, a smile crossing her lips. "But I still can't stay."

"Please."

"Why?"

"Because I love you."

"I know; that's why I can't."

"What's that got to do with it?"

"Right now, I'm attracted to you. I think I might even be in love with you. But when this is over, one way or another, it might change. I don't want to hurt you, no promises, remember?" she said, tears now streaming down her small pretty face.

"No promises, Maggie," he returned, getting up and walking toward her. "I just want tonight, whatever happens after that happens," he whispered, leaning over and kissing her softly on her warm, tear salted lips.

Maggie didn't answer, she didn't have to. She just held him close. Connor felt she wanted to love him; she wanted him to help solve the puzzle that had become her life and end her nomad journey for answers. This was what she wanted, but there were no guarantees that getting the explanations would absolve her of the quest. He knew no promises could be made, because none may be kept, all she could offer, she did and that was surrender.

Feeling her melt into his arms, he lifted her in the air and carried her toward the bedroom. Laying her gently on the bed, he could feel her breathing increase while he continued his seduction by kissing her neck. He unbuttoned her shirt and began suckling on her erect nipple; he could feel her excitement when she pressed her hips against him. He wanted her, but it wasn't the sex, it was the peace of having her near, it comforted him in a way he couldn't explain in words, only feelings. It bombarded him in waves that just continued to roll over him.

As he undressed her and entered her body, there was no other place on earth he wanted to be, she was home to him, the thought of life without her seemed unbearable and that scared him. But tonight she was his again; he knew what it would take to have a chance to win her for good, but even if successful, there were no guarantees, no promises.

~ ~ ~

Chapter 27

Saturday Morning around 8:30—Connor was awakened from a sound sleep by the buzzing of his doorbell. He opened his eyes and glancing at the clock, realized he had passed out and slept through the entire night, he couldn't remember the last time that happened. He looked over to see if Maggie was still asleep, his groggy brain registering that she must have left sometime during the early morning hours. When he didn't feel her pressed against him, it should have been obvious; she always kept body contact whenever they slept together. He felt a little distressed that she had left without him knowing, but that was not out of the ordinary, it was just that he hardly ever was unaware of her departure.

When he got up to answer the door he felt a strange sense of calm, a kind of bliss hangover from their time together, he hoped it would last for awhile, but knew it probably wouldn't as the stress was already beginning to creep into his morning. As he pulled on some sweats and headed to the front door, his course was interrupted by the sound of his ringing phone.

"Hello," he answered, picking up his cordless phone on his way to the door.

"Why didn't you return my call last night?"

"Who is this? Susan," he returned, a little annoyed at her tone, as he opened the door to see Alex standing there.

"Yes, it's Susan. Why didn't you call?" she asked sternly.

"I'm sorry, I didn't listen to my messages last night, why didn't you just call again?" he said, motioning for Alex to come in.

"I did call again, three times and you didn't answer."

"I must have been in a deeper sleep than I thought. I guess I slept through it. Is anything wrong? This is not the first time you haven't been able to reach me."

"I don't know if anything is wrong or not, why don't you tell me?"

"What do you mean?" he returned, making a face for Alex's benefit.

"You've been acting so weird and you said you were going to call and you didn't. Then when I called there was no answer. So you tell me if anything's wrong?"

He hesitated before answering. He wanted to tell her the truth about what was going on and how he felt, but this wasn't the time. Doing it over the phone was the coward's way out; he was going to have to see her in person. He just didn't know when.

"I saw Wes last night. He had more information about my Dad and the gold."

"You're not seriously thinking about going over there are you?"

"I'm thinking about it."

"Oh—My—God! Have you lost your fucking mind? Connor, don't be an idiot, you could get killed doing this."

"My choice, Susan."

There was a long moment of silence. He was perplexed as to what else to say. He wasn't used to people questioning what he did, almost as much as he knew Susan wasn't used to not having complete control in her relationships.

"You're right—as usual, it is your choice," she said coldly. "I guess we all have choices to make."

Before he could answer he was greeted to the sound of a phone being banged hard on its receiver. He stood there with the phone held to his ear, not quite believing she had hung up on him and surprised by the realization that he was hardly even disturbed by it.

"Not the most cordial conversation you've had in a while I gather," Alex concluded, a mischievous smirk on his face."

"Was it that obvious?" he returned.

"Nah, most people would have hardly picked up on it."

"I thought so. What are you doing here this early anyway?" he asked, heading back to the bedroom.

"Man, are you brain dead these days or what? Don't you remember, I said I would meet you to go over to Pauley's and call off the fight, then we could go over the numbers for our little gold safari."

"Yes, I remember. I guess I just got preoccupied with Susan's call."

"Yeah, by the way. What was that shit about you sleeping through her call? You sleep so light that a fish fart would wake you. What's up with that?"

"I just slept through it, that's all."

"No, really Con. I've known you forever, I figured that with everything going on and calling off the fight, which by the way, if you haven't figured it out yet, I'm here so you don't change your mind, you'd be awake all night."

"I did have a little help going to sleep last night," he surrendered, winking at Alex, while he got dressed.

"Maggie?"

"What can I tell you?"

"You can tell me how you do it. You get caught with another woman the night before and the next night the one that caught you is back in your bed. You're my hero."

"That's not how it is with her, Alex."

"Please, allow me my delusions. They help get me through the day."

"Whatever you need, delude away."

"Thank you."

Connor finished dressing and they headed to Pauley's. The conversation was non-specific and light discussing how they would wind down the rehab business and segue into property management. Connor knew all the numbers and felt without the Philippine operation and some help from the bank that they might actually be able to break even, get jobs and hold out till the market changed. As good as that sounded; he was having a hard time fathoming it as an option. He had made up his mind that he was going to pursue the gold, anything else wasn't another choice; it was failure.

Pulling into the lot, he couldn't help notice the large number of cars. Getting out of the truck, he headed into the building, past reception, through the Fitness Factory and into the main room at Pauley's, followed closely by Alex. When he made his way toward the ring, he was met with a wild round of applause from the hundred or so members that were camped out at ringside. He gave them a half-smile and headed toward Pauley, who was talking to a couple of people including Leon Harris, the black heavyweight Sid was sparring with the day he orchestrated the confrontation.

"Lot of people here, Con," Alex said.

"Yeah, once they hear I'm calling this off, they'll probably throw tomatoes."

"Funny. You aren't going to let them effect your decision. Are you?" he asked, sounding concerned, as they neared Pauley.

"Not a problem, Alex."

"Good."

When they reached Pauley, the men he was talking to, with the exception of Leon Harris, offered their words of encouragement and then dismissed themselves for spots at ringside.

"Hey, Pauley," Connor said, feeling a bit subdued.

"Good morning C. Mason, how are you?"

"I'm fine."

"Yeah, he's fine and he's calling off this circus," Alex chimed in.

"That true, Connor?" Pauley asked, looking somewhat relieved.

"Yes, I'm sorry to say it is," he returned, having a hard time getting the words out.

"I think that's a good choice."

"Is it?" he questioned, starting to second-guess his decision.

"That g-g-guy is a b-b-bad m-m-man," Leon stuttered slowly. "S-s-staying away from h-h-him is a g-g-good thing."

"Going to disappoint a lot of people here, Pauley," Connor returned.

"Don't worry about that, they just wanted a show. They'll get over it."

"Alright," Connor conceded.

"I'll take care of this with Frank. Believe me, Connor, he won't be disappointed."

"Thanks, Pauley. Come on Alex, let's go before we end up making a scene."

"That's going to be a little difficult, bud," Alex returned, motioning in the direction of the hallway leading into the gym.

Connor turned to see Frank Handrahan and Sid coming toward them. He had the look of a fighter about to do battle. His chin was down as two beady eyes glared up in Connor's direction, his face was sullen and serious. Connor knew this was much more than a sparring session; he had called him out in public and ridiculed his manager. With his dyed blonde hair and tattooed arms, his mug shot could easily pass him off as a serial killer. Connor started to walk in their direction when he felt a hand grab his elbow.

"Wait here C. Mason, let me handle this," Pauley said, quickly moving to intercept Handrahan and his menacing protégé.

Connor settled in, leaning against Pauley's desk, where he watched him talking with Handrahan while Sid listened. He could see Sid's face begin to redden as he started shaking his head. It was clear that he was upset about not getting his chance at Connor, even though both mentors looked quite satisfied that this little testosterone explosion was no longer going to take place. Connor took note that based on what he was observing, he had Sid in the frame of mind he had expected and wanted for the fight, he was obviously mad as hell.

"Come on, Con. We've got lots to do," Alex said, motioning to him to leave.

"Wait just a minute, Alex," Connor returned, not taking his eyes off the discussion happening about twenty feet in front of him.

"Wait for what, let's go—now," Alex replied, tugging on his shirt.

Connor didn't say anything; he didn't have to. He gave Alex the look and that spoke a thousand words about what was in danger of happening.

"Don't do this, Connor. We had a deal, remember?"

"Sorry, Alex. I'm sitting on the fence here. I can't guarantee which way I'm going to fall."

"Connor, you need to let this go. Think of it as a test. If you can't walk away from this, how would you ever leave a cave full of gold? We have to be prepared to do that in order to stay alive. Here you may just get your ass kicked, but over there you may get it blown off. Show me you can do it—let's walk away.

"It's not the same thing, Alex," he returned, feeling all emotion leaving him.

Alex was losing him and Connor sensed he knew it; his mind was going to a place that warriors go before battle. He was heading for a netherworld, where life, death and fear have no meaning—destroy is the only objective, a world between human and savage behavior. He knew that place; it would transform him to beast, enabling him to release a controlled fury inside a square ring surrounded by colored ropes. Once the mind goes there, the body has no choice—but to follow.

"Connor, please! This is not the important issue."

Connor looked over at Alex. He was engulfed in a bitter inner conflict, everything was moving in slow motion. His psyche was ready to engage, but his heart was telling him that it's not necessary. It was a distraction he didn't need, not with what was at stake—friendships, business, fortune and most importantly—Maggie.

"You're right, Alex. Let's get out of here."

"Thank you," Alex returned, letting out a sigh of relief.

They started to head out of the club in the direction of Pauley and his adversaries. Connor brushed past them without incident while Alex followed. A clear path to the door was in sight; he felt they were home free—almost.

"Hey golden boy. What happened, your mum wouldn't let ya come out dancin' today?" Sid yelled, loud enough for all to hear.

"Frank, control your boy," Pauley said sternly, obviously not wanting an ugly incident with members present.

"Let it go, Chris," Handrahan directed Sid.

Connor stopped, but didn't turn around. He hesitated for a second and then continued toward the door.

"I see ya got your Shelia with ya. Ya going home to play house?" Sid continued. "She's a sweet thing, be gentle, ya faggots."

Connor shook his head. He could only imagine the look Pauley must have given them both when he heard Handrahan pipe up.

"That's enough, Chris. Golden boy had something come up, let it go, we've got work to do," he directed half-heartedly.

"Ya know what came up, Frank? The yellow streak on his back," he said, laughing loudly.

Connor spun to face them. He wanted to stand and trade barbs with Sid, but even though it was like shooting at an unarmed man, it served no purpose unless he was willing to back it up in the ring. He stared at them for a moment, then turned and headed out of the gym.

"Ya come back anytime, golden boy. Just make sure ya get my permission first, wanker," Sid shouted, as Connor and Alex exited.

They left Pauley's, and made their way out of the building. Connor walked with a sense of purpose as he headed toward his truck followed by Alex in hot pursuit.

"I'm proud of you, Con," Alex said, upon reaching the vehicle.

"Are you, Alex?"

"Damn straight I am. You didn't give into that guy, you didn't let him get to you."

"Sorry to disappoint you."

"What are you talking about?"

"I'm going back," he returned, reaching behind the seat and grabbing a large duffle bag.

"You had that with you all the time. You never intended not to fight him."

"I had every intention of not fighting, I just wanted to be prepared—in case I changed my mind."

"Which you have, I take it."

"Yes."

"Why?"

"It's something I can't explain, Alex. It's just my nature," Connor returned, heading back.

"I know," Alex yelled, watching him walk away. "I'm afraid your nature is going to get us killed someday—someday soon," he finished, the last two words falling on deaf ears.

~ ~ ~

Chapter 28

Saturday Night, Army Commander's Head-quarters, Bukidnon Province, Mindanao—Colonel Vadula, ignoring the twinge in his back, sat uncomfortably upright behind his large pine desk. He had his two pearl handle revolvers dismantled in front of him while he meticulously cleaned and oiled every movable part. It was a ritual he performed every evening, regardless of whether or not he had fired them that day; the guns were as much a part of him as the appendages he held them with.

He glanced around his long, narrow office, housing his desk and eight wooden chairs split up evenly on each sidewall, forming a makeshift corridor. The labored hum of a rusted air conditioning unit drowned out the noise from the nearby barracks while he watched countless tiny red ants, common invaders to every dwelling on the island, quench their thirst from the dripping condensation. The spotless bright, white walls were just painted in order to keep the bleeding brown stains caused by the relentless humidity at bay. They were adorned with aerial views of the camp, awards, maps and pictures of other military paraphernalia. A large bookcase sat behind his desk, against the back wall, home to countless trophies, ribbons and medals, all attesting to his proficiency with a wide variety of firearms.

There were over a thousand men under his command, most dispatched throughout the province, keeping a presence to insure some stability in a land of chaos. He had his own private contingent, whose sole purpose was to serve his whims and funnel any information on the activities of people, foreign and domestic, that he had put under surveillance in an effort to improve, what he had long since realized was a miserable existence and unsure future.

He felt the overwhelming need to escape from his preordained destiny of uncertainty that he could no longer intellectually accept. His options were limited despite the military resources at his fingertips. As he polished his pistols, he wondered about George Fall, the latest target in his quest for a financial windfall. The American's whereabouts were the subject of his intense scrutiny, having no intention of letting his quarry slip through his fingers like he had six months ago. He had ordered him watched twenty-four hours a day since their meeting at the Pryce Plaza hotel.

The thought of kidnapping and ransom had come to mind, in case the business arrangement he lobbied for didn't pan out. He would have some of his men, posing as rebels, perform the desired task and no one would be the wiser. Of course, his men would have to be eliminated, but life was cheap here and that was a small price to pay for a comfortable retirement he rationalized. George in and of himself, was of no value; anyone who had spent as much time "in country" was not likely to have friends or relatives willing to pay to insure his safety. But the wealthy speculators considering financing his mine would make a prime target. His thoughts of how to escape his inevitable poverty were brought to an abrupt halt as Corporal Vega, one of his underlings assigned to watch George Fall, entered his office.

"Good evening, Colonel," he said, coming to attention and saluting his superior.

"Good evening, Corporal," he returned, not bothering to acknowledge the salute, instead going back to cleaning his weapons. "Do you have anything to report?"

"Yes, sir," he replied, still standing erect. "Mr. Fall returned to the hotel and asked if there were any messages."

"And corporal, were there?"

"No, sir."

"What was his reaction?"

"I am not sure of your meaning, sir?"

"Was he angry, upset, happy?" he asked, beginning to reveal his rapidly deteriorating patience in his raspy tone.

"He did not seem upset, sir," replied the Corporal nervously.

"I see. Where is Mr. Fall now?"

"He is at his home, sir."

"Who is watching the home?"

"I have stationed men to watch the house and perimeter, sir."

"Are they good men, Corporal?"

"I think so, Colonel."

"If I were you Corporal, I'd make sure they were good men. If Mr. Fall escapes our observation of him, you will answer to me. Understand?"

"Yes, sir."

"For your sake and that of your family, I sincerely hope you do. You're dismissed Corporal."

"I will not disappoint you, Colonel," he returned cautiously, leaving to return to his men.

Colonel Vadula placed the guns in front of him and admired the sparkling metal. He began to slowly and delicately reassemble his prize possessions back to their functioning form. It was an exercise he could perform in the pitch black in a matter of seconds, but this was not a field drill, it was an obsession. Obsessions require time, and he knew he had nothing but time—time to wait for George Fall and his financiers to fall under his influence.

~ ~ ~

Chapter 29

As Connor made a rapid reentry, several exiting members, informed the exhibition had been canceled, made an about face and followed him back into the gym. He was sure many of them had been surprised that he took the verbal abuse being doled out without a response. On most occasions he was as quick witted as he was quick fisted. A murmur started to rise when those who had not yet left, noticed him coming down the short hallway. Having heard the commotion, Pauley, still in conversation with Handrahan and Sid, looked up, and moved quickly to intercept him.

"What brings you back, C. Mason?"

"Forgot something, Pauley."

"What was that?" he returned, a smug smile coming to his face.

"I forgot to kick somebody's big mouth Australian ass before I left," he yelled, loud enough for the entire room to hear.

"What took you so long?"

"Traffic."

"Thought so."

~ ~ ~

Pauley directed Connor into the men's locker room before he turned to address the opposition.

"Have your boy ready in twenty, Frank."

"We'll be ready in ten to kick that faggot's arse," Sid bellowed, his face reddening.

Pauley followed him into the locker room, no more explanations, the fight was on and that was it, no more questions, no more second guessing; just preparation. Pauley knew Connor would never be able to walk away after Sid's crowing. He was the cock of the block, and like that proud bird who fights to the death, no matter the odds, Pauley knew he'd be back—it was his nature.

He spotted Connor at the far corner of the locker room where he had begun peeling off his clothes. Pauley opened a nearby locker and removed several rolls of tape and some punching mitts. He waited while Connor unzipped his bag and pulled out his shorts, protector, gloves, shoes and headgear. As he pulled on his protector and shorts, Pauley couldn't help notice his body, he was leaner and more defined than he had ever seen him and was also looking a lot stronger.

"You look good, C. Mason," Pauley offered.

"Thanks, I've done a lot of weight work the last six months."

"Looks like it paid off," he returned, knowing full well how good his body looked had little to do with his survival in the ring, but also realizing this was not the time to cast any doubt.

"Twelve ounces and no hats, Pauley," Connor asked, referring to the weight of the gloves and the fact he didn't want to use headgear.

"Not sure I can make that happen, but I'll try," Pauley returned, as he started to tape Connor's hands.

Most sparring sessions utilized a more padded mitt and Pauley knew that Handrahan was expecting sixteen or eighteen ounce gloves, but seeing how his guy was a big hitter, he probably wouldn't put up too much of a fuss. As for the headgear, he never liked them, they didn't always protect a fighter, as more often than not it was better to get knocked out with one punch then absorb several dozen mini-concussions. He often thought more fighters got their brains scrambled sparring with headgear than they did in real fights. Some boxers got a false sense of invulnerability and took a lot more punishment because they were less cautious; feeling the headgear gave them more protection than it actually did.

Handrahan wouldn't care about the punishment. For the same reason he'd accept the lighter gloves, he'd wave the headgear. Some guys were so predictable, Pauley thought. It was a wonder they ever won a bout, although this confrontation was tilted more in the opposition's favor than he would ever admit to his fighter.

"How does that feel?" Pauley asked, finishing his tape job.

"Feels real good," Connor returned, while he alternated pounding a fist into his open palms."

"Good, go loosen up with some shadow boxing and I'll go see how our opponents are fairing."

"Who's going to ref?" Connor asked, starting to throw combinations in an effort to break a sweat and get limber.

"I asked Leon to ref," he returned, disappearing through the locker room door.

~ ~ ~

Connor nodded his approval and went back to work. It was time to get his mind right. He knew what lay ahead was no easy task, but what fights were? He needed to block out everything in his world and enter another, the world of a gladiator, where he could take all his demons, manifest them into the shape of an opponent and then do battle. He liked that place, maybe too much, at least that's what Maggie would say; a needless distraction, an addiction—maybe she was right.

As he felt his mind grow cold, removing all reason and compassion, he became more and more relaxed. He relished in the eerie calm as he continued to throw punches, feeling the beads of sweat form on his forehead. Glancing in the mirror he could see his body start to glitter from his perspiration, highlighting the newly formed definition in his chest and arms. His shoulders loosened while he continued ripping combinations into the air, his jab felt like a snapping rubber band, he was entering that place—his mind was getting right.

~ ~ ~

Pauley stood for a few minutes while he watched Sid's manager tape the two large slabs of meat he had for hands. The crowd was getting a little restless as Sid tried to entertain them with his pre-fight predictions. Pauley knew most saw him as a vile bully and paid little attention to his ramblings; they were there to see Connor and support him against this seemingly unbeatable force. Fans love an underdog, especially when it's the home team, he thought. When Handrahan finished, he approached them.

"Frank," Pauley said getting his attention. "What do you say to twelve-ounce gloves?"

Handrahan hesitated before answering. Pauley knew he wouldn't want to agree to anything that would give Connor an edge, even though in this case the request seemed to favor his man.

"I'll fight that punk bare knuckles," Sid yelled.

"What do you say Frank?" Pauley asked, ignoring his protégé's remarks.

"Who asked for twelve's, Pauley?"

"Connor."

"Not you?"

"Nope."

"Twelve's will be fine then," he returned, his lack of confidence apparent in his tone.

"One more thing, Frank."

"What's that?"

"No hats."

"What a dolt that bloke is, this just keeps gettin betta and betta," Sid chirped, bouncing around the ring to get loose.

"Anything else, Pauley?" Frank asked.

"Six rounds, okay with you?"

"Six rounds will be just fine."

"Have your man ready in ten minutes, Frank."

"Pauley, you may not want to have your man that ready."

"What's that supposed to mean, Frank?"

"What it means, Pauley," he said walking closer so only he could hear. "Is that you may not want to be so helpful to someone who doesn't figure in your financial future."

"Is that so."

"Think about it. Mason doesn't stand much of chance and if things get a little tough, you could not be so forth coming with the right advice. Right now I pay to use your gym and I'm thinking very seriously about having you help me train Chris. We wouldn't want anything unfortunate to disrupt his progress, would we?"

"You seem a little worried about someone who doesn't stand much of chance, Frank."

"Even a blind squirrel finds a nut from time-to-time. All I'm saying is, in this business you need friends to make a go of it, that's all."

Pauley stood and looked at Frank while he contemplated his not so subtle message. He was irritating to say the least and his boxers were usually the loutish and bullish types that lacked the heart anytime they were stood up to. That being the case, he was a constant revenue source and did attract some fighters with talent and God knows he could not afford to lose the income by alienating him from the club. The logical course would be to play along, so if Connor did lose as expected, it would seem to Frank that he didn't really help him—but there's not much logic in the fight game he thought, and every so often it gets displaced by pride and principal. "Frank, in this business, there are no friends. You've been around long enough to know that. Be ready in ten minutes," Pauley replied, turning and heading back to the locker room.

Pauley left Handrahan standing while he disappeared through the doorway. He was glad to deny him the added insurance he was looking for. He was sure that Handrahan wasn't that concerned, he probably felt his man was the superior talent although their had to be a shadow of doubt because of his past experiences with the way Connor handled some of his other fighters. But that was a long time ago, before he was a manager and trainer of a world champion. Things were different now—at least that's what Pauley thought he hoped as he smiled to himself.

Pauley entered the locker room to a sight that always made his adrenaline pump, an athlete in full sweat preparing to go to war. Nothing mattered now, not the opponent, not the money, not the state of his business, nothing but one thing— the fight. He walked over to the bench and picked up a pair of boxing gloves and punching mitts. Connor, still shadow boxing in the mirror, managed a slight focused grin, noticing his approaching reflection. Pauley walked up behind him when suddenly he whirled around still throwing punches.

"You got it all, Connor, twelve's and no hats. We're going six rounds."

"Good."

"Let's get these gloves on," Pauley said, holding open one end.

Connor pushed his right hand in while Pauley pulled it on; then repeated the procedure with the left. He tied both gloves and wrapped the laces with wide athletic tape.

"How do they feel, C. Mason?" Pauley asked, putting on the punch mitts.

"They feel good," he returned. "Let's tak'em for a test drive."

"One," Pauley barked, holding up the right-hand punching mitt.

Connor snapped off a left jab into the mitt as a grunting sound released some air from his lungs.

"One, two."

A snapping jab followed by a hard right hand and more grunting.

"One, two, three, two."

A quick jab, right hand, cracking left hook, ending the combination with a banging right hand.

"Two, three, three, slip two."

A right hand followed by a left hook, then recoiling and throwing the left hook again as he ducked to his right while

212

Pauley threw a left over his head and popping up, Connor finished with a stinging right hand.

He looked good, Pauley thought. For the next five minutes he continued to call out combinations. He wanted him really warm before entering the ring, although billed as a sparring session; he knew it was much more than that. This was a turf war, the big dogs had pissed on the same tree and now they were defending their territory.

"You ready?" Pauley asked.

"Let's do it."

~ ~ ~

Connor followed Pauley out of the locker room and into the main gym, much to the delight of the partisan membership who clapped and yelled their shouts of encouragement. He saw Alex standing quietly, leaning on Pauley's beat up wooden desk. Connor knew he didn't want this to happen, but now that it was, he hoped he was going to support him.

As he climbed up on the apron, Sid was already in the opposite corner receiving some last minute instructions. Leon Harris held the ropes open for him while he entered the squared circle. Bouncing to continue to stay loose, he spotted Alex bulling through the spectators.

"Connor," Alex yelled.

Connor looked over, feeling the perspiration pouring down his forehead.

"Kick his ass, brother."

Connor nodded as Pauley shoved his mouthpiece in place.

"You know he's going to come out fast, Connor. If he charges, stay low and block the punches with your arms, he can only keep that up a minute or so, then once he eases off start picking him apart with your jab," Pauley advised.

Connor nodded, then turned and faced his adversary. Leon Harris was already in the center of the ring waiting to start the fight. He pointed to Sid's corner, where he was pacing like a trapped animal, and received his signal that he was ready to start, after getting the same affirmation from Connor; he waved them to the center of the ring.

Sid rushed across the ring as Connor circled to his left to avoid the charge. Sid made a rapid move to his right cutting off the ring and swinging with a wild left hook that Connor easily avoided. Continuing his charge, he banged Connor into the ropes and fired a left and right to the body as his opponent rebounded off them. Connor stayed low and picked off the shots with his arms while Sid continued to throw wide hard punches at his head and body; nothing made a solid connection but Connor could feel his power. Even the blows he was blocking hurt. He looked into Sid's eyes and could see he was wild with rage. He had stopped cutting off the ring and was now chasing after him, while Connor kept him at a distance, snapping crisp hard jabs off his head. He looked furious when the round ended with Connor landing a pretty three punch combination, jab to the face, right to the chest followed by a hard left hook to the body, causing the pro-Connor crowd to cheer wildly. At the bell, Leon had to step in to keep Sid from pursuing him back to his corner.

"Good round, C. Mason," Pauley said, while he removed his mouthpiece and gave him a drink.

"He's strong, Pauley," Connor returned, breathing hard.

"Yeah, but he's slow. Stay away and keep jabbing, let's take him into the later rounds and see how he reacts in the deep water. Now relax and breathe, you're doing fine."

"Okay, Pauley," Connor replied, taking a few long deep breaths.

When Connor got up from the stool, the crowd shouted as Leon waved for them to start the second round. Sid again charged toward him. Connor sidestepped and threw a hard left to the body followed by a right hand up the middle that grazed off Sid's chin. It hardly slowed him down as he bore in, catching Connor with a left hook to the rib cage that took his breath long enough for Sid to land a wide hard right that deflected off his neck and shoulder. He was strong, stronger than anyone Connor could ever remember fighting, a couple of clean punches could end this he thought, maneuvering out of harm's way and attempting to regroup. Sid followed quickly after him while Connor kept him at bay with a stiff jab, having felt his adversary's power he was hesitant to open up with anything more substantial.

Suddenly Sid slipped under his jab and stepping in, landed a hard left hook to his liver. The shot went right through him, paralyzing him with pain; he couldn't get out of the way when a hard right to the chin sent him tumbling to the canvas. He lay on the ring floor hearing the crowd pleading for him to rise; his head was ringing when he looked up at Leon who was counting over him. He struggled to his feet at the count of seven, trying to look less hurt than he was; knowing Pauley would stop the fight. Sid, who was mugging for the crowd and raising his fists in the air as they were signaled to continue, closed in for the finish.

Connor was still feeling a little disoriented as he threw out a couple of light jabs. Sid dove in at him as Connor stepped inside the wide left hook he threw and grabbed his arms, holding on till Leon broke them apart. Leon stopped the action and warned Connor not to hold, giving him a few more precious seconds to recover. The round came to a merciful end as his regained mobility and jab thwarted off another damaging blow.

"You can't run from him C. Mason, you've got to fight or he's going to walk right through you," Pauley said, toweling him down and straightening his legs to increase the blood flow.

"That's kind of what's going on out there, Pauley," he returned, becoming a little frantic.

"Relax, you wanna fight this guy or do you want me to stop it?"

"Don't stop it."

"Then use your head. Double and triple up on the jab and then follow it up with something hard. Move in and out and throw punches. You wanted him, you got him, now fight him." Connor nodded, while Pauley squirted some cold water on his neck and head.

Sid was looking confident in his corner, his beady brown eyes burning a hole in Connor seated across the ring.

215

Frank Handrahan rubbed his thick neck and gave his instructions so loud that Connor had no trouble overhearing them.

"You got him hurt, Chris. Get in there and finish him this round."

"Not yet, Frankie. I'm gonna punish this punk a bit more."

"Don't fool with him," he returned, slapping him to get his attention. "He's still dangerous, don't fucking mess around, end it."

"That wanker's got nothing. I could beat him with one hand tied around me back. He's getting a lesson."

"Chris!" Frank yelled, as his protégé, ignoring him, waded back out to continue his carnage.

Connor threw out a jab that connected to Sid's forehead, snapping his head back. Sid smiled in an obvious effort to dismantle any confidence being built while he continued to press forward. Connor was feeling pressured as he circled to his left in order to avoid any damaging left hooks to the body. Sid was bobbing side-to-side, forcing Connor's jab to miss while he worked his way inside. He feigned a left hook, causing Connor to flinch, enabling him to throw a hard right to the chest that drove his rival into the corner. Sid rushed in, trapping him with hard lefts and rights to the body. Connor could hear Pauley yelling to get out of the corner, but the ferocity of the attack had him pinned. He continued to turtle up and absorb the painful infliction as his mind searched for a way out of the onslaught.

Finally a hard right to the ribs dropped him to the canvas, momentarily ending his dilemma. Leon knelt down next to him and asked if he wanted to keep fighting while Connor used the ring ropes to struggle to his feet. He motioned his desire to continue something he knew a fighter did instinctively, not taking stock of the gravity of the situation or his physical well-being. Connor took a deep breath while he stared at Sid, who was smiling; his black mouthpiece exposed while he readied to rain down more pain. He could hear Alex at ringside yelling to stop the fight; the crowd was much quieter as they watched a friend, not just a pugilist taking a beating.

Pauley yelled to Connor to double the jab as Leon waved the combatants back into battle.

Connor popped quickly out of the corner, not wanting a repeat of the last thirty-seconds, he circled to his left and began to snap out jabs at Sid's face. He doubled and then triple jabbed, stopping his charging antagonist who tried without success to work his way back inside. His body was in agony; but the strategy allowed the round to end without Sid being able to mount another significant attack. Sid appeared somewhat frustrated and breathing hard when he returned to his corner.

"I told you to finish him, Chris. Now do it this round," Handrahan yelled.

"I will," Sid choked out, taking a seat.

Connor collapsed on his stool while Pauley stepped through the ropes. He knew Pauley must be having trouble separating himself from the fact that this man he had a deep concern for was taking a horrific beating and focus on giving him the direction he needed to get out of this mess in one piece. Pauley held the water bottle to his lips as Connor could feel him peering into his deep blue eyes. He knew he'd have to convince him he had the heart to continue.

"I'm not quitting, Pauley. If you're thinking of stopping this you can forget about it."

"I'd never do that to you son," Pauley replied, looking satisfied for the moment. "How do you feel?"

"I hurt all over."

"You've got to block out the pain."

"No shit, Pauley, but it's a lot easier said than done."

"This round, we've got him where we want him. Double and triple up on the jab, then go left hook to the body and right to the head and move out. You've got to take it to him, he's ready to fold."

"How do you figure that, Pauley? He's beating me to a pulp in there," he gasped, noticing Leon walking over to his corner.

"D-D-Do you w-w-want to continue, C-C-Connor," Leon asked.

"Don't stop this, Leon."

"He's not going to unless I tell him," Pauley answered. "Tell him why he's going to take it to him this round, Leon."

Leon hesitated for a moment. He looked a little strangely at Pauley. Then as if a light came on, he spoke. "H-H-He d-d-don't breathe when h-h-he punches."

"That's right, " Pauley said, nodding in agreement. "Look at him sitting over there, he's going to cave."

Connor was feeling tired and sore when he peered around Pauley at the source of his agony. He could see Sid was breathing heavily, unable to obtain a comfortable rhythm, realizing both Pauley and Leon had noticed that Sid was so intent on hitting him with as much force as possible, he was holding his breath when he threw punches. That, coupled with his intense anger, seemed to be sucking the energy from his body. Connor knew that if he didn't breathe, he wouldn't relax, if he didn't relax; he'd get tired—dog-tired.

He felt a glimmer of hope when he rose to start the fourth round. His rib cage was killing him and he certainly didn't want to absorb any more punishment, but he knew he had to mount some kind of offense so his adversary would continue to struggle for oxygen—at what cost, he wondered.

Sid looked like he was going to charge, but after a few rapid steps he slowed, eating a jab to the face in the middle of the ring. Connor continued to jab for the next minute, circling to his right and staying off the ropes. A couple of wild hooks found Sid no longer breathing though his nose, his mouth was open exposing the black plastic guard that he was sucking air around. Connor noticed his difficulties and moved in behind a double-jab, right-cross combination and then, stepping to his left, landed two vicious left hooks to the short rib. He could see the pain in Sid's eyes when he backed off to the chorus of the wildly cheering patrons. He then quickly ventured close enough to snap a series of jabs off Sid's large head while sweat flew with every landed blow. With around thirty-seconds left in the round, Sid muscled him against the ropes and began to fire hard shots to the body.

Connor could hear Pauley yelling to get off the ropes,

but instead he leaned back against them and let Sid pound away, protecting his aching rib cage and head. The pain started to subside as he used the cradling physics of the ring restraints to help cushion the punches. Everything suddenly felt like it was in slow motion, as he slipped several head shots and returned a hard, one-two combination up the middle. The force of the blows sent Sid staggering back to the ring center as the round ended.

Connor knew what was happening when he made his way back to his stool, he was about to enter a higher plane—a place athletes visit all too seldom, but the memory of time spent there could stay with them a lifetime.

When he took his seat, everything in his mind was blank, his psyche eliminating all but the task at hand. The crowd was no longer in focus, Pauley was giving instructions and rubbing his neck, but he couldn't hear him or feel his touch. He didn't feel tired or sore, his arms and legs were weightless as he enjoyed the euphoria of his journey. He was traveling to another level. A place sportsmen called—the zone.

When a basketball player went there, the hoop looked as big as an ocean, and no matter what shots were taken, they were going in. When tennis players got there, the ball looked like a watermelon and nothing seemed out of reach. It was a land where legends were made and stories were forever told; when an athlete excelled so far above his opponent that no matter what he tried, the onslaught could not be stemmed. He knew when a boxer made the trek, his adversary seemed in slow motion, he could see punches before they were thrown, those that missed him by inches seemed like feet and openings to attack looked as big as picture windows. The problem, he realized, came from getting overconfident and the resulting consequences, in basketball, he'd take bad shots, in tennis, he'd miss some balls—in boxing, he'd get his head knocked off.

As Connor rose, the labored condition of his rival was apparent from his heaving chest muscles and the heavy-legged movement that brought him within range. Wasting no time, Connor threw a four-punch combination, jab to the head, hard right to the cheek, stinging left hook to the body ending with a solid right uppercut that deposited Sid on the seat of his pants.

When Leon motioned him to the opposite side of the ring he caught Frank Handrahan, suddenly looking very displeased, pacing just below his corner while the crowd was screaming for blood and Pauley was shouting to keep attacking. Connor ignored all of it, as the commotion brought more curious spectators from the attached health club.

Sid struggled to his feet, looking more confused than hurt while Connor closed the distance to solidify his new position as aggressor. Sid managed a poking jab, followed by a tired straight right hand that was well short of his target; Connor advanced behind a series of triple jab combinations that created an opening to his opponent's body. Seizing the opportunity he double left hooked, landing hard to the liver and kidney area. Sid, in distress, retreated backward until the ropes halted his escape leaving him trapped. Connor followed and began banging hard to the body with left and right hooks. When his adversary lunged forward in an effort to stop the barrage, he absorbed a left-right uppercut combination to the face and chin; the last shot splitting his lip wide open. He stumbled forward, dazed, as Connor sidestepped and landed two chopping rights behind the ear that sent him face first to the canvas.

Connor, thinking the fight was over, was more than surprised at his opponent's resolve while he watched Sid slowly rise to his feet, his face looking puffy and red as he wobbled on unsteady legs. Leon gave him an eight count, while those viewing from ringside urged Connor to continue the onslaught, their cries reminiscent of ancient Rome he thought, where patrons would scream for the execution of the defeated opposition.

By the time the referee motioned them to continue, Connor's focus was already broken, as was the body and spirit of his adversary. Sid reluctantly moved forward, not looking anxious to absorb more of a beating; what he didn't realize was that his opponent had lost interest in administering one.

Boxing was a hard game, one that tested courage and

perseverance. It was not Connor's chosen profession. He had other options, but it was his antagonist's and he respected the dedication and sometimes the desperation that went with his choice. The first message had been sent and received, not to bully those weaker; Connor felt any further abuse was not necessary, in spite of the lynch mob atmosphere. The next message was one of compassion, he wasn't sure if it would be understood, but any continuation of punishment would do nothing to communicate it.

Connor met him at center ring as Sid tried to mount an attack. It was a slow awkward attempt, but valiant given his debilitated state. Connor threw out some light jabs to keep him at bay, choosing not to complete the total destruction he had built the foundation for. When the round ended, Connor went back to his corner where Pauley stood waiting.

"What's up C. Mason?"

"It's over, Pauley. I've had enough."

"You mean you've given enough."

"Whatever."

"You're a good man, C. Mason," Pauley returned, placing an arm on his shoulder. "I'm proud of you."

"I couldn't have done it without you," Connor replied, leaning on the ring ropes.

"I'm not talking about the fight."

"I know."

Connor looked over toward Sid's corner where Handrahan was berating his performance and trying to pump him up for a strong finish. He was just ending his lecture when Pauley called over to him.

"Fight's over, Frank."

"What do you mean the fight's over, there's still one round to go?"

"Connor called it, he's had enough."

"He's quitting?"

"If it makes you feel better, you can call it that."

"It does."

"Fine, he quit."

"Never thought I'd see the day you'd give up, Golden

Boy," Handrahan crowed at Connor.

"Like I know I'll never see the day you get a brain, Frank."

"What's that supposed to mean?"

"I'll write you a letter," Connor returned, while Pauley cut the tape from his gloves.

"Smart ass."

"Half-me, half-you, Frank," Connor retorted, as he exited the ring.

"Do you believe this guy?" Handrahan said turning to Sid still seated.

"Let it go, mate," Sid returned, clearly grateful that the bout had come to an end with him still able to walk out on his own power.

Handrahan just shook his head while he walked over to his protégé to remove his gloves. The rhetoric he was spouting was for his own benefit and in defense of his fighter. Connor knew that in his heart Handrahan realized that his man was whipped, and that was a fact his ego was unlikely to allow his mind to accept—at least for a while.

Connor made his way through the crowd with Pauley and Alex following close behind. He graciously accepted the accolades bestowed on him for standing up to this daunting figure. Heading toward the locker room, he wondered if he had any broken ribs. The high of the moment was passing and the reality of the punishment he absorbed was slowing inching to the forefront, the pain increasing with every breath. Before he could totally evaluate the extent of the damage, he noticed Maggie leaning against the wall, just beyond the still buzzing crowd. She gave him a kind of half-smile when he approached.

"Thought you decided not to do this?" she said, folding her arms.

"I did."

"That's not what it looked like."

"Some thing's are never what they look like."

"Some thing's are."

"That's true enough. Anyway, I came here to call it off

222

and things escalated to a point that I couldn't."

"What things?"

"I don't know exactly, just things."

"Things like your pride, one-sidedness, or is it just what you do?"

"Kind of like that, I guess."

"This is the type of thing that makes me believe you'll go and get yourself killed."

"What is, Mag?"

"This fight, it's a perfect example. You decided not to do it and then you let other—things, get in your way. It made no sense and you did it anyway."

"I can differentiate between what to do and what not to," he returned, suddenly feeling very tired and a little aggravated.

"You haven't shown me that yet."

"You've only been watching six months, stick around, maybe I'll surprise you."

"I'm afraid you won't live long enough."

"Look, I'm sorry I disappoint you, but it's my life. If I start thinking like someone I'm not, then I will be in trouble."

"Don't go, Connor."

"Don't go where?"

"You know, after the gold."

"I appreciate your concern, Mag, but I'm going."

"Don't do it for me."

"Of course not, Mag," he replied, trying hard not to sound condescending. "Look, I've got to go grab a shower. Can we talk about this later?"

"I don't know."

"Whatever," he returned, feeling too tired to argue. He turned and headed for the locker room, leaving her standing against the wall. As he reached the door, he wanted her to understand how he felt, he wanted to talk it out and get both of them on the same page, but the fight had sucked every ounce of energy he would need to accomplish that task. What he really wanted was to get some rest and renew himself; then he would tackle Maggie.

Alex was waiting for him when he entered the locker room. He managed a smile, as he approached.

"Nice job, Hoss," Alex said.

"Thanks, bud."

"Maggie give you a little gas out there?"

"Not too bad."

"How are you feeling?"

"Kind of beat up, my ribs are killing me."

"Yeah, you took a lot of body shots," Alex returned, pointing to the discoloration around his rib cage. "You had me a little worried for a while."

"You're not the only one," Connor returned, peeling off his shorts and wrapping up with a towel.

"I know you're probably tired, but we need to go over the numbers. If we're going to do this, we only have a couple days before we have to be on a plane. The thirteen- hour time difference coupled with the twenty-four hour travel time gives us a go-no-go date of Monday at the latest."

"Let me take a shower, then we'll grab something to eat on the way to the office."

That's fine, I'll need to pick some things up this afternoon, if we decide to go."

"I kind of think we've already decided, don't you?"

"Just leaving you room to back out, you know, if you're getting cold feet."

"Right," Connor returned, trading mischievous looks, as he went to pour hot water over his sore and battered body.

~ ~ ~

Alex sat and waited for his friend. He appreciated what he had accomplished. He knew it wasn't just for his benefit, but his previous altercation with Sid was definitely the catalyst behind what took place. He realized that Connor would go to the mattress for him; he just hoped that someday he could return the favor. While he ran mental scenarios of their upcoming adventure, he wondered if the opportunity would come sooner than later. He just prayed that if it arose he would be brave enough to answer the call as Connor had done many times for him. Maybe a half-a-world away, he would get his chance.

~ ~ ~

Chapter 30

As they pulled in front of the Capital Rehab office, Connor was visibly wincing with every breath. He couldn't breathe, move or God forbid, laugh, without pain surging through his entire torso. The over the counter medication wasn't even touching his misery when he gingerly slid out of his truck and onto the pavement. He slowly made his way to the front door while Alex followed, carrying the food they had picked up. He couldn't help but wonder if Alex was also going to have to lug him up the stairs to his office.

"We're not doing so good, are we?" Alex inquired, stepping in front of Connor to unlock the office door.

"We're doing just fine, it's me who's dying here."

"You think they're broken?" he asked, pointing at Connor's ribs.

"Maybe, I'm not sure," he returned, entering and making his way slowly up the stairs.

"How about we get some X-rays?"

"What for? If they're cracked, they'll only wrap them anyway. I'll do it later, besides we're running short on time."

"Well, I'm just not sure we. . . ."

"Let it go, Alex," he interrupted. "I know what I'm doing."

"Fine," Alex replied.

"Look," Connor said, slowly easing into his desk chair. "I can come up with a hundred and fifty thousand between borrowed funds and credit card advances. I could also make another fifty happen if we pledged the remaining equity in the properties. What can you get hold of?"

"Between now and Monday, probably around fifty thousand or so, between my home equity and credit cards. I figure we can use the corporate American Express card for tickets and hotel. Where are you going to get the additional financing on the properties?"

"Don't ask?"

"You're going to see the Greek aren't you?"

"Yeah," he surrendered. "He's the only one I know with cash that will lend on short notice."

"He's a fucking loan shark, Con."

"I know, I know, but we've got time constraints here, bud.

"What we've got is a mind constraint here, cause you're not thinking straight. What's the vig on that?"

"Standard deal, ten percent up front and then two percent during the outstanding period?"

"A month."

"A week."

"A week, that's a thousand bucks a week interest, Con."

"Do you have a better idea, Alex?"

"Yeah, let's not do this."

"That's always been your choice," Connor returned, looking in his desk drawer for more Tylenol.

"Alright, give me the whole load. We go over there and somehow make it back alive with no gold, what's the worst case?"

"Got it right here," he returned, grabbing a note pad from the corner of his desk. "Here's the deal, we've got a two hundred thousand dollar credit line with the bank to pay back, payroll taxes of around thirty thousand not including on-going interest and penalties. Then there's the new investor cash of a hundred thousand, credit cards and equity lines of a hundred thousand and the Greek at fifty thousand plus the vig. That's not to mention some dough to keep Nancy and the place intact till we get back. Let's say ten grand to be safe. On the asset side, if we liquidated all our properties in a fire sale, before the bank takes them in foreclosure, maybe two hundred and fifty thousand.

So in best of all worlds, it's two hundred and fifty thousand, but that would mean paying the bank first and normally, given our list of creditors, I would look to pay them last. No matter what, someone nasty is going to be chasing us; the IRS or the Greek, in addition to our creditors and the investor, who I'll take care of."

"Jesus Christ, Connor. What a mess," he returned, now holding his head in his hands. "What do you think?"

"If we don't go, eliminate the Greek, the investor and our credit cards, we most likely break even. Button up everything and go get jobs. Not all that bad."

"Who put up the hundred thousand investor cash?"

"My Mom."

"Connor, you're not going to risk your mother's money on this?"

"Does it make me a bad son, Alex?" he returned, attempting a little levity.

"Noooo, what it makes you is a fucking psychopath."

"I can live with that."

"I hope you can. What else?"

"On the bright side, we still have half-million dollar insurance policies, so if we don't make it or even if one of us doesn't make it, the other could get out of this debt free."

"That's not very reassuring."

"Sorry."

"I bet."

"Moment of truth, big guy. What do you say, in or out?"

~ ~ ~

Alex took a long pause. He was watching his entire financial future flashing before his eyes; things were crumbling and the only way to get whole was to smuggle gold out of a third world country. The chances of it all working out was one in a thousand or worse. Everything in his head was screaming to walk away, get even, start over and stay alive. This was not a good idea; as a matter of fact it was a very bad idea. The problem was that Connor was his best friend in the whole world and that he realized, was a bond stronger than any amount of common sense.

"As Adam said to the snake, I'll bite."

"We'll be alright, Alex," he returned sincerely, trying to reinforce his decision.

"I wish I could share your confidence. What now?"

"I'll call Wes and Billy Hilliard to let them know we're on. You go collect the equipment and get our plane tickets."

"What are you going to do after that?"

"I'm going to see the Greek and then find a hot tub and see if I can get some relief for these ribs."

"Fine, I'll call if I need you, otherwise let's touch base tomorrow," he returned, getting up and heading out to perform the appointed tasks.

~ ~ ~

Connor watched while Alex disappeared down the stairs. It seemed like he'd been looking out for him all his life and in his heart he hated the thought of placing him in danger, but he knew he needed someone to watch his back. Alex was the only one he could trust and that alone made him worth his weight in gold. He was glad he left because he didn't want him to see how bad he was hurting, the pain radiating around his rib cage when he shifted in his seat.

The suffering caused him pause to relive the time a few short hours ago, when he was locked in combat. As the encounter played out in his head, he smiled to himself. He had journeyed to the brink of his ability and survived; he now would have an opportunity to play that game again, an opportunity he reveled in. His moment of euphoria was brief when the reality of what was required to make it happen leapt into the forefront of his mind. He reached out and dialed Wes's direct line. The phone rang and an unexpected, but familiar voice answered.

"Wes Adams."

"Wes, Connor. I didn't expect you to be in on Saturday. I was calling to leave you a message."

"Well, don't let the fact that I'm answering stop you."

"Funny."

"I thought you'd see the humor."

"We're going, Wes."

"That, I don't find humorous."

"I didn't think you would."

"I take it you contacted Mr. Hilliard and were able to work things out."

"I did."

"What else can I say then, good luck and keep me informed."

"I have a question if you don't mind."

"Go on."

"Does George know my father is missing?"

"I doubt it. I haven't contacted him other than wiring the monthly funds to keep the operation going."

"How much is left in the fund?"

"Less than ten thousand, enough for a few more months, your Dad left a year's worth in the account when he departed."

"So with the money still coming, he had no reason to question my father's whereabouts?"

"Precisely."

"Thanks, Wes. Anything else I should know?"

"Just one thing, Connor. You're on your own, trust no one and above all—be careful. Remember, wherever there's greed, there can be no justice."

"Thanks for the advice, Wes," he returned, a little puzzled by his offering. "I'll be in touch."

~ ~ ~

Wes hung up the phone, shaking his head. The news from Connor filled him with a mix of emotions. It was disturbing that a young man had elected to put himself in extreme danger, but at the same time it was exciting that the most amazing situation he had ever been involved in was being brought back to life. He took a moment to reflect on his relationship with Guy Mason. He had been a beacon of intrigue for him, in what otherwise was a rather mundane existence, and he was grateful for that. Now the son had replaced the father and he felt renewed again, but without the same sense of loyalty. It was different now he thought, as his own life swirled through his head. Money had always been an issue that directed his actions.

Opening the top drawer of his desk, he removed a leather bound binder and flipped the pages to a series of phone numbers he had not dialed in many years. He found the number in question and started to make the call that he knew could alter the outcome of Connor's adventure, not to mention his own financial destiny.

~ ~ ~

Chapter 31

Connor lowered his aching body into the hottest water he could stand. He lay back and placed a hot cloth over his head, waiting for the soothing warmth to give him the relief he longed for. The day had gone as well as expected considering his physical condition. He had made contact with Wes, Billy and the Greek. Wes was notified of his intent and would handle anything that came up on this end. Billy had assured him, in his own southern, cryptic phone speak, that he would meet them in Cebu, one week from Wednesday. Given the required proof along with confirmation the one hundred and fifty thousand had been wired to his account in Thailand, Billy, his planes and men would be ready when needed. Connor decided he would handle all the banking on Monday morning before his scheduled departure at 11:00 a.m.

His muscles were beginning to feel the positive effects of his bathroom spa as he leaned forward to add more heated liquid without the same restricted movement. He was excited and nervous, but his biggest concern was the financial hole he was digging. He had gone over most of the numbers with Alex, but failed to mention the additional one hundred and fifty thousand dollar note he had to sign with Billy, if at their meeting in Cebu they gave the project a go-status. It really went against his grain. It was a high risk envelope whose success hinged on the word of a desperate man, fifteen years removed from the first failed attempt, and a father who's secret life had just recently been exposed.

As the steam caused sweat to bead up on his forehead,

he thought of the thin line he was walking and the reasons for it, none of which were compelling enough for a logical person to go forward. Logic, unfortunately, was no longer a player in this drama, he realized. It had been displaced by something far more powerful—desire.

When he rose from the soothing heat of his bath, he couldn't help noticing the increased discoloration of his battered rib cage; the area seemed to darken with each passing minute. As he toweled off, the relief he had been experiencing was passing quickly. By the time he finished dressing, he found himself in the same labored state that caused him to seek his initial reprieve. Succumbing to the pain, he rifled though his nightstand and retrieved a bottle of prescription pills, remnants of a back injury he sustained lifting weights a few months earlier. He hated taking any kind of medication, so the thirty-day supply was almost entirely intact. He swallowed two pills and sat on the edge of his bed; finally giving into the exhaustion brought on by the physical and mental stress of the last three days. He lay back and stared at the ceiling, thinking of his final bit of business before returning home. He had stopped by the diner after making his phone calls and saw the Greek.

Michael Andros, a.k.a.—The Greek was easy to find. He sat in a booth in the back of his brother's Central Avenue diner and conducted business just like he had for the past nine years. Connor always received a warm welcome from him and his brother; they were both boxing fans and had seen him fight in the Golden Gloves. He became aware of the Greek's avocation from some gamblers that he met at Pauley's. Pauley always tried to discourage that type of activity around the club, but the fight game was a magnet for seedy sorts, a hazard of the sport that was difficult, if not impossible, to police.

Andros was rumored to have access to unlimited amounts of money from Greece and while his association to organized crime was suspected, it was never an issue. He didn't have the reputation as a leg-breaker; although Connor was savvy enough to realize that this was not the type of man to have an outstanding obligation that you couldn't pay. He was a businessman who had been known to assist people in repaying their debt in ways that were both risky and distasteful. Connor had borrowed from him on a few occasions when he needed quick cash to close a deal or to bridge a cash flow gap. He never used the funds for more than a week due to excessive interest rates.

As expected his loan request and collateral were well received, repeat customers that paid were always the best kind in the loan sharking business. After a few cursory questions regarding the use of the money, which Connor found humorous, considering the shady types that he observed having coffee and dropping off their weekly vig. He guessed it was just the Greek's way of doing his due diligence, regardless of the lack of substance and in depth analysis. He believed it just made him feel better to have a conversation before parting with his cash, maybe he had an innate way of telling who was a good risk or not. No matter, after their brief interview, in which Connor lied about his use of the funds, a waiter returned with a small paper bag filled with cash and a piece of spanokapita, a Greek cheese and spinach filled pastry that he was fond of. Connor accepted his hospitality and the money; he had punched the interest clock and it was now ticking.

Starting to drift off, he thought of calling Maggie. She was the last loose end before boarding the plane. He didn't know if they had a future, or even if he wanted to pursue one with her. She was a handful and it seemed his hands were always full. He thought about Susan, his mother, his Dad, Alex; all the people he would make happy, disappoint or maybe never see again.

He wasn't rational regarding this whole expedition; maybe Maggie was right, he was being drawn to this place. It would help explain why, despite his best judgment, he couldn't seem to steer himself away. It was like an addiction he couldn't control. The path to avoidance was clear, he just couldn't bring himself to follow it, hoping if placed in a position where lives depended on him, he could rise above this funk and do the right thing. He only had till tomorrow to slay his demons and make amends, the following day a plane would transport him thirteen thousand miles from home to confront the monster he had inherited. Those were his last thoughts as he surrendered to his uncertainty and a restless sleep.

~ ~ ~

Chapter 32

Inside his castle retreat, located near Marseille, on the Mediterranean Sea in the South of France—Charles Morgan convalesced from his procedure at the Swiss hospital the day before. He was feeling energized while he sipped tomato juice from expensive crystal and studied the reports laid out in front of him. He removed his glasses and ran a bony hand over his bald head. His entire life had one purpose and one only, he thought; protect the legacy he inherited and pass it down intact, to the next heir deemed worthy. Tradition was an important component of his existence, and one that needed to be upheld at all costs with blatant disregard for all sacrifices, his and others, as well as anyone who needed to be sacrificed. He was basking in the deification of his empire and the intoxicating power he wielded whenever a threat, real or imagined, was posed to it, when suddenly he was interrupted by the entrance of Jonathan Ames.

"Good morning, Mr. Morgan."

"Good morning, Jonathan. Is there something pressing that requires my attention on a Sunday?"

"Sorry to disturb you, sir. But we received some information I think you will find most interesting."

"Very well," he returned, motioning him closer.

"Remember the other day when we were discussing the Philippine operation and George Fall."

"Of course I remember, proceed," he returned, revealing his impatience at being bothered.

"You asked me to keep you updated in case a 'Guy Mason' surfaced with regard to this activity."

"Yes, go on."

"It has come to our attention that the operation is going forward and Mr. Mason's son is spearheading the effort."

"Really," he returned, pausing to rub his pointed chin while he absorbed this intelligence. "Do we know anything about this young man?"

"Our source depicted him as very resourceful, sir."

"Pity. What was our source, Jonathan?"

"It was a barrister from America, I'm told, with direct knowledge of the operation."

"What possessed them to pass on this information, Jonathan?"

"Looking for a leg up I imagine, sir."

"Quite," he agreed.

"How would you like to proceed, sir?"

"Given the limited time and less than successful negotiation we experienced previously with the father, I think it best to eliminate the son from the equation. Would you agree, Jonathan?"

"Yes, sir. I believe that would be the logical course given our limited access and influence on the target."

"Do we have contract players in the Asian Theater at this time?"

"Yes, sir. We have a most capable consultant out of Hong Kong, who recently completed a contract for us."

"Good, make it so, Jonathan. I do not want to use any of our people on this."

"As you wish, sir. It will be taken care of."

"Expediently."

"Of course, sir," he returned, turning to exit and put the wheels of his appointed task in motion.

"Jonathan."

"Yes, sir," he replied, whirling around.

"What is the status of the rebel activity in the area?"

"Our field operatives have planted a rumor that a plane filled with weapons went down in the Province. That should increase the rebel activity there, at least enough to dissuade any followers of the soon to be late Mr. Mason."

"I agree. While you're here—the Russian Mafia fellow, Chernov, any news yet?"

"Mr. Chernov met with a most unfortunate accident, sir. His boat exploded while fishing with associates on the Sea of Azov. All hands were lost I'm afraid."

"I see; when did this tragedy take place?"

"Tomorrow, sir."

"Very good, keep me in the queue on this Philippine activity."

"Yes, sir."

With that, Morgan dismissed his underling to the confines of his spacious state of the art office located just down the hallway. He knew the drill all too well. Ames would use one of several secure computer and phone hookups to e-mail instructions as well as downloading a computer-generated dossier on his intended target. Copies of a driver's license, passport and recently purchased airline tickets were available with the touch of a button. If information was computerized, they had access to it. He smiled, knowing that there was no escape from Morgan Gold International's vast web. As had been experienced with many of his victims, there was nowhere to run and nowhere to hide, where he couldn't reach them. His own resourcefulness and power gave him a warm glow with regard to protecting his domain. It was his destiny, and he relished in his ability to function at an extremely high level with no regard for conscious or consequence, the only thing that mattered was survival and enhancement of the entity he ruled.

~ ~ ~

Chapter 33

Sunday Morning, ten o'clock—Connor was awakened, still fully clothed, by the loud buzzing of his doorbell. He opened his eyes to a splitting headache and the feeling that he'd been run over by a tractor-trailer. He attempted to rise; his progress hindered by the give in his mattress when he used the unstable platform for balance. Finally, after some painful maneuvering, he managed to get upright and began the tedious journey to answer the impatient visitor on his porch. Reaching the door, he unlocked and slowly opened it, revealing Alex with two large duffle bags and a medium-sized, gray brief case.

"Hey, bud. How ya feeling?"

"How do I look?"

"You look like shit."

"Well, I don't feel half that good."

"Could you drag your crippled ass out of the way so I can get this stuff inside?" he asked, a big smile crossing his face.

"Why are you in such a good mood? Yesterday you were Mr. Doom and Gloom."

"I've accepted my fate and decided to go into this with a positive attitude," he returned, dragging the bags into the living room.

"You had sex with Nancy last night didn't you?"

"That too."

"I can always tell when you get laid, you're always unrealistically happy the next day."

"Not all of us posses your forte with the opposite sex. We lesser men are allowed to celebrate our foray of women due to the infrequent nature."

"Whatever you need."

"Thank you, your grace," he replied, giving him a deep bow and a wide arching swoop of his hand.

"You're welcome, asshole," he returned, trying his best to avoid additional pain by not laughing. "What's in the bags?"

"Equipment your father suggested, plus some other things."

"How much did you spend?"

"Around twenty grand or so?"

"Twenty thousand!"

"Yeah, twenty thousand, we need good stuff and it's expensive, besides I charged it."

"Good thinking."

"Thank you."

"What's in the gray brief case?"

"That information my friend, is on a need to know basis and. . . ."

"You don't need to know," they repeated in unison, nodding and smiling at each other.

"I don't really care, you know."

"Yeah you do, but I'm not telling you anyway."

"Fine, what's the rest of the stuff?"

"Just things on the list. I figured we have a long plane ride we can discuss it all then."

"And the gray briefcase?"

"Maybe, I'll decide on the plane."

"Oh goody. What's the flight itinerary?"

"Leave Albany International at 11:00 a.m., arrive in Detroit, then Detroit to Tokyo and Tokyo to Manila. The next morning we grab a local fight to Cebu and we're there Wednesday, before noon, Philippine time."

"What are we flying?"

"Northwest to Manila and Philippine Airlines to Cebu."

"Philippine Airlines have frequent flyer miles?"

"Not sure, I didn't think it was that important, seeing how for less than a hundred bucks American, you can fly first class from one end of the country to the other."

"Good point. Do we need anything else?"

"A prayer would help."

"Amen, brother, amen."

"What are you going to do the rest of the day, Con?"

"I'm going to plant my sorry ass back in the tub, then I'm going to pack and just rest up till tomorrow."

"Sounds like a plan. What about Maggie?"

"What about her?"

"You going to see her before we leave?"

"I don't know. I never know with her."

"True," he returned. "Alright, I've got a few more things to take care of. I'll pick you up here at 9:00 a.m."

"Fine, if I'm not here, I just went to finish some banking. I'll put money in the operating account, so Nancy can keep things going till we get back."

"If we get back."

"No Alex, when we get back. Positive attitude, remember?"

"Guess I better get some more horizontal reinforcement tonight."

"Whatever you need, brother."

"Don't worry, I'll be okay."

"I know you will."

"I'll see you in the morning."

Connor watched as Alex left. The dye was cast and wheels were in motion, they had acquired the necessary cash and credit from a variety of sources, family, credit cards, banks, smugglers, and loan sharks. It made him smile when he reflected on the eclectic rationale behind the rapid accumulation of funds. Once the initial fee was wired to Billy Hilliard, he realized there would be no turning back; up to this point the adventure was more surreal, come tomorrow morning that would all change. What lay ahead was one more day and one more restless night of soul searching—after that brief period for rescission, a physical and financial commitment would cement the mental one he had made days before.

~ ~ ~

Chapter 34

Monday Morning, seven o'clock, City of Cagayan De Oro, Mindanao—George Fall busily packed a small bag for the short flight to Cebu. Having not received a message to the contrary, in two days he expected to be reunited with his old friend and partner, Guy Mason. He had done his part, made the sacrifice, stayed behind, all in order to ensure their success after a decade and a half hiatus. Having brought the operation full circle, he was now ready to pass the baton and let Guy take it the rest of the way home.

His Filipino girlfriend and their four children were still sleeping while he made his way out of their dilapidated stucco and stone home and into his car. The neighborhood was one of the better ones, but with little to no landscaping, eroding roads and abandoned houses, it had the look and feel of an East L.A. ghetto after the riots.

Slipping behind the wheel of his rusted relic, he wondered what he would do after this was over; he cared for his family, but had no intention of taking them back to the States with him. He would make sure they were comfortable, but in his mind that was the extent of his obligation. After all, he had supported them for years and gave them a better life than they could ever have hoped for, he had done his part for others, at least recently, and now it was time to do for him.

The temperature was already in the mid-eighties and rising when he turned onto the main road leading to the airport. He was feeling the increasing humidity, evident by the cloudy mist rising off the broken pavement as a hot sun evaporated the last bit of morning moisture. Even with the windows down and driving along at a brisk pace, the breeze offered little relief from the suffocating dense air, the source, he imagined of his labored breathing. He squirmed in his seat, the sweat on his back causing him to stick to the threadbare upholstery, while his stubby hand with the missing index finger adjusted his rear-view mirror.

As he looked behind him, he couldn't help notice a familiar vehicle that he had seen over the last several days. Taking a few unscheduled turns confirmed what he suspected; someone was having him followed and while it was disconcerting, it didn't take a rocket scientist to figure out who was behind it. It was a concern he had ever since the Colonel surfaced at the Pryce Plaza Hotel, but not something he would let jeopardize the operation; he had come too far and waited too long to have anything stop him now.

After pulling into the stone and gravel airport lot, he parked and headed toward the terminal building. The structure was the size of a small ranch house with no back wall, just open air that led out to the runway. Making his way inside he noted the miniscule, under-stocked coffee shop and lone clerk who handled ticket sales inside. The airport had no tower and no support systems, other than the crews that arrived on each government subsidized Philippine Airline landing. With less than a half-dozen daily flights, he knew there was no need or funding.

George purchased his ticket and waited to board the airbus that was already on the runway, having just arrived from Davao, on the southern end of the island. He watched as three men exited the vehicle that had been tailing him and entered the terminal. They were dressed in army fatigues, a sight not uncommon in the province and final validation that they were part of the Colonel's private force.

Deciding to board the plane, he figured he had at least two days to lose them before he met with Guy. He took a seat near the back of the aircraft and peered through the window while they questioned the ticket agent. As the remaining passengers finished arriving and the crew prepared for takeoff, there was no sign that they would be accompanying him on his journey.

The plane taxied down the runway and lifted off into a bright, blue cloudless sky. George sank back in his seat, enjoying the air-conditioned reprieve from the steamy heat and the fact he wouldn't have to expend any energy on evading his military skip tracers. He knew it was a luxury he would not be afforded again; certain there would be hell to pay when the Colonel found out he had left the island unattended. But for now there was only a short flight to a quiet hotel room, cold beers, available women and sweet dreams of an affluent life in the not too distant future. Nothing else mattered—at least not for another forty-eight hours.

~ ~ ~

Chapter 35

The loud sound of gunfire followed by scattered partisan applause broke the Monday morning silence at the Bukidnon Province command post. A small crowd of enlisted men and their families had gathered on the firing range to witness the impromptu exhibition before heading off about their day's business. Colonel Vadula loved an audience, captive or not, to display his talent as well as the opportunity to subtly enhance his already menacing image.

He watched while a small child picked his way through the broken glass and lined up another half-dozen empty bottles on a large rock around thirty feet away. After setting the last bottle, he moved quickly out of harm's way as the Colonel drew his two pearl handled revolvers from their tied down, holstered resting place, releasing a hail of bullets and obliterating his glass targets with the speed and precision of a western gunfighter.

Without missing a choreographed beat, two soldiers behind him launched four more bottles high into the air, as he swung around, firing as he moved to a crouched position, decimating the air borne objects. Standing upright, he punctuated the display with a mesmerizing thirty-second gun twirling exercise, ending with a slick holstering of his shiny weapons. The crowd showed their appreciation with the obligatory cheering and clapping. The Colonel waved in acknowledgment, before signaling them to disburse, when he noticed Corporal Vega and his men hurrying toward him. He reloaded his pistols and waited.

"Good morning, Colonel," he said, breathing heavily and saluting as he and his men came to attention.

"Good morning, Vega," he replied, offering a half-hearted salute in return. "Why are you and your men here and not watching Mr. Fall?"

"He has left the island, sir."

"You have not answered my question?"

"Sir?" he returned, sounding confused.

"Why are you not watching Mr. Fall?"

"He is no longer on the island, sir," he answered, a sudden unset of nervousness causing his voice to crack.

The Colonel just stared without answering, an exercise he had perfected, knowing full well how it raised the anxiety level. Suddenly, he let out a yell of frustration as he drew his side arms and let fly a volley of gunfire in the direction of his underlings, sending them flying to the ground in all directions. The chaos subsided a few brief seconds after the last bullet had left its clip. Both guns were smoking, as the Colonel felt himself slipping into an eerie fervor, continuing to click the hairpin triggers while walking toward the men cowering beneath him. Snapping himself out of his anger induced state, he knelt down and placed the hot barrel of his revolver on the sweaty temple of the terrified corporal.

"Corporal Vega," he said, fighting to control his rage. "Do not say a word. You and your men are to find Mr. Fall and follow him to hell if necessary, but you are not to let him out of your sight. Leave and do not return until you have found him and if you lose him again, we will repeat this exercise, but with you and your men having many holes in your bodies. Do you understand me?"

Corporal Vega looked away and shook his head in acknowledgement. His men, frozen with fear lay face down near him.

"Good. I'm going to turn around, and when I look back I don't want to see you until you know the whereabouts of Mr. Fall."

The Colonel rose and headed back toward his office. He could hear Vega and his men scurry to their feet and rapidly retreat in the other direction. Vadula knew that George Fall would return; of that he was certain, and when he did, hopefully he would have his speculators with him.

Time ticks slowly in a place where the future was filled with uncertainty, he thought. Once George Fall and his financiers fell within his web, it would be necessary for him to speed up the clock with regard to his plan for financial gain—and God help anyone who would come between him and his anticipated windfall.

~ ~ ~

Chapter 36

Wednesday Morning, eleven o'clock, high above the City of Cebu, Cebu Island—Connor looked out the window of the Airbus 300 while it circled and readied for landing. He had spent the remainder of the day Sunday and early Monday taking care of last minute details to ensure a smooth transition from businessman to treasure hunter. The only thing he was unable to accomplish was to find Maggie. A level of emptiness had accompanied him when he boarded the plane on Monday morning, hoping she would show up to see him off and give him the lift that only came from seeing her smiling face.

On the other end of his emotional spectrum he consciously decided against contacting Susan; with everything else going on he couldn't bring himself to deal with her before leaving. By the time he returned she would be back in London. He kept telling himself he would go there to give her the explanation she deserved, but in the back of his mind he wondered if he would ever get that chance.

When he had landed in Manila the day before, after traveling for twenty-four hours and downing painkillers like they were candy, the heat, humidity and strange surroundings assaulted his senses as being more foreign than any place he had ever experienced. That was a major city; he couldn't imagine what lay ahead in the less civilized locales he was bound for.

When he looked over at Alex, sleeping in the first class seat next to him, he marveled at how calm he had remained.

He had figured he would have to nursemaid him during this entire ordeal, but so far it had been the exact opposite. Alex was the pillar of strength while he wrestled with his own self-doubts. He was feeling more vulnerable than usual, but he attributed it to his battered body, the long trip and the fact he had very little sleep. Keeping it light, Connor had not even pressed him about the gray briefcase, whose contents Alex continued to playfully, but zealously guard.

As the plane sat down on its tropical runway, lined with palm trees and armed guards; Connor shifted his thoughts to George Fall, and the task he would have, to convince him to let a total stranger take control of his destiny. Based on the desperate situation he seemed to be in, it shouldn't be an insurmountable problem, but he could never be sure.

Exiting their air-conditioned confines, they were greeted by an even hotter environment than they had experienced during their evening landing in Manila, less then twelve hours earlier. The heat reinforced the unfamiliar location. From his father's notes he knew Cebu was a manufacturing and shipping haven, with the exception of Luzon, it was the most industrial island in the archipelago. Due to the industry base, it was not unusual to see a wide variety of foreign faces involved in import-export, hence it served as a fairly discreet meeting place, unlike Mindanao, where their presence would definitely garner more attention.

After retrieving their luggage, with the assistance of a multitude of local porters, all of whom expected payment for their minimal services, it was loaded into the cab of one of the several drivers who accosted them. Directing the taxi to the Cebu Plaza Hotel, Connor could feel the adrenaline begin to kick in, helping to negate the exhaustion he was feeling from the trip. Despite his sore ribs and aching muscles, it was time to put his game face on, they would only get one chance and he wanted to make sure to take his best shot.

"You ready for this, bud?" Connor asked.

"I'm ready, I'm glad were doing this, but for the life of me, I don't know why."

"I can't imagine, but I hope you still feel that way a week from now."

"Me, too. How are you?"

"Still real sore and tired, but I'll be fine."

"Fuck, it's hot here."

"You can say that again," he returned, wiping the sweat off his forehead.

When the taxi pulled up to the Cebu Plaza, Connor thought it had the look of any major chain outlet. It was a high-rise building with lots of glass and metal, the grounds were meticulously manicured, with large palm trees lining the street leading to the entrance. Several Filipino men in white linen shirts and long dark pants were attending to arriving passengers. The surrounding area they had passed through was industrial and dank; it made the establishment stand out like an oasis in a desert. The hotel maintained a high standard in order to give foreign businessmen, investors and entrepreneurs a comfortable place to escape the riggers of doing business on the island. Comfortable lodging, he imagined, was a necessity for attracting outside capital, always a high priority of developing nations.

Entering the lobby, the climate-controlled environment offered a welcome reprieve from the relentless heat. Connor was sure they would get used to it in time, but for now it felt refreshing to escape from its wearing effects. Checking in was not a problem, despite their lack of a reservation, he figured most higher end hotels outside the capital, had few, if any overcrowding problems. Not many natives could afford the nightly rate and while foreign investment looked like it was becoming more prevalent, as he expected capacity had not yet been compromised.

Connor inquired at the desk about George. An attractive young woman verified that he was a guest and had offered to ring his room, when a co-worker informed her that Mr. Fall had left a message that he was expecting visitors and would be waiting in the bar. From his reputation, Connor was not surprised by his choice of meeting venue. He and Alex were directed to the bar, located off the lobby, after s

251

ending their luggage ahead to the rooms.

The lounge was bright and open with a tropical décor and large floor-to-ceiling glass windows that overlooked the floral grounds, but purposely blocked off the less than picturesque surrounding neighborhood. It had succeeded in accomplishing the desired illusion of an island paradise.

Connor scanned the room in search of George, who wasn't hard to spot, sitting near a window, accompanied by two women who looked to be no older than twenty. Approaching the booth, it was apparent by the number of empty beer bottles, that he and his guests had been there for quite some time, despite the early hour. Talking here would not be a problem, Connor thought. The bar was suffering from a noticeable lack of patrons, except for a few early lunch customers.

"Excuse me," Connor interrupted.

"Yes, what can I do for you?" George returned, his voice betraying the effects of the alcohol, as the two young women whispered and giggled.

"Are you George Fall?" Connor asked, a mere formality; with the exception of thinner, graying hair and a few extra pounds, Connor recognized him from the pictures he had received from Wes Adams.

"Maybe, who wants to know?"

"I do, I'm Connor Mason. This is my friend, Alex Litowski. You knew my father."

George sat up straight in his seat as if slapped in the face. He was obviously caught totally off guard by Connor's introduction. The drinking appeared to have dulled his senses enough, that he needed a moment to gather himself before attempting a coherent conversation.

"You're Guy's boy. The last time I saw you, you weren't ten years old."

"I'm sure it's been a long time for you."

"Where's your Dad? Is he checking in?"

Connor hesitated; knowing this was going to take some explaining and remembering that he should trust no one, especially the two intoxicated young locals seated at the table.

"I think we should talk in private, Mr. Fall."

"These girls here, they barely speak a word of English," he returned, playfully grabbing the leg of one of the women causing her to squeal.

"Still," he returned, motioning with his head.

"Alright, girls here's some money, why don't you go out to the pool and I'll catch up with you later," he returned, tossing a handful of colorful local currency on the table.

The women quickly scooped up the Philippine pesos, straightening the crumbled bills and laughing while they walked arm in arm in the direction of the outside facilities.

"Sorry to break up your party," Alex said, a little sarcasm sneaking into his voice.

"You boys didn't break up anything, you just postponed it a bit."

"I'm glad," Alex replied, his tone betraying how unimpressed he was.

"I appreciate your concern. Now as I was asking, where's Guy?"

"He's not coming," Connor answered.

"What do you mean, not coming?"

"He's been missing for over ten months now."

"What?" George replied, the shock apparent even in his condition. "He's not coming?"

"Bingo, give the man a prize," Alex chimed in.

"Cut it out, Alex."

"Manny," he yelled, getting the attention of one of the bartenders. "Coffee, please, strong coffee. Tell me what happened?"

Connor spent the better part of an hour explaining about his father, the tapes and the events that led them to him. He made sure to emphasize their one-week time deadline to obtain a sample for Billy Hilliard. Alex reinforced the risk they had shouldered in order make the trip and get involved in the operation. George listened before he voiced his concern about the health of the activity now that Guy was not in the picture.

"Boys, I need to think this over," George said.

"Think what over? There's not much to fucking think

over here," Alex returned, sounding very under appreciated.

"You may think that, Alex, but I've been doing this a lot longer than anyone else and I've got things to consider."

"That's bullshit, how could you possibly get this done without us? You got three hundred thousand lying around to pay for planes?"

"Give him the time, Alex. He just laid eyes on us an hour ago," Connor interrupted.

"Yeah, and we just risked every cent we have or will have for the next twenty years, not to mention flew half-way around the world to get what? 'I need to think about it.' I don't think so."

"I do," Connor answered. "Come on, let's get some rest."

"Fine," he surrendered.

"Sorry, Connor. I just want a little time," George reiterated.

"It's alright, George, take your time. We'll be in our room." Connor winced visibly when he rose from the table.

"You look like you're in some pain there, Connor," George observed, watching his struggle.

"Had a little accident before we left and I'm still sore. The trip didn't help."

"I might be able to get you some relief for that."

"That would be great," he returned, having no idea what he had in mind.

Connor and Alex made their way to the elevator. Alex had a tendency to snore and with Connor being a light sleeper, whenever possible he got a separate room. In this case they were separate, but adjoining. Entering their quarters, they looked to Connor like any other hotel accommodations, two double queen beds, desk, chair, television etc. In addition, each had a small concrete balcony overlooking the pool. All in all it was comfortable and most welcome after their exhausting journey. Alex unlocked the inside door separating them and opened it wide.

"Do you believe that guy, who the fuck does he think he is?"

"He's the guy who knows where the gold is."

"Well, that's true enough."

"Besides, we're his only option, you know it, I know it and most importantly, he knows it. He'll come around, be patient," Connor returned, settling down on the bed after grabbing the remote.

"That's why you always handle the negotiations, Con. You've got a nose for this stuff."

"Then take the word of your favorite bloodhound. By nightfall we'll be up to our long dangling ears in this deal."

"You're probably right, but his attitude just pissed me off."

"Get over it, it's not important."

"Wow, there's the pot calling the kettle black."

"Maybe I'm learning something,"

They both hesitated for a moment, looking at each other with a sly smile and then in unison,"Naaaahhh."

"What are you going to do till we hear from him?"

"Take a nap," Connor returned, finding the only interesting available channel to be CNN.

"Sounds like a plan. I'll see you in a few," Alex returned, going back into his room.

Connor, placing his head on the pillow, could feel himself immediately start to surrender his consciousness. His body was aching, but his tired state was quickly overtaking the pain and he knew he would soon fall into a deep sleep that only sheer exhaustion could bring on. All that could be done had been—the decision to proceed was obvious to him, but of course nothing was ever a given, especially if it involved a fortune in Japanese bullion. He would have to wait for George Fall to give his blessing.

~ ~ ~

Chapter 37

Wednesday Afternoon, Cagayan De Oro—Andy Wai caught sight of his slender, very tan, mid-thirties physique in the mirror of the dismal airport restroom. He had just exited the Philippine Airline 737 that had arrived from Manila via Hong Kong. His reflection revealed a tall five-foot ten or eleven oriental man, with dark hair and eyes, wearing a recently purchased expensive, blue custom silk suit accented with a white crew neck shirt and handmade black shoes. He grabbed his black leather bag when he exited and entered the small terminal building, lowering his sunglasses while he peered around, looking for transportation. The pricey watch on one wrist, and thick gold bracelet hanging from the other silently advertised his well-to-do status about as subtly as a neon billboard.

When several taxi drivers vied for his business, he selected the one cab that had working air conditioning, and with the assistance of several porters, only one of whom actually carried luggage, the rest of his custom bags were loaded into the vehicle. Taking out a thick wad of bills, he overpaid his helpers causing them to squeal with delight. It was rare that Asian visitors were this generous with the poorer class, especially a Chinese businessman of means like he wanted to appear to be.

As his ride pulled out of the unpaved parking lot, he suspected that more than workers, travelers or their entourages had noticed him. It had been his experience that in most third world countries there were always several informants, who frequently observed all incoming and departing flights. He knew he was someone that they could not help but notice; someone their benefactor would want to know about. He made sure they would take note of the cabbie he contracted, taking his time and flashing lots of cash. Someone would most likely be looking to interrogate him upon his return as to the final destination of his seemingly wealthy passenger.

He directed the driver to the Royal Palm Hotel located in the heart of downtown Cagayan De Oro. The intelligence he received prior to his arrival informed him that it was a well-known local establishment, frequented by many travelers who chose not to pay the markedly higher rates of the ritzier Pryce Plaza. It was a three-story wood structure, offering air conditioning units in over half of its thirty-five rooms, most of them in working condition. There was no swimming pool and no common areas to speak of, except for a small coffee shop annexed to the tiny lobby that was operated by a third party, not associated with the hotel. Each room housed a well-worn double bed, one chair, nightstand and dresser. The rooms were clean, and while there were televisions in most, very few could boast any reception worth watching. It was a poor country cousin to the Pryce Plaza, the difference in ambiance and service was like the distance from Hong Kong to New York; that said, based on his information, it was still by far the second best overnight lodging available on the northern end of the island.

A young barefoot street porter, who, like he expected didn't work at the hotel, but freelanced customers, much the same as those working the airport, helped unload his luggage and carried it into the lobby. Andy paid the driver, giving him a tip that he suspected would have him bragging about his fare for months. The cabbie thanked him over and over before departing.

He entered the lobby and secured a room on the third floor in the back, offering an additional fee to insure the quieter location, as most of the customers were occupying the air-conditioned rooms on the first two floors. The streets surrounding the hotel were bustling and noisy, so he figured

257

requesting quarters buffered from that activity would not be deemed as a particularly unusual request.

The porter led the way up the three flights of stairs to the assigned room, his pack mule status necessitated by the fact that the elevator in the lobby hadn't been operational in several years. Andy followed, maintaining possession of the leather bag he had kept in close contact since he left the airport. The porter opened the door and placing his bags on the bed, turned on the air conditioning unit in an attempt to alleviate some of the stifling heat that seemed to increase with each flight they ascended. Andy hardly noticed the current conditions when he pulled out a hundred pesos bill and paid his young helper. Offering his service in the future, he left in much the same state as the elated cabbie, seeing how the payment he received was almost twenty times the norm.

Finally alone, he settled into the single chair, placing his leather carry-on at his feet. There was no need to unpack, if he had done his job correctly, he would not be staying the night. He had accomplished all he set out to; the only thing left to do now was wait. He had made as grand an entrance into this third world apocalypse as possible, without being so obvious as to seem severely out of place. Being noticed was his goal, as well as leaving an easy trail to his location. The bait had been cast, now it was time to see what fish would be reeled in.

In his line of work, he knew it was almost as important to know who else was looking for who he was looking for, than finding them. Once he located them or they him, there was an excellent chance he would be led to his target—a good thing for assassins to remember, he thought, while he waited for his prey to come calling.

~ ~ ~

Chapter 38

Connor was suddenly awakened from his jet lag induced slumber by a loud knock. He looked at his watch, which verified he had been sleeping over three hours. He couldn't believe the time, having felt like he had just shut his eyes a few moments ago. The knocking continued while he struggled to get his foggy brain to engage and his fight and flight abused body to its feet. He made his way slowly to the door, when Alex, having heard the commotion entered through the adjoining passage.

"Who the hell is making all the racket?" Alex asked, his alertness appearing in much the same debilitated state as his partner.

"It's someone at the door," he returned, opening it.

"No shit."

They stood like two children rubbing their eyes. The open door had revealed two attractive Filipino women dressed in white uniforms. They were all a little dumb-founded while they shared an awkward moment of silence.

"Can we help you?" Connor asked.

"Sir George send us to give massage," answered one of the young women in broken English.

"He sent you to give us a massage?" he confirmed.

"Yes," she returned, as they barged past their exhausted looking clients.

"Look ladies, this is not a good time. We're very tired."

"Make you feel better."

"Yes, I'm sure it will make us feel better, but. . . ."

"What the heck, Con. It's not like we're in a hurry or anything," Alex interrupted. "Let's get a massage, what can it hurt?"

"You want to deal with this right now?"

"Deal with what? It's a rub down, we're awake now anyway."

"Fine," Connor agreed.

"Alright, girls. What do we do?" Alex asked.

The girls whispered to each other and then one of the young women took Alex by the hand and led him back to his room.

"See you in a bit, bud," Alex said, smiling as he disappeared.

"What now?" Connor directed to the remaining woman.

"Go in room and take off clothes."

"Fine," he returned, going into the bathroom and re-entering in a towel.

While he was undressing, the overhead light had been turned off and replaced by a softer one from the desk lamp. Mood lighting he thought while he lay, stomach first, on the bed that had been stripped down to the sheets.

"What's your name?" Connor asked.

"My name is Imee," she answered, sounding flattered. "What is your name?"

"Connor."

"That is a nice name," she returned, removing a bottle of oil from a pocket on her uniform. "You relax now, Imee take good care of you."

Why not, he thought, closing his eyes.

Imee started at his shoulders, her hands felt strong when she dug into his tense muscles. With his eyes shut, his mind drifted to Maggie and how she would relieve his sore shoulders after a hard workout. For the next thirty minutes she worked his neck, back and legs, the lotion she applied felt like baby oil, except for a more flowery scent. It smelled distinct in its odor, but pleasant, the consistency allowing her hands to flow without friction across his body. Connor

260

flinched when she rubbed near his rib cage. She eased up, as his sudden reaction and the discolored area alerted her to the injury.

"What happen to you?"

"Took a bad fall before I came," he replied.

"Hurt you?"

"Oh yeah, it hurts."

"I careful, you please turn now."

"Sure," he returned, rolling over on his back.

She straddled across his chest and leaning forward she massaged his head and temples, her long hair brushing against his face. She was firm, but gentle, and she smelled really good to him. He could feel his entire body reaching a new level of relaxation while she rubbed his shoulders, arms and hands. She then slid to the end of the bed and began to massage his feet and ankles. After ten minutes she applied more oil and started to work up his legs, digging hard into his quads and then with less force over the inside of his thighs, brushing gently on occasion, but he suspected not totally by accident over his genital area. Leaning over she whispered in his ear.

"Close eyes and relax," she said, slowly removing the towel that was covering him.

Connor lay motionless on the bed, feeling relaxed even though he was now totally exposed. Imee took the towel and covered the desk lamp, further darkening the room. Standing on the side of the bed, she unzipped her uniform and slid it off. She was wearing no under garments, as she lay down next to him and placed her soft hand on his chest.

"Would you like sensation?" she asked in a soft whispery voice.

"Sensation?" he questioned.

"Yes," she replied, sliding her hand down his chest and resting it on his manhood.

It startled him a bit, but not enough to make him jump; the scene had prepared him for some kind of sexual advance. He slowly reached down and removed her hand.

"Not today," he said, now looking into her dark brown eyes.

"You not like me," she returned, looking a little upset by the rejection.

"No, I like you just fine. I'm just very tired. You made me feel a lot better already," he reassured her.

"Sir George already pay for sensation."

"No one has to know but us. You keep the money," he returned, sensing the concern in her voice.

"Thank you, thank you," she said, getting off the bed and putting on her uniform.

Connor got up and grabbed his towel off the lamp, wrapping it around his waist. He went into his pants and pulled out an American twenty-dollar bill and handed it to her. "This is for you," he said.

"I already paid, I cannot take, sir," she returned, seeming a little embarrassed by his generosity.

"Please," he insisted, placing the money in her hand.

She gave him a big smile as she walked over, kissing his chest while she hugged him tightly. Suddenly a voice from the other bedroom interrupted their friendly embrace.

"Connor."

"What Alex?"

"She's asking me if I want sensation, what the hell is that?"

"She wants to polish your knob for you brother," he replied laughing.

"We talking a rub and tug session here," he called back.

"You got it, bud."

"Excellent," he returned, giggling like a schoolboy.

"Enjoy yourself pal. I'm going to grab a shower."

Connor let Imee out of the room and went into the shower. He popped a couple of pain pills and turned the water on very hot, letting the soothing liquid pour over his relaxed body. After about ten minutes he felt the best he had in days, he was still sore but right now it felt tolerable, the pills mixed with the rub down had done the trick—at least for the time being he thought.

Connor got out and dried off. He put on a pair of boxers and went into Alex's room to find him alone, lying prone on the bed, covered partially by a sheet. He broke into a wide grin when his friend entered.

"How you feeling, bud?" Connor asked.

"I feel like I was rode hard and put away wet, brother." He was not able to keep the smile off his face. "I think I'm going to like this place."

"That's a surprise."

"I mean, maybe old George isn't so bad after all."

"A guy buys you a massage and a hand job and now he's your best friend."

"You never bought me one," he kidded. "Maybe you could take care of me in the morning."

"Keep dreaming, Romeo."

"It was worth a shot," Alex conceded.

"By the way, if you recall I put your own private concubine on payroll."

"That's a low blow, throwing Nancy in that way."

"When you start talking low blows, I'm not even going there with you, big guy."

"As well you shouldn't, just let me enjoy the afterglow."

"Enjoy away, if your new friend George decides he doesn't need us, your next afterglow will be the result of your own hand."

"Man, you sure know how to kill a mood."

"Sue me."

Their banter was abruptly halted by another knock on the door. Connor opened the door to find a much more sober appearing George Fall.

"George, come on in."

"Thanks, did you boys enjoy the welcoming committee?"

"I liked it," Alex chimed in.

"How about you, Connor? I hope it helped you feel a little better."

"I found it to be a very invigorating, George. Thanks for your hospitality," he returned, deciding not to tell him he declined the highlight of the offering.

"You're both welcome," George returned. "Look, I've

been doing some thinking and I would like you to help me with the operation. Your Dad was my friend and partner, if he believes you can do this, I owe it to him to give you the chance."

"No offense, George," Alex interjected. "But you don't really believe you had any other option?"

George stood silently, obviously a little taken back by Alex's comment. He seemed to be waiting to see if Connor would come to his aid like he had done earlier. Connor had no intention of letting him off the hook, he had to realize that they were his saving grace, conceding anything less could put them and the project in danger. He had to know his place and that place was no place if he didn't accept them as equals. They all just looked at each other waiting for someone to speak.

"I guess you're right about that," George conceded, breaking into a half-smile.

"I'm glad you feel that way," Connor returned. "If this is going to have a chance for a successful outcome, we're going to have to work together and trust each other, part of that is realizing we need one another."

"You're right," George agreed. "Let's shake on it."

"That's okay, George, I've already been shaken," Alex interjected.

"Man, you're just a barrel of laughs, today," Connor retorted.

"How true."

"I'll shake for both of us, George," Connor said, extending his hand.

George took his hand and administered a hearty midwestern shake. He looked relieved that someone actually showed up to help him. He wasn't his father, but Connor felt like George now saw him as the next best thing.

"We need to get back tomorrow," George said. "I don't like to be away from the mine for long."

"Well, we also need to get the sample and be back here in a week."

"It shouldn't be a problem. Why don't we eat something and then get some rest. I think it's going to be a long week."

"Sounds like a good idea, we'll meet you down in the lobby in ten minutes."

"Good," he returned as he left the room.

"What's your read on this guy, Connor?" Alex asked.

"I'm not sure, but what I am sure of is we need to keep as much control as possible. He's desperate for this to work."

"And we're not?" Alex returned.

Connor had no comeback; he just shrugged his shoulders and smiled before returning to his room to finish getting dressed. He knew they were every bit as desperate as George was; they just hadn't been in that state as long. He wondered, when the riches of kings are within your reach, can you still hope to be objective if the need arises? That was a question that remained to be answered—and the wrong response he knew could cost them all considerably more than a cave full of gold.

~ ~ ~

Chapter 39

Having not moved in over three hours, Andy Wai was interrupted from his self-imposed meditation by a loud banging on his hotel room door. The hum of the air conditioning unit belied the current room temperature, as it was still engulfed in a stifling heat, the antiquated window unit being too small to effectively contend with the blast furnace conditions of mid-day. Despite the torrid environment, he displayed no ill effects. The heat had failed to raise even a bead of sweat on his well-acclimated person. He waited for the second, more enthusiastic assault on the barrier, before rising to answer the summons. While he walked slowly toward the door, he skillfully slid a four-inch stiletto blade, handle first, up his suit coat sleeve. He smiled to himself, as he knew the game was about to begin.

Opening the door and stepping away, he retreated to the far wall while three native soldiers invaded the tight confines of his quarters. He leaned back against the wall and folded his arms, as he sized up his unwanted, but expected guests. The man who appeared in-charge was large for a Filipino, he thought, almost six-feet tall and at least two hundred pounds. He had a straggly beard and a half-moon crescent scar that ran from the corner of his eye, down his cheek, and ended at the tip of his mouth. His two charges were somewhat smaller, but appeared comfortable with this confrontation as they gripped their M-16 army issue weapons. Andy gave them a quizzical and confident look, a reaction to their usually intimidating presence he was sure they had not experienced.

"My name is Sergeant Cruz and we need you to come with us, Mr. Li," the large man directed.

Andy surmised he must have read his assumed name from the hotel registry while he made no move, just tilted his head to one side as if half-attempting to understand or hear what the Sergeant was saying. The men seemed anxious by his strange response to their instructions.

"Colonel Vadula, Army Commander of Bukidnon Province requires you to come with us, now," he commanded.

"That not possible," he returned softly, maintaining his posture. He knew most third world military thugs were not usually exposed to anyone defying their directions. Like he expected, it left them unprepared to recognize a clear danger signal when confronted with it. Following orders was a soldier's job; it was universal regardless of the country of origin. Their duty was clear to Andy; bring this uncooperative foreigner to their superior. He watched as the Sergeant hesitated for a moment before he removed his pistol and trained it on him. Then with a sudden head movement, he silently directed his men to take him by force.

When the soldiers approached, they momentarily blocked the sight line between the Sergeant and his intended target. Andy with one rapid, underhand motion released the blade he had let slide from his sleeve into his left hand. The knife found its mark, lodging in the throat of the startled commander, causing him to drop his weapon as he fell to his knees. That assault was followed by a lightning fast strike to the neck of the closest soldier, crushing his windpipe. As that antagonist dropped to the floor, the remaining soldier fumbled to get his weapon into firing position when a kick to the groin caused him to double over in pain. Without hesitation, Andy positioned himself behind his distressed adversary and grabbing his head, ended his earthly being with one quick violent wrench.

He then turned his attention back to the Sergeant, who was slumped on his knees. A loud gurgling sound was emanating from him while he unsuccessfully tried to clear the rapidly rushing blood from his throat, as he fought desperately for the air he was in fatally short supply of. His eyes looked wild while he instinctively battled for a life that was slipping rapidly beyond his grasp. Andy watched as his victim fell to his side and after a few labored gasps lay motionless, death having won their struggle.

After surveying his work, he was now well aware that the military was likely to be in the vicinity of his target. It was not unexpected, considering the locale, but in his business still necessary to confirm. He opened his expensive suitcase and removed two common canvas duffle bags and a set of nondescript clothing, common to residents of the area. Accenting his disguise with a tattered baseball hat and inexpensive dark glasses, he knew he could now easily pass for a native, despite his foreign extraction.

He packed the contents of his luggage and his leather carry on into the canvas bags. Throwing one over his shoulder and carrying the other, he left unnoticed down the fire escape, blending into the hustle and poverty of this third world chaos.

~ ~ ~

Chapter 40

Thursday Morning—Connor found himself, George and Alex boarding a late morning flight to the island of Mindanao. Dinner that evening had been uneventful and short as they decided to plan the next few day's activities with clearer heads after a good night's rest. He was hoping to be feeling better, but the difference in pain was immeasurable from the previous day. The pills he took with breakfast had taken the edge off enough for him to be comfortable as long as he wasn't too active.

They were the only passengers in first class. Most of the other fifty or so travelers, Connor imagined, could not afford the ten-dollar upgrade. This would give them a chance to talk during the forty-minute flight and evaluate some of the reconnaissance information that George would have been privy to.

"What's the situation regarding the military in the area, George?" Connor asked.

"Pretty much token forces, we should be able to buy them off without much of a hitch."

"How much?"

"How much for what?"

"To buy off the military."

"Around five thousand U.S. I think would do it," George returned, so cavalierly that Connor immediately suspected he was tossing out a number he thought they'd find palatable.

"We can do that," Alex replied.

"How much cash do you have on you?"

"We've got around sevvv. . . ."

"We've got enough," Connor interrupted, not wanting George to know the exact amount.

"Yeah, we've got plenty," Alex contributed.

"I hope so," George responded.

"How about rebel forces, have you run into them near the mine?"

"In the past two years, our lookouts have only spotted one rebel squad. Most of their activity is in North Cabato, one province to the south."

"What about the uncle who witnessed the gold being put in the cave?" Alex asked.

"The old guy died about a year ago."

"What happened?"

"He was up at the mine site and took a fever. By the time I got word, he was already gone."

"That's too bad, he got so close."

"Yeah, he didn't even want the money for himself, he wanted it to improve the life of the people in his mountain village. You know, better schools, a hospital, better housing. He had this dream, it's a shame he didn't live to see it happen," George recounted, sounding less than sincere.

"Maybe we could help make his vision happen," Alex said.

"You're free to do what you want—with your share," George returned coldly.

"Is the nephew still in the picture?" Connor inquired.

"Lido. He's in charge when I'm not there. He'll meet us at the airport, he's a good man."

"You're sure he can be trusted?" Alex asked.

"I've trusted him for fifteen years, I'm not about to stop now."

"Alright, first order of business is to secure the sample and arrange transport with Billy Hilliard. Are we in agreement?"

Alex and George both acknowledged their approval.

"It sounds like from what you've told us George, that

the military and the rebels are not an issue at this time. The only other player to worry about is Morgan Gold and I don't see how they could be in the picture yet."

"Looks like we may have some clear sailing on this first step," Alex contributed.

~ ~ ~

George just nodded. He knew that there was no such thing as clear sailing in this operation and Colonel Vadula would still be a problem even if they did offer him a payoff. But they were so close, closer than he'd been in fifteen years, and he wasn't about to cast a shadow on their obvious naiveté. He would keep the truth from them as long as possible, by then he figured they would be as deeply intertwined as he was.

While the plane circled the Cagayan De Oro airport, the scene he viewed from his window would make it necessary for him to amend his story sooner then he expected. Coming in and touching down, he observed over a hundred military troops lining the runway, along with a dozen heavily armed vehicles.

"Is that what you call token forces, George?" Connor asked sternly, sounding more than just a little concerned.

"You guys have to believe me, I've never seen this many soldiers here. Something must have happened, something big," he returned, suddenly feeling very uneasy.

"Is there anything else we should know? Tell us now, it may be your last chance."

"There's nothing else, I swear it," he said, not able to bring himself to discuss his meeting with the Colonel, fearing they would never get off the plane.

"You better fucking be telling the truth," Alex stated, nervously rubbing his hands together.

Not another word was spoken. They deplaned and headed for the small terminal, where they would wait to collect their luggage. George spotted Lido through the dilapidated wire fencing that surrounded the tarmac; he had a very worried look on his face. George held his breath when they

271

reached the building, thinking that the heavy occupation of the airport was due to him ditching his tail a few days ago. But that didn't make sense—he hoped.

As they entered the terminal, they joined the other passengers lining up to have their luggage and their person searched. Native travelers, regardless of sex were being stripped naked and their belongings strewn about. George was concerned that the contents of their luggage would raise a raft of unanswerable questions. While they waited, he noticed a man approaching that could alleviate this inconvenience. Unfortunately, he realized it would be at a much greater risk than any search would cause.

"Good morning, Mr. Fall," said a heavy, raspy voice, sounding pleased his pigeon had returned to the coop.

"Hello, Colonel," he returned sheepishly.

"Are you going to introduce me to your companions?"

"Of course. Connor Mason, Alex Litowski, this is Colonel Marquez Vadula."

"Nice to meet you, Colonel," Alex returned, extending his hand.

The Colonel stood staring at his new acquaintances. He smiled slightly, but made no attempt to accept Alex's greeting. George recognized this behavior immediately, this was his chance for maximum intimidation, despite his diminutive statue, he was a force to respect and that message had now been clearly sent. Finally Alex withdrew his offering, he looked more pissed off than scared, but considering the number of armed troops surrounding them, George was afraid that his companions must be feeling like he did; that their fate was not in their control at this moment—and possibly not from this point on.

"What's going on here, Colonel?" George asked, not sure he wanted the answer.

"We are searching for an assassin who killed three of my men, I'm afraid, Mr. Fall."

"Why do you think it was an assassin, Colonel?" he returned, relieved the commotion had nothing to do with him.

"My men were highly trained soldiers and they were

killed at close quarters without a shot being fired. In addition, our investigation has uncovered that the killer was of Oriental origin arriving yesterday from Hong Kong," the Colonel replied, glaring directly into the eyes of his new guests.

"Do you often allow assassins in your province, Colonel?" Connor pointedly directed, his choice of words leaving George feeling very uneasy.

"Not often, Mr. . . ."

"Mason."

"Mr. Mason, I won't forget again," he retorted, his upper lip quivering slightly. "This man was of exceptional skill, he must be in search of a special target."

"Really."

"Most really, Mr. Mason."

"Well after the search here, we're going to go get settled in, Colonel," George said, attempting to change the tenor of the conversation.

"You don't have to wait, Mr. Fall. As I have discussed with you before, you do for me and I can do for you."

"Thank you, Colonel."

"I expect so, Mr. Fall," the Colonel returned. "Please identify your luggage and my men will retrieve it for you. Your associates will be staying at the Pryce Plaza?"

"Yes, Colonel," he returned, having hoped to bring them to his house unnoticed and avoid the high profile hotel on the hill.

"Good, I'll meet you there for a meal. We can discuss business."

"Of course, Colonel. We'll be waiting for you."

"That would be the wise thing, Mr. Fall. Goodbye until then," he directed at the small group before returning to supervise the search of the remaining passengers.

They gathered up their luggage with the help of a couple of soldiers and twice as many porters. They loaded it into George's vehicle and climbed in for the eight-mile trip to the Pryce Plaza Hotel. George had noticed that Lido had kept his distance, blending in with the crowd, knowing it was not the best place or time to be associated with him and his entourage.

When they pulled out of the parking lot, George spotted Lido tailing close behind on his 250cc dirt bike.

"What was that all about, George?" Alex asked pointedly, wiping the sweat from his forehead, already looking like he was feeling the combined effects of the recent stress and the hot humid conditions.

"You heard him, they're looking for an assassin."

"No they're not," Connor interjected. "What they're looking for is his target and he found them."

"Us?" Alex questioned.

"Who else could it be? It's not like there's a lot going on here."

"George, is there someone else he could be after?" Alex asked, suddenly sounding a little panicked.

"I don't know, Alex. I just don't know."

"You can't be sure about this, Con?"

"Of course I'm not sure, but on a scale of one to ten, we're an eight."

"Jesus Christ, who sent him, not that Morgan Gold Company?"

"Who else?"

"How the hell could they possibly have found out so fast?"

"Someone told them, Alex."

"No kidding, but who?"

"Someone who had lots to gain and nothing to lose."

"Who's that?"

"Wes Adams. He knew what was going on and he would know how to contact them."

"I know, but he was your father's friend. Why? It doesn't make sense."

"Sure it does. My father's probably dead; it's not like he would have to face him. He tried to talk us out of this. Chances are far greater it's not going to work, than it is. If he sells us out, he has a better chance of coming out ahead."

"I think it's thin, Con."

"I don't believe Wes would do something like that, Connor," George chimed, feeling a little relieved that his deceptions were being overlooked for now.

"I don't want to believe it, but it adds up. And, there was one thing he said before we left that bothered me."

"What was that?"

"He told me that 'wherever there's greed, there can be no justice. Trust no one.'"

"Sounds like good advice to me, Con."

"Me too, but at the time it just struck me as odd. Now when I look back, I think he was trying to warn me in some perverse way about what he intended to do," Connor concluded.

"This is really fucked up; what now?"

"I don't know yet, but we went from a clear path to having an assassin and a pint sized Colonel with a voice like the exorcist on our tail."

"Can I make a suggestion?" George asked.

"NO!" They both said in unison.

"No really, I have an idea."

"I got a better one, George. Book us on the next flight back to the U.S.," Alex stated.

"What is it, George?" Connor conceded.

"As long as we stay close to the Colonel, the assassin is not going to try anything, that is, even if he really exists and is after you."

"After us."

"After us," George agreed, not believing for one second that anyone would waste a highly paid professional on him.

"I don't know, George. At some point we're going to need to slip away from the Colonel and his men to get this done."

"Not to worry, boys. This is the Philippines, everyone can be bought, even the Colonel's men, trust me."

"I never believe anyone who says trust me," Alex contributed.

"Alright don't trust me, but I know what I'm talking about."

"We'll see, George. We'll see," Connor said, as they arrived at the Pryce Plaza Hotel.

275

Pulling up to the front door, they were assisted in unloading their luggage by the doorman. Entering the air-conditioned lobby, George was grateful to be out of the smothering heat, sure his companions would be duly impressed by the level of accommodations. George decided he would stay and wait for the Colonel while Connor and Alex checked in and headed up to their rooms. They had told George they were going to get some rest and make a decision on whether they would continue with the operation.

After seeing to it that his associates were comfortable, George ventured into the parking lot in search of Lido, who had been following them, incognito, from the airport. He spied his five-foot six-inch frame waiting under a tall palm near the rear of the lot, his long black hair hanging out from under his ever present red bandana wrapped tightly around his head. He had dark eyes and a flat medium size nose, underscored by a very sparse, black mustache. His darkly tanned skin that highlighted his thick physique was tough from many hours digging in the hot sun. He stood upright when he saw George coming towards him.

"Hi Lido, how's everything at the mine?"

"Everything is good, but we have a problem."

"What's that?"

"You have not paid the men in two months and they are growing restless, plus there is more rebel activity in the area."

"The men will be paid in a day or two; I've been a little short on cash, but I have it now," he returned, anticipating liberating the funds from his new partners as he had spent most of their wages on personal pleasures.

"That's good. Where is Sir Guy? I did not see him with you."

"He's not available, so he sent his son to help us."

"Is he not well?"

"No one knows Lido. He went to Mexico on business and has been missing for over ten months according to his son."

"Was his business, gold business?"

"I think so."

276

"That is a dangerous business."

"Don't we know it. What's the report on the rebel troops?"

"My men have reported many armed rebels. They are looking for something in the area. Based on the way they are searching, they could be at the mine in seven to ten days."

"That's not good, not good at all," he returned, with obvious concern. "When you meet Guy's son and his friend don't say anything about that, understand?"

"Should they not be informed? It is very dangerous for them."

"Lido, old friend, I'm afraid if we tell them they will leave and your uncle's dream to help the people in the village will be over. Besides, we'll keep our lookouts and get them out before there is any trouble."

"Okay, Sir George, I will say nothing."

"Make sure the workers don't mention it either."

"Yes. What about the Colonel?"

"Don't worry about him, he'll be taken care of," he said, having no idea at that moment how that task would be accomplished. "You head back to the mine and I'll meet you in a couple of days, tell the men I'll bring their money."

"Thank you, Sir George. I will tell them," he replied, seeming happy to go back with good news.

Lido mounted his motorcycle and headed out of town, in the direction of the jungle mine. George watched him leave knowing that the entire situation was now very dicey. Between the military, the rebels and now possibly an assassin in the mix, it couldn't get much worse—he hoped. No matter, he was not about to quit, this needed to get done, it was his last chance to escape his hellish life; he couldn't face another failure. He wouldn't; one way or another this would be the end of it.

~ ~ ~

While George headed through the parking lot and back into the hotel, Andy Wai, wearing a tattered baseball hat, smiled as he observed his every move hidden behind his inexpensive sunglasses. He had been staking out the hotel, pretending to be working on the grounds when they arrived. So far everything had gone as planned; all he needed to do now was wait—wait for his opportunity to complete his deadly assignment.

~ ~ ~

Chapter 41

After getting settled and a brief nap, Connor, with Alex
in tow, made his way down to the pool area, which was built
into the hillside overlooking the city. He noticed several guests
mulling around both in and out of the water, lounging on
chairs or ordering refreshments by the bamboo poolside
bar. The pool was large and the surrounding bright white concrete patios were tiered with plenty of lounge chairs and tables.
It could easily handle several hundred patrons, but looked
almost deserted with the less than two-dozen people currently utilizing the facility. He spotted George sitting at a table
talking to one of the waiters who had just brought him a
beer.

"Hey, George," Connor said.

"Hi boys, did you get some rest?"

"A little," Connor replied.

"Pretty nice place wouldn't you say?"

"Yeah, it's one of the nicest hotels I've seen anywhere,"
Alex returned, gazing around the grounds.

"You've been here all this time?"

"Yup, just waiting for you guys to get up or the Colonel
to arrive, whichever happened first."

"You said the nephew, Lido, was following us from the
airport, where is he?"

"I talked to him in the parking lot, the hotel makes him
a little uneasy. He went back up to the mine to make sure
things are okay."

"What's the plan, George? You must have thought of

something while you were sitting here," Connor asked, wanting to get his take on the situation.

"I did. What we need is a two-stage operation, but once we leave we cannot come back here, where the Colonel can get to us. We need to get the sample and arrange for transport shortly after meeting with Billy."

"How the hell are we going to get back to Cebu? We can't fly in or out of that airport without him knowing," Alex said.

"We're not going to fly out of the airport."

"How are we going to get off the island?"

"Boat."

"Boat?"

"Boat. I'll arrange a charter to take us to Cebu for the meeting. The Colonel won't expect that," George explained.

"Yeah, but once he finds out we're missing, he'll know there's something going on."

"That's the key. Once we leave, we need to make sure we don't see the Colonel again."

"What's your plan for that?" Connor asked.

"Once we have things settled with Hilliard, we'll fly back in and move the gold to the transport location. It can all be done within two to three days."

"Are you brain dead? You just said we can't fly back in here," Alex contributed.

"We can fly back, we just can't fly into this airport. We'll fly to the southern end of the island in Davao. We'll have Lido meet us and we'll drive to the mine from the backside."

"How long a trip?" Connor asked.

"Probably eight hours by car, the roads here are not what you'd call reliable."

"We taking your car, George?"

"Yup."

"I don't think so, that piece of junk won't make it over tough terrain," Connor stated.

"You'd be surprised."

"I don't want to be. Let's see if we can rent some kind of jeep."

"You won't be able to return it."

"Think about what your saying, George. I don't think I really care right now if the rental makes it back," Connor scolded.

"Of course," he conceded.

"I take it we won't be smelting the gold?"

"No time and I don't even know if the smelters are still operational," George returned.

"No matter, how are we going to move it?"

"We need to purchase three jeepneys. It's going to be around twenty-five thousand."

"What else?"

"We need a couple of dirt bikes. It's the only way to get to the mine quickly and get the gold to the jeepneys."

"We can't get vehicles to the mine?" Alex inquired.

"We can, just not all the way. We need the bikes to move the gold from the mine to the vehicles."

"What do you mean not all the way?" Alex asked.

"It's hard to explain, you'll see when you get there."

"How much for the bikes?" Connor demanded.

"Twelve thousand."

"Alright, what else?"

"Money for the Colonel to keep him off guard and I owe some back payroll at the mine."

"How much?"

"Around another ten thousand?"

"That's over fifty grand, George," Alex calculated.

"You said you had plenty of money, I hope you do, there could be other expenses that come up."

"Let's hope not," Alex said, listening to their nest egg dwindle down to near nothing.

"You also need to get some flash money for the mountain people."

"What's that?"

"We go to the bank and exchange around four or five thousand into small denominations of pesos and put it in a duffle. If we have any trouble at the mine, you flash open the bag and promise to pay anyone that's a problem. Once they see all that money, they'll do anything we need them to, it's just a precaution."

"When do we do that?" Connor asked.

"We'll do it when we land in Davao, on our way to the mine."

"Sounds like you've thought this out pretty well, George. When do we go?"

"I'll need a couple of days to arrange the boat, jeepneys and motorcycles. I can have Lido and a couple of men get them up to the mine."

"We can help, George," Connor offered.

"I don't think so, guys. It will be hard enough for me to move around. You need to stay in plain sight and keep a high profile until it's time to go."

"How do we slip away?" Alex inquired.

"There's a cock fighting tournament in town starting on Saturday and running all week. The place will be packed, so I'll arrange to get us out during the fighting."

"We talking fighting birds, George?"

"Yeah, it's huge here. Awful bloody sport, they put these razor sharp spurs on them and they fight to the death."

"Sounds like something the Colonel would like," Connor deduced.

"He loves it."

"Why am I not surprised?"

"What do you think?" George asked, seeming a little anxious.

"I think we need to talk it over," Connor said.

"Don't take too long, boys. Wednesday is coming fast and everything here moves slowly. We need as much lead time as we can get."

"One more question, George," Alex asked.

"What's that?"

"Do you have any weapons?"

Before George could answer, Connor noticed a familiar and threatening figure approaching. As he came nearer, the sun glinted off the two highly polished silver revolvers slung low on his waist. From afar he had the look of a child, playing with toy guns, but this was no child and Connor doubted that playing was ever part of his youth.

"Good afternoon, Colonel," George said. "Any news on the assassin?"

"Not as of yet Mr. Fall," he returned, removing his hat and joining them at the table. "But I have my informants, and we will find him. I'm just not sure if it will be in time."

"In time for what, Colonel?" Alex asked innocently.

"In time to stop him from killing whoever he has come for, Mr. . . . ."

"Litowski."

"Yes, Mr. Litowski."

"What can we do for you, Colonel?" Connor asked.

"That is the very thing I would ask you, Mr. Mason."

"What can you offer, Colonel?"

"Anything and everything."

"Could you be a little more specific?"

"Yes, I can offer you protection, armed escorts, safe transportation, entertainment and many other things that young men such as yourself may desire."

"I see, what is the fee for these services?"

"I can be very reasonable, it all depends on what you like?"

"Maybe this will serve as a suitable retainer," Connor returned, removing a sealed envelope from his pocket and sliding it toward him.

The Colonel took the envelope and pulling out a pocketknife slit the top and peered inside. Using his thumb he fanned the twenty-five American hundred dollar bills. What equated to roughly six months salary made him seem very pleased, as a slight smile crossed his usually pursed lips. Unfortunately, Connor knew that like an animal getting its first taste of blood, the initial thrill of his new found cash would quickly pass and he would long for more—much more.

"Most generous of you and your associate, Mr. Mason," the Colonel acknowledged as he nodded at them.

"If things go well there will be more, Colonel."

"I'm counting on it, Mr. Mason," he returned, rising from his seat. "Now if you don't mind I have some very pressing business and will be unable to join you for a meal, but I would like to extend an invitation to visit me at the compound tomorrow. I have an exhibition planned I think you may find most interesting. I will send my men to pick you up at eight o'clock."

"Thank you, Colonel. But we have some important business to take care of. I'm afraid we'll have to do it another time."

"I must insist Mr. Mason, it is not polite to refuse your first invitation in the Philippines, especially from your new partner."

"I totally understand, Colonel, but we. . . ."

"I don't think you do, Mr. Mason," he interrupted. "My men will get you in the morning."

"That's fine, Colonel. See you in the morning," George chimed in.

"In the morning then," the Colonel replied as he turned and took his leave.

They watched while his smallish but intimidating figure left the pool area and disappeared through the glass doors leading to the lobby. Connor couldn't help notice the pains people took to avoid him. The workers around the pool would not make eye contact, obviously fearing they may, for no particular reason, become the brunt of his ire. He was both a powerful and unpredictable force. And that, Connor realized, made for a very dangerous combination.

"We got real problems here with this guy," Alex said.

"We'll handle him," Connor returned, looking at George for a reaction.

"He's a fucking psycho, Con. He really scares me," Alex replied, his voice resounding with genuine concern.

"Don't worry, I've been dealing with him awhile. You gave him some money and that will buy us enough time to get in and out before he knows what happened."

"You really believe that, George?" Connor asked.

"I do."

"What about weapons, George. Do you have any?" Alex revisited.

"We got plenty. They're hidden at the house."

"What do you have?"

"We got handguns, mostly 45 caliber automatics, rifles, shotguns, whatever you're looking for."

"I'd like to see them," Alex requested.

"No problem, I'll pick them up at the house tomorrow after we're finished with the Colonel. But, I never carry a gun here."

"That's your choice, George. Given the climate, I'd rather be in position to defend myself if necessary. What do you think about being armed, Con—Con?"

He didn't answer; he was totally distracted by a new guest who had just entered the pool area. Between the pain pills, jet lag, heat and stress, he kind of zoned out and the first thing he fixated on was an exotic beauty situating herself on a nearby lounge chair.

"Hey bud, you with us here? This is important stuff," Alex said, snapping him out of his daze.

"Sorry, I just spaced out for a second. What were you saying?"

"I was asking what you think about being armed?"

"I think it's a good idea."

"There's your answer, George. If we go forward with this, we want guns."

"Suit yourselves."

"What now?" Alex asked.

"I'm going to go make arrangements for the vehicles we discussed. Why don't you boys take some time and make a decision about what you want to do. I mean, you're here now, if I were you I'd give it a shot," he returned rising from his seat.

"No offense, George. But you're not us," Alex responded.

George just shrugged and departed for town to make the necessary preparations. He seemed satisfied with himself for concocting a feasible plan. Connor wasn't sure it would work, far from it, but given their current financial situation, he was willing to give him the benefit of the doubt—for now.

"Well, what's the verdict partner? Are we going for this or are we getting out of Dodge?"

"George is right, Alex. We're here, we might as well give it a shot."

"You're being just a little blasé aren't you?"

"Maybe, but I'm not going to analyze this to death. Let's take it one step at a time. We can always bail."

"Yeah, but come tomorrow we have to give old George fifty large, that's almost our whole stash. How do you feel about handing him that much cash?"

"Fine, because we're not handing him anything. One of us is going with him."

"He'll go ballistic."

"Not if he wants to get this done and if he does freak, fuck'im."

"I'm with you brother."

"Alright, let's go get some rest, we've got a big day with the military tomorrow," Connor said, getting up from the table. "By the way, when you turn around, check out the babe at the pool, she's to die for."

Alex got up and turning around, his eyes were treated to a very special sight, made all the more enjoyable, Connor figured, by the courtesy of his ever raging hormones. Stretched out on a nearby lounge was a six foot tall, dark skinned goddess. She was Eurasian, although it was difficult to determine if she was half Japanese or Vietnamese on the Asian side; one of her parents was definitely black. No matter, the combination yielded a woman of stunning beauty. Her silky, jet-black hair hung almost to her waist as it framed a perfect body, highlighted by a rippled mid-section and long shapely legs, one of which bore a colorful snake tattoo, starting at her ankle and traveling up the inside of her thigh. She was one of the most visually, captivating women Connor had ever seen.

When they walked by, she lowered her sunglasses and catching their glances with her own pair of beautiful emerald green eyes, offered them a wide inviting smile. Connor returned the gesture as he headed to rest and reflect on the day's activity, as well as this foreign poolside beauty.

~ ~ ~

A half-mile away, Andy Wai's less inviting eyes watched their every movement. From his vantage he had a partial view of the terraced pool area. As he adjusted his tattered baseball hat, turning around the bill after removing his sunglasses, he focused in on his target through the scope of his high-powered rifle. Deciding his position was less than optimum he surrendered to the need for a better location, while Connor and Alex disappeared into the hotel. They were safe—for now, but for how long, was a question he knew he would play a major part in determining.

~ ~ ~

Chapter 42

Friday Morning, eight o'clock—Alex found himself, Connor, and George being loaded into a green and brown camouflage patterned Humvee accompanied by three soldiers, one of whom was perched in a suspended hammock seat with his head and arms exposed through the top, manning a roof mounted large caliber machine gun. All in all, Alex thought it was an impressive sight, although he imagined mostly for show. Finding a seat next to Connor required him pushing several long bands of ammunition and loose weapons to the side. It looked like enough artillery to fend off a battalion of rebels, in what he perceived as the highly unlikely event of an incident. They finally got settled and were transported east, toward Maltibog and the army command compound.

Arriving at the base, they were taken to Colonel Vadula's office, where their host was waiting.

"Good morning, gentlemen," he said, his voice sounding especially raspy at this early hour.

"Good morning, Colonel," George said, as they made their way toward his desk.

"Did the hotel accommodations suit your needs?" he asked, while they found a seat in one of the eight chairs that lined the walls in his narrow space.

"They were fine, Colonel," Connor answered.

"You've won lots of awards for shooting, Colonel," Alex said, noticing the case of trophies and ribbons behind him."

"Yes, Mr. Litowski. I take great pride in my skill as a marksman. Do you shoot?"

"A little."

"We must have a contest, it is not often that I get to test my skills against a competitor."

"We'll have to do that some time, Colonel."

"Yes, we will do it now."

It took a few seconds before Alex realized he was serious. George gave Alex and Connor a distressed look as they sat dumbfounded. Alex knew he had inadvertently hit a hot button with the Colonel and his reaction displayed the volatile nature that made him so unpredictable. From what Alex had witnessed in their short association; his whims were law, and the law had said, it was time for a contest.

"I thought you brought us up to see an exhibition, Colonel. We don't want to disrupt your plans," George offered, obviously not wanting to be exposed to both him and firearms.

"It will be no disruption, Mr. Fall. I had planned a shooting demonstration; this will just serve to make it more interesting—much more interesting. Please follow me."

The Colonel rose and his guests followed him out into the compound and onto the rustic shooting range. They quickly attracted a crowd; his foreign entourage helping to peak the interest of what would otherwise be the apathetic viewing participants of the barracks. The Colonel barked out some instructions in his native tongue of Tagolag and two soldiers hurried off in the direction of a nearby Quonset hut. He then walked over to a large rock and lined up six empty bottles before rejoining the group.

"Do you like pistols Mr. Litowski?" he asked, while he lightly rubbed the handles of his ever-present side arms.

"Never did use handguns very much, Colonel," he returned.

"That is too bad, I long to test my skill against another pistol marksman," he returned, not sounding terribly disappointed.

"Sorry, Colonel. I prefer shotgun or rifle."

"No need to apologize, Mr. Litowski. We will explore these other disciplines."

Without warning, the Colonel spun around and drawing his weapons smoked his glass targets. It seemed to startle George and Connor, but Alex remained composed, having spent a lifetime around the sound of gunfire. The Colonel finished off the display with his well-practiced gun twirling and holstering much to the delight of his partisan cheering section.

"Very impressive, Colonel," Alex said.

"Thank you, I am the fastest quick draw artist in the country."

"I don't doubt it, Colonel."

"It would be a mistake to doubt it, Mr. Litowski," he returned, his so far pleasant enough demeanor changing again in the blink of an eye.

"I won't make that mistake."

"Good," he returned. "Here are the weapons for you to choose."

Alex turned toward the metal building and observed two soldiers carrying an assortment of firearms and ammunition. Reaching the group, they deposited them on a nearby bamboo table. The Colonel motioned Alex to the table, where he handed him a silver-plated, automatic, pistol-grip twelve-gauge shotgun.

"Probably not the sportsman gun you're accustomed to, Mr. Litowski."

"It'll do, Colonel," he returned, holding the gun and testing the weight and balance.

The Colonel motioned for the two soldiers to follow, one picked up several boxes of shells and the other grabbed a container filled with empty bottles. Alex and the Colonel walked ahead while George and Connor followed, with the increasing crowd of currently forty or so lagging close behind.

The Colonel stopped and motioned to the men assisting them, to stand on either side while he loaded four shells into the chamber. He nodded and the soldiers launched four bottles high into the air. The Colonel mounted the weapon and swinging it from one side to the other blasted the targets. He motioned for Alex, who stepped forward and proceeded to match the Colonel's effort. He smiled, appearing pleased with his guest's ability.

Alex imagined that engaging an opponent of skill would make any victory the Colonel could muster all the more meaningful. For the next half-hour more bottles were lofted in a variety of patterns, all with the same results. It seemed that word had spread through the compound as the crowd swelled to more than a hundred. They cheered for both participants, but seemed to Alex to be favoring him. Based on what he'd been exposed to, he imagined that the Colonel was not the most popular of figures, even among his own constituents.

He was relishing in his newfound celebrity, a podium usually reserved for his best friend when he decided it was time to up the ante and give the crowd something to really cheer about. The Colonel had just finished another successful round, when Alex asked for his weapon. His opponent gave him a peculiar look, but then handed the gun over. He looked over to the soldiers as he loaded both weapons, motioning them to launch four bottles each, double the previous rounds. He took the guns and crossed his hands resting one wrist on top of the other, making them easier to lift. The Colonel wore a look of concern. Alex was well aware that if he was successful, there was no way he could imagine the Colonel matching his feat, and that would be a very hard thing for him to swallow, especially in front of a crowd. Regardless of the potential consequences, he still felt compelled to proceed.

Alex nodded and the eight bottles were thrown high into the air. Using his right wrist as the base and pivoting his left hand, he lifted the guns into firing position, easily breaking the four bottles to his left, using the bottom gun in his right hand while he simultaneously fired at the bottles to his right. He broke three of the bottles at their apex, then dropping the gun in his right hand while grabbing the barrel of the other, swung around blasting the last bottle less than a foot from the ground. The attending soldiers and family members erupted in applause. Alex turned and bowed as he soaked up their very vocal praise. The Colonel appeared impressed as he joined the crowd in a more subdued expression of his appreciation, even though, Alex was sure it was eating him up inside.

"Congratulations, Mr. Litowski. A most impressive display of shooting and good fortune."

"Thank you, Colonel, sometimes it pays to be lucky."

"Yes, sometimes. It looks like we have a tie, me having the edge with handguns and your victory with shotguns. I propose we break the tie with some long distance shooting."

"That would be just fine, Colonel. Bring your paycheck."

"What did you say to me?"

"Nothing, Colonel. It was just an American expression," Alex returned, enjoying the fact he was getting to his opponent, but still aware of the danger he represented.

~ ~ ~

George and Connor watched from a ways back. Connor was enjoying the high skill level of both participants, but was becoming increasingly anxious about the possibility for an incident if Alex continued to press the Colonel in front of his people. Another defeat could send his fragile ego over the edge, resulting in a level of mayhem they could not comprehend or afford.

"Alex is good, don't you think, George?"

"Yeah, maybe he's too good."

"You think we may have a problem here," Connor asked, sensing George's concern was similar to his own.

"If he dusts the Colonel again, we just may. How good is he?"

"He's a man among boys, George. My boy is a shooting fool; we're in trouble."

"You'd better tell him not to shoot so good then."

"I know Alex, George. I don't think he'll tank."

"Convince him, we don't want that little motherfucker on us more than he already is. That man is not stable, there's not much to hang onto when you live your life here, no telling what may set him off."

"All right, I'll try."

"Try fucking hard," George returned, seeming close to becoming unglued.

Connor started to walk toward Alex, who was busy sighting in the rifle that had been handed to him. He and the Colonel were using the leaves on a palm tree around two hundred and fifty yards away as practice targets. Before Connor could reach them a soldier stepped in front impeding his progress. When he tried to go around, the soldier motioned to stay back. Connor just looked at George and shook his head.

~ ~ ~

"Are you ready Mr. Litowski?"

"Whenever you are, Colonel."

"Good," he returned, motioning to his men.

The first target was a pineapple, set on a bent palm around three hundred yards away. The Colonel situated himself in a prone position, using a tripod stand to steady his gun. After several deep breaths, he took aim. Getting his breathing right, he fired and the pineapple exploded as the local contingent raised a loud cheer, appearing to be thoroughly enjoying the competition. The Colonel acknowledged the crowd, which had now grown to better than two hundred, while Alex readied to take his shot.

This was not a particularly demanding shot Alex thought, other than the fact he didn't have his own gun. The pineapple was replaced and he decided he would make it a little more challenging by standing to shoot. He took one breath, held it and squeezed the trigger, blasting his target to pieces. The cheers were even louder. He knew most of the military crowd realized the difficulty of the feat he made look easy. The Colonel, however, did not look impressed.

"Should we move the target back, Colonel," Alex asked, trying not to gloat, but feeling there was no way the Colonel could outshoot him.

"Would another two-hundred yards be okay with you?"

the Colonel returned, his raspy voice cracking as his upper lip quivered.

"Let's make it interesting. Why don't we move the target back four-hundred yards," he suggested, knowing full well that the distance would test the Colonel, but was still well within his envelope.

"Fine," he returned, motioning for his men to reset the targets.

While the Colonel got into position, Alex looked over at Connor and clinched his fist, relaying that he was about to put him away. Connor caught his eye and gave him a subtle head-shake that left him a little confused. He knew he was trying to tell him something, but what?—he wondered. Alex was keeping eye contact, when a roar went up from the crowd signaling that the Colonel had been successful in his attempt. His eyes were asking what, as Connor made a slow turn of his head, accented by dragging his forefinger slowly across his throat. Alex gave him a disgusted look confirming that his message had been understood, but he didn't like it.

"Your turn Mr. Litowski," the Colonel directed, sounding a little more confident having hit his target.

Alex made his way into position, deciding if he was going to miss, he might as well make a production out of it. He got to his stomach and taking the shell in his hand, blew the dust off his bullet and slowly loaded it into the chamber. Just as he was about to complete his charade, the Colonel interrupted.

"Are you not going to shot this from a standing position, Mr. Litowski?"

"Not this time, Colonel," he returned.

"I guess at this distance you don't feel as sure of yourself," he badgered.

"I guess not," he replied, seeing through the Colonel's mind game and getting more pissed off by the second. Alex settled in on his target, the Colonel's comments and his overall smugness running through his head. He knew Connor and George were counting on him to miss and not upset their unpredictable host, that was the smart thing to do, the right thing given this circumstance, the type of decision he had been preaching to Connor for the last week.

In his mind the message was playing over and over again, do the right thing; don't let pride interfere with common sense. Those were his last thoughts as he pulled the trigger, he didn't even bother to follow the path of the bullet; the erupting crowd signaled the result. When he looked up, the pineapple target was nowhere to be seen. He felt a momentary rush of guilt, but he wasn't ready to lay down without turning the screws on the Colonel at least one more time, it was stupid he thought, but a damn sight more satisfying.

As he rose, the smug look from his opponent was gone, replaced by an expression of very real concern mixed with a healthy portion of disdain. Alex finally turned to look at his companions; their faces reading like a road map to disaster. He had had his little reprieve, now it was time to get down to the business of not making their life anymore difficult, it was time to tank.

Another target was put in place while the Colonel readied himself. He appeared a little more nervous as he pondered over the shot. After what seemed like an eternity he pulled the trigger, missing his target. He said nothing when he rose from the ground. There was a murmur growing from the onlookers as Alex settled in for what could have been the winning effort. He took a little extra time in order to make everyone think he was bearing down before he fired and missed. There was a loud groan from the crowd. When he looked over at Connor and George, he was comforted by the relived look on their faces.

"Always hard to make a shot when it really counts, wouldn't you agree, Mr. Litowski?" the Colonel said, his cockiness resurfacing.

"Sure, Colonel," he returned half-heartedly.

The Colonel got in position, suddenly looking much more relaxed than during his previous attempt. He performed his breathing ritual as he squeezed the trigger, hitting his target. He rose to a round of applause while he vacated the area in favor of his adversary.

"Champions make shots when they have to," he said, as Alex passed by him.

"I could out shoot you standing on my head you little fuck," Alex returned under his breath.

The spectators were buzzing as he readied. He looked over his shoulder at the Colonel who was smiling confidently and accepting accolades from some of the by-standers. Alex was thinking of prolonging the Colonel's anxiety, he just wasn't sure if his fragile psyche could handle the pressure of shooting another round. There was only one way to find out he thought, while he took aim, smiling to himself. He took a couple of deep breaths, then held and fired. The crowd fell silent as he failed to hit his mark. He rose, shaking his head in mock disbelief as he approached the Colonel.

"Nice shooting, Colonel," he said, extending his hand.

"Try not to be too disappointed, Mr. Litowski. You could not have been expected to outshoot a professional," he returned, accepting his hand and looking relieved.

"You're right of course," Alex returned, biting his tongue.

"I must get on with my day's activities now. My men will return you and your friends to the hotel," he said, abruptly dismissing them.

Alex smiled at Connor and George when he returned. He hated to lose to the Colonel but he had done the right thing, finally. They were directed to the Humvee for transport back; they had met the enemy in his lair and were returning in one piece. Alex felt the defeat was a Trojan Horse, meant to give a false sense of superiority to his enemy. He was feeling smarter and somewhat more in control of their fate as they were deposited at the Pryce Plaza. A feeling, he worried, that may propel him and his best friend a bit more recklessly down the path of their high-risk operation.

~ ~ ~

Chapter 43

George followed his new partners up to Connor's room to discuss the plan. He was quite familiar with the suite when he entered, boasting a bedroom with two queen size beds and a sitting area that included two chairs and a love seat with matching coffee and end tables. The rooms were larger than he remembered, accented in shades of peach and white, including curtains, bedding and furniture. It was a well-coordinated, light and airy feeling environment, enhanced further by a sliding glass door leading to a balcony overlooking the pool area and city below. In general, he thought it showed very little signs of wear since he was a guest; a result of limited usage he rationalized. He took a seat and contemplated the next few days' activity. After recounting the morning's festivities and praising Alex, not only for his ability, but also for his prudent judgment, they were ready to focus on critical matters.

"What have you decided?" George asked, confident they would agree to move forward.

"We're in, George," Connor returned.

"Great," he replied enthusiastically. "I've secured the vehicles and I'm going to need the money to pay for them."

"That's fine, George. But we'll handle the cash."

"What do you mean?"

"I mean one of us is going with you to make the purchases."

"That's not a good idea," he argued.

"Maybe not, but it's that way or no way."

George didn't answer. He had hoped to skim a little

extra while he was waiting for the gold to be cashed in. Five or ten thousand would allow him the kingly existence he felt he deserved. Now they would know the actual prices he had negotiated, leaving him out in the cold with regard to his attempted enterprising. He knew he had to agree, what other choice was there? Maybe after seeing the gold they would be open to an advance against proceeds.

"Alright, one of you can come, maybe I can do a little better on the pricing."

"We thought that might encourage you to make your best deal," Alex added.

"What's our time frame, George?" Connor asked.

"I can have everything arranged, but we don't want to leave till Monday. We'll head to the mine, retrieve the sample and meet with Billy. If we board the boat by Tuesday, we can be in Cebu no later than Wednesday morning. By leaving Monday we won't be missing long enough for the Colonel to alert the other airports and keep us from flying back into Davao."

"What's the plan for exiting the hotel?"

"We'll head out on Monday afternoon to the cock fighting tournament in the city. The place will be packed and it will be easy enough to get lost in the crowd."

"What about our equipment?" Alex asked, pointing to the two duffle bags and his mysterious gray briefcase.

"We'll need to take it out over the next couple of days. I'll have it in the car when we head up to the mine. You're not going to check out. If things work out you won't be coming back, so don't leave anything behind you need, especially passports."

"We're not dummies, George," Alex returned.

"Just making sure, I don't want to leave anything to chance."

"So after we meet with Billy, what's the timeline?"

"Meet with Billy, arrange transport, be back at the mine Friday, have Billy fly in and pick up the gold no later than Monday and we're out of here—for now.

"What do you mean for now?" Alex questioned.

"It's not important, I'll explain it to you later."

"Are you sure?"

"I'm positive."

"You better be, George. I don't want any surprises," Connor added.

"Relax, there won't be any surprises."

"How will the rest of the vehicles get to the mine?"

"While we're on our way to meet with Billy, Lido and some of the men will take care of that detail."

"Can't they load up the vehicles while we're in Cebu?" Alex asked.

"This is the Philippines, Alex. If we let them into that mine while we're not there, we'll come back to a thousand people picking through that place and more military then you can shake a stick at. Nothing stays quiet here for long, the only ones that can go in are us and maybe Lido, no one else."

"What's keeping them from walking in there right now and getting the gold?" Alex inquired.

"Believe me, no one that doesn't have to would go in there," George replied.

"Why?"

"You'll find out when you see it."

"Anything else you want to tell us, but not tell us, George?" Connor asked; starting to sound a little agitated.

"No, that's it."

"Fine, let's get to work. You take Alex so he can inspect the weapons, pay for the vehicles and the boat. I'll stay here in case we get any unexpected visitors," he said, referring to the Colonel or his men.

"Okay, let's go Alex."

"Yeah, let's go. Con, how you feeling?"

"I've been better," he returned, rubbing his aching ribs.

"I'll see you this evening, Con," he returned, as his friend just nodded.

~ ~ ~

Connor watched them leave, wishing he felt better so he could have joined them. Maybe it was better that someone stayed behind. They definitely would attract less attention that way, he rationalized. He walked over to his nightstand and removed the pain pills from the drawer. Grabbing a bottle of water sitting nearby, he downed three pills and lay back on the bed, waiting for the pain to pass. He was still not accustomed to the thirteen-hour time change. That, coupled with the effort it took to move at all, had him exhausted.

As he stared at the peach and white wallpaper, he realized that in a matter of hours their money would be spent and they would be alone and deeper in debt. All for a dream of adventure and the love of a woman he wasn't sure would be waiting when, and if, he returned. He closed his eyes and let all the energy sapping variables, along with the medication, usher him off to sleep. He knew the train was on the track moving full speed ahead—the next stop, a familiar one—uncertainty.

~ ~ ~

Chapter 44

Sunday Morning, Pryce Plaza Hotel—Connor paced in his room while he contemplated their final hours before beginning the operation in earnest. George and Alex had used the past two days to secure the vehicles and charter the boat for Tuesday's trip to Cebu, so far without incident. Alex had figured they saved almost eight thousand dollars by accompanying George, well worth the decision to inconvenience their partner. Lido and his men were supposed to make sure everything was on site by the time they returned, that was if they could shake the Colonel's spies, possibly avoid an assassin and get the sample to Billy. The problem was, after two days of hanging around the hotel he was beginning to go a little stir crazy, the good thing was, because of his forced convalescence he was actually gaining some pain free mobility and adjusting to the time change.

It was almost 10:00 a.m. He decided before meeting with George and Alex to go over any last minute details, he would try to reach Maggie. Having had no contact for over a week, he missed her. Yet, with everything going on, the pain of separation had dulled somewhat, but in no way disappeared. He picked up the phone and dialed. It was about 1:00 a.m. in the States, so he would probably wake her up, but he was sure she would be glad to hear from him. After all, she was partially responsible for him being here.

The phone was ringing. He held his breath and felt his heart pounding in anticipation; his head swirled with emotions when he heard the receiver being picked up.

"Hello," answered a tired sounding male voice. "Hello, hello, who is this?"

Connor hung up the phone, a sick feeling engulfing his body. It had only taken a week for her to spend the night with someone else he thought, as he tried to ward off the emotional jolt. She had said she thought she loved him, he guessed that was just till he left, then she found someone she liked better. Alex was right; she was a nutcase, a nutcase who unfortunately he was still head over heels for.

He needed to take his mind off of her; maybe there was a good explanation why a strange man picked up, he attempted to rationalize. Considering Maggie only had one phone, and the fact that it was on her bedroom nightstand, flew in the face of anything other than a new lover.

Walking out on the balcony, he looked down at the pool already buzzing with thirty or so guests catching some morning sun. Most were Chinese or Japanese businessmen looking for business opportunities or checking on current operations he imagined. He saw a few new faces, suspecting by their Caucasian features, in this part of the world, they were probably Australian. While he continued to survey the area, a familiar and most welcome figure caught his attention. The Eurasian beauty from the other day was swimming laps, clad in the tiniest bikini he had seen in quite sometime.

Watching her exit the pool, she turned more than a few heads, ringing out her long black hair while the water dripped off her lean, hard body. Feeling the need for some diversion, he grabbed his bathing suit, towel and lotion and headed poolside, figuring Alex and George would find him when they were ready.

Entering the pool area, he spied the source of his new desire sitting on a lounge chair drying in the sunshine. The water, pooled in little beads, seemed to evaporate off her rock hard mid-section as he inspected her. She was a magnificent specimen and exactly the medicine he needed, regardless if their liaison would turn out to be real or imagined.

He took a seat about twenty feet away, ordering several beers as he drank up the courage to approach her. It wasn't like a rejection would be impossible to deal with; after all, he was thirteen thousand miles from home, why would it matter other than to ruin a fantasy that could easily have lasted the rest of the afternoon. He decided to engage her, getting off his chair to shorten distance between them. When he drew near she acknowledged his presence with an intoxicating wide smile.

"I thought you'd never get here," she said, in a sultry voice revealing just a trace of an Asian accent.

"Excuse me," he returned, caught totally off guard.

"You did come over to put lotion on my back. You would not want me to get burned would you?"

"Of course not," he returned, deciding to play along.

"Good then, lather me up would you?" she said, handing him a tube from her bag.

"My pleasure."

She turned around and reaching back unfastened her scant bikini top, letting it drop into her lap. Her newly exposed breasts were full and perky. He rubbed the lotion on his hands and then down her neck and shoulders. She pulled her long black hair out of the way so he could have unobstructed access to her back, her skin was soft and smooth, but firm to the touch. As he continued to apply the protective ointment she started making a quiet sighing sound when he stroked her skin.

"Could you do my legs, please," she said, moving to lie on her stomach.

"Sure," he returned, squirting more lotion onto his hands.

Starting at her ankles he ran his salve drenched hands up the back of her legs, covering every inch of exposed skin including the long snake tattoo that adorned one of her shapely limbs. He went slowly and deliberately, as the sounds she was emitting gave him the impression she was enjoying this little seduction as much as he was. Finally finishing his appointed, albeit, pleasurable task, he reached for his towel and removed the excess lotion from his hands.

"Thank you for taking such good care of my body," she said, rolling over on the lounge to face him. "I like your touch."

"I liked touching you," he returned, feeling that he sounded like a bad cliché.

"I'm glad, maybe we could do it again in a more private setting."

"That may be able to be arranged," he returned, not quite believing what he was hearing. "What's your name?"

"Jade. What's yours?"

"Connor. Connor Mason."

"That's a nice name, Connor."

"Thank you."

"You're welcome."

"What are you doing in this place?" he asked, truly interested in how this beauty came to be in this part of the globe.

"I'm here on business, and you?"

"Business."

"I'm glad we got that out of the way," she returned smiling.

"Yes, but what do you do?" he asked, still curious.

"Anyone I want, Connor."

"Really."

"Yes, really. Why don't you meet me in town tonight, we can have some fun."

"I don't know. I've got some things to take care of."

"Are you playing hard to get, Connor Mason?"

"I assure you, that's not the case."

"Then meet me, tonight."

"Where?"

"There's a local club on Mapa Street."

"What's it called?"

"Love City."

"Seriously, Love City?"

"That's it. I'll be there after eight."

"Why don't we just go together?"

"That would not be appropriate, to go on a date without a chaperon, seeing how we just met."

"Are you kidding?" he asked, surprised by her answer after being exposed to a more suggestive demeanor.

"No, I prefer to be proper. Properly picked up at a club and properly seduced by a handsome young—American?"

"American," he confirmed smiling.

"I'll see you tonight then," she returned, replacing her bikini top and rising to leave.

"How do I get there?"

"Just get a driver from the front desk to drop you off. I'll bring you back to the hotel."

"Can I bring a friend?"

"I think," she said, taking her soft hand and starting at his forehead, running a finger down his face and lips, "that in this case, three would be a crowd. Don't leave me waiting."

"I'll try not to."

"Try hard, Connor. I promise you a night in the Philippines you will never forget," she said, as she walked away."

He watched her depart, lean, tall, sexy and to him, and he imagined, to many who encountered her, totally mesmerizing. Wait till Alex hears about this one; it will blow him away he thought. Settling in, he closed his eyes; lost in an erotic Asian daydream. The sting of Maggie and her unknown amour crept into his head as he used his new acquaintance to help erase the hurt of betrayal. He wanted to see her tonight; it was therapy. If this project was going to end in disaster, she would be a sweet memory to carry with him. Just as he was retreating into a deeper stage of relaxation, his mental exodus was interrupted by a familiar voice.

"Hey, Con. Where you been? We've been looking for you."

"Couldn't have been looking too hard," he returned, reluctantly opening his eyes to Alex and George walking in his direction.

"Hard enough," Alex replied as they both took seats on either side of him. "What have you been up too?"

"I've been talking to the girl we saw at the pool on Friday."

"The one with the snake tattoo?"

"That's her," he returned, a smile piercing his lips.

"Fuck you, the sun's boiled your brain out here."

"Meeting her tonight."

"Meeting her where?" His voice echoed his concern.

"A club called Love City. Do you know it, George?"

"Yeah, it's a dance club on Mapa Street. Mostly Jap businessmen and hookers go there."

"You think that's a good idea, Con?"

"Just killing time, brother."

"If you don't mind then, I'll go with you."

"I asked her about that already, she implied that three would be a crowd. Sorry, bud."

"How about the assassin that's supposedly out there?"

"You've been out and we've been here for going on four days without incident; besides, the Colonel's men will most likely be following."

"Yeah that's true," George contributed. "They pretty much followed Alex and I the whole time we were out. But they keep quite a distance."

"We were followed," Alex said, sounding somewhat surprised.

"Yeah, we were followed. That's why Lido and his men have to pick up the vehicles. Don't worry, they don't know what we were up to and by the time they figure it out, we'll be long gone."

"How are we going to lose them tomorrow?" Alex asked, suddenly seeming less concerned about his friend's scheduled tryst.

"We'll lose them at the tournament," George returned.

"I know that, George. But exactly how are we going to lose them?"

"That's what we're here to discuss, isn't it?"

"Quit stalling," Connor returned. "You're not sure are you?"

George hesitated, making it clearly obvious to Connor that he hadn't thought it all out. He probably figured they would easily be able to slip away in the crowd, but that wasn't the elementary level of sophistication that Connor wanted to hear.

"It will be a large crowd. We'll just get lost in it and Lido will meet us with the car a few streets over," he returned nervously, wiping the sweat from his balding head.

"Man, that is way thin," Alex returned, looking over at Connor and rolling his eyes.

"You got a map, George?" Connor asked.

"Yeah, what for?"

"So we can all get on the same page here. We need to have a primary and a secondary pick up location in case we can't shake the Colonel's men."

"Okay," George agreed, spreading out a crumpled local street map he had stuffed in his pocket.

"Where's the arena?"

"It's here," he answered, pointing to a spot near the out-skirts of downtown.

"Alright," Connor replied, studying the area. "Primary pick-up spot on the corner of Tiago and Elias, secondary corner of Hizon and Musa. If we can't shake the tail, we'll regroup back here and try again."

"What do you mean regroup?" Alex asked.

"We can't all sneak out together, Alex. We'll be too easy to follow."

"I don't like the idea of being separated."

"Connor's right, Alex. We've got a better chance by splitting up."

"Fine."

"What's the layout, George?"

"The place is like a big wooden circular theatre. The fighting pit is made of thick glass in the middle, with the best seats reserved for foreigners surrounding the pit. The rest of the seating are wooden bleachers, separated from the pit area by barbed wire. Surrounding the good seats are the bettors, they take your bet and lay it off into the crowd. Just before the fight starts, the noise level gets deafening with everyone yelling out wagers. When the fight begins the place goes nuts, people standing, cheering, screaming."

"How long do the fights last?"

"Hard to say. Some last a couple of minutes, others are over in seconds."

"Okay, just as the last fight ends, we'll leave through three separate exits. Got any ideas, George?" Connor continued.

"Yeah, the soldiers will be in the crowd, so they will have to fight through, which will buy us some time. They'll be watching the main exit into the parking lot, so that's out. I can get us out through the fighter's staging area and a window in the bathroom. Those are the only ways that make sense."

"Where are we in relation to the arena?"

"Here and here," he returned pointing at the map.

"Okay, you and Alex exit through the fighter's entrance and I'll leave through the bathroom window. When you get outside, split up and head for the first pick up point. Alex, you take this route; George, you go this way," he said, tracing the two separate egresses with his finger.

Alex and George both nodded in agreement.

"Can you go into town and get me six dozen of the brightest colored t-shirts you can find tomorrow morning," Connor asked. "All the same color, yellow would be nice."

"Sure," George replied, looking a little curious.

"Also, stop at the bank and exchange five hundred dollars into small pesos denominations."

"Okay, but why?"

"Insurance."

"What do you mean?"

"You'll see if we need it."

"Fine."

"Also, we'll need copies of the map so we all have one, including Lido."

"I'll take care of it," George confirmed.

"Well, if all the equipment is in your car, we should be set for tomorrow."

"Everything's there. Along with Alex's guns."

"Thanks, George," Alex acknowledged.

"You're welcome."

"Alright, let's get some beers and kick back," Connor said, hoping to keep the stress level as low as possible, knowing tomorrow it would reach heights that neither he nor his partner had ever experienced.

"Sounds good," Alex agreed.

George ordered more drinks and general small talk diminished to silently relaxing in the hot sun, interrupted only by cooling dips in the pool. Connor was enjoying these luxuries now, like his companions seemed to be, not knowing when, if ever, they would be afforded any of them again. What lay ahead had him feeling both nervous and excited, while he contemplated the many potential outcomes in his mind.

~ ~ ~

Chapter 45

Around 7:30 p.m.—Connor, after a long shower and a couple of more pain pills, made his way down to the lobby to secure a ride to Love City for his clandestine rendezvous with Jade. Maggie had consumed his thoughts since going back to his room. He was feeling some trepidation, but at the same time he was putting on his game face, getting his mind right for what lay ahead. Unfortunately he was still in need of something to relieve the hurt and the countless visions he had of Maggie and another man. He tried to clear his head of it; it didn't make sense to be upset, but sense had little to do with love, he reasoned.

As he approached the desk clerk, he saw a familiar and daunting figure that was bound to upset his plans.

"Good evening, Mr. Mason," came the vexing voice.

"Hello, Colonel," he returned, looking into his cold, dark eyes.

"Going somewhere?"

"As a matter of fact, I was just about to hire a car for a meeting."

"Please let me take you."

"No, that won't be necessary."

"I insist—partner."

"What I mean, Colonel, is that I'm in no hurry," he returned, not wanting to subject Jade to this philistine if he decided to accompany him beyond the transportation he offered.

"If you're not in any hurry, we must have a drink and discuss our future together."

"Of course, Colonel. Lead the way," he surrendered.

For the next three and a-half-hours, Connor sat in the piano bar and drank Chevas Regal while he skillfully fielded the Colonel's inquiries regarding his business and their activities over the next week. Much of the conversation focused on the good life in America; a subject his guest seemed hopelessly obsessed with.

Around two hours in, he had given up on his meeting with Jade, another time and preferably another continent, he hoped. She was only a distraction and one he could definitely sacrifice, although her company would have been much preferred to that of his current and most unwanted companion.

An hour earlier he had caught Alex's eye, who after seeing who he was entertaining, made a beeline, he imagined, for another social venue, either with George or preferably Amy Menendez, who he told Connor he had taken an instant liking to upon seeing her working the front desk. No matter, he didn't see the need to subject anyone else to the ramblings and intimidation of this pint-size Machiavellian dictator. In a way it was good he was the only one with the Colonel, he could keep the damage control to a minimum by not having to worry what someone might let slip out under the influence of several scotches. The Colonel was already starting to show the debilitating effects of his consumption.

"I'm sorry your friends could not join us, Mr. Mason," the Colonel slurred out in a raspier voice than usual, thanks to the smoky liquid.

"I think they're just getting some rest tonight, Colonel," he lied.

"Well, it is getting late and I must get back to the compound," he returned. Losing his balance when he rose, he steadied himself on the table.

"Drive safely, Colonel," he said, hoping that maybe he'd drive off a cliff or worse.

"Mr. Mason, would you mind taking care of the bill. I'm a little short."

311

"Yes, you are Colonel," he returned, smiling at his innuendo.

"What am I, Mr. Mason?" the Colonel replied, sounding a little confused.

"You're leaving, Colonel and I'm paying the bill."

"Yes, thank you," he returned.

The Colonel staggered his way out of the bar and into the lobby, much to the relief of the staff who seemed to have been on pins and needles since his arrival. It was almost 11:30 p.m. when Connor decided to pack it in and head back to his room. The night was shot and the next day would be here before he knew it. He had drunk plenty, but was not as inebriated as his departed guest, not quite.

Entering his room, he noticed the flashing message light on the phone. It was from Alex who thanked him for not making him deal with the Colonel. He had met with George briefly and then spent the rest of the evening with Amy down by the pool. If he needed to talk he could call the room; otherwise he would see him in the morning.

Connor needed to talk, but his buddy wouldn't quite fit the bill. He wanted to talk to Maggie. He picked up the phone and dialed her number. The phone kept ringing with no answer, Maggie didn't believe in having a recorder or voice mail, she always said if you were supposed to talk to someone, they'd answer, not a machine.

He lay on his bed and tried to fall asleep, but it was no use. He couldn't get his mind off her and the possibility that she was with someone else. The drinking had just magnified those feelings, instead of dulling them like he had hoped. He called room service, ordering some cold San Miguels before heading out onto his balcony. There was a slight breeze, but with the air temperature still in the mid-eighties, it offered no relief to his heightened emotions. The fact that he couldn't reach Maggie made him think hard about what he was doing; if it was just the money, it suddenly didn't seem worth it.

He continued to dial her number for the next two hours, but with no success. He was not going to reach her tonight, his heart was aching and his head was starting to pound. He reached for a couple of pain pills and downed them with a swallow of cold beer. He felt like he was heading for a meltdown and couldn't seem to get hold of himself. He was feeling even more woozy from the pills and additional beers when he decided to take one shot at getting some relief, going into his toiletry bag, he took out a condom and put it in his pocket before heading down to the lobby.

The night clerk was sitting behind the front counter and music was still emanating from the piano bar, even though it looked like most of the patrons had either left for home or returned to their rooms.

"Excuse me," he directed at the clerk.

"Yes, sir. May I be of help?"

"Yes, I think you can. I need to know the room number of a young lady staying at the hotel."

"Yes, sir. Who would that be you are looking for?"

"I only know her first name, it's Jade. She is very tall, dark skin with a snake tattoo on her left leg. Do you know who I'm talking about?"

"Yes, I know her room, sir. I will dial it for you."

"No," he said stopping him. "I just need to know the number—I want to surprise her."

"I am sorry, sir. I can't do that."

"Why not?"

"We are not allowed to give the room numbers of guests."

"Maybe this will help," he said, reaching into his pocket and pulling out an American twenty-dollar bill.

"I'm sorry, sir. I would lose my job. I cannot tell you, but I will ring the room.

"No, that's all right," he said, desperately trying to think of something. "I don't suppose more money would help my cause."

"No sir," he returned unwavering.

Connor thought for a second before deciding to play his trump card, as distasteful as it was to him.

"What's your name?" he asked.

313

"Jacinto, sir."

"Jacinto, do you know Colonel Vadula?"

"Yes, I do, sir." He was suddenly sounding very nervous.

"Colonel Vadula is my partner and I don't think he will be happy when I tell him you didn't help me."

Please don't tell the Colonel sir, please," he pleaded, looking very upset. "Her room number is 412."

"It's okay, I won't tell him," Connor reassured, feeling guilty in spite of his pill and alcohol induced condition.

"Thank you, sir. Thank you."

"No problem, don't worry," he said, leaving the twenty on the counter. "Take this for your trouble, no one will find out I promise, okay?"

"Yes, sir."

Connor got on the elevator and headed up to Jade's room. He wasn't sure she would be there, but given his state of mind it was worth a shot. He walked down to the end of the hallway and knocked softly on her door; half-hoping she wasn't there or wouldn't hear his summons. There was no answer; he turned and started to leave when the sound of the door unlocking stopped him.

"Hello," said a soft voice from behind the slightly cracked barrier.

"Hi," he returned.

"Can I help you?"

"I don't know, but I'm here to find out. Can I come in?"

"I don't know, you stood me up tonight."

"I'm sorry, something unexpected came up."

"Then you're here now because something else came up?"

"Something like that," he grinned.

"Come in," she offered opening the door. She was wearing nothing but tiny black panties and a smile.

"You look great," he said, admiring her beautiful, mostly naked body.

"Thank you," she returned, taking his hand and leading him to the bed. "How did you get my room number?"

314

"I bribed the night clerk," he returned, deciding not to get specific about his methods.

"I see," she said, sitting him on the bed in front of her.

"Look, I want you to. . . ."

"No more talking," she interrupted. "You didn't come to my room to talk."

"Yes, but I. . . ."

"Shhhhhh," she scolded, placing a long finger to her lips.

He stopped talking while she walked over and turned off the light, leaving only the glow of the full moon shining through the open balcony door to illuminate the room, giving it a shadowy and tropical feel. The breeze had picked up, but the air conditioning was off and the room was fifteen degrees hotter than the rest of the hotel. He felt engulfed by a warm sensation, a combination of pills, alcohol and desire as he watched her kneel in front of him and unbutton his shirt. She removed his shirt, shoes, pants and underwear leaving him sitting naked on the edge of the bed. She stood in front of him and slowly removed her one scant item of clothing. She was magnificent he thought, her six-foot frame highlighted by the sparse light coming in from outside.

She stepped forward; settling next to him as her full warm lips met his neck he fell softly back while she wrapped her arms around him. She kissed his neck, chest and stomach while her hands moved up his leg and gently stroked his already excited genitals. She slid up his body and took hold of him, about to let him enter when he stopped her and gently rolled her off.

Fumbling at the bedside for his pants, he removed the condom from his pocket. Rolling back over towards her, she took it and guided him to his back. She unwrapped the plastic protection and placing it in her mouth, she leaned down and covered his erection, causing him to arch his back in anticipation. Making her way back up his body, she straddled him and reaching down guided him inside her. As she rocked back and forth, he could feel the sweat running down her body when he stroked her breasts. She leaned over, biting his neck

315

and ears as she increased her pace. He was feeling like he would pass out from the heat and alcohol as she continued to make love to him, each time he was about to climax, she would stop till he regained his composure and then start again.

For the next hour, he was lost in her spell, she was in complete control and he knew it. She was a very skilled pleasure giver, almost too skilled. But in his altered mental state nothing mattered; he was all too happy to be the receiver of her expertise. Finally she allowed him to complete the act as his entire body convulsed. He felt completely exhausted. She collapsed on top of him letting his final release, in concert with the mood altering substances he'd ingested, rob him of his consciousness.

~ ~ ~

Chapter 46

The next morning—Connor awoke to a hammer in his head and a reaggravated rib cage, thanks to his early morning bedroom gymnastics. While he fought to clear his brain and move his aching body to an upright position, it dawned on him that this was not his room. Looking around the site of his sexual escapade, it became rapidly apparent that he was alone, not only that, but the room had been cleansed of any trace of his partner's previous habitation. He got up and searched the drawers, closet and bathroom, finding nothing. The only thing left was him, and just barely. After getting dressed, he headed back to his room, wondering what happened to Jade and why she left so abruptly.

Alex was sitting in the hallway as he approached. A relieved look crossed his face when he saw his friend. "Man you had me worried," he said.

"How come?"

"The last time I saw you was with the Colonel at the bar, and you said before, you were headed into town to meet that babe, so when you weren't in your room this morning, I didn't know what happened. So what happened?"

"You don't want to know."

"Yeah, I do. So tell me."

"I hooked up with the woman from the pool last night."

"The one with the tattoo?"

"Yeah, did you forget already?"

"No, I just have a hard time keeping all your women straight."

"That's very funny."

"So go on. Did you do the nasty?"

"Yeah, it was wild."

"I hate you."

"Why? Weren't you with Amy last night?"

"Yeah, we talked at the pool and I ended up with a kiss goodnight. You on the other hand take a tumble with probably the best looking woman on the continent."

"I think we are all given the tasks we can handle," Connor returned grinning.

"You're an asshole, you know that."

"Yes, but I'm an asshole who got laid last night."

"True, but an asshole none the less."

"If it makes you feel better."

"So are you going to see her again?"

"I don't know."

"You know, I mean after this is over, are you going to contact her?"

"No, I mean I don't know period. She was gone when I woke up this morning."

"Maybe she just went to breakfast or confession."

"Funny. No, she was gone, her and all her things. It was like she was never there."

"That's weird," Alex added.

"Tell me about it. We can't worry about that now. What time is George picking us up?"

"He said around eleven. You got an hour and a half or so."

"Alright. I'm going to take a shower, grab a couple of things I don't want to leave behind and I'll meet you in the lobby."

"You got it, brother. This is really it, isn't it?"

"We're headed down the rabbit hole, Alice. This is the real deal now. You ready?"

"Ready."

"Good, I'll meet you downstairs."

Connor went into his room and took a couple of Tylenol for his headache and three pain pills to take the edge off his damaged ribs. Looking at the bottle, he only had nine pills left and he prayed by the time they ran out, he'd feel better. If not, it was going to be a long trip.

Savoring the hot shower made him realize he was about to abandon the creature comforts that the hotel offered. It had buffered the reality of what life was really like here, he thought, a hectic struggle for survival. In a few hours, he and Alex would be hurled into the middle of that unfamiliar phenomenon. No time for second thoughts, it was coming and there was no stopping it; not that he would have even if he could.

~ ~ ~

Chapter 47

George pulled his rust eaten Toyota up to the front of the hotel as Connor and Alex got in. Connor had inquired at the front desk about Jade's mysterious disappearance and was told that she checked out early this morning, leaving no forwarding information. He decided he'd give some time to finding her when this was over. He liked her and held out for the possibility of getting to know her, even though the odds were long that it would ever happen. For now there was gold in his future and that and that alone was his first priority. The night with Jade had sharpened his focus, he would get done what he needed to and then deal with the Susan's, Jade's and Maggie's in his life. Until then, he knew he could not afford them any of his concentration.

"Did you get the shirts, George?" Connor asked.

"Got them right here, six dozen bright yellow. I also got the pesos," he returned, pointing to two large paper bags.

"God, that's a lot of bills," Alex observed.

"At a twenty-five to one exchange rate, you can get a lot of worthless paper," George replied.

"That's fine, lots is what we need," Connor added. "You got the maps too?"

"One for each of us with the routes marked," he returned, sounding proud of himself for taking care of things."

"Perfect. Everybody knows the plan, if you can't shake the soldiers, head back to the hotel and we'll regroup."

"We won't have much time if it doesn't work," Alex contributed.

"I know, but we can't risk not getting away clean."

They all agreed. Connor reinforced that time was running out to get the sample to Billy Hilliard. This would probably be their only shot to get away, after this attempt the Colonel would be even more on guard.

As they drove into town, the place was alive with open-air markets, brightly adorned makeshift vehicles and legions of people hustling in the streets. The arena housing the cockfighting tournament was a large round wooden structure that according to George held eight to nine thousand spectators. The outside was covered in colorful banners that helped to disguise the fact that the building was badly in need of repair. At least a thousand patrons were lined up outside either trying to gain entrance, talking with friends or dealing with street vendors. Connor noticed that the surrounding area was largely poor residential and industrial, evidenced by the many abandoned structures and lack of street traffic, other than in the direct vicinity of the arena.

A steady line of jeepneys, the brightly decorated open air taxis, were picking up and dropping off passengers when George pulled into the large parking lot. He parked near an exit as planned, so Lido would have no trouble getting out in order to complete their rendezvous. They exited while Connor watched George hide the key under the front seat mat. Connor took the money and shirts as George led them through the crowd to a separate entrance reserved for foreigners, the few wealthy Filipinos and local dignitaries. They paid the fifty pesos entry fee, roughly two bucks, and were taken to chairs directly in front of the glass combatant's enclosure. Once they were seated, a man named Pio approached them and offered to handle their bets. After enlisting his assistance, Connor scanned the rapidly filling arena for the soldiers he knew would be following. They were easy to spot, having positioned themselves among the crowd directly on either side of them. Opening the bag he was carrying, Connor took out three of the bright yellow t-shirts.

"Here, put these on," he said, handing the shirts to Alex and George.

"You got to be kidding. We stand out enough as it is without these. They'll be able to spot us a mile away," Alex stated.

"Precisely, now just shut up and put them on."

"You better have a good reason for this."

"Trust me."

"You know I hate people who say trust me."

"That's why I said it, for your benefit."

"No jokes, Con. Not now."

"I have to Alex, it's the only thing that keeps me from messing in my pants whenever I think about what were doing here."

"This is kind of fucked up isn't it?"

Before he could answer, the screaming crowd interrupted him, as two Filipino handlers brought their cocks into the ring area. A third man in the glass circle, who George had explained, acted as a referee in order to ensure the animals suffer no more undue inhumanity than necessary. The birds were paraded for the hoards of spectators as the noise built to a fever pitch. Connor observed that the bettors, surrounding the hundred or so privileged observers seated inside the barbwire barriers, were busy laying off wagers to people in the crowd. The cocks were stroked and kissed by their keepers while they were intermittently thrust at each other in order to increase their rage. Alex handed Pio five hundred pesos to bet on the jet-black bird and he went to work, making the wager and securing odds for his American clients.

After ten minutes of betting and the accompanying posturing by the handlers, Connor watched while the razor spurs were attached to one leg of each of the cocks. This was a fight to the death; the sharp spurs were four inches long, enabling the combatant to deliver a lethal blow within seconds of the battle beginning. Connor was engrossed; it was a cruel, bloody sport that he knew was outlawed in most civilized nations, but a national obsession in this third world. The birds were bread for battle, it was their nature, they would engage in this behavior regardless of the entertainment value this inhuman sport fostered. Connor couldn't help but feel a strange kinship towards them, but he didn't feel sorry, they were just doing what they were meant to, not many of us could say that he thought, as the fight began.

The handlers took their birds to the center of the ring as the noise rose to heights that Connor didn't think possible. He looked over at George, who appeared caught up in this wild frenzy despite having experienced it before. Just when he thought it couldn't get any louder, the birds were released, treating the action thirsty patrons to an explosion of blood and feathers. The cocks attacked each other feet first as the razor spur on the black fighting bird pierced the torso of its game opponent, sending fourth a gusher of blood and killing it instantly. The crowd applauded. No one seemed disappointed by the limited duration of the match; there would be more to come Connor imagined, many longer and more gruesome to satisfy the paying spectator's lust for death.

As the commotion of the first encounter ended and the noise level decreased, Connor watched while the handler of the dead bird gingerly lifted his fallen hero from the sandy pit. He caressed him much like one would a child, before discarding his lifeless body into a bin, the first of many corpses that would end up in someone's pot at the end of the day he figured. In a country this poor, the transition from loved fighting pet to food was a way of life.

According to George, the handler had most likely raised and trained the cock for at least two years; he could see there was a definite emotional connection between the trainer and his champion that defied the logic of subjecting it to this violent ending. But the reasons for why things were done in different cultures could make all the difference between success and failure, a lesson that Connor was hopeful of learning in order to avoid a fate similar to the fighting birds he was viewing.

Prior to the next match, Pio retrieved Alex's money. He looked excited. Custom dictated a winning client meant a generous fee; Connor knew he had no idea how much good fortune he was really in store for. The spectacle continued to repeat itself throughout the afternoon. Connor kept tabs on the

Colonel's men as he figured the bright yellow shirts must have given the soldiers a relaxed sense of security. They definitely stood out among the more subdued garb of the other spectators.

~ ~ ~

While the soldiers watched their quarry and the quarry watched the soldiers, Andy Wai was sure that neither was aware that he watched them both. Dressed in jeans, a red and green plaid shirt, work boots and a tattered baseball hat, he blended perfectly with the working class crowd behind the barbwire barrier. His eyes were hidden by the same pair of cheap sunglasses he used to augment his disguise after eliminating the Colonel's henchmen at his hotel. He was very close to finishing his work, he thought as he made his way toward one of the exits in order to avoid being detained by the soon to be exiting crowd. All that remained now was for his prey to be revealed in a vulnerable area so he could complete his assignment and then return to the shadows, until a time his highly paid services would again be required.

~ ~ ~

Upon being informed that the next contest would be the last, Connor got up and approached Pio, asking for a special favor and punctuating his request with an American hundred-dollar bill. His puzzled look turned quickly to a smile, as he accepted the money and the bags he was handed. Enlisting the help of one of his associates, he quickly dispersed the brightly colored shirts among the people near the center ring, encouraging them to put on the gift from the generous Americans.

By the time the last fighting cocks were displayed, almost seventy people had donned the same yellow shirts as the Americans, rendering them practically invisible. They had taken the opportunity to separate and change seats during the commotion, blending in with the brightly garbed constituency near the glass pit. When the contest began, Connor noticed the men assigned to them were in somewhat of a panic as they tried to make their way through the wildly cheering crowd. Having seen this, he caught Pio's eye and gave him a nod. Simultaneously upon receiving the signal, the last fight came to a merciful end just as Pio reached into the paper bag and pulled out a large handful of pesos. The bleacher crowd had just begun it's decent when he launched the cash in the direction of the slowly exiting patrons. Once they realized it was money being thrown like confetti, a mad scramble ensued, blocking all egresses with a mass of rabid humanity. He continued to strategically disperse the bills per Connor's instruction throughout the arena, effectively blocking their pursuers.

Connor, Alex and George used the human pile up to effect their escape. As Alex and George made their way through the handler's entrance, Connor watched them shed the yellow shirts, leaving them on the floor. They were to split up and follow the preplanned routes laid out on the maps to the rendezvous with Lido.

Connor discarded his shirt on the dirty bathroom floor and after popping out a flimsy wooden screen held in place by two rusty nails, he exited through the window. He took out his map and walking briskly headed for his first left turn on Victoria. The street was long and lined with empty warehouses. He looked back over his shoulder, as he thought for a second that he noticed someone on one of the parallel streets. He broke into a jog heading for his next right on Ruiz Avenue, quickly dismissing his misgivings, seeing no one unusual when he turned and headed for Ortigas.

His heart was pumping. Only two streets to go he thought, and he would have successfully eluded the Colonel's men. He could feel the sweat running down his back as the temperature was well into the nineties. He hadn't noticed the heat in the arena because he wasn't moving around and the days in country had helped him become more acclimated. But the stress, combined with the exertion, was beginning to take its toll as his ribs began to ache and he felt his breathing becoming labored.

Suddenly, a small dark sedan coming straight for him took his focus. It stopped a block or so up ahead and the slender figure of a woman got out of the driver's side. As she walked toward him she began to look very familiar. Her tall, lean physique gave away her identity, even before he was close enough make out her face, it was Jade. She broke into a wide inviting smile as he closed the distance.

He was surprised, but happy to see her despite the situation, although he wondered why she left the hotel without telling him and what brought her to this desolate section of the city. Had she been at the fights? Was it a coincidence or did her business have something to do with it? All of these explanations were firing through his head along with his desire to get to the pickup spot, cluttering his senses. So much so, he neglected to give a second thought to the man in a tattered baseball hat and cheap dark glasses standing partially exposed in the doorway of a building on the cross street he had just past.

~ ~ ~

Stepping out from shadows sheltering his presence, Andy Wai had hidden behind his back his current choice for destruction, a custom nine millimeter with a silencer. He was within point blank range when without any hesitation he raised his weapon and fired—the bullet making a muffled sound while it traveled through the dense air before striking its target.

~ ~ ~

Chapter 48

The bullet found its mark, instantly separating the target from its most precious possession—life. Connor slumped to the ground, sure that his was about to end. He sat frozen with fear while the woman in front of him lay dead, a bullet to the forehead erasing her beautiful smile forever. In the seconds he had left, he wanted to lash out and avenge this senseless act. Who were they anyway to deserve this type of ending? —terminated at the hands of a paid killer. It wasn't fair, it was a crime against reason; his life would end to protect the unearthing of a shiny yellow metal; it defied all rational logic.

The reality of his helplessness made accepting death all the more intolerable when he turned to face his killer and prepared to meet the same fate as Jade. Had he never pursued her she may not have been involved in this needless and tragic event. He watched, listening to his own shallow breathing, while the assassin moved quickly toward him, his weapon dangling from his left hand. His eyes never left the lifeless body of his target, as he reached down and grabbed Connor by the elbow, pulling him to his feet.

"You must go, hurry," he said, releasing his arm.

Connor stood stunned, his legs felt like they were cast in cement. He had his chance to attack, but in his confused state he couldn't bring himself to move.

"Who are you?" he managed to blurt out.

"My name is Andy Wai, a friend."

"Why did you kill her?" he questioned franticly.

"Come here and look," he returned, walking quickly over to his victim on the pavement in front of them.

Connor followed him to Jade's fallen body. It was painful to look at the women who last night was so full of life. He watched while the assassin rolled her over, revealing a sight that gave him a chill, despite the stifling heat and humidity. A hypodermic needle was on the ground hidden by her torso. It was obviously in her hand, concealed behind her as she approached him.

"What's going on? Please tell me," he pleaded.

"She is assassin, sent here to kill you, she had poison, make it look like you had heart attack," he returned, while he scanned the street.

"By who?" he asked, knowing in his heart, it was Morgan Gold.

"Someone with a lot of money. She is very expensive."

"Why did you help me? How do you even know me?"

"Billy Hilliard sent me to watch out for you."

"Billy."

"Yes. You must leave now," he insisted.

"Wait, I was in her room last night, why didn't she just kill me then," he asked, trying desperately to make some sense of this unfathomable event.

"She is professional. Wanted no witnesses. Someone must know you go to her room."

"The night clerk."

"Yes, maybe save your life."

"Jesus Christ, Jesus Christ," he lamented, the reality of the event crashing in on him. "I slept with that women last night."

"Congratulation, you last one."

"That doesn't make me feel better," he said, his exasperation mounting.

"Sorry, you go now—NOW!" he yelled. "I make sure no one follows, go."

Connor took off running, not thinking about the heat, his ribs, Jade or anything else. His mind was blank with fear as the adrenaline of this terrifying event was fueling his body.

All he wanted was to get to the pick up point and get out of the city—and maybe the country.

As he rounded the last corner his feet were flying when he saw George's car at the corner in front of him. Alex and George were already in the vehicle with a Filipino behind the wheel; he deduced as being Lido. Alex, seeing him approach, was leaning out of the window waving. He opened the door allowing him to dive inside. Lido took off and they headed out of town in the direction of the mine.

"What kept you, Hoss? We were just about to head to the second pickup spot," Alex said, sounding relived.

"Just took a little longer to get out than I expected," he panted, trying to catch his breath.

He decided that no one needed to know what happened, figuring it would only be upsetting and disrupt their focus. The assassin had struck without remorse or hesitation. Anything less would have been a liability that could not be afforded in the profession, and there was no mistaking Andy Wai as anything but professional. Complete the assignment in an expedient manner, with as little suffering as possible to the victim. While it was a distasteful experience at best, in it's truest expression, quick, accurate and deadly, he could not help but be in awe of his savior. He decided he'd tell the story when they met up with Billy Hilliard. He'd have to then; he'd need to thank him for saving his life, he thought, as Alex's voice brought him back to reality.

"The shirt thing was a stroke of genius, Con. Not to mention the flying cash routine our man performed."

"Yeah, it did work out pretty well."

"Like a charm," George added. "I can't imagine the pile up the money caused. I bet the soldiers are still trying to get out."

"I doubt that," Connor concluded. "But at least they're not following us."

"Excuse my manners," George said.

"You mean your lack of them," Alex chimed in.

"Yeah, something like that. Anyway Connor, this is Lido. Lido this is Connor, Guy's boy."

"Good to meet you, Sir Connor," Lido offered.

"It's good to finally meet you, Lido."

"I am truly sorry about Sir Guy. He was a good friend. I wish he was with us."

"Thanks, Lido. I wish he was too."

"Man, I bet the Colonel will be mad as hell when he finds out we slipped his guards," Alex said, obviously trying to change the topic from Connor's father.

"He will be, when he finally finds out," George added.

"What do you mean when he finally finds out?"

"We are fortunate that the little bastard is as scary as he is. None of his men will be in a real hurry to tell him they failed."

"How does that help us now?"

"Tomorrow, we have to get to the boat and there is only one way down the mountain. If the Colonel doesn't know we're missing, he won't alert any checkpoints that may be set up."

"And if he does find out?" Connor asked.

"We'll have a little problem. We'd have to hike out through the jungle."

"Are you fucking kidding me?" Alex said, looking displeased.

"Don't worry, we should have plenty of time."

"I sure as hell hope so."

Finally leaving the city limits, Connor breathed a sigh of relief when they reached the mountain road leading towards the town of Malaybalay and the mine. George had said it was a two and half-hour ride to the town and another hour to cover the three miles of jungle road to reach the base of the mine.

The trip had been rather uneventful. George's wreck of a car had labored up the step road until they reached the first plateau where the terrain mercifully leveled out. The hills were a luscious green as from his vantage Connor could see the rich rolling landscape, highlighted by lush valleys and jungle covered peaks. It had a regal feel to him, in stark contrast to the bleak appearance of the poverty ridden, dank city below.

They had passed several remote villages, evident by the grass roofs and pine board walls of the small flimsy dwellings, made more conspicuous by the lack of any noticeable civilized infrastructure. Despite missing those luxuries, it still had a more peaceful feel than anywhere else in the country he'd seen so far.

Reaching the one street town of Malaybalay, Lido turned off on a dirt road a little over halfway into the quiet village. He followed the road till it ended at the edge of the jungle, where they parked the car, out of the way, near some large mahogany trees. Removing the weapons Alex had chosen, along with his two duffle bags and gray briefcase, they covered the vehicle with a thread bare, leaf-green tarp, completing the camouflage. They then followed Lido down a small embankment through some trees about a hundred feet until the undeterminable trail widened into a crude jungle road. Sitting off to one side, covered with brush was a beat up jeep, looking in worse condition than George's car. They loaded themselves and the equipment into the dilapidated vehicle and proceeded on the bumpy journey toward the mine.

Connor was feeling nauseous from the humidity and the bouncing he had endured for the last hour. His improving rib cage was relapsing into pain as he used the muscles in his still vulnerable torso to steady himself during the ride. He was relieved when their excursion came to a halt at what appeared to be the mine site.

Where the jungle road ended was a clearing with several large canvas tents and one long bamboo table under a tarp, sheltering it from sun or rain. Connor, scanning to his right, saw two cave entrances cut into the mountainside, around a hundred feet apart. Hanging above the nearest opening was a sign that read Bukidnon Mines, Ltd. About a dozen Filipino men that were mulling around the area, in and out of the tents and the mines, came out to view the new visitors. Lido had told them that they were all residents of the surrounding villages. They appeared in various stages of dress, some with shirts, some without, some in short pants, some long, and most with either bandanas or baseball caps. The clothing they wore had one common theme, Connor observed; it highlighted the poverty they lived in, as their work attire was tattered and well worn. Several of the men had no footwear to speak of and those that did were either missing laces or grossly miss-sized. They had the look of a rag tag lot to say the least, but every sun-baked face was wearing a large smile when they greeted Connor and his companions.

After the obligatory introductions, Lido hustled the men back to their tasks. Connor was anxious to get to the job of securing the sample and seeing what a cave full of gold looked like.

"Well this should be easy. Which one of the caves has the gold in it, George?" Alex asked, sounding excited and eager.

"It's not in any of them," George returned.

"What are you talking about?"

"These are decoys, in case the wrong people come snooping around."

"Where's our mine?" Connor asked.

"About a mile in that direction, up on top of the hill over there," he said, pointing to a mountaintop in the distance.

"How do we get there?"

"Do you really have to ask, Alex?" George returned, shaking his head and smiling.

"No, I guess I don't."

"We need to hurry though, it's going to be dark soon."

"We won't have any light to get back," Connor contributed.

"We're not coming back till tomorrow morning," George returned, heading toward one of the tents. "By the way, are you boys wearing boxers or briefs?" he yelled back.

"Who cares?" Alex responded. Sounding a little perplexed by the need to furnish that information.

"You will in a few hours, so what is it?"

"Boxers," Connor called out laughing. "Don't be bashful, Alex. Tell him what you're wearing."

"Briefs," Alex surrendered, making a face at Connor.

"Lose them," George said, returning from the tent with a backpack.

"Fuck you, George. What are you, a pervert underwear collector? Take Connor's boxers and put those on your head instead."

"Seriously, Alex. You've got to take them off. If you wear them walking in the jungle, the seams are going to rub you raw once they get wet with sweat and you're going to have the worst case of jungle crotch rot you can imagine. That, my friend will not heal without a prescription steroid ointment."

"Don't bullshit me, George. You're making that shit up. Do you believe him, Con?"

"I don't know, Alex. But given the choice of taking off my underwear or potentially getting Philippine crotch rot, I think you know what I'd choose."

"Fine," he said in a condescending tone, unfastening his shorts to remove the briefs.

Connor couldn't help laughing while Alex peeled off his undergarments. He wasn't sure if George was telling the truth or just busting his chops for giving him a hard time in Cebu, but he had a feeling that he was serious about the potential affliction. George organized Lido and a couple of men to haul Alex's equipment up to the mine as they began the journey on a single person path through the jungle.

The light was just beginning to fade when they made their way up the final incline to the mountaintop. It took them a little over an hour to reach the two grass huts that marked the mine site. Connor was feeling the effects of the day's activity, including his earlier brush with death. He was down to his last six pain pills as he took three of them with a mouthful of water. The men they used as porters deposited the equipment and were given a flashlight and sent back. There was no opening anywhere and Alex was looking concerned.

"Alright, George, where's the gold?" he asked impatiently.

"You're standing on it," George replied.

"What do you mean, I'm standing on it?"

"It's about four hundred feet or so below you."

"That's great, how do we get to it? You got a shovel?"

"We already did the digging; follow me," he returned, walking into the grass hut closest to them.

George and Lido removed a large piece of plywood flooring from the middle of the hut revealing a large, well-like, hole whose opening was around four feet across. There was a narrow bamboo ladder visible about a foot down, other than that it was pitch black, except for two colored wires coming up from the darkness and coiled neatly near what looked like a large battery. Alex gasped out loud as Connor viewed the opening, somewhat in awe of its existence.

"How deep is it?" Alex asked, sounding nervous, now that the prospect of having to go down there was apparent.

"It's almost four hundred feet as best as I can tell," George answered.

"Is it that wide all the way down?"

"Lido tells me it's narrower in spots where the rock was too hard to carve through."

"Is that ladder four-hundred feet long?" Alex inquired.

"Hell, no. There's a bunch of ladders, all twenty to twenty-five feet in length. When they dig they allow for ledges to secure the ladders. We've made around twenty of them, so that's how we estimated the depth."

"So this is what Billy meant by a Filipino mine?" Connor concluded.

"This is what he meant. A lot of the mines are dug straight down because you don't need to reinforce the walls and ceiling, it's a lot cheaper and faster. The men work on top of each other like ants handing baskets of ruble up the ladders. Sometimes during the monsoon season you'll hear about a mine like this collapsing and killing up to a thousand miners, it's gruesome, but effective when you're pressed for cash and time."

"It's like a big dark smokestack."

"That's exactly right, Alex. That's why they call it a chimney mine."

"Now I know why Connor's Dad suggested some of the equipment he did."

"What kind of equipment?" Connor asked, having not paid much attention to the list after handing off its procurement.

"Ropes, harnesses, carabineers, headlamps, two-way radios, stuff like that."

"Looks like it was a good call."

"Yeah, from the looks of this we'll need it all."

"You been down there?" Connor asked.

"Nope," George responded.

"Are you going down?"

"Nope."

"Don't you want to see it for yourself?"

"Not bad enough to go down there. I made sure it got dug, your Dad was the one to check it out, you're taking his spot, so now it's up to you."

"Fine," he returned, not feeling all that anxious to head down the shaft, after seeing it up close.

"See what I meant when I said no one would go down there unless they had to."

"I do now," Alex replied. "What do you think, Con?"

"I think one of us has to go and get the sample. You want to go?"

"Honestly?"

"Of course, honestly."

"I can't, Con. I'm sorry, but it's too claustrophobic for me. I'd freak out, I know it."

"Okay, I'll do it," Connor volunteered, as confidently as anyone he imagined, agreeing to descend into a deep, black, unknown abyss would.

"You all right for this?" Alex asked, obviously concerned about his friend's physical condition.

"I'll be fine, Alex. Besides this is one of the reasons I came, I wanted to see what my Dad saw, first hand."

"In the morning, then," George said. "We'll get some rest and go for the sample at first light."

"Sounds good to me," Connor returned, knowing he'd need to rest before attacking this undertaking.

The four of them settled into hammocks strung up in

335

the two grass roofed huts. There was some makeshift netting they used to keep the various jungle bugs off of them during the night. It really wasn't the insects that Connor was concerned about, but poisonous snakes that liked to curl up next to a warm body.

He also was dealing with a different dilemma; the sight of Jade, lying dead, kept running through his head. He felt bad about her death, even though she'd been sent to kill him. It didn't make sense. Why should he feel anything? She was good at what she did, everything she did. She had him manipulated to a point he would have trusted her with his life and she'd almost succeeded in taking it.

That event was bothering him so much that he wanted to talk about what happened. Maybe Alex could help sort it out, but this was not the time and he knew it. Nothing about this place was as it seemed and that made him extremely uncomfortable. Wes Adam's warning played over and over in his mind, "*wherever there's greed, there can be no justice, trust no one*"—not even one of his father's best friends, he thought. He was determined not to make that mistake again; he wanted to make sure he'd be around to confront Mr. Adams.

~ ~ ~

Chapter 49

The smell of coffee brewing allowed Connor to momentarily forget where he was, as he opened his eyes and struggled to get out of his cocoon-like hammock. Once his mind settled he had fallen into a deep sleep, not sure if his peaceful rest was a product of the soundless accommodations or his sheer exhaustion. No matter, he felt surprisingly renewed, despite the contortionist position his suspended bed required. As he stepped out of the hut he saw Alex was already up, drinking Lido's coffee with George, while he sorted out the equipment for his foray into the chimney mine.

"Good morning," Connor directed at the group surrounding Lido's makeshift jungle kitchen.

"Hey, Con. How'd you sleep?" Alex asked, while all present acknowledged his greeting.

"Not bad, considering I felt like a caught tuna."

"Yeah, not quite the Pryce Plaza, is it?" George added.

"Not quite. We got anything to eat?"

"How about some dehydrated scramble eggs?" Alex asked, pulling a silver pouch from one of his bags.

"Is that what you're eating?"

"Yeah, why?"

"How come they're orange?"

"How the fuck should I know, they taste fine and this ain't the Ritz, big guy."

"Fine, I'll have the orange eggs and any green ham, if you got it."

"Coming right up."

For the next thirty minutes Connor joined George and Alex as they ate the dehydrated offerings, while Lido had a traditional fish and rice breakfast. They discussed the plan for getting him into the treasure cave, while Alex prepared ropes, harnesses, headlamps and communication equipment. The idea was for him to get in, get the gold bar and get out as quickly as possible. They needed to make their way to the port and on the charter before the Colonel's men worked up the courage to inform him they lost their charges. Connor knew time was a precious commodity they were always trying to conserve.

Lido and George went into the hut to remove the plywood flooring. Alex helped Connor get on the necessary gear to begin his descent. The heat was already climbing along with the humidity when Connor made his way into the hut and prepared to enter the dark shaft.

"Alex, what is this thing?" he asked, pointing to a silver gear-like piece of equipment on the rope attached to his harness.

"That's a decelerator. Squeeze this cam here and you go down, stop and you stop. You can go as fast or as slow as you like depending on the pressure you apply."

"Good to know. But why don't I just use the ladders?"

"You want to trust'em, be my guest."

"No, that's okay," he returned, having had inspected the fraying vines holding the bamboo structures together.

"Alright, you've got the ear piece hooked to the two-way so we can talk, headlamp and extra flashlight, digital camera. Looks like we're good to go."

"One thing, George, what are these wires coming out of the mine for?"

"Try and stay away from that side of the mine, Connor."

"And why would that be?"

"Cause we've got it wired with explosives."

Connor paused, as he gave him a look of disbelief. "When were you going to share this little gem, Mr. Fall? Before or after I blew myself up?"

"I was going to tell you. I just didn't want to spook you

338

before you were ready to go. It's scary enough just to go down there without thinking it could blow. Don't worry, just don't bang into the dynamite, it gets a little unstable in the heat."

"What do you mean a little unstable?"

"You'll be fine, just be careful around the charges."

"Anything else I should know, George?"

"When you get to the bottom, you'll find some tools on a ledge near you. You'll need them to make the opening big enough to get into the cave. Once Lido's men started breaking through we made them stop before they broke into the chamber. It should be easy to bust through seeing how you're entering though the ceiling."

"That it?"

"All I can think of right now, good luck."

"Thanks."

"Be careful, Sir Connor. You will do well I know this."

"Thanks, Lido. See you guy's shortly."

Connor began to lower himself into the darkness. The light from his headlamp revealed the slow painstaking effort that went into chiseling through hundreds of feet of dirt and rock; it was a monumental task to say the least. He was glad to have the manmade ladders within his reach. They gave him the added security of being able to have another way down or up, along with the proof that others had ventured into this dark subterranean world and emerged intact. It felt hot and steamy, like he was being lowered into a furnace. He could feel the sweat forming on his neck while the dust that hung, suspended in the shaft attached to his moist skin. His stomach was a little queasy as he struggled to get air into his lungs, the lack of any natural ventilation more evident the deeper he descended.

At around two hundred-feet, he spotted the dynamite that had been set into the wall as he followed the wires up toward the dimming light at the surface. His ribs felt about the best they had since he left, but he was sure that would be short-lived. The chimney seemed to narrow the deeper he went, giving him a bad claustrophobic feeling; in some spots it was so tight that he was just barely able to squeeze through. Just when he was beginning to doubt his effort, a reassuring voice came over his earpiece.

"Hey, bud. How you doing down there?" Alex asked.

"Not bad, considering I'm hot, sweaty and can barely catch my breath. How the hell do people work in conditions like these?"

"Don't know, bud. But from up here it looks like you're doing just fine."

"Can you guys still see me?"

"No, that's why from here you're looking good."

"Thanks a bunch," he answered, appreciating the humor more than he let on.

"How's the decelerator working?"

"The gizmo?"

"Yeah, the gizmo you ass."

"Works like a charm, is it going to pull me outta here too."

"Not quite. We figured you could use the ladders and just keep pulling up the slack in case they can't hold your weight."

"If they can't hold my weight you're going to have to pull me up."

"We got enough workers, we can do that if we have to."

"Get them ready," he returned, looking down as he eyed the bottom of the mineshaft. "Look I gotta stop talking for a minute, I'm near the bottom."

"Anything else we can do?"

"Send down an elevator?"

"I'll work on it. Over."

Settling on a ledge that served as the foundation for the final ladder, he was about four-feet above the small opening that would supposedly lead him into the treasure chamber. Nestled against the wall was a pick and long pointed metal bar. The shaft was wide enough near the bottom that he felt he would not have a problem swinging the pick if he had too.

Resting on the ledge, he gathered himself, trying to slow his breathing and fight off the panic he was beginning to feel as a result of his extremely constricted environment. He was struggling to remain composed as he grabbed the metal bar and positioned himself over the opening with his legs spread, pushing against the sidewalls for balance while he attacked the partially exposed entrance. A couple of hard pokes and the light from his headlamp revealed the rock dropping into the chamber. His hands were slippery with dirty perspiration, a product of the heat and dust, as he managed one final thrust, breaking through, causing what rock remained and the bar to give way into the manmade cavern below.

"Connor, what's going on down there?" Alex's voice reverberated in his ear, startling him momentarily.

"Why don't you come down and see for yourself," he returned, trying to slow his racing heartbeat.

"You're a funny guy. No really, are you in yet?"

"I just broke through. It looks like the cave's not very high, unless there's something blocking my view," he returned, flashing his light into the opening. "It looks like something metal about six feet below me."

"George says it's probably a truck. Your Dad told him that there's a bunch of them in there."

"It could be. I guess they dug the shaft right over the top of it. I'm going in, I'll be back to you in a minute."

"Okay, but don't keep us hanging."

"I'm the one who's hanging here," he returned, dangling on the end of his four hundred foot lifeline.

"Good point. Over."

Connor lowered himself into the dark cavern. Despite having no natural light it was a welcome liberation from his recent tight quarters. Landing on a flexible metal surface, he quickly realized that he was on the hood of a vehicle. Trying to gain some sense of perspective, he removed a larger flashlight he had attached to his belt and began panning the area. There were several trucks in front of and behind him; some of those to the rear were partially buried in what looked like a previous cave in. He unhooked his harness and made his way carefully toward the far sidewall where he jumped off the truck on to some uneven ground that made a crunching sound under his feet. Pointing the flashlight below him revealed a sight that sent an unnerving sensation through his body.

"Jesus, Jesus," he shouted into his attached microphone as he stumbled forward to the sound of more crunching beneath his feet.

"What is it, Con? What's wrong?" Alex questioned, sounding concerned by his friend's startled tone.

"Fuck, Alex. There's skeletons all over the ground here," he returned franticly.

"Try and relax, Con."

"You try and relax a mile underground in a cave full of human bones."

"I know. But you've got to calm down."

"Alright, I'm calming down," he replied, momentarily controlling his anxiety.

"What else do you see?" Alex asked.

"So far a lot of dark."

"I know that, what else?"

"There's a lot of trucks down here and there's probably more than I can see, but they look like they were buried in a cave-in toward the back of the cavern," he returned panning his light.

"Okay, George says your father told him that there were torches lining the cave wall. Do you see any?"

Taking his light, he illuminated the far wall and revealed a line of torches every ten-feet or so. Some seemed to still have material capable of burning; others were no more than thick bare sticks.

"I see some," he answered, returning his focus and his light to the skeletons under his feet.

"Try and light some of them, Con. It will help to give you some perspective."

"A lot of people were killed down here, Alex," he returned, as he closely examined a skull, poking his finger through what looked like a bullet hole.

"I know, bud. Go light the torches."

"No Alex, I mean a lot of people. They were shot I think. Maybe this has something to do with what Maggie was

342

talking about. I know from his tape that this must have gotten to my Dad."

"Connor, forget about the skeletons. You've got to get the sample, take some pictures and get out of there. We've got a schedule to keep."

"I know, I know," he returned, refocusing, but at the same time trying to remain open to his surroundings in hope that a clue to Maggie's plight would emerge.

"Good, now light the damn torches."

Making his way down the wall he lit several torches, which helped to eliminate some of the tension of being in a totally blacked-out environment. As he made his way forward, he could see three long high stacks in front of him. The cave had an eerie shadowy feel. The lack of any natural light gave the illusion of his man-made sources being swallowed up by the overwhelming darkness. His eyes widened and his heart pounded when he neared the stacks, he had seen the pictures, but nothing could have prepared him for what he was now witnessing.

"What's going on, Con? What are you seeing?"

"You wouldn't believe it, Alex," he calmly spoke into his mouthpiece, the gold diverting his attention from his foreign habitat.

"Try me, try me now."

"I'm standing in the middle of three stacks of gold bars. They're six feet high, six feet wide and look to be at least thirty feet long. This is a lot of gold, bud. A lot of gold," he repeated.

"YES!" Alex yelled into his earpiece. "Alright, alright. Calm down," Alex said, suddenly breathing very heavily into the two-way radio.

"I am calm," Connor returned, smiling to himself at his friend's excitement.

"I know, I know, it's me."

"No shit."

"Okay, get the sample and get back up here."

"Fine. Over."

Grabbing the small digital camera in his pocket, he

began firing off several photos of the gold and the cave. The ancient material on the torches was already beginning to burn out, casting flickering shadows over his subject matter. His heart was beating franticly while he held the camera at arms length and took several shots of himself with the gold bars in the background. Turning his attention to the stacks, he quickly located the Burmese finger bars that Billy Hilliard had alluded to. Taking one of the small two-pound bars, he placed it in his pocket, before deciding to take another, just in case. In case of what he wasn't sure, but it seemed like a good idea to have an extra.

~ ~ ~

Alex waited patiently, along with George and Lido, trying not to bother their intrepid explorer in the treasure cavern below. He was excited by Connor's report, like he was sure the others were. He imagined they were daydreaming of the fortune and its impact on their lives as he was, while they anticipated Connor's return to the surface.

The silent peace was suddenly interrupted by one of Lido's men intruding on the small hilltop encampment. Lido made his way out of the hut to intercept him. Alex and George watched the exchange of dialogue with interest. After a few highly animated minutes, Lido returned to the group, just prior to dismissing the emissary and directing him to return to the main camp.

"What's going on, Lido?" George asked.

"We have a problem, Sir George. My men have reported a checkpoint outside of the village on the way down the mountain."

"Military or rebel?"

"They are not sure, sir."

"What do you mean, military or rebel?" Alex asked.

"Sometimes the rebels pose as military in order to rob or kidnap foreigners."

Alex nodded, remembering his conversation with Billy on the subject. "What if it's military; is that better?"

"Depends."

"Depends on what?" A feeling of real concern coming over him.

"Depends on whether the Colonel has found out that we're no longer under his surveillance."

"Is there another way to get to the boat?"

"We can cut through the jungle, but we'd never make it there on time without the car," George conceded.

"This isn't good."

"Do not worry, Sir Alex," Lido comforted. "Everything will be all right."

"How do you know that, Lido?" he asked, hoping for some local perspective.

"The night before last I sacrificed two chickens."

"You sacrificed two chickens?" he questioned.

"Yes, sir."

"And that will make everything all right?"

"Yes, sir."

"I feel better already," he returned, rolling his eyes at George as he returned his attention to the dark hole and his friend below the surface.

"Good," Lido replied.

~ ~ ~

In the cavern, Connor was exploring the canvas, covered backs of several trucks. Most were filled with gold bars, while others contained gold Buddha shaped statues of various sizes and jewel encrusted artifacts such as knives and swords as well as several clay jars of loose precious stones. He fought back his desire to grab a handful and stuff his pockets, knowing the fewer items he returned to the surface with, the less likelihood of the fortune being accidentally discovered by hostile parties. He was becoming numb to the riches surrounding him when his light caught a silvery glimmer on the seat of the truck he was inspecting. As he moved to retrieve the shiny objects a voice in his ear interrupted him.

"Con, where are you?"

"Disneyland, where the fuck do you think I am?"

"No, I mean did you find the bar and are you on your way back?"

"I found the bar and I'm ready to start getting out of here."

"Good, hurry up. We need to talk about some things."

"What things, what's wrong?"

"Nothing. We just need to get you out and get to Cebu."

"Fine, I'm on my way. Over." He had been around Alex too long not to sense the concern in his voice. Not that it mattered; he had his own immediate worries, getting out of this subterranean death tomb.

He knew the way back would be more taxing than the way down, although he was sure he would have a lot less anxiety knowing he was heading for the surface. The more he tried to relax, the more he became aware of the pain in his ribs and his difficulty breathing in the sparse air available. The adrenaline rush of his recent discovery, that had masked the pain and lack of oxygen, was beginning to subside, conjuring up new concerns that he would have to expend more energy on his ascent.

As he headed for the mineshaft and the long exodus, his mind wondered to Maggie's insinuation that he would not be able to recognize the clue to help ease the supernatural affliction that had invaded his life and haunted her. He stopped himself from leaving while he fought to take in his surroundings in an attempt to discover something more precious than the yellow metal and jewels he shared space with.

Suddenly, he felt drawn to the truck and the shiny, silver objects he was reaching for when Alex had radioed. Making his way back he found the vehicle, and reaching in the window he snatched two tiny flat metal sheets from the seat. He quickly inspected them, and discovering they were dog tags, placed them in his pocket and headed for the funneled opening; hopeful that he had found the clue he was seeking.

He felt a deep sense of satisfaction while he replaced the harness and began the tedious process of hoisting himself up through the mine roof and onto the ledge, home of the first of many bamboo ladders he would use to assist his ascent. Focusing his attention directly in front of him, he painstakingly made his slow methodical rise, one step at a time through the dense, hot, dark air, stopping only to sip water from his canteen. He resisted the urge to quicken his pace, knowing full well that under the circumstances he was making maximum progress, any faster would only impede his ability to take in and process the precious oxygen he craved.

After over thirty grueling minutes he emerged in a dirty, sweat soaked, exhausted state. Alex and George helped him out of the hole and poured water over his head to cool his body temperature while he struggled to regulate his breathing in the already oppressive mid-morning jungle heat.

"You going to be all right, Connor?" George asked.

"I'll be fine, I just need a minute," he returned, a little breathless.

"You got the bar, Con?" Alex asked.

"Right here, bud," he replied, pulling one of the two small yellow bars from his pocket.

Alex reached out and took the bar. "Man, it's got some heft to it," he returned, bouncing the diminutive ingot in his hand.

"It's one of the densest metals on earth," George contributed.

"It's amazing that after all these years it still holds its shine," Alex continued.

"That is one of the great things about gold, dust it off a little and it looks brand new, no matter how old."

"I don't mean to break up the geology lesson," Connor interrupted. "But Alex said we had something to discuss, so I take it there's a problem."

George and Alex looked at each other for a moment, before explaining the report from Lido's men and the ensuing peril it could potentially represent. The best they could hope for was the checkpoint consisted of a routine military check in search of rebels and weapons and not them.

"What do you think, Con?" Alex asked.

347

"If we can't get around them, someone has to get the car through. Lido can lead you around the blockade through the jungle Alex, while George and I try to get the car past them. You carry the guns and the gold."

"What if they're rebels or the Colonel has alerted his men to stop us?"

"Then you need to be in position to take them out," Connor returned, looking at Alex with his deep blue piercing eyes. "Can you do it, bud?"

"I don't know. I came to get gold, not kill people. Is that why we're here, to kill people?"

"No, Alex. We can pack it in right now if you want."

He waited as Alex hesitated for a moment. Connor knew he could make almost any shot from a thousand yards in, but he wasn't sure if he could take someone's life. George was biting his lip. Connor caught his look and figured he was visualizing his dream crashing down around him. He was sure that if George could shoot like Alex, he would kill a thousand men to realize emancipation from his life here and delivery to the opulence he had made clear he felt deserving of.

"I'll do whatever needs to be done," Alex assured him.

"Are you positive, Alex? We don't have to do this."

"I'm sure, I can do it," he returned, taking a deep breath.

"Let's take a walk," Connor suggested.

Connor led Alex to the far end of the small hilltop encampment, out of earshot of George and Lido. They both stood, staring off into the jungle mountain range visible from their lofty perspective. This was a big time gut check for both of them and Connor knew it. Taking a life for money was way out of their rational envelope and they needed to come to grips with that before continuing.

"I know this is a hard thing for you Alex," Connor said. "But we can't do this without you being a hundred percent sure."

"I know, Con. I said I can do it," he returned.

"But are you sure?"

"Not a hundred percent," he replied, looking away as he scratched his neck.

"Life is tough here, Alex. People struggle everyday just to survive. We can make a difference, not just for ourselves, but for them. I think I understand a little more, what my father meant by do the right thing with the money. We can do the right thing, Alex, or we can stop right here. Whatever you want, I'll back you."

"I want to help, Con. I just don't know if I can kill someone to do it."

"I understand, bud. Let's call it then, I'm okay with that."

Alex didn't respond as he looked up, seemingly searching for inspiration. Finally he focused back on his friend. "I'll do it."

"Are you sure?"

"Yes, let's go before I have any more time to think," he said, as they both headed back to the others.

"Okay. Lido, take Alex and get him into a position above the checkpoint where he can have a clear shot. George and I will make our way back to the car. What should they be watching for, George?"

"If they make us get out of the car, it's a good bet we're being taken hostage or to the Colonel, depending on if it's rebels or soldiers," George replied, starting to sound a little shaky.

"How many soldiers at the checkpoint, Lido?"

"My men reported three, Sir Connor."

"What do you think, Alex?"

"I can definitely get at least two of them. The third is a wild card, I just don't know."

"I'll take care of the third one then. I'll keep a forty-five in the back of my belt and wait till you drop the farthest one from us before I shoot the closet. By then you should have a bead on the third one."

"That's the plan then," he agreed.

"Alright. Radio George and I when you're in position. When it's over, we'll pick you up down the road. Good luck."

"Thanks, you too."

Connor watched while Alex and Lido headed toward the next mountain carrying a high-powered rifle and both gold bars. He and George made their way down through the jungle to the decoy mine site. Taking the old jeep, they began the bumpy one-hour journey to the car. Arriving at the vehicle, they waited an additional hour before Alex radioed that they were in position, about six hundred yards above the checkpoint, informing them he had a clear line of sight for a shot, if needed. Upon receiving this confirmation they began making the trip toward their fate. Connor knew no one was comfortable with the scenario; it was simply a necessity given the circumstances.

He wondered if his father would take someone's life in pursuit of riches; he thought not, but harbored little doubt he would do whatever he had to in order protect his life or liberty; of that, he was sure. The next few minutes would bring him closer to the fine line he was about to cross; he understood in order to survive he would have to act without hesitation, there was no room for a last minute moral dilemma. He had learned that lesson well from the man who had saved him from the beautiful assassin. His gullibility at her hands continued to haunt him as well as the memory of her lifeless body.

George was driving as they neared the checkpoint, about a mile outside of the village limits. When they pulled up, a soldier waved them to the side. A second soldier, stationed directly across the two lane road, pointed a large caliber machine gun, mounted on the back of an army jeep, in their direction. Connor could feel his heart pounding as they came to a stop.

~ ~ ~

Alex stared through the scope of his high-powered rifle as the soldier approached the open car window and began, what appeared to him to be, the standard interrogation of his captive audience. Lido sat quietly beside him, looking through a pair of binoculars while Alex trained his sites on the

350

machine gunner across the road. A third soldier positioned himself in front of George's car and stood ready with an army issue M-16 rifle. Alex could feel his pulse begin to quicken and his breathing become erratic. The seconds passed like minutes. He planned to take out the machine gunner first, followed by the soldier in front of the car; Connor would have to get the one talking in the window. His hands were beginning to sweat and he could feel a trembling come over him as the thoughts of killing another human being invaded his fragile psyche.

Suddenly the soldier pulled the car door open. He looked to be directing George and Connor to vacate the vehicle; initiating the signal they agreed on. Alex moved his sights toward Connor, who, by getting out on the opposite side of the car, helped conceal the fact he was positioning his hand behind his back as he prepared to draw the pistol hidden in his belt. The sweat was now running down Alex's face and into his eyes while he struggled to maintain his poise. He watched George and Connor hand their passports and identification over to the soldier. Alex could feel Lido moving restlessly next to him, he knew he had to be troubled, wondering why he had not yet acted.

"Sir Alex," Lido said softly. "You must shoot. They are out of the car."

Alex focused in on his target, trying to find some rhythm to his breathing. As he started to depress the trigger, his hands began shaking so badly, he knew he would miss, placing them in more danger than they were in already. He released his grip, wiping the salty sweat from his eyes in an attempt to gain control and revisit his target.

~ ~ ~

Connor was growing anxious. The soldiers were yelling back and forth in Tagalog. He could hear George's shallow breathing, as he knew they both anticipated a shot at any moment. His heart was beating so hard he could hear it pounding. He wanted to radio and find out what the hell was

351

wrong, but couldn't, knowing it would alert the heavily armed targets to another presence.

~ ~ ~

Alex was now wringing his hands in an effort to stop the shaking and the ensuing numbness that was following. He just couldn't seem to control himself; it was like buck fever he thought, an affliction, hunters suffer when they site a live animal. He couldn't bring himself to pull the trigger. He could sense Lido was becoming more and more concerned.

"Please, Sir Alex. Fire the gun, you don't have much time."

"I can't, Lido," he surrendered. "I'm shaking and losing feeling in my hands. I can't make the shot."

"You have to. It is taking too long down there. Something is going to happen."

Alex nodded in agreement while he attempted to settle himself. He knew he only had one chance to hit the machine gunner clean. He bore down and started to slowly depress the trigger of his rifle when the trembling started to increase again. Just as he was about to fire, he released his finger grip and dropped his head, not able to bring himself to take the shot.

~ ~ ~

Suddenly with one rapid jerk, the machine gunner pulled back the bolt to arm his gun; the alarming sound startled George so badly that it caused him to flinch noticeably while Connor readied for the worst. Just when Connor was about to draw his gun, the soldiers began laughing. One of the men came toward George and handed him the identification and their passports, motioning them to continue on their way. He then turned and walked back to his fellow militia, still laughing at their joke. George and Connor quickly got into the car and headed down the windy mountain road. Connor was relieved at the turn of events, but wondered why Alex had failed to fire.

~ ~ ~

Alex watched them get back into the vehicle. He was experiencing more guilt than relief; still he was glad he didn't have to kill anyone, glad he waited, even if it was not by his own choice. As he packed up his weapon and followed Lido down the heavily treed hillside towards the road, he was now filled with doubt. He knew that he couldn't pull the trigger; if he had and missed he would have elevated the danger. Despite the outcome, he had been tested and failed miserably. They could have been kidnapped or killed and it would have been on his shoulders. Suddenly he was feeling more like a burden than an asset to the operation.

~ ~ ~

About forty-five minutes later and another mile down from the checkpoint, Lido and Alex emerged from the jungle, walking across a small grassy field to the road where Connor and George were waiting. As they got into the car, Connor was grateful that no shots were fired, but was still feeling uneasy as to why.

"What happened up there, Alex?" Connor asked.

"Just waiting to see how it played out, bud," he sheepishly returned, passing him the two gold ingots.

"I thought we agreed, if we exited the car that was the signal."

"I had it under control. Everything worked out didn't it."

"Yeah, this time," conceded Connor, deciding to continue this conversation in private.

"Well, I'm glad it didn't come to violence, and when we get a chance I need to change my underwear," George admitted, still sounding shaken.

"How far to the boat?" Alex asked.

"We'll be there in three hours, give or take," George returned.

"Cool," Connor replied, still very concerned about Alex's failure to act.

During the trip, Connor described in detail his descent into the treasure cavern and what he uncovered in the back of the disabled vehicles. He shared the digital pictures with his companions, viewing them through the camera. A few military looking trucks passed them along the road causing some momentary concern, but no confrontations. Connor began to feel better about their chances for success, nearing the pier and their transportation to Cebu and Billy Hilliard.

Pulling up to the busy dock area, they turned more than a few heads as they unloaded their bags from George's trunk, including weapons, and proceeded toward a twenty-eight foot tugboat shaped wooden vessel nestled at the end of a rickety pier. The inhabitants of the area looked to Connor to be mostly poor fisherman who depended on their boats both as a source of livelihood and living quarters. Many were busy storing supplies for their next outing while others were fixing nets or just taking in the sun and kibitzing with their neighbors. Tuna was the fish of choice, but as Lido had informed him, anything taken from the sea would be sold or made into a meal.

Approaching their charter, Connor noticed the paint peeling from her reddish bow and the weathered white wheelhouse when the captain of the small boat came forward to greet them. His name was Ramon Roxas, a local fisherman and friend of George's. He was five-seven with dark hair and eyes, a barrel chest and big white teeth highlighting his deeply tanned round face. He was wearing a horizontal red striped shirt, blue jeans and a lime green baseball hat as he assisted their boarding.

~ ~ ~

It was just after four o'clock in the afternoon; the Captain had informed them the trip to Cebu would take at

354

least twelve hours, having to proceed more cautiously once it got dark. George was giving Lido some last minute instructions. He directed him to pick up the jeepneys and motorcycles during their absence and secure a dependable rental vehicle in Davao for the eight hour plus journey to the mine. He told him to be at the airport on Friday morning, before returning to Connor and Alex who were resting on the boat while Lido waited.

"Guys, I'm going to need some money," George informed them, walking toward the boat.

"How much and what for?" Connor asked.

"Around three thousand, payroll for the men and money to lease a vehicle in Davao."

"Fine," Connor replied, reaching into his pocket and pulling out a wad of bills. He peeled off three thousand in American currency and handed it to him.

George figured he wouldn't quibble about the amount, after what he just saw in the cave, everything in comparison would seem insignificant. George watched Connor settle in next to Alex on a makeshift bench located near the bow of the boat. The captain had pulled out a cooler filled with San Miguel beer, priority cargo obtained under his direction. They hoisted a cold brew and appeared to be toasting the operation as George turned to give Lido his final directions while they prepared to depart.

"Here's the money for the men and the car lease. Meet us at the Davao Airport on Friday morning; okay?"

"Yes, Sir George."

"Lido, do not pay the men in American money, make sure you exchange it first," he instructed, pulling out the cash and handing him two thousand. He then folded up the remaining thousand and put it in his pocket.

"Yes, Sir George."

"It's up to you to get everything done. Don't let me down."

"I won't, Sir George. Sir George there is something I should tell you about what happened on the mountain when Sir Alex was to shoot the soldiers."

"Doesn't matter, Lido. You just take care of what you need to. I'll worry about Alex and Connor," he returned, not in the mood for a long conversation, since the sight of his partners drinking cold beer had captured his attention.

"Yes, sir."

"I'll see you Friday at the airport," he said, dismissing him as he turned and walked towards the boat.

Lido returned to George's rust bucket of a vehicle and drove off to carry out his appointed tasks. George boarded the boat and joined Alex and Connor in a cold one, while Captain Roxas navigated the vessel towards open water and the island of Cebu. For the next several hours the beers flowed and they enjoyed the reprieve from the jungle heat, basking in gentler, late afternoon sun, tempered by refreshing ocean breezes. George let his mind wander to a better place and the riches he was close to acquiring. The only reminder of his current reality was the rocking of the vessel and the strong smell of diesel from the engines.

~ ~ ~

As they cleared the bay of Macajalar, with the small island of Mambajao in sight off their right, Connor watched George retreat to the stern of the boat to take a nap. He was feeling tired, but was way too juiced by recent events to even consider going to sleep. He figured now was an appropriate time to get Alex's version of what took place on the mountain.

"Alex, what went on with the soldiers back at the checkpoint? Why didn't you shoot?"

"I don't know, I just didn't. It all worked out. What's the problem?" he said, casting his eyes away.

"It all worked out this time. What if we're faced with another situation, can I count on you?"

"I don't know," he surrendered, hanging his head.

"Well, I need to know. What happened up there?" Connor returned sternly, in search of commitment.

"I got buck fever. I had the machine gunner in my

356

sights when I started shaking so bad, I just couldn't pull the trigger."

"You may have to pull a trigger before we're done, how do you feel about that?"

"Not too good, Con. I didn't come here to kill people. Is any amount of gold worth a human life?"

"Probably not, brother. But what we're talking about is doing what's necessary to save our lives. Given a life threatening situation can I count on you?"

"I think you can," he returned, lifting his head and staring him in the eye.

"I hope so, Alex. I hope so," he returned, raising the cold beer to his lips and taking a long swallow.

As they passed the island of Mambajao, Connor was enjoying the tranquility of the open sea, when his relaxation was suddenly broken by a loud bang and erupting water to the right of the bow. He and Alex jumped to their feet only to be abruptly jerked backward when Captain Roxas rammed the engines to full throttle. George, who came running towards the bow of the vessel, appeared in a panic.

"Ramon, what the fuck is going on?" he yelled up to him.

"Jump buddies," he called back, pointing toward the small island.

"Oh shit," George exclaimed, hurrying to the protection offered on the other side of the wheelhouse.

Another explosion in the water sent the three of them diving to the safety of the deck. Peering through his binoculars, Connor could make out two speedboats, each filled with heavily armed men, closing rapidly.

"What's going on, George?" Connor screamed, grabbing him by the arm.

"Jump buddies," he returned, cowering on the deck.

"What the hell are jump buddies?"

"Pirates, they're after the boat."

"What can we do?"

"I don't know, shoot I guess. Ramon will try to outrun them," George returned, clearly distressed.

"He can't outrun them in this tub," Alex deducted, getting up and heading into the wheelhouse.

"What are you doing, Alex?" Connor called out.

"Getting the rifle."

"Good idea."

~ ~ ~

Alex removed the rifle from the blanket that covered it when he brought it on board. He used the open window of the wheelhouse to steady his aim while he attempted to get this new enemy in his crosshairs. Placing one of the marauders who was manning a mounted deck gun in his sights he could feel his body start to tremble, as an all too familiar debilitating sensation assaulted him. The attackers, he estimated were around five hundred yards out and their speedy vessel offered very little cover. He could have easily picked off enough of them to dissuade their pursuit, if he could only bring himself to pull the trigger.

The man in his sights fired the deck gun and another explosion erupted in the water, close enough for the ensuing funnel to splash over the bow soaking George and Connor. Alex could feel himself retreating into an anxiety ridden panic. He had to do something, he thought, not able to stomach the idea of letting them down again. Suddenly he came to grips with a solution to his dilemma.

"George, tell the captain to stop the boat," he yelled from inside wheelhouse.

"We're not stopping any fucking boat, Alex. Are you crazy? Ramon can outrun them," he screamed, sounding more scared than convincing.

"I need him to stop the boat so I can get a shot off, they're bouncing and we're bouncing, at this distance I need it a little steadier to make the shot. Now tell him!"

"Are you sure, Alex?" Connor yelled. "Once we stop they'll be on top of us in minutes."

"Connor, tell him to stop the god damn boat," he demanded, feeling his friend had lost confidence in him, but still knowing he was their only chance.

"George, tell him to stop the boat," Connor instructed.

"Fuck that, Connor. If we stop they'll be in machine gun range in seconds. At least we've got a chance while were moving."

"Con!" Alex yelled, attempting to site his new target.

"I'm trying Alex, give me second will you. George, tell him to stop this boat now or I'm going to blow your fucking head off," he said, as Alex watched him aim his forty-five automatic, right between George's eyes.

~ ~ ~

George stared straight at him, shaking his head, not believing for one minute he'd actually pull the trigger. On the other hand, he had witnessed Alex's ability and decided it may be in their best interest to let him try as it was becoming more evident, by the rapidly closing vessels, that they would not be able to outrun their pursuers.

"Okay. Okay," he surrendered. "Ramon stop the boat," he yelled, as another shell exploded into the water, drowning out his request. "Ramon, stop the boat," he repeated.

The Captain, hearing his command, pulled back the throttle and brought the small craft to a drifting halt. George looked back as the pirates opened fire with their Russian manufactured AK-7's, the bullets landing about thirty-yards short of the hull. He knew they would be within range in less than a minute. George and the others waited for the boat to settle so Alex could shoot. He was becoming more and more uneasy while he watched Alex concentrating on his target.

"Take the shot, Alex," George cried.

"Keep quiet, he'll take it when he's ready," Connor scolded.

"When's he going to be ready, when were already dead," George returned, retreating to the deck and covering his head.

~ ~ ~

Connor was peaking over the side, watching the bullets land closer to their motionless ship when he heard Alex fire. He deduced that he must have missed, as neither boat showed signs of slowing. He could feel a knot in his stomach, realizing they didn't possess the firepower necessary to outshoot this foe; Alex was their only chance.

He grabbed the binoculars laying near George's cowering hulk and zeroed in on the raiders, who were now he estimated within a hundred yards, as a second shot from Alex's rifle rang out. Connor could see a large billow of black smoke emerge from the back of the lead boat, causing it to suddenly veer off to the right. The inhabitants started abandoning ship as a fire broke out on the deck. The trailing vessel broke off its pursuit, electing to pick up their distressed comrades. Captain Roxas returned the engines to full throttle. The chase appeared to be over.

"Nice shooting, Alex," Connor said, observing his exit from the wheelhouse sporting a relieved grin.

"Thanks, I owed you guys one," he returned, seeming to enjoy his much needed redemption.

"Great shooting," George acknowledged, attempting to get his round body up from the deck of the rocking vessel.

"What the hell did you hit, bud? I think you missed the first one."

"No, I didn't. The first shot hit what looked like a gas container; it must have soaked the deck. The second shot hit the outboard engine, disabling the boat and starting the fire. I have to admit the fire was an unexpected bonus."

"Well, whatever, it did the job."

"Amen to that."

"Hey, George. Did you know about these pirates?" Connor asked, turning his attention back to him after glancing in the direction of the recent encounter, reconfirming their escape.

"Yeah, I knew about them," he returned, having finally gotten himself situated on the bench and rearmed with a fresh San Miguel.

"Why didn't you let us in on this little tidbit?"

"I didn't think we'd have a problem. They hardly ever come after a boat in open water; they usually operate further north around clusters of small islands. Pickin's must be slim for them to be this far south, sorry," he apologized, taking a huge gulp of nerve steadying brew, causing some excess to escape out of the corner of his mouth, which he wiped with the back of his sweaty hand.

"Why did you call them Jump Buddies?" Alex asked.

"It's a nickname. After they board and rob you, they tell you to jump in the water. They say 'jump buddy.' That's where the name came from."

"Very cute," he returned, shaking his head.

"Anything else we should worry about between here and Cebu?" Connor inquired, now skeptical of any information regarding potential risk coming from his father's former partner.

"Nothing other than this Filipino beer makes me fart," George returned, nervously giggling at his attempted humor.

"That may be the most dangerous hazard we've run into yet," Connor retorted.

"Send him to the back of the boat, Con," Alex added.

"Good thinking, brother," he said, nodding at his friend.

Dusk turned to night and calm, moonlit seas marked the next eight hours. To the best of his knowledge, Connor thought there were no other small islands between Mindanao and Cebu, until they reached the Bohol Strait and by then they would be within spitting distance of the port. He did not expect to be accosted by any other sea-faring raiders on the remainder of their voyage; after recounting their close call, he and his companions poured back a few more beers before trying to find a comfortable place to sleep.

Connor lay awake, starring at the star filled sky. He thought back to the night on his front steps, when he wondered if the night sky would look the same on the other side of the world. It looked pretty similar, but that was about the only thing his home and here had in common. It was very foreign, oppressively hot and extremely dangerous; all and all it was about the most exciting place he had ever been. No one in their right mind would want to submit themselves to this, he thought, as the rocking of the boat began to usher him off to sleep. Why then did his father like it so much? Maybe for the same reasons he did.

~ ~ ~

Chapter 50

The next morning—Connor awoke to the cries of seagulls, while the faded red and white tug pulled into port on the island of Cebu. The dock looked big and bustling, highlighted by huge container ships dwarfing their small craft as they shared the waterway. Unlike the small fishing dock in Cagayan de Oro, to him this harbor seemed a portrait to capitalism, at least as much a portrait as he could expect from third world commerce. When they motored into their slip, even at sunrise, the pier was alive with workers loading furniture, mahogany, produce, fish and other products for export on the large sea-going vessels.

After exchanging farewells with Captain Roxas, they hailed a cab for transport to the Cebu Plaza and their meeting with Billy. Alex was not thrilled with being forced to leave his rifle behind. Connor had informed him there was no way to board the plane to Davao and remain inconspicuous. Although not his weapon of choice, he settled for the fact that their handguns would not pose the same problem. They could be more easily concealed and were legal on local flights, as long as you remember to empty the ammunition, George reminded them.

Connor sat back in the taxi already feeling the heat and humidity starting to creep back in the further they traveled from the water and its cooling winds. An inland breeze was non-existent, stifled by people, traffic and large factory buildings that lined the streets. George was already squirming in an attempt stop the sweat from affixing him to the seat. As

Connor observed him wipe the perspiration from his brow using the back of his stubby fingered hand, he unconsciously fumbled in his pocket, pulling out the metal tags he had extracted from one of the abandoned treasure trucks. In all the excitement, mixed with his exhaustion, his possession of them had slipped his mind. This was the first time he had studied them carefully, identifying the names of the two American soldiers whose skeletal remains he figured he trampled across during his underground excursion. For a brief moment the gold was forgotten, his mind conjured up visions of their suffering, causing him to cringe as the cab pulled up in front of the hotel.

George was the first one out, obviously anxious to be reunited with his old friend as well as the more comfortable air-conditioned confines the hotel lobby offered. Connor and Alex followed close behind while he accosted a clerk, who seemed to recognize him. They hung back as George continued his negotiations, rejoining them wearing a familiar Cheshire cat grin.

"Old Billy is here, room 314," George announced proudly.

"Well, let's ring his room," Alex suggested.

"Forget that, we're going up to his room," George returned, looking more energized than Connor had observed during their brief association, as he hurried toward the elevator.

"Let's go," Connor agreed, following him.

"Are you sure he's not going to be upset?" Alex asked, reminding Connor of their first encounter and how uneasy Billy made him feel, as the elevator door closed.

"Billy's a good shit, Alex," George reassured him. "He'll be glad to see us, trust me."

"There's that saying I hate," Alex mumbled to Connor.

George led the charge to room 314, assaulting the door with an enthusiastic pounding. Realizing it was just before 7:00 a.m., Connor wasn't so sure that old Billy would be happy to see anyone at that hour. Before he could suggest another tact, the door flung open to one of the scariest sights he could imagine; standing before them with blood-shot eyes, disheveled hair and unshaven face was a six-foot six, two hundred and eighty pound, naked Billy Hilliard. He was clutching his cowboy hat, his enormous manhood in a ready for action pose. Connor was speechless. He tried to keep from laughing while waiting for someone to say something. George seemed totally unfazed as he launched into conversation.

"Billy, how the hell are you?" he asked.

"I was a site better a few minutes ago, before y'all got here," he returned, rubbing the back of his neck with one of his huge hands, as he appeared to be attempting to regain his senses. "Don't just stand there, come on in," he said, turning around and placing the large hat on his head.

They followed Billy into his room. It contained a spacious sitting area with adjoining bedroom. Passing by the open bedroom door, Connor could see two naked brown skinned, young women sprawled on the king size bed. The bedding was twisted and contorted so; he could only imagine the activity that took place prior to their arrival. He turned his attention back to Billy as he took a seat in one of the upholstered rattan chairs.

"You want some of that, boy?" he said, looking at Connor.

"No thanks," Connor returned. "You want a towel?" he asked, growing rapidly tired of looking at Billy's grotesque, unclothed form.

"Am I turning you on, son?"

"No, it's early, I usually don't throw up before noon. Just trying not to interrupt my schedule."

"You're a real smart ass, ain't ya?"

"Just my nature, Billy."

"I'm surprised it hasn't gotten ya kill'd yet."

"Speaking of which, thanks for sending Mr. Wai."

"Mr. Wai, who the hell is Mr. Wai?" Alex asked, obviously surprised.

"The chin help you out, son?"

"That he did, I guess I owe you my life."

"Owe him your life, what the fuck happened I missed, Con?" Alex blurted, now sounding totally confused.

Connor took the next fifteen minutes and recounted the whole tale about Jade, the seduction and her death after the cockfight. Alex sat with a betrayed, yet astonished look on his face. George gave no marked reaction, after fifteen years over here, Connor doubted anything surprised him anymore.

"You must have been one miserable fuck if she wanted to kill you afterwards," Billy joked.

"Regardless of that comment, I want to thank you, sincerely."

"Before you go gettin' all misty eyed youngster, I can't take credit for all of it."

"What do you mean? He said you sent him."

"I did send him, boy. But it was because Wes Adams called and asked me too."

"Wes?"

"Yep."

"Guess that kind of blows our theory about him, huh Con," Alex added, referring to his suspected sellout to Morgan Gold.

"It does and I'm glad," he returned.

"What was your theory about Wes?" Billy asked.

"Nothing," Connor said, not wanting to get into with him, considering what happened left his suspicions unfounded.

"How do you think they found out, Con?"

"I'm not sure, Alex. Maybe we'll never know."

"Anywho," Billy interrupted. "Wes said to send my best man, so I sent Andy. He's a deadly little motherfucker, that chink, and he's the best. I'm glad he helped ya, even though you-all a smart ass little bastard."

"Really, thanks again for sending him."

"You're welcome, son. I owed it to your daddy. By the way, do you have something for me?"

Connor hesitated for a moment, before he broke into a wide smile. Alex and George were smiling too. The answer was in his pocket and they all knew it as they watched him reach for the bar.

"Here it is." He tossed Billy the small gold ingot.

"Nice job, son," he returned, snatching it with a swipe of his massive hand. "Looks like we're in business."

"Sure does," Connor returned.

"Why don't you boys get a room and a shower and we'll meet downstairs for some breakfast."

"Sounds like a plan, Billy," Connor returned getting up from his seat.

"Hey, Billy. You always get two at a time?" Alex asked, referring to the women in his bedroom.

"Naah, last night I was a little beat. I usually get three or four. They're sturdy, but little, they tire out kinda fast, so when one gets tired, I toss her off and toss another one on."

"See you downstairs, Billy," Connor said, shaking his head and smiling at Alex who was staring wide-eyed at his new sexual hero. "Come on Alex, before you make a bigger ass of yourself."

"What?" he asked, following him out the door.

They went back to the lobby to check in. Alex and Connor secured their usual adjoining rooms. Connor wanted to sleep, but decided to keep moving. After taking a long shower, he got dressed and went down to meet his partners for breakfast. They exchanged some small talk and then got down to the plan regarding the gold transfer. Billy would land on the Del Monte golf course at first light on Monday morning. The course was around seven miles from the mine heading toward Valencia, the next town after Malaybalay. They would pass by it when they journeyed the back way from Davao, on their return trip. George said he was very familiar with the pick up point; he had played the course on many occasions, a few times bringing the Colonel as his guest.

Billy had his three planes and a dozen mercenaries ready to go into action; they would land and deal with any resistance that may arise. He explained to them that once they delivered the gold, they were to stay out of the way and let him and his team do their job. He didn't mix words, someone could get hurt or killed and as long as it wasn't them, be thankful.

Connor knew that once the operation was passed over to Billy, things could get very dicey in a hurry. He was sure when you put seventy million in gold bullion in the hands of highly motivated, highly compensated soldiers of fortune, it would take an act of God for them to abandon that kind of wealth without first starting a small war. He had been a beneficiary of their expertise, and while he was grateful, he didn't want to be responsible for the loss of innocent life. He was sure Alex felt the same, as he was sure his father would, if he were here. George on the other hand, he knew would have no misgivings about the loss of innocent lives; there could be bodies strewn everywhere as long as he got, what in his mind, was his long overdue reward. People could die and he wouldn't lose a single night's sleep over it.

They were close, so close Connor could taste it, but at what cost? That bill, he thought, still remained to be tallied.

~ ~ ~

Chapter 51

Colonel Vudula paced impatiently on the compound firing range while he awaited the arrival of Corporal Vega. His informants had recently gotten word to him that George Fall and his associates had not returned to the hotel since leaving on Monday afternoon. He wanted a report from his man as to their whereabouts, but had been unable to find him until dispatching men to his home. The fact that he had not answered his radio made the Colonel suspicious; then having to have him picked up confirmed those perceptions. Had they not been able to accost his family, he was sure that the Corporal would have remained unreachable in the foreseeable future. He could feel his blood pressure rising as his men, with Corporal Vega and one of his charges, approached.

"Corporal Vega, I have been worried about you. You have not been very accessible as of late."

"I'm sorry, Colonel. My men and I have been searching for Mr. Fall," he returned sheepishly, looking away from his superior.

"Why are you searching for him? Hasn't he been under your surveillance since he returned with the other Americans?"

"No sir, we have not seen him since the cock fighting tournament on Monday," he answered, his increasing anxiety apparent.

"Why was I not informed of this, Vega?" the Colonel asked, feeling his upper lip starting to quiver as he fought to control his escalating rage.

"I was afraid," he returned, barely audible.

"Speak up, Corporal. I cannot hear you."

"I was afraid, sir," he repeated, just slightly louder.

"Afraid of what, Vega?"

"Afraid you would kill me, sir," he said, taking a deep breath.

"Well, Vega. You are right to be afraid of that," he hauntingly replied. "Have you anything to say for yourself?"

"Yes, Colonel. We have the name of a man who may be working for Mr. Fall."

"And who might that be?" he asked, rubbing the pearl handled revolvers at his side.

"His name is Juan Romauldez, he lives on the mountain in the village of Malaybalay, sir."

"What is it that makes you believe he works for Mr. Fall, Corporal?"

"My wife's cousin owns a store in the village and Romauldez came in to buy things."

"And what about that makes you think Mr. Fall is involved?"

"He paid him with an American hundred dollar bill, sir."

"Is that so," the Colonel said, rubbing his chin while he processed the value of this information.

"Yes, sir."

"You may have just saved your miserable life, Vega," the Colonel returned with some disdain.

"Thank you, Colonel. Thank you," he said, sounding relieved.

"Don't thank me yet, Corporal. All you have to do is outdraw me."

Vega stood frozen. The Colonel could only imagine the fear that he was experiencing when he realized he was about to die. The soldiers surrounding the Corporal, including his man, backed away while the Colonel stood staring through two black lifeless eyes at his prey. He readied, at what he knew was point blank range, his smallish hands poised just above his guns.

"Please, Colonel," he begged. "I have a wife and children, please do not do this."

The Colonel said nothing, as over a minute passed; finally his overmatched opponent made a move for his sidearm. But before he could clear his weapon, the Colonel had both revolvers drawn and pointing at his underling. He tipped his head to one side and smiled slightly, before pulling the trigger, the bullet striking the terrified Corporal in the left eye socket and exiting thru the back of his skull. His men backed further away when their superior approached the lone remaining soldier who was under the late Corporal Vega's command.

The man stood at attention as the Colonel neared, he imagined that Vega's underling hoped for an opportunity to plead his case; but there was nothing to be gained by that futile exercise he thought. He nonchalantly placed the gun barrel on his forehead and without any hesitation or hint of conscious, pulled the trigger.

As the lifeless bodies lay, still warm, on the blood soaked ground, the Colonel was already planning his next move, a move that required him to pay a visit to the mountain village of Malaybalay—and a villager named Juan Romauldez.

~ ~ ~

Chapter 52

Wednesday Evening around nine o'clock—
Connor was resting in his room after having spent most of the
day going over last minute details with Billy. On Monday
morning if the pick-up area was clear, they would light a red
flare as a signal for the first plane to land. At that point Billy
and his men would secure the area. Anytime from now until
Sunday night, Billy could be reached at the hotel and the operation could be aborted or the rendezvous time changed.
Connor had signed the one hundred and fifty thousand dollar
note, after Billy verified that the Saudi buyer was in place and
awaiting delivery. He was now deeper in debt and could see
only one way out, or at least only one way to get whole.

George and Billy had disappeared a few hours ago,
most likely for some horizontal entertainment. Alex was sleeping in the next room while Connor thought about Maggie and
the dog tags he retrieved from the treasure cave. They were
scheduled to fly to Davao on Friday morning, and from that
point, they would have less than three days to remove the bullion and transport it to the rendezvous. He would have
tonight and tomorrow to recuperate; that part he wasn't worried about, it was the mental part he needed to work on.

As he rubbed the metal tags between his thumb and
forefinger, he slid to the side of the bed and picking up the
phone dialed his office. The thirteen-hour time difference
would make it around 8:00 a.m. back home, Nancy should
be in he thought, while he listened to the ringing in the
receiver.

"Hello, Capital Rehab," a familiar voice answered.

"Hi, Nance."

"Boss, is that you?"

"In the flesh."

"Thank God, you guys had me worried sick. Is Alex with you? Are you okay?"

"Alex is here and we're both fine. Nance, I need you to do something for me."

"Sure, anything."

"This is going to sound like a strange request, but this information is very important."

"Good ahead, Connor. I'm used to strange requests from you two."

"Which one of us are you used to stranger requests from Nance?"

"You're not funny, boss."

"Just kidding."

"What do you need?"

"I've got two names I need you to investigate for me. One is Jesse Hamilton, the other is Jacob Thomas, they should both come up as army personnel, missing in action during World War II in the Pacific."

"Okaaay, what exactly are you looking for?"

"That's the strange part, I'm not sure. I need to know everything you can find about them and their families, past and present. In my rolodex you'll find a number for Ben Cole, he's a private investigator, ex-state trooper and ex-military, he'll be able to help, just mention my name."

"No problem."

Connor relayed the rest of the information on the dog tags to Nancy. He had her read them back, verifying the spellings and serial numbers.

"Alright, you win the prize, boss."

"What prize?"

"The strangest request prize."

"For now, just wait till Alex gets back."

"You take care of him and yourself."

"Don't worry, Nance. I will."

"I know you will. I'll get this info for you. You can count on me."

"I always knew I could."

"Hey, I almost forgot."

"Forgot what?"

"Maggie stopped by yesterday. She told me if I heard from you to tell you to call her."

"She did, huh?" he returned as dispassionately as he could, considering she had just jump-started his heart.

"Yeah, she did. Call that girl, I think she likes you—a lot."

"Thanks, Nance. It's good to hear your voice, I'll be in touch."

"Bye, boss."

Connor hung up and immediately started to dial Maggie's number before something made him stop. He sat, tapping the phone receiver against his cheek trying to decide if this was the most prudent time to contact her. She probably wouldn't be at home now, he rationalized and if she was, at this early hour, maybe she wouldn't be alone and that was something he didn't want to know, not now, not with what lay ahead. He had another thirty-six hours to recover before they would be on a plane, traveling back to the mine and into who knows what kind of peril. He wasn't sure if the dog tags had anything to do with her supernatural contact; he would wait till he got an update from Nancy and then, maybe he would have enough information to shed some light on her dilemma.

It was possible, he thought, that the puzzle may never be solved. The likelihood that Maggie was not mentally competent loomed as a much more plausible explanation than her so-called ghostly invasions. He wasn't sure and he didn't want to be blind to the obvious, guarding against a repeat of the Jade incident, even if the consequences did not carry the same finality. He needed to have a clear, objective mind when he spoke to her. Anything less would not allow him to evaluate a future with her on any level.

Deciding definitively not to call, he settled in. One more day in Cebu and the operation would begin again in earnest. He needed to be ready; knowing his actions from that point on may impact his and his companions' very survival.

~ ~ ~

Chapter 53

Friday Morning—Connor, along with Alex and George boarded the plane for the short flight to Davao at the southern tip of Mindanao; their arrival to be followed by an extended journey back to the mine. Connor had spent most of the last twenty-four hours going over the plan for the air removal with Billy, who reinforced the point, that once on the ground and his men took control, they were not to interfere or question any actions by his team. After internalizing that message, he used the remainder of the time to relax and prepare for what lay ahead.

He tried to keep his mind clear and focused, despite his acute awareness of all the obstacles that stood between them and a successful excavation, not to mention keeping his own personal problems compartmentalized. He imagined that Alex fought to maintain his own even keel considering his previous failure at the checkpoint and their narrow escape from the pirates. If his special skills again were required, Connor wondered if he would be able to defeat his demons and not let them down.

George's position, on the other hand, was crystal clear. He had no doubt, that not long from now, he would be vindicated from his sins, the type of vindication that only money can buy. He had teamed up with Billy for a premature celebration of drinking and whoring. Connor had witnessed their cavorting with more than a little disdain; even though he was hardly a missionary, something about a country that was so poor it was forced to prostitute its daughters to survive, did not sit well with his conscious. Even Alex, who was suffering from perpetual hormone rage couldn't bring himself to participate in their brand of sexual debauchery.

Landing in Davao, there was no sign of the military that had greeted their arrival in Cagayan De Oro a few days earlier. As they deplaned, George alerted them to Lido waiting in the parking lot. Connor spied him leaning against an early nineties model Toyota Land Cruiser. Connor and Alex smiled at each other, approving of his choice of transportation.

From what George had told them, the City of Davao was a tourist town. Travelers from Japan, Australia and Europe were common visitors to the pristine beaches and one large luxury hotel, the Insular Continental, located on the southern shore of the island. The wealthiest Filipinos would also take holidays here, while others stayed in town or at one of the less expensive beach hotels. Fishing was the other industry, besides tourism, that dominated commerce. Just southeast of Davao was the city of General Santos, renowned for its tuna cannery.

With little or no notice as far as Connor could tell, they grabbed their bags and loaded them into the rental. Lido had the air conditioning cranked. They welcomed the abrupt change in temperature upon entering the vehicle.

"Nice truck, Lido," Alex said, settling into his seat.

"Thank you, Sir Alex," he returned proudly. "I got a very good deal."

"When we're done Lido, you'll be able to buy ten of these things," George bragged.

"I would only need one, Sir George," he said, wheeling the truck out of the lot.

"Whatever. How's everything at the mine?"

"Everything is ready, Sir George."

"Are the vehicles in place?"

"Yes, my men cleared the entrance to the road and they are at the mine."

"Did you get the equipment I wanted set up on the hill?"

"Yes, sir."

"Do the men know what we're going to be moving, Lido?" Connor asked.

"They do not know for sure, Sir Connor. They are poor mountain people and are not educated in these types of things. They are happy to have a place to work and food to eat."

"You didn't answer my question."

"They know something of value will be moved. They are poor and uneducated, but not stupid. If there was not anything of value, they know you would not be here. They just don't know what it is."

"Fair enough, that answers my question. What do you think, George?"

"We need them to load the jeepneys, Connor. When we get out what we want, we'll blow the mine, so we can come back again."

"What do you mean? This is it, George," Alex blurted out.

"It may be it for you boys, but I'm going back and set up the mining operation we originally planned. We own the damn mine."

"Do what you want, George," Connor surrendered. "But you're just bucking for trouble."

"If we don't go back and control the area, they may dig the rest of it out themselves."

"So what? We got ours, why would you care," Alex retorted. "Be happy to get some and get out in one piece."

"I will be, but then I'm getting more."

"Man, you're a greedy bastard," Connor said, shaking his head.

"Don't worry about me."

"We won't," Alex replied, sounding a little disgusted.

"Good. By the way, we need to stop at the bank and exchange some money. We need to get our flash cash, in case we need to buy someone off."

"Fine," Connor agreed. "Let's do it."

Lido drove to the National Mindanao Development Bank in town, a local branch of a large institution found throughout the southern region. It was just before 8:00 a.m., when Connor, with Lido at his side, rang the bell. After a brief conversation with the bank manager, they were allowed to enter prior to regular hours and exchange their money. It made sense to Connor that foreign currency, at a profitable rate of exchange, was a commerce opportunity entertained at any hour. About thirty minutes later, Connor and Lido reappeared with two large sacks full of Filipino pesos.

"I feel like we robbed the place," Connor said, getting back in the truck.

"How much did you exchange?" Alex asked, looking at the amount of bills they carried out.

"Only around four thousand, but it buys a lot of pesos."

"I guess it does," he agreed, taking the sacks and positioning them on the floor.

The remainder of the trip was thankfully uneventful, the rented vehicle making all the difference in comfort to Connor during the eight-hour excursion. At a little past 3:00 p.m., they passed through the town of Valencia on their way to Malaybalay. Alex joked that they better not blink or they'd miss the whole place. Lido had packed a cooler of chicken sandwiches and cold beer, which they devoured on route. Connor wondered if any of the meat was courtesy of the cock-fight they attended a few days ago.

Just outside of Valencia, they passed the Del Monte compound, a subsidized housing development for employees working in the pineapple fields that lined the opposite side of the road for as far as the eye could see. About a mile further down the road the golf course came into view. The fifth and sixth holes converged to offer a suitable landing area for the DC-3's that, if every thing went according to plan, would be making their unexpected arrival on Monday morning. Del Monte executives and their guests used the course mostly on weekends according to George. Occasionally military higher ups, such as Colonel Vudula would try their skill, as long as some unsuspecting civilian was picking up the tab.

All looked quiet to Connor on this Friday afternoon, as they drove by unnoticed. A far cry from the ruckus he expected they'd create three days from now when the sleepy course would be turned into airport runway. Connor could only imagine the resulting mayhem Billy Hilliard's private army would create if any early morning golfers attempted to interfere with the transfer. He decided to warn them away if possible, but also realized from the point of touchdown it would be out of his control. He pictured the potential slaughter and that made him feel very uneasy.

Less than twenty minutes later they reached Malaybalay, taking the turn on the dirt road and following it to the recently uncovered crude vehicle path to the mine. After a brief discussion, they decided to shift their rental to four wheel drive and leave their usual mode of transportation, the dilapidated jeep, in its resting place, still covered with jungle vines.

Connor was concerned that the route to the mine was now totally exposed. Lido's men had cleared away the heavy brush that camouflaged the entrance to allow the Jeepneys access to the road. He assured Connor that his men would keep look out and alert them to any potential intruders. Connor reluctantly accepted the situation, knowing it was too late to change anything or turn back, even though he felt the operation was now more vulnerable because of it.

Reaching the base mine, they were greeted by a familiar cast of characters, looking happy to see Lido, George and their new American benefactors. The recent arrival of the three jeepneys and several dirt bikes seemed to have raised the level of curiosity among the workers with regard to the longevity of their employment. They quizzed Lido in their native tongue as Connor observed them pointing to the vehicles and the returning Americans. He appeared to have calmed their concerns and hustled them back to work.

"What's going on Lido?" George asked.

"They are very worried, Sir George. They think that you will leave soon and they will have no more jobs here."

"Tell them that they will not lose their jobs, even if we have to go away for awhile."

"I told them already, but they still worry."

"Show them the money, tell them we'll leave it with them when we go."

"Are you sure, Sir George?"

"Yes, I'm sure. Go ahead."

Lido took the sacks and called his men. He showed them the money and Connor, Alex and even George couldn't help but smile at their child-like reaction. They seemed much happier as they headed back to their unproductive labor. Connor could see that Lido was clearly enjoying his statue as rainmaker; they seemed to look to him as their bridge to a better life, having delivered steady employment for almost two years. Connor felt glad for Lido, imagining the juggling he must have had to perform each month to secure their wages from George.

"Everything okay now?" George asked.

"All is well, Sir George," he returned smiling.

"Good, let's get up to the mine. We've got lots to do."

They all agreed as Lido directed some of his men to carry their things while they made the one-hour ascent. It would be dark soon and they wanted to get settled in so they could get a good night's sleep before they started the operation. Lido, under instructions from George, had earlier transported a gas-powered winch and tackle in order to assist in hauling the gold out of the abyss. They had estimated being able to move around a hundred pounds at a time. Working steadily they should be able to unearth the desired amount over the next forty-eight hours, as long as Connor and Lido could hold out in the cavern depths.

Upon reaching the hilltop, Lido directed his men back to the base camp. They decided to start unearthing the gold at first light. Once they had brought up the amount to be transferred, they would get the workers to bring it down and load it in the jeepneys for transport. At that point they would blow the mine, telling the men they had unearthed all the gold that was there. They would leave them the cash from the bank, and after would return to help Lido finance the promsied housing, schools and hospital.

As they prepared the evening meal, Connor wondered

381

if George had any intention of fulfilling that end of the bargain. It was obvious he felt he deserved more than the rest; he had suffered much longer. The uncle's vision clearly was not his, and any promises from his father's former partner, he suspected were just lip service at this point.

They dined on the freeze-dried food Alex had left behind, along with the equipment and gray brief case, whose mysterious contents Connor realized he had still not pressed Alex to divulge. It wasn't that he refused to tell him it was just that, in all the excitement of recent days, Connor hadn't even bothered to ask.

After eating, Connor and Alex settled into their hammocks, covering themselves with the makeshift mosquito netting. Connor was feeling the best he had physically since their arrival; it was the mental aspect he was having trouble with. His brain was swirling while he tried to locate a peaceful thought, Maggie, the dog tags, his father, his debt, Jade and the next day's monumental undertaking filled his head. He was worried and excited all at the same time; his body was vibrating with emotions that just kept pouring over him. The heat and humidity were no longer a concern, just a minor inconvenience as his body had acclimated better than expected to his jungle environment. He clutched the three remaining pain pills, saving them until they were really needed. Tomorrow was the moment of truth. He was ready—he knew he had to be, what other choice was there?

~ ~ ~

Chapter 54

Early Friday Evening—Colonel Vadula stared from the makeshift window of a tiny, three-room, plywood shanty. He was watching Juan Rumaldez's slender, five-foot-seven frame approaching on the dirt and rock road that led to his home. It was clear that the sight of a military vehicle parked near-by had startled him, as his gate slowed considerably as he neared. The Colonel, anticipating his entrance, returned to his position when he heard him climbing the ladder like-stairs into his home. He knew he wouldn't flee, despite all the obvious signs of trouble. His main concern would be for his pretty young wife Belinda and his two young daughters.

Once inside he came face-to-face with what the Colonel knew had to be the worst of fears for a father and husband. Two heavily armed soldiers stood over his wife and youngest daughter, sitting bound and gagged on an old mattress, while his oldest girl was held tightly on the lap of the self-proclaimed most dangerous man on the island.

The Colonel sat on a rickety wooden chair, with the young girl, stroking her long black hair with one hand and rubbing one of his pearl handled pistols along the smooth skin of her leg with the other. He didn't speak. He just waited, giving Juan time to take in the whole shocking scene, wanting to reinforce his total helplessness and his family's grave danger. Terror was an emotion, best elevated in silence he thought. After what he was sure seemed like an eternity to his prey, the Colonel's raspy voice broke the eerie quiet.

"Juan Rumaldez?" the Colonel asked, running his gun

barrel along the cheek of his frightened hostage.

"Yes, sir," he returned softly, casting his eyes downward.

"Juan, you have some information I need. Will you help me?"

"Yes, sir. I will do anything, please don't. . . ."

"QUIET," the Colonel shouted. "Don't speak unless I ask you to. Do you understand me?" he said, clutching the child tightly against him, feeling his upper lip begin to quiver.

"Yes, sir."

"Good," he returned, calming himself. "You recently cashed a large American bill. Where did you acquire this money?"

Juan hesitated, the Colonel was sure he had been told by his benefactors not to reveal the source of his income or the location of the mine site to anyone if he wanted to keep his job. He was also quite confident that employment was hardly his primary concern at this moment.

"I got the money from my work."

"And where is it that you work, Juan?"

"At a mine in the mountains."

"Now, this next question is very important, so think carefully before you answer. Do you work for an American named George Fall?"

He didn't answer; he just nodded.

"Very good, Juan. You may just get out of this alive yet," the Colonel acknowledged.

For the next hour he grilled Juan on the location of the mine, the stationing of the lookouts and the whereabouts of the Americans. Juan told him everything, including the existence of the hilltop huts and the fact that, although he had never been, George and his new associates spent a lot of their time there.

"Are you sure that's everything, Juan?" the Colonel demanded, squeezing the arm of the child so tightly it made her cry.

"That's all, please don't hurt her," he pleaded.

Having gotten what he came for, the Colonel released

the sobbing child from his grasp and watched while she rushed to the outstretched arms of her father. He held her close, obviously not sure if their nightmare was over. The Colonel signaled to his men and they exited the hut-like house, walking briskly toward their vehicle.

The Colonel paused, as he still wasn't quite sure if he had created enough of an impression to dissuade Juan from trying to warn the Americans. Looking over at his pretty wife, still gagged, with her hands tied behind her back, he walked over and knelt down, placing his revolver on her temple. She cringed when the metal pressed against her skin. Juan looked terrified as he clutched his daughter.

"Juan, don't get any ideas about heading up to the mine to warn anyone of our visit," he said, sliding his free hand inside his victim's flimsy sundress and roughly fondling her breast.

"I wouldn't do that," he answered sheepishly.

"Good," he returned, as he leaned forward and touched her cheek with the tip of his tongue, wanting to taste her fear. "I will be back tomorrow, make sure you're here, and your wife. We have a little unfinished business," he smiled, removing his hand and getting up to leave. "Do you understand me?"

"Yes, sir."

"Don't make me come looking for you, Juan. You wouldn't like what happened if I found you."

"No, sir."

"Good, tomorrow then," he said, getting up to leave. As he headed for the door, he watched while Juan hurried to untie his family. They all clung to each other and cried. He was sure there was now a monster in their lives; tonight he imagined they would pray for deliverance from his deadly grip—what else could people as powerless as they possibly do.

~ ~ ~

Chapter 55

Daybreak, Saturday Morning—Connor was rudely awakened by the unnerving sensation of cold steel being pressed against his cheekbone. He struggled to focus while a shadowy figure stood over him. He was just barely able to make out the silhouette of his assailant due to the rising sun shining through the doorway, partially obstructing his vision. When he looked to his right, he observed Alex suffering the same fate at the hands of another man. Starting to come to his senses, he recognized the intruders and his heart sank, realizing their dream and maybe their lives were now precariously close to ending.

He slowly got out of his hammock and was escorted along with Alex out of the hut. Leaving the small confines, he saw George and Lido, heads hanging, as they stood in the middle of the camp, guarded by a familiar menacing figure.

"Good morning, Mr. Mason," came the unmistakable signature, raspy voice.

"Hello, Colonel," he returned, trying not to show any fear, but feeling he wasn't doing a very good job.

"Good morning to you also Mr. Litowski. I am glad to see that all my partners are well," he stated, the sarcasm dripping from his scratchy vocals.

"To what do we owe the pleasure of your visit, Colonel?"

"I think you know, Mr. Mason. You and my other partners are continually trying to make my men look foolish. By doing this, you make me look foolish, too. Where did you go when you slipped away Monday afternoon?"

"We had some business to take care of."

"What kind of business?"

"The type that is no concern of yours, Colonel."

"That is where you're wrong, Mr. Mason, dead wrong. Why are you up here and not down at the mine?"

"We like to get away from the mine, so we come up here," he returned, trying to think on his feet.

"I don't believe you—partner."

"That's your choice."

"Of course it is," he returned, as he looked at his two guards and nodded.

Connor watched while the soldiers interpreted his silent direction and closed in, motioning for him to raise his arms. One kept their rifle trained on him while the other began conducting a search. As the guard began to pat him down, Connor instinctively jumped back; suddenly realizing the second gold bar he had retrieved from the cavern was still in his pocket.

"What's this all about, Colonel?" he yelled, backing away from his bodily invader.

"You're being searched for contraband," the Colonel returned calmly.

"What contraband?"

"I'll let you know, Mr. Mason," he said, withdrawing one of his pearl handled revolvers and pointing it directly at him. "It is much easier to search a dead man, they don't resist as much. Please allow my man to continue his job."

Connor reluctantly succumbed to his inspection; not believing the Colonel would actually shoot a valuable commodity that could be ransomed. The rest of the captives looked uncomfortable. Connor knew they were all too aware of what would momentarily be discovered. The soldier moving down his pant leg encountered the hard metal object in his pocket, reaching in he pulled out the small gold ingot. Realizing what he had uncovered, he discontinued his search and brought the distinctively, molded bullion to his superior. The group was dead silent while they watched the Colonel inspect the bar.

"This is contraband, Mr. Mason," he said, holding the gold at arms length. "Where did you get it?"

"I don't remember."

"Think hard, Mr. Mason. Your answer may save your life and those of your companions."

"Sorry, Colonel. It's just not coming to me."

"Maybe this will help you remember," he returned, pointing his weapon at George. "I will count to three and then I'm going to shoot Mr. Fall, somewhere in the groin, and we'll watch him bleed to death.

One. . . ."

"Jesus Christ, Connor," George yelled. "Tell him!"

"Shut up, George. He's not going to shoot. We're his meal ticket."

"Two."

"We got the gold from a mine below the hut," George blurted out.

"Fuck, George," Connor yelled, knowing that once the location was revealed, they were as good as dead.

"I'm sorry, Colonel," George pleaded. "There's lots of gold down there, plenty for all of us."

"Show me where it is, Mr. Fall."

"Right over here, Colonel," George said.

Connor watched in disbelief while George led the Colonel into the hut and assisted him in removing the floor covering. It was a deadly mistake and everyone knew it, except George it appeared. Connor listened to their conversation as George spilled all he knew about the contents of the cavern. When they came walking out, George had a nervous grin on his sweaty round face; the Colonel bore a more sinister expression.

"It will be all right," George assured, as he rejoined them.

"Stop kidding yourself," Alex returned.

"How did you find us, Colonel?" Connor asked, trying to stall for time, although he didn't know what more time would do for them.

"You can't have mountain peasants walking around

with American hundred dollar bills up here and not get noticed, Mr. Mason."

"Lido?" Connor questioned, looking toward him.

"I am ashamed," he returned, looking away. "I had so much to do, I didn't have time to exchange the money and the men wanted to be paid."

"Oh God, Lido," Alex exclaimed.

"I'm sorry," he returned, sounding exasperated.

"Forget about it, Lido. It's not your fault, we all had a hand in creating this mess," Connor said, knowing that everyone had made mistakes, including him, by keeping the gold bar instead of leaving it in the cave.

"So you see, once I got word about the money, we simply visited the family and they were gracious enough, at my insistence, to show us the location of the road leading to the mine. We thought the early hour would find everyone surprised by our visit, including your sleeping lookouts."

"What would you like us to do now, Colonel?" George asked.

"You should make your peace, Mr. Fall."

"Make my peace, for what?" he questioned.

"That's what men do when they are about to die, Mr. Fall, as you and your friends are."

George stood motionless, as if in shock. Connor knew he was having a difficult time believing that anyone who he had just identified a king's ransom for would have him killed. It just didn't make sense. It did, however, make perfect sense to Connor; having the location of the gold, why would he leave any witnesses, especially ones with means to cause problems.

"Colonel, we can help you sell the gold. Set up offshore accounts, whatever you need," George proposed, his voice starting to crack.

"First of all Mr. Fall, I control planes and men, and can very easily circumvent any inspections. I know wealthy men who will buy it and still be afraid of me, a combination that I find most inviting. Secondly, why would I trust you to do anything you're telling me? You have not so far, you have only mocked and ridiculed my authority."

"I understand how it looks, Colonel, but we. . . ."

"Do you, Mr. Fall, do you really understand what it is to live my life," he growled, staring at him with his dark beady eyes.

"Look, I'm sorry, we're sorry," he pleaded, his tone revealing he was near the breaking point.

"I'm sorry too, Mr. Fall," the Colonel returned.

"You can't just kill us, we're Americans for Christ sake."

"I didn't kill you, Mr. Fall. I tried to save you and your friends from the rebels who captured you in the jungle. Unfortunately, my men and I were too late, you had already been executed."

"Save your breath, George," Connor said. "This little coward would have killed us no matter what we did."

"Who are you calling a coward?" the Colonel growled at him.

"You, you little hypocrite; you have all your shooting medals and commendations and you're going to gun us down in cold blood. Go ahead then, hero. Show your men how brave you are, we're not armed, it's safe, go ahead," Connor badgered, trying to play on his bravado.

The Colonel hesitated as the two soldiers with him eyed their commander. Connor's knew his words were cutting through him; sure that he wanted to kill him now, before it was just business, but now he'd been insulted. Still he counted on the fact that he'd like the idea of making a contest of it, one that Connor imagined would be extremely tilted in the Colonel's favor.

"I'll tell you what, Mr. Mason. Why don't you and I have a competition, you can draw against me. If you win, you and your friends can go free, if you lose—well it won't matter, because you'll be dead," he said, rubbing his hands confidently over the pearl handles of his holstered pistols as his upper lip quivered betraying his rising anger.

"You're on, Colonel," Connor returned, his adrenaline pumping. "Give me a minute, will you?" Turning his back, he faced Alex.

"Can I beat him?" he whispered.

"Not a chance, bud," he returned.

"Thanks for the vote of confidence. Maybe he'll miss."

"Not likely, Con. You don't have a prayer."

"Any suggestions?"

"Let me have a go at him."

"You haven't had much luck shooting people over here, Alex. I can pull the trigger, can you?"

"I know you can pull it, brother, but you won't have enough time. You can't outdraw him."

"That's not what I asked."

"I know. I can do it."

"I'm sorry I got you into this," he surrendered; knowing only Alex had a shot at besting the Colonel.

"It's not your fault, Con. Hey, you know me; I'd follow you anywhere."

"Are you ready, Mr. Mason?" the Colonel called out, his impatience obvious.

"There's been a change of plans, Colonel. Alex is going to take my place."

"As you wish. I'll kill him first and then you," he returned, taking off his hat and handing it to one of his men.

Connor looked at Alex and after giving him a nod and a word of encouragement stepped aside, joining Lido and George. The Colonel instructed one of his men to place the 45 caliber pistol they had confiscated from the hut into Alex's belt, as they faced each other about twenty-feet apart. Suddenly a look from the Colonel signaled the soldier, who drew back his rifle and delivered a sharp blow to Alex's right elbow causing him squeal in pain.

"You bastard," Connor yelled, lunging forward, before a pointed rifle halted his advance.

"I'll be alright, Con," Alex assured him as he rubbed his arm.

"So this will be the ultimate shooting contest, Mr. Litowski, with each other as the target."

"I guess you're right about that, Colonel." He flexed his right-hand looking like he was trying to restore the feeling.

"What is it like being so close to death?"

"I don't know how you're feeling, Colonel. Why don't you tell me?"

"That's the American way, brave on the outside, but shaking like a schoolboy on the inside. I commend you for the front you're putting up. Maybe if you drop to your knees and beg, I may spare you," the Colonel offered.

"That's not going to happen, Colonel," he returned, still shaking his hand.

"You really can't expect to defeat me, Mr. Litowski. I'm the fastest draw on the islands and you have no chance in light of your—unfortunate accident."

"First of all Colonel. I'm not from the islands and secondly, I'm left handed," Alex's tone so confident that Connor thought from the look on the Colonel's face, he was suddenly having a moment of doubt.

Connor, George, Lido and the Colonel's men watched in anticipation. Both combatants seemed tense, as their lives were dangling in the balance of this encounter. Connor was sure that Alex had the Colonel thinking that maybe this would not be as easy as orchestrated, although he had no illusions about the level of his skill, and the fact that he was a killer and Alex was not. Whatever the outcome, one thing he was sure of; it would be over soon, not just for Alex, but for all of them.

~ ~ ~

Chapter 56

It was just after 11:00 p.m. in downtown London, at the Morgan Gold Corporate Offices, located in the heart of the financial section near Trafalgar Square. Charles Morgan watched while Jonathan Ames, a fax message tucked neatly under his arm, entered his penthouse office through the heavy mahogany doors. Morgan was sipping tea and waiting for his next phone call, knowing that in his business working hours are never dictated between nine and five; world commerce goes on twenty-four hours a day. He was anticipating an update on a gold vein at their mine near Kuala Lumpur, when his underling's entrance captured his attention.

"Working late this evening, Jonathan," he said, reaching for his glasses.

"Yes, sir."

"Is there something that requires my attention?"

"Yes, sir. I have some news about the Philippine activity."

"Go ahead then, what's happening?"

"I'm afraid we've had a bit a bad luck regarding the termination of Mr. Mason."

"Is that a fact," he returned, running a hand over his baldhead. "What kind of bad luck?"

"It seems our operative has been removed from the equation."

"Is this a temporary removal?"

"No, permanent I've been informed."

"Really?"

"Yes, sir."

"Do you think we've underestimated young Mason, Jonathan?"

"It is a possibility, sir."

"Do we have anyone else we can send in?"

"Another contract or our people?"

"Outside contract, Jonathan. If people are going to be disposed of, I would like to not have any trail back to us."

"I understand, sir. We, unfortunately do not have anyone available for at least seventy-two hours."

"That's a lifetime with regard to this situation. Can't we do better?"

"Not at this time."

"How about the rebels in the area?" he asked, taking another sip of tea.

"We have been informed that they are sweeping the province in search of the plane load of arms we rumored to have crash landed there, sir."

"Well, we're going to have to hope that they keep things disrupted until we can find a more competent consultant to complete the contract."

"I understand, sir. I'll get right on it."

"Do we have a clue where Mr. Mason is, Jonathan?"

"Computer records show that he purchased a ticket for Davao, Mindanao yesterday morning, Philippine time."

"What was the origin of the flight?"

"Cebu, sir."

"Did we have any record of him leaving Mindanao by plane previously?"

"No, sir."

"Then it's highly unlikely that he flew to Cebu, he must be using other forms of transport."

"It would seem that way, Mr. Morgan."

"Yes, it most certainly would, Jonathan. You know what to do. Keep me informed," he said, dismissing him.

"Yes, sir," he returned.

As Ames exited, Morgan was more than a little miffed by his victim having had eluded the web he'd cast. He was not satisfied with the outcome so far. The longer it remained a loose end, the more vulnerable they would be to a potential market glut disrupting their profits and stranglehold on the commodity he relished. This was not acceptable; it was now taking more time than he was interested in spending. How Mason was able to escape their highly paid assassin was a mystery he longed to have answered. No matter, he thought, in a short period of time, young Mr. Mason would be fertilizer in some Asian farm field. The mental image of that brought a smile of anticipated satisfaction to his otherwise stoic features.

~ ~ ~

Chapter 57

The sound of gunfire echoed through the jungle hillside, breaking the morning calm. The Colonel had cleared his weapon first, but fired second, as he stood momentarily before dropping in a heap to the ground. A gaping hole in his chest, compliments of the 45 slug that now released a stream of red, darkening his pressed tan shirt.

Alex zeroed in on the Colonel's men, looking as though in shock, obviously not believing their superior had been bested while blood continued to pool around his lifeless body. When he turned to his companions, they too seemed frozen in place, as the entire event took only a fraction of a second to play out.

The Colonel had lost a split second by straightening his arm before firing, while Alex cleared his weapon and fired from the hip; that was all that separated them from life and death. He had observed that flaw in his opponent's technique at the army base; tucking it away in the event of a confrontation, it gave him the physical and mental edge he needed to preserve their lives—for now. He had traveled full circle from the previous day's potential disaster. In this place at this time, he had achieved more than vindication, for now he was the man—the man that saved their lives.

Alex knew there was no time to waste. There were still two armed men to deal with. He was still feeling his adrenaline high when he took an armed stance, pointing his weapon at one of the soldiers, as he noticed Connor draw back his fist to attack the still stunned guard closest to him. Suddenly a volley of shots rung out, cutting down their would be foes. George dove to the ground while Alex watched twenty or so armed Filipino men emerge from the jungle. He took note of their various stages of dress, everything from jeans to fatigues, dark green t-shirts to open button shirts, army boots to sneakers and sandals, one thing they did have in common, all were wearing bright yellow bandannas around their heads.

One man, carrying a smoking machine gun, appeared to Alex to be the leader as he dispatched his followers to secure the perimeter of the camp. He was dressed in boots, camouflage fatigues, army green t-shirt and bandanna. At around five-foot ten and maybe one hundred and eighty pounds, he looked to be one of the larger of the intruders. His long dark hair and unshaven leather brown face was highlighted by a black eye patch that partially hid a scar starting just above his eyebrow and ending on his cheekbone below, probably remnants of the wound that cost him the eye, Alex imagined.

"Who are they?" Alex asked Lido.

"Rebels, Sir Alex. The one in the front is named Dato."

"You know these men?"

"Yes, some of them. Some are from the village. They would rather steal than work."

"What's their cause, why are they fighting?"

"They are fighting for a better life, like we all are, they just do it with guns and terror."

No one moved as Dato and his men completed their infiltration of the small encampment. His men searched the first hut while their leader stood over the fallen Colonel, about fifteen feet from Alex who still held his gun, now dangling in his right hand. George was maintaining his position on the ground; looking too petrified to stand.

One of the rebels exited the first hut and leaning close to his superior, reported his findings. Suddenly Dato turned his attention from his comrade to Alex, still armed, standing to his right.

"Drop your weapon, please," he asked politely. Alex did not hesitate; opening his hand and letting the pistol fall. "Thank you. Did you kill the Colonel?"

"Yes," Alex answered, feeling very vulnerable.

"Do you know of a plane that has crashed in these mountains?"

"No."

"Are you an American?"

"Yes."

"And your friends?"

"Yes."

"There is a deep hole in the hut, why was it dug?"

Alex hesitated for a moment, not sure what he should say, he knew the Colonel had the gold bar in his pocket, if they searched him, it would certainly raise more questions.

"It's an abandoned mine shaft. We were going to close it up with an explosion, when the Colonel appeared demanding money we didn't have," Connor said, intruding on the conversation.

"I see," Dato returned, turning toward this new source of information. "When the soldiers find the Colonel's body, they will be searching everywhere for the people that did this. This will be a big problem for me, when I'm looking for the plane."

Connor hesitated for a moment before answering. "They don't have to find the body."

"What do you mean?"

"We can drop it down the abandoned mine shaft, before we blow it."

~ ~ ~

As soon as he made the suggestion, George shot him a look like his life had come to an end. Connor caught his gaze with his piercing blue eyes, returning his stare that reinforced that this was their only way out alive. The thought that George would try and make a deal for the gold raced through his mind. Connor was sure he couldn't stomach the thought of starting all over again, he could only hope that he learned his lesson from the Colonel and know that that course of action would only end in disaster.

"Yes, that is a good idea," he agreed motioning to his men to get the bodies.

"We'll help," Connor said, as he moved toward Alex and grabbing his arm directed him toward the Colonel's lifeless form.

Bending down to pick up the body, Alex, like Connor hoped, caught on to exactly what he was doing when he stepped between him and Dato, blocking the rebel leaders view while Connor removed the small gold bar and slipped it back in his pocket. He knew Alex had to be wondering why he would risk this, when he could have dropped it down the shaft with the Colonel, but he had his reasons and was just thankful he backed his play.

They dragged the corpse into the hut and dropped him head first down the dark shaft. Once his body had disappeared out of sight, the lifeless forms of his henchmen were disposed of. Connor then grabbed the battery and wires and unrolled them out into the yard, stopping next to a deflated and pitiful looking, George Fall.

"How do we do this, George?" he asked.

"You're not really going to collapse the mine, are you?"

"Fuck yes, you idiot," he whispered harshly. "We're not out of this yet, not by a long shot. If they even have a hint that something of value is down there, we're dead men. So either you show me how to blow this or I'm going to kill you myself."

"Alright," he reluctantly agreed. "Take the blue wire and connect it to the negative terminal, then just touch the positive electrode with the red wire. That should set off the charge, same as before."

"What do you mean same as before?"

"We had problems the first time we tried to move the gold. Rebels and the military were closing in and your father did the same thing you're doing now. That's why some of the trucks were buried near the back of the cave. First the father, now the son, I hope I don't live to see any of your kids."

"Sorry, George, but we have no choice," he returned, feeling some empathy for him. "Stand away from the hut," he yelled.

Connor, following George's instructions, ignited the explosives setting off a blast deep in the chimney mine, causing dirt and dust to come bellowing out of the hut. After it cleared, they inspected what was left of the hut to verify that the mine had indeed collapsed in on itself. Connor watched as Dato conferred with some of his men, before walking over to address them.

"My men think we should hold you for ransom, but since you killed our enemy, I would like to give you the chance to buy your freedom."

"How much?" Connor asked.

"Whatever you have."

"We have vehicles down below at the other site."

"I'm afraid they are no longer there, we observed your men driving off in them after the Colonel's arrival."

"We have the rental vehicle, give him the keys, Lido."

Lido reached in his pocket and pulled out a set of keys, tossing them to the rebel leader, who snatched them with one hand.

"That will buy you some time," he returned, smiling and dangling the keys in front of them before sticking them in his shirt pocket.

"I've got something," Alex interrupted. "May I get it?"

"Certainly," Dato answered, motioning for one of his men to accompany him.

Alex went into the other hut that Lido and George were occupying and brought out the two large sacks of pesos.

"How much time will this buy us?" he asked, reaching into a sack and tossing handfuls of pesos into the air. The pesos were flying everywhere as he dispersed thousands of bills in all directions around the camp. Dato motioned to his men, who put down their weapons and began stuffing their pockets with the cash.

Dato looked at his four captives. "Very clever," he acknowledged. "That will buy you until my men have collected the money from the ground. If I were you, I would leave now. When we catch you, and we will, you will be held for ransom."

"Fair enough," Alex said. "Come on, let's get out of here."

The four of them quickly prepared to leave while Connor followed Alex back into the hut, observing him rummaging through his bag. He watched him grab the disk with the pictures from the treasure cave, a small electronic device, which he activated, and his mysterious gray briefcase. Connor waved George and Lido ahead when he stepped out of the hut to wait for his friend.

"Come on, Alex," Connor yelled.

"I'm coming, I'm coming," he answered, running out of the hut with the briefcase in hand. None of the rebels seemed to notice the case, as they, including their leader, were busy picking up the scattering bills.

"Forget that thing, Alex," Connor said, while they hurried to catch up to George and Lido. "It's only going to slow us down."

"We need it."

"What the fuck is in there that's so important."

"You'll see. Now let's pick it up," he returned, increasing his pace.

"Hey, clever idea to throw the money, how'd you ever think of that," Connor kidded as they ran.

"You're a funny guy, C. Mason. I hope we live long enough to joke about it," he returned, overtaking George and Lido.

Twenty minutes later, Connor could see that George was really hurting; his round out of shape body was heaving in an effort to process more oxygen. Connor was feeling his rib cage scream as he downed the last three pain pills he'd been saving. From their position he could see the rebels beginning their pursuit, obviously not wanting a potential payday to slip thru their fingers. They were practically carrying George when they neared the decoy mine.

"I can't make it," George said, struggling to get out the words.

"We need to make it to the camp, Sir George. Everything will be alright, then."

"How do you figure, Lido?" Alex asked. "Did you kill some more chickens the other night?"

"What are you talking about?" Connor asked, as he helped Lido drag George's now limp, exhausted body.

"Don't ask, it's an inside joke."

"No, Sir Alex. The other night I sacrificed a whole pig."

"Now that makes me feel better," Alex returned sarcastically.

"I am glad," Lido replied.

"What are we going to do when we get to camp, Lido? The jeep's another three miles away, we can't outrun them, they're not more than ten minutes behind us."

"Please don't leave me," George begged.

"Shut up, George," Alex said. "Don't worry we won't leave you, I want the pleasure of kicking your stupid, out of shape, ass once we get out of this."

"You think we're really getting out of this?" Connor questioned, hurting badly, a result of the human load he was hauling.

"Of course we are. Weren't you listening, Lido killed a pig, we're going to be fine."

Connor just shook his head, as they broke out of the jungle and into the abandoned mine site. Everyone was gone; all that was left was a few huts and the rental vehicle. They collapsed to the ground in order to catch their breath, it was now three miles to the jeep and the heat and humidity had them almost wiped out and George reduced to human baggage.

"What now Lido? The rebels are right behind us. Do you know anywhere we can hide, or a short cut or what?" Alex gasped.

"We get into the rental vehicle, Sir Alex?"

"What are you talking about, you gave the rebel guy the keys?"

"No, sir," Lido said, standing in front of them dangling a set of keys. "I gave him the keys to Mr. George's car."

"You're shittin' me," Alex exclaimed.

"No, sir. I wouldn't do such a thing," he returned, heading to the vehicle.

"I love you, " Alex said, catching up to him and giving him a big kiss on the lips.

"I like you too, Sir Alex," Lido replied, looking a little stunned, but smiling.

They loaded into the Land Cruiser and took off down the trail. Connor would have liked to have seen the look on Dato's face when he realized Lido had given him the wrong set of keys, it must have been priceless, he thought. As they proceeded on the rougher than usual ride, due to their haste, Connor knew they still had the problem of getting off the island and back home. He was sure that prior to his early morning invasion, the Colonel had set up road blocks along the one mountain road leading to the airports, in case they escaped his clutches. He was also positive that George would never hold up under intense questioning about the whereabouts of the Colonel and his men. Even if by some miracle they made it to an airport or the docks, the odds were they would be swarming with soldiers. If they hid around Malaybalay, the rebels or the military would eventually find out, they stood out too much and people were poor, that combination made for easily solicited information.

"How are we going to get off this island?" Connor asked. We can't use the airports or the docks and I don't think we could hide effectively long enough for the search to die down. Any ideas?"

"I do," Alex returned. "Just get me to a clearing and I'll get us out of here."

"How are you going to do that?"

"I'm going to call Billy and have him pick us up at the golf course."

"We'll never make it to a phone, Alex. There's no service up here."

"I brought my own," he returned, pointing to the gray briefcase.

"Is that what I think it is?" Connor asked.

"Portable satellite phone, good on ninety-seven percent of the earth's surface."

"Amen."

"Exactly that, brother."

"Looks like you saved our bacon again, Alex. By the way nice job up on the mountain, no one else could have beaten the Colonel. You saved our lives."

"Thanks, I just wanted a chance to step up. You were always the one there for me, I wanted to return the favor."

"Well you did and more, I owe you. We all owe you."

"It's not about owes, it's about friends. Even though it didn't work out, I wouldn't have missed it for the world. It was an adventure, even if we are in the financial dregs for the rest of our lives."

"Yeah, an adventure for you. Just the end for me," George lamented.

"We're not done yet," Connor contributed. "I've got a plan that may just get us whole. I'm not sure it will work and it's risky, but worth a try. I will, however need the exact location of the mine."

"That's not a problem," Alex answered. "Got it right here on my GPS," he said taking a small electronic device from his pocket. "I took the exact mine coordinates just before we left, to use as a direction point in case we had to escape through the jungle. I've got latitude and longitude to within three feet."

"What the hell is GDS," George asked.

"It's GPS, global positioning satellite. It uses satellite signals to triangulate your position. Planes and ships have used them for years, now that they're affordable and handheld, hunters use them all the time."

"That'll do," Connor returned smiling.

"What's the plan, Con?"

"Let's call Billy first and then I'll explain it to everyone," he returned, as they came to the end of the path and exited the jungle and onto the dirt road leading to the village of Malaybalay.

Alex got out and quickly set up the small satellite dish and hailed an operator, who put him in touch with the Cebu

Plaza Hotel, where they hunted down Billy. After explaining what happened, he agreed to pick them up on the golf course in two hours. They loaded back into the vehicle and proceeded to the rendezvous. They waited in the parking lot while Connor explained his plan; it was a long shot, but under the circumstances, the only shot. With everyone in agreement, they waited for Billy to swoop down and fly them to safety.

The next hour and a half was tense. Connor almost expected the military to surround them at any time or the rebels to emerge from the jungle that encircled the course. There were very few golfers in the heat of the midday sun when they drove out to the fifth hole once they saw a plane circling. Connor watched while Billy and his co-pilot made a perfect landing, although the fairway would require some repair from the ruts left by the tires.

No one approached when they climbed aboard and took off. Connor never thought he'd be this glad to see good old Billy as he lifted him and his friends into the relative safety of the friendly skies of Air Asia.

~ ~ ~

Chapter 58

Three days later, late afternoon—Connor was sitting in the busy international terminal at London's Heathrow airport. He felt rested, although still somewhat jet lagged after being jostled around the globe. Billy Hilliard had delivered them safely to Cebu, where they said their goodbyes to Lido, assuring him that they would see him soon, and boarded a plane for Manila and then on to Hong Kong. They spent the next day and a half, resting up, getting new clothes and going over the new initiative he had devised.

He had contacted Wes to assist with the preparations and he'd been surprisingly supportive of the plan. Wes agreed to meet Alex and George in Grand Cayman, while Connor took the point and flew to London. He had been here half a day, checking out the area, and had returned to the airport to meet an international courier who had been contracted to deliver a package to him.

As he leaned back, reflecting on the activities of the last few weeks and how they'd affected his life, he realized how close to death he'd come, how close to riches and how broke he really was. He wondered then, why he was feeling so content, more content than he'd remembered being in his whole life. Maybe his father was right, "a life without adventure is a life not lived"; he'd never felt more alive and more grateful for his life than he did right now. Why was it? It wasn't something that was explained in words, he thought, only feelings. While he waited for the plane and his package to arrive, he took his newly acquired cell phone and dialed the office. He'd been in touch with Nancy from Hong Kong, but she still hadn't received the information on the dog tags from Ben Cole. The phone was ringing as he waited for her to answer.

"Good morning, Capital Rehab."

"Hey, Nance, it's Connor."

"Morning, boss."

"It's afternoon over here."

"Where are you?"

"I'm in London and Alex is in Grand Cayman, same time zone as you."

"Got it, I'm having a hard time keeping track of you jet setters lately."

"With a little luck, we'll be home soon."

"I hope so."

"Me, too. Did you get any information from Ben Cole?"

"Sure did, just got an e-mail an hour ago."

"Let me hear it," he said, hoping for a clue to Maggie's perceptions.

"Jesse Hamilton, black enlisted man, missing in action in the Philippines. Worked in a slaughterhouse in Chicago prior to the war, no known relatives currently living. Jacob Thomas, corporal; missing in action in the Philippines. Worked on the family farm in Indiana, farm is currently in foreclosure and set for auction in two weeks. Guess they couldn't make it, although it did last over fifty years, someone must have been good at farming."

"Thanks, Nance."

"Anything else?"

"Yeah, get me an address for the Thomas farm and find out who holds the mortgage and how much."

"That it?"

"That's plenty. I think I got what else I needed. I'll talk to you soon."

"Okay, bye boss."

"Bye."

Connor contemplated the information. He remembered what Maggie had told him about why people on the other side make contact with the living. It made perfect sense

407

that Jacob Thomas wanted to help his descendents and save the family farm. Maybe that was what he was supposed to do, no matter how far out there it seemed; something had made him go back and pick up the dog tags. He decided now was the time to make the phone call he'd been putting off. He dialed Maggie's number, trying to stay calm as her phone rang.

"Good morning," a man answered, the same one he recognized a week earlier. He wanted to hang up, but fought the urge as the voice inquired again. "Hello, is someone there?"

"Yes," he said reluctantly. "May I speak to Maggie Andrews, please?"

"Sure, just a second."

There were a few moments of silence followed by a voice that still lit up his heart.

"Hello," she answered.

"Hi Maggie, it's Connor," he said a little sheepishly. "I hope I'm not disturbing anything."

"Connor, I've been worried sick about you, are you all right?"

"I'm fine."

"Are you still in the Philippines?"

"No, I'm in London."

"Are you there with her?"

"With who?" he questioned, caught totally off guard.

"You know, that girl, Susan," she returned, her voice sounding a little colder.

"No, I'm not here with Susan. I'm here on business, relating to the Philippines," he replied. The thought of seeing Susan after he had finished his business was on his agenda, but only to bring some closure to their relationship. "Do you care?"

"Maybe."

"You have a strange way of showing it."

"What do you mean?"

"You know what I mean, having someone staying with you already."

"Makes you jealous, doesn't it?"

"It did at first, but not anymore," he lied.

"Good, well maybe you can understand a little how I felt when I saw you with her."

"You said that stuff doesn't bother you."

"I know what I said. But it's not always how I really feel," she returned her voice softening a little.

"Well, it doesn't matter now, you obviously have found someone else."

"Is this why you called?"

"No, I wanted to tell you that I might have the answer to why you had those feelings around me."

"Please go on," she replied. He could sense her urgency.

"When I was in the cave with the treasure, I found a pair of dog tags. One had the name Jesse Hamilton, the other Jacob Thomas. Hamilton has no family living, but Thomas has a family farm, currently in foreclosure. Maybe he's the contact and he wanted me to use the money from the gold to save the farm. It's all I can think of."

"God, Connor, God," she said sounding distressed.

"What is it, Maggie? Are you all right?"

There was no answer. After a few moments, a man's voice came on the line.

"I'm sorry, whoever this is, Maggie can't come back to the phone right now. She seems to have taken ill."

"Is she all right?"

"I think she will be, she went to lay down."

"Take care of her and don't let her get hurt, please, she's a little fragile. She acts tough, but she's not that tough."

"You seem to know her pretty well."

"I thought I did."

"Don't worry, I'll take care of her," the voice reassured him. "After all, what are big brothers for?"

"You're her brother?"

"Yeah, came down to visit her from Michigan. My wife is in Florida with the boys. I hadn't heard from her since the accident, so when she called I flew in about a week ago."

"Really?"

"Really."

"Tell her not to worry and I'll talk to her soon."

"I will, goodbye."

"Goodbye."

Disconnecting the phone, he hoped she was all right as he felt renewed hope for their relationship. It was possible that it was true, her sensations, maybe Jacob Thomas was the key. This time he was glad he called, his heart felt lighter while he continued to wait and watch for the courier.

~ ~ ~

Chapter 59

In a large apartment in an upscale section of downtown London, Charles Morgan reviewed his reports, while waiting for his late afternoon update from Jonathan Ames. Work and meeting places were never kept to the same schedule, men in high places have enemies, and he knew that following a routine could make him vulnerable. No matter his place on the food chain, someone could always get to him if they were moti-vated and willing to make sacrifices. Long ago a random schedule of movements and locations were devised in an effort to protect the keepers of the flame. Today, a secure apartment in downtown, tomorrow a villa in the French countryside, the next day, a private plane at thirty-five thousand feet and so on, technology had given him the freedom to not be predictable.

He turned the page of his latest mining report and compared the figures to projections on his computer screen, frowning at the difference. He had just started to scratch down some notes when his underling appeared.

"You're late, Jonathan," he said, without picking up his head to acknowledge his arrival.

"Sorry, sir. I was taking care of an incident."

"Important one, I hope," he returned, being short, as the rejuvenating effects of his treatment had long since peaked and he knew he would soon be feeling all of his seventy-nine years.

"Quite."

"Any word on the whereabouts of young Mr. Mason?"

"As a matter of fact, sir, we have been able to track his movements."

"Where has he been, Jonathan? Did he remove any of the gold?"

"Were not sure if any gold has been removed, sir. If it has, we are not aware of any major transactions as of yet. As far as where he's been, he went from Mindanao to Cebu, by some form of transport we haven't identified, and then by commercial air to Manila and on to Hong Kong for two days. Our contract player just missed catching up to him there."

"Where is he now?"

"He's in London, sir.

"Splendid, it shouldn't be much of a problem finding him now."

"No problem at all, sir."

"Why are you being so smug, Jonathan?"

"Mr. Mason is currently in the lobby of our downtown offices. He is insisting on seeing—let's see how did he phrase it—oh yes, the head honcho."

"Did he say what he wanted?"

"Said he had important business to discuss. He was quoted as saying lots of tons and lots of dollars. I believe you know what he's alluding too, sir."

"Yes of course," he answered tersely. "Well, don't just stand there. Send a car for him. Let's have the meeting in the secure flat on Kensington."

"Very good, sir. I'll make the arrangements."

As Jonathan Ames left to arrange the transport of their guest and prepare the Silver Dawn Rolls Royce that would take them to the rendezvous, Morgan could not help but be impressed by this young man. To have the courage to show up on their doorstep to propose a deal was a noble and most likely, a fool hardy effort. He clearly had too much knowledge to be allowed to roam freely. He was a potential problem already at his tender age and given a chance to season, he may become much more, he thought. If it was determined he had intimate knowledge of the legendary Tunnel Hoard, he would not let that happen. However, anticipating what would take

412

place at the meeting was not necessary. He would assess the information, directing his underling to take the desired action—with no concern or remorse for the welfare of young Connor Mason.

~ ~ ~

Chapter 60

Riding in a late model, chauffeured Mercedes that had picked him up outside of the Morgan Gold office building in London's Financial Center, Connor sat back while he was driven to Kensington, a very posh, residential section of the city. The driver directed him to a flat, where he was instructed to take the private elevator to the penthouse using the code on the card he was given. Getting out of the car, the tree lined, tranquil streets, with large white apartment buildings and fenced in gardens was in sharp contrast to the hustle of the business district.

As he walked up to the doorman, he felt no false sense of security from the comfortable surroundings. He was going into a world far deadlier than one he had just left in the jungles of Asia and he needed to remain frosty. He was entering a place he may not leave alive, even though the expensive trappings surrounding this clandestine meeting belied that possibility.

Using the numbered code and clutching a valise, which contained the package from the courier he had met at Heathrow, he entered the private elevator for the short eight-floor ride to the penthouse. He imagined it contained state of the art metal detectors and debugging sensors, sure no weapons or concealed transmitters would escape their scrutiny. The door opened and a tall, silver haired man wearing a three-piece, gray pinstriped suit greeted him.

"Mr. Mason?" he inquired. *A Brit formality* Connor thought. Based on the ruckus he caused at their headquarters and the fact they tried to have him killed, he obviously knew full well who he was.

"Yes," he answered.

"My name is Jonathan Ames. Please follow me, Mr. Morgan is expecting you."

He was led down a long hall into a large room, it was at least thirty by sixty, with high ceilings, gleaming wood floors and large windows on the outside wall, all draped with heavy cream colored floor to ceiling window treatments. At one end of the room was a large, highly glossed wooden desk with one chair situated in front of it, the one he assumed that was meant for him. Behind the desk was the bent, aging figure of the head honcho, Charles Morgan. Jonathan Ames ushered him to the wooden chair, where he was invited to sit across from his venerable host. Connor took his seat, while his escort remained standing, taking a position just to the right of his elder statesman.

"Nice to meet you, Mr. Mason. You have been on our minds lately," Charles Morgan said in an emotionless tone.

"I'm sure I have," he returned, offering no other customary gesture as he stared into his coal-dark eyes.

"What can we do for you?"

"May I?" he asked, pointing to his valise.

"By all means," he returned.

Connor reached in and removed a small digital camera, cell phone, and two manila folders. Picking up the camera, he nonchalantly pressed the shutter taking a picture of his hosts. Plugging the camera into his phone, he punched in a long distance number and waited for conformation. Morgan and Ames sat patiently while he completed his task. He then picked up the first folder and handed it across the table to Mr. Morgan.

"I understand you're in the gold business and I would like to sell you a mine. In the folder you're holding are pictures of our most recent strike."

~ ~ ~

415

Charles Morgan opened the folder and viewed the pictures that Connor had taken during his subterranean excursion. He could feel his aging heart beating like a youngster on his first date, as he was face-to-face with the legend. He did nothing to show any emotion, but it was a sight seen by few men, most of them dead and most likely the one sitting in front of him would be joining them soon. He was however, impressed by the discovery. After viewing the photos, he handed them to his underling in order to keep him up to speed on the negotiation.

"Very impressive vein you struck, Mr. Mason. However, pictures can be doctored in this day and age, anything is possible with computers, wouldn't you agree?"

"I certainly would, sir. That's why I brought along a little added proof of the mine's validity," he returned, reaching into his pocket and pulling out the small finger bar minted in Burma and handing it to him.

Charles Morgan took the bar and cradled it like it was a child. It offered proof positive of the discovery, it could have come from nowhere else. He rubbed the soft shiny metal with his bony white hand like he was stroking a lover. The feel was intrinsic to him, like no other, as if gold ran in his veins; it was his oxygen for survival. At the core of his empire was the substance he held, it was a symbol of power and money; the most intoxicating inanimate object he knew. To him, it was an abbreviated form of his sole reason for living.

"What is the price for your mine, Mr. Mason?"

"Fifty Million, American. Transferred to an offshore account before I leave, and one other piece of information."

"What would that be?"

"We can discuss that once we've come to an agreement on the mine."

"What if we say we're not interested, Mr. Mason?" he asked, testing his resolve.

"If you're not interested, I've got a team of attorneys ready to go with me to negotiate with the President of the Philippines. It's a fairly corrupt administration, I'm told, probably need to sell most of the gold; it is a poor country after all.

I'm sure the people would realize at least ten percent of the fortune, although I can hardly imagine what the price would drop to considering the glut that would be dumped on the open market.

"I see. What if you were to have an accident, Mr. Mason? Let us say before leaving this flat," he said, seriously contemplating that option.

"First of all, the latitude and longitude would be delivered to the Philippine president along with the pictures you have in the folders, my posthumous gift to the islands. Secondly, I have a half-million dollar insurance policy, which pays double in case of accidental death, which I'm sure you're alluding to. I recently made my beneficiary the gentleman that terminated an assassin that was trailing me in Cagayan De Oro. She was very good at her job, I was told; he, on the other hand, is the best. You can use your imagination as to his targets. Also, I took into account that your photos were not readily available, so I took the initiative to take your picture a few minutes ago and e-mail them to my associates. That's what I was doing before showing you the pictures. Ain't technology great? So I think we can agree that neither of us is fucking around here," he returned, maintaining his poker face demeanor.

"Mr. Mason, you're not so naive to not believe we can't circumvent everything you've put in place, here. We can command Presidents and assassins, with a lot more negotiating muscle than you could ever imagine."

"I'm sure you can. I have no illusions about your influence, but why bother? We can settle this right here for fifty mill. You don't think a President is going to settle for that, especially when it's in his own back yard. My offer is chump change compared to what's in the mine, and you maintain control of the market. I didn't come here to threaten anyone, I just want to make a deal that's good business."

"That's a lot of money, Mr. Mason."

"It's a fair price."

Charles Morgan sat, staring at his young adversary. He imagined him popping up again somewhere before his life and

417

seat of power had ended, but what he said made sense and did get him what he desired.

"We have a deal, Mr. Mason. How do you wish to proceed with the transaction?"

"In this envelope I'm holding bearer shares for Bukidnon Mines, Ltd. as well as coordinates for the location of the mine. Here is my account number, wire instructions and ABA number for Cayman National Bank. Effect the transfer and once I have confirmation from my associates, the shares are yours."

"Agreed. Carry out the transaction, Jonathan."

"Yes, sir," he returned, leaving to complete the contract.

"Wait," Connor said, stopping him. "There's one more piece of information I need."

"Yes, what would that be?"

"I want the name of the person that gave you the information about my activity."

"As a rule we never divulge sources, Mr. Mason," Jonathan Ames answered.

"I'm sure, as a rule, no one brings you a cave full of bullion. Make an exception."

Ames looked at his leader for direction, receiving a subtle nod of compliance. "I'll affect the transfer and bring you the name, Mr. Mason."

"Thank you."

~ ~ ~

Connor sat across from Charles Morgan in silence and waited for Jonathan Ames to return. He knew there was no pleasant, small talk to exchange. All they had was a transaction; that's where their common ground began and ended. Their worlds were as different as day and night, so he waited quietly for consummation and the inevitable separation. After twenty long minutes, his underling returned to acknowledge the transaction had been completed and verified.

"Excuse me one minute," Connor requested, as he dialed his cell phone. "Hello, Wes. Did we get it? Great, I'll see you all soon." After disconnecting his call he had only one more question left unanswered.

"Can I have the name please?"

Jonathan Ames looked quickly to Charles Morgan who again nodded his approval.

"The name you are looking for is Susan James, a barrister here in London."

"What?" He sat feeling stunned.

"Stings a bit, doesn't it Mr. Mason? When someone you know betrays a confidence."

"Yes it does," he agreed, quickly regaining his composure.

"If it makes a difference, the information was obtained without any malice towards you. She simply told a senior partner and word got back to us. I'm sure if she had known the repercussions to you, she would never have divulged the information."

"Did she make partner?"

"I'm told she has a leg up on it."

"If it meant making partner, I'm sure she's had both legs up."

"Quite," he returned, seeming for the first time at a loss for an appropriate response.

"Here's the certificates," he said, handing them to Morgan.

"Thank you, Mr. Mason. I hope this concludes all our business together—forever."

"Me, too."

"Mr. Ames will show you out."

Connor rose from his chair to follow Jonathan Ames, when his superior called him back. After a brief discussion, he rejoined Connor and led him to the elevator. When the door opened he reached in his pocket and took out the gold bar Connor had confiscated from the mine.

"Mr. Morgan wanted you to have this," he said, handing him the tiny ingot.

"What for?" Connor questioned.

"A reminder."

"A reminder of what?" he asked, taking the bar.

"To stay out of the gold business."

"I see."

"The driver is at your disposal. He'll take you wherever you need to go."

"I appreciate that."

"Good bye, Mr. Mason," he said, flashing him a slight grin.

Connor nodded to him as the elevator door closed and he proceeded to the waiting car. He wanted to yell at the top of his lungs, but maintained his professional demeanor. There was one more piece of business to finish before leaving London. He gave the driver directions to Susan James' law firm.

Stopping across the street from her office, he exited the car and waited for traffic to clear enough for him to cross. As he watched the front door, a beautiful brunette appeared, wearing a long designer woolen coat, expensive high heels and carrying a leather brief case, arm in arm with a well-dressed, medium-height, pleasant looking young man. Connor recognized her immediately; she was just as stunning as the first time he laid eyes on her. She and her companion were hailing a cab, when she looked up and saw him standing across from her. It was obvious that she didn't believe it at first, but once she realized it was him; she said something to the man with her and making eye contact with Connor started to cross the busy street. As she took a step off the curb toward him, he slowly shook his head and opened the car door. She saw the sign and stopped dead. One picture can say a thousand words, this one said just two; it's over. There was nothing else left to discuss. He raised his hand toward her and got back into the vehicle. She nodded in his direction and turned to rejoin her friend.

Connor took a deep breath and directed the driver to take him to the airport; it was time to go home. There was still one final piece of business to finish.

~ ~ ~

Chapter 61

Arriving at Kennedy Airport—Connor was more than juiced up at the thought of getting off the plane and meeting his friends. Alex, Wes and George should already be there, he thought, after flying in from Grand Cayman. He looked forward to seeing their smiling faces. The whole negotiation with Morgan Gold had not sunk in yet. It was a risky and brilliant plan that at this moment seemed to have paid off. While they weren't filthy rich, they were much better off than two weeks ago—much, much better off.

As the doors of the United 747 opened and he headed down the walkway, his mind drifted back to Maggie. He couldn't wait to get home and see her. He wanted to get things square with her, now that he appeared to have uncovered the source of her ghostly sensations. Before he could fall any deeper in thought about their anticipated reunion, he saw Alex standing just outside the door. When he stepped through the doorway, Alex ran to greet him, accosting him like schoolgirl with a crush. He wrapped his arms around him and held him tight as Wes came into sight.

"You did it, Con. You did it," he shouted, still holding onto him.

"We did it, bud," he returned, smiling widely. "Now you gotta let me go or people are going to start talking."

"Let'em talk, I don't care," he kidded, giving him a big kiss on the check.

"You two better get a room," Wes contributed, extending his hand.

"Great to see you, Wes," he returned, shaking Wes's hand after finally being released by Alex.

"Nice job, son"

"Thanks, I appreciate that. Are we good?"

"Money is in the bank."

"Yes," he said, clinching his fist. "I'm not sure I believe it yet."

"Believe it, brother," Alex chimed in. "We got bank accounts with lots and lots of zeros in them."

"Alright. We better mosey over and grab our connecting flight then," he returned. "Hey, where's George at?"

"George already caught his flight. He's heading back to Columbus to do some catching up with his kids and relatives."

"Did he say anything?"

"Yeah, fuck it's cold here," Alex returned, as they all laughed.

The three of them headed for their connection and the short one-hour, puddle jump to Albany International Airport. It was still early afternoon when they landed. They had spent the flight talking about the financial arrangements that were yet to be made, with particular attention to Lido, George's ex-wives and the survivors of one persistent spirit, Jacob Thomas. As they gathered their luggage in the terminal, Connor had one piece of pressing business that needed immediate attention.

"Wes, can you give Alex a lift?"

"That's no problem," he answered.

"Where you going partner?" Alex inquired, sounding as if half-knowing the answer.

"I've got to see someone, bud."

"You're not dumping me for a girl are you?" he returned, sporting a wide grin.

"Sorry, but if it's any consolation, I still respect you," he kidded.

"Who gives a shit about that? Go then, you—bitch. Get out of here."

"I'll call you guys later," he said laughing.

"I think you two need some professional help," Wes chided.

"No doubt about that, Wes. But at least now we can afford it," he returned, smiling.

"Yes, we most certainly can," added Connor, disappearing through the door and into the mid-November sunshine. His feet were barely touching the ground as he reached his truck. He wheeled out of the lot after paying the two hundred plus parking fee. *Chump change* he thought, when he handed the money to the attendant. His heart was racing as he hurried to Maggie's apartment. He was determined to find her and that was the most logical place to start.

Pulling into the parking lot, he didn't bother to look for her vehicle. He just ran to her building and pushed the bell.

"Hello," came a strange older woman's voice.

"Hi," he returned, a little taken back. "Is Maggie there?"

"Who?"

"Maggie, Maggie Andrews," he repeated.

"No, there's no one by that name here."

Connor took a second to check the building number and then looked at the names opposite the doorbell. Maggie's no longer appeared across from her buzzer. It had been replaced by "Carson."

"Are you still there?" the voice asked.

"Yes, yes I am," he answered. "Are you Mrs. Carson?"

"Yes."

"Did you just move in here, Mrs. Carson?

"Yes, last week."

"Do you know what happened to the woman who was here before you?"

"I'm afraid I don't. Why don't you ask at the office?"

"Thank you, I will," he returned. "Sorry if I troubled you."

"No trouble, good luck."

He was beginning to feel a little panicky while driving over to the manager's office. He thought that maybe she had decided to change apartments within the complex, but given her fondness for the view, he knew it was doubtful.

As he walked into the office, a heavy, older gentleman sitting behind a desk greeted him. He had thick glasses and a large mustache, giving him the look of a walrus. One hand clung to one of his suspenders and the other rested on his pot-belly. He lowered his rimless spectacles while he watched Connor enter.

"Can I help you, son?" he asked.

"I hope so," he answered. "I'm looking for Maggie Andrews, building nine, apartment 5b."

"I know Maggie. Cute little thing."

"Is she still here?" he asked nervously.

"Nope."

"Do you know where she went?"

"Nope."

"Can you tell me anything?"

"Moved out last week. Young guy, maybe a little older than you helped her."

"She didn't leave a forwarding address?"

"Nope, paid her rent in full and took off. Sorry son, that's all I know."

He didn't say anything. He just nodded to him as he left. His stomach had an empty feeling as he got in his truck and picked up his cell phone. He dialed her number and waited while a recorded voice informed him that the number had been disconnected. He sat there, berating himself for not calling her sooner. He felt lost, and it hurt; it hurt bad. After all he'd been though, after all he attained, he knew she was what he wanted most of all. Finally after a few long minutes, he decided to try the club and see if they knew anything. He dialed the number and listened to the ringing phone.

"Good afternoon, Fitness Factory. Judy speaking, may I help you?"

"Judy," he returned, remembering the fit-red head who worked the front desk. "You probably don't remember me, but this is Connor Mason. . . ."

"Oh, I remember you," she interrupted. "How are you? We haven't seen you in awhile."

"I'm well, thanks for asking. I'm looking for Maggie Andrews. Is she there?"

"I'm sorry, Connor. Maggie doesn't work here anymore."

"Do you know where I can find her?"

"No, she didn't leave any forwarding information."

"Did she say anything before she left?"

"She just said goodbye and it was time for her to move on."

"Thanks, Judy."

"You're welcome. Will we be seeing you soon?"

"I'm sure you will be, bye," he returned disconnecting.

Suddenly he felt exhausted. The adrenaline high had run its course. She was gone, he could feel it, but without at least some closure, he was finding it hard to deal with. He decided to head back to his place and get some rest. He needed to sleep and then maybe with a clear head and the help of Ben Cole, he could find her. Even if she didn't come back, he still needed to know how she felt about him, before he could move on.

Pulling up to his home, he parked and went in. The house was empty, almost as empty as he felt his life would be without her. He knew he'd get through it and he also knew that this was what it felt like to be heartbroken. It was a feeling he wouldn't forget anytime soon.

Entering his bedroom, he was greeted by a sight that made his heart stop. Lying on his pillow was an envelope with his name on it. His hands were shaking when he picked it up. Tearing it open made him realize what it was like to need answers. How helpless it could make you feel. How Maggie had probably felt for the last five years. He took a deep breath and read the letter:

Dear Connor,

I hope this letter finds you well, as I know it will. I can tell about things like that you know. I had to leave. It was time, I'm sure you understand. I can feel that you have almost finished what you set out to do. I'm sorry I ever doubted you. You are stronger than I ever imagined, that's why I know you'll survive me not being there. Thank you for everything, but now you must finish the rest for yourself. Your peace is within your reach and the answer is close by. I think you know what I mean.

Smile when you think of me, baby. I do when I think of you and what you've done for me. Please don't try and find me, It's better this way.

Forever Yours, Love,
Maggie

He could feel a tear run down his cheek as he laid the letter on the bed next to him. He knew what had to be done; it was time to finish it. He owed that to both of them, he thought as he surrendered to a peaceful sleep.

~ ~ ~

Chapter 62

Five days later—Connor found himself, in a black 1996 Carrera 4, somewhere outside Bloomington, Indiana, tooling down the back roads of America on his way to the Thomas farm. The window was part way down and the music blearing while he passed the farms on Route 54. He was glad to be back. His adventure seemed a lifetime away, so far beyond normal everyday life that the memory of it had its own surreal place in his mind. At times he couldn't quite believe it happened. But whenever he required substantiation, he'd just reach down and rub his new good luck charm, the small gold bar he'd taken from the tunnel.

He had spent the last few days with Wes and Alex celebrating their good fortune. Unfortunately without Maggie, it didn't offer quite the same satisfaction for him like it did for his partners. They divided up the booty; half of the money was set up in a trust for Lido and his village. The fund would be used to build better housing, schools and a new hospital that had been the wish of Lido's late uncle. All the workers at the mine were paid a huge bonus and would be retrained in the building trades. A new major employer was about to have a positive economic impact on the small mountain village, and they all felt very good about that.

Wes Adams had spent the better part of the week negotiating with George's ex-wives. It was going to take somewhere around four million to square up fifteen years of neglected child support and alimony. In the end, money did buy happiness for them. They could care less about George, but they loved his money. A two-million dollar bonus was paid to Billy Hilliard for getting them out alive as well as a much smaller one to Nancy, for what he wasn't quite sure, but she was part of the team and could use the cash to discard her useless spouse.

After all outstanding debt was retired and the dust had cleared there was somewhere around fifteen million left, which they agreed would be distributed equally in six shares, George, Alex, Wes, Connor, his Mom, based on his father's involvement and the Thomas estate. That was a hard one for him to get by George as well as convincing him that the lions share should go to Lido and the people of his village, but in the end, he went along with the group, it was the right thing to do. He really wasn't such a bad guy, Connor thought.

Having spent part of the time in some soulful after thought regarding Maggie and her letter, he could only imagine that something in their last conversation must have prompted her to go. He wasn't sure, all he was sure of was he missed her. But, it was different than before, not as intense. She had been part of his life and for that he was grateful. Some birds were never meant to be caged and he had come to realize that Maggie was one of those. He wasn't hurt because she left, just sad. He understood her better for what she went through; he had experienced his own life-altering journey. Now-a-days, he slept soundly, the highs weren't as high and the lows weren't as low. He felt happy with the balance he'd found, sometimes the thing you need most was something you don't even know you want. He would always be grateful to her for that gift.

Despite the fact that she was gone, he still felt obligated to complete their journey and satisfy the spirit who brought them together. He wasn't sure if any of this afterlife stuff was true, but for now, it was his perception, and as for most people, that was reality.

He knew he had to address the finances relating to the Thomas homestead before the foreclosure was completed. Nancy, with the help of Ben Cole, had gotten the address as well as the information about the bank holding the mortgage.

Before he left, the money to pay off the mortgage was wire transferred to the bank, close to eight hundred thousand including interest, penalties and attorney fees.

He was happy to learn that Jacob's wife, Sarah, was still alive. He wanted to give her the rest of the money and talk a little about Jacob. He had no intentions of telling her that it was his ghost that precipitated his actions, that was more than a woman of her age could take, he figured. Plus, even though he was a believer, although still somewhat skeptical, he didn't want to came off as an eccentric nut case.

Taking the turn on south Route 67, he enjoyed the crisp air of the late autumn day. Winter would arrive soon and it would be a welcome change from the jungle climate he had labored in. He was glad he decided to drive; he couldn't bear the thought of getting into another airplane. It made him smile when he went into the Porsche dealer and bought his car. It was a steal; low mileage, in mint condition and only fifty thousand. When the salesman asked him how he wanted pay, he just handed him a gold card from Cayman National. He enjoyed recalling the look on the salesman's face. He had always dreamed of buying a car with a credit card. It's just the little things in life that can make you happy, he thought, laughing to himself as he spotted the turn leading to the Thomas farm.

The long road was bordered on both sides by large, recently harvested fields, giving the landscape a somewhat barren look. There were no trees to speak of, just earthen brown land. Pulling up to the large, white house, there were several children, dressed in overcoats, playing in the yard and an older woman rocking in a chair on the faded front porch. She was accompanied by a mixed bred, medium sized black dog. There were two large red barns on the property as well as several high silos. Various modern farming equipment was displayed outside the barn, all tagged and numbered, apparently for the auction that was no longer going to take place. As he got out of the car, the woman on the porch smiled while the older children ran to admire Connor's car.

"Can I help you, young man?" she called out from her rocker.

"Yes, am I at the Thomas farm?"

"This is the Thomas farm," she answered. "But if you're here about the auction, it's been called off. We've been blessed with a bit of a miracle."

"I'm not here about the auction, Ma'am, I guess I'm here about the miracle."

"Is that so?"

"Yes, I'm looking for Sarah Thomas."

"That would be me, young man," she replied. "Children," she yelled. "Don't touch that man's car." Some of the kids were obviously venturing too close for her comfort.

"It's alright, Mrs. Thomas. Could we talk for a minute?"

"Certainly, please come in," she said, getting up from the rocker.

Connor walked up the front porch stairs while Sarah waited for him by the door. She was small, not more than five-foot-two with flowing silver gray hair. She had pretty features, despite her wrinkles that seemed to disappear as she flashed him a wide, warm smile. What he noticed most however, were her big, emerald green eyes that seemed to sparkle when the light caught them. He followed her through a wide foyer, past the living room and into a large country kitchen.

"We do most of our talking in the kitchen out here, Mr. . . ."

"Mason, but you can call me Connor."

"Well, Connor, everyone is in town, trying to get to the bottom of our good fortune. We kinda think someone made a mistake. But for now it sure feels good."

"It's no mistake, Mrs. Thomas. My associates and I paid your note to the bank."

"Why would you do such a thing?" she asked, sounding like she was not sure if she believed him.

"We did it because of your husband."

"Jacob?"

"Yes, we found something that belonged to him and

430

that's what led us to you. I'm here because I have some information about his death."

"His death?" she said, suddenly looking very distressed. "What happened to him, please tell me, was it his
heart?" she asked, her eyes starting to well up.

"I'm sorry," Connor offered. "I didn't expect it to upset
you so."

"Well, why wouldn't you?" she scolded, the tears starting to run down her face.

Connor was confused by her reaction, after over fifty
years he didn't expect it to be this much of a shock, when
abruptly his bafflement was taken to new heights by the sound
of a man's voice.

"Sarah," a voice rang through the house. "Whose car is
that out there? And why ain't you watching those young-uns,
they're all over that vehicle."

"Jacob, is that you?" she called out.

"Yes, it's me, who were you expecting?"

"You're alive," she said, getting up from the table to
greet him.

Connor sat totally perplexed, stunned by the entrance
of the man who he was sure was his ghost. Before him stood
Jacob Thomas, a vibrant eighty-year old, six feet tall, still sporting a full head of white hair. He was dressed in tan pants with
suspenders and a white shirt with no tie, buttoned at the collar. Connor noticed he walked with a bit of a limp when he
came forward to meet him.

"Of course I'm alive, woman, he returned, hugging her
tightly. "I promised you that I wouldn't let you outlive me, and
I keep my promises."

"This young man told me you were dead."

"Well, young fella," he said, turning his attention to
Connor, now feeling flush from embarrassment, still sitting at
the kitchen table. "What the hell are you doing scaring my wife
half to death?"

Connor couldn't speak, he was totally mystified by this
discovery; all he could do was smile and shake his head.

"Speak up boy, cat got your tongue?" he returned, his

engaging smile taking the sting out of his comments.

"I'm glad you're not dead, sir."

"That makes two of us. What are you doing here?"

"I guess I came to give you something."

"He says he's the one that paid the bank, Jacob," Sarah said.

"Is that true?" he asked, lowering his voice.

"Yes, sir."

"Why?"

"Maybe this will help explain things," he offered, reaching into his pocket and pulling out the two sets of dog tags, then handing them to Jacob.

"Where did you get these?" he asked, wide-eyed, as he examined them closely.

"Where do you think?" he returned.

"In a cave, on the other side of the world, a lifetime ago for me."

"That's where."

"You were in that cave, son?"

"Yes, sir."

"How long ago?"

"Just a few weeks ago. Can I ask you some questions?"

"Sure, son. Sarah, go out and watch those kids, please and keep them away from that car," he said, sitting down at the table next to Connor.

"Okay, Jake," she returned, trotting out to the front porch.

"She's the only reason I'm alive today. I love that woman more than life. I went through hell to get back to her and I'd do it all again. You find a good woman, hang onto her."

"I've been trying," he returned. "Can you tell me what happened over there?"

"Sure. What's your name anyway, son?"

"Connor, Connor Mason," he said, reaching out to shake his hand.

"Well, Connor Mason. I'm going to tell you, what I haven't told anyone but my wife in over fifty years."

Jacob recounted his story with Connor hanging on

every word. He told of his capture and the tunnel, the large Japanese officer and the small boy as well as the mysterious contents of the cave. Connor stopped him now and then to add what he knew and compare landmarks, locations and time frame. It seemed to do the old man good to finally have some one to confide in about what had happened. He seemed amazed that the young child hanging on the waist of the large officer had been the catalyst to Connor finding him and the contents of the cave after all these years. He recounted the kindness the child had shown him. He was sad to hear he had passed.

"So when they were ready to leave, the officer, who you tell me is this General. . . ."

"Yamashita."

"Yes, Yamashita, he walks me into the jungle and I'm pretty sure we ain't coming out together. So I turn and face him and start telling him about myself. I don't think he under-stands, but then he says a few words in English and I know he knew what I was saying. Next thing I know he takes his pistol and fires two shots in my direction, but he misses me by a mile. I fall to the ground and when I finally get the nerve to look up, he's gone. All that's left is this white sack filled with food. I wait a couple of hours and then go back to the campsite, but they're all gone. I ate the food and went down to the stream that ran nearby for water. I was really weak and I passed out there. Some Filipino natives found me and took me back to their village. They nursed me back to health and around four weeks later I hooked up with an American recon unit and six weeks later, I was shipped home. I never expected to get back alive."

"Why are you still listed as missing in action?"

"Record keeping was never the strong point of the U.S. Army. The war had ended and lots of us went home; paper-work was avoided whenever possible. Plus I didn't want a lot of attention, because I didn't want to do a lot of explaining about my whereabouts, so I never corrected the mistake."

"Did you know what was in the cave?"

"Not for sure. I never laid eyes on it, but I figured it was

433

something important or valuable. A lot of men died because of it, including my friend, Jesse Hamilton," he said, holding up his dog tags.

"It was filled with gold bullion."

"That doesn't surprise me, but to tell you the truth, I didn't care. I promised that Japanese officer that I'd never tell anyone about that place, and except for my wife, I haven't."

"Well, Yamashita had a treasure and my partners and I want to share part of it with you."

Jacob hesitated for a moment before responding to his offer. He smiled soulfully at him before he finally spoke.

"He already gave me his treasure, Connor."

"What do you mean?" he asked, a little confused.

"Follow me," he said, slowly getting up from the table.

Jacob led Connor into the living room and over to a gallery of pictures. They covered the mantel over the fireplace; two large bookshelves built into the wall, a sofa table and several end tables.

"This was the treasure he gave me," Jacob said, pointing to the pictures.

"I'm not sure I understand, sir."

"This is my family, Connor. Five children, eighteen grandchildren, at last count a dozen or so great-grand children and a wife, who after all this time, still takes my breath away. They're my treasure. That man spared my life, so I could grow old with them. There's no amount of money or gold on God's green earth that's more of a treasure than that," he said, his voice cracking as his eyes started to tear up. "Do you understand?"

"Yes, sir. I do."

"So you can keep the money or give it to me, it makes no difference. I'm already a rich man," he returned, wiping a tear from his check.

"Yes, you are Mr. Thomas, richer than most will ever be, but if it's all the same to you, I'd like to give you your share. After paying off the farm, it comes to over one and a half million. Here's the bankbook and a name to contact. They can wire you the money. It's in a Cayman Island account. If you don't want it for yourself, take it for your family."

Jacob reflected a moment before reaching out and accepting the bankbook from his young benefactor. He then mumbled something that Connor could not make out.

"Did you say something, sir?"

"He said everything would be all right."

"Who did, Mr. Thomas?"

"I'd like to tell you, but I don't want you to think I'm a crazy old war veteran?"

"Try me."

"I've had this dream for the last week," he started to say and then stopped. "No, it's just a dream, it's not important."

"Please, sir. What is it?" Connor pleaded.

"Jesse Hamilton."

"What about Jesse Hamilton," Connor asked, suddenly feeling a cold rush over his body.

"For the last week, I've had this dream. Jesse is standing in front of me, just as I remember him, he's telling me that everything will be all right and I'm not going to lose the farm. I've had it for a week straight; I ain't never had the same dream for a week straight."

"Go on," Connor prodded, feeling the hair on his arms starting to rise.

"Well, it's weird. It's not like a dream; it seems too real, like he's in the room with me. It's almost like he's. . . ."

"A ghost," Connor contributed eagerly, now tingling all over.

"Yes, like a ghost, but not the scary kind. Anyway, last night is the first night I don't have it and I wake up this morning to find someone has paid the bank and then you show up."

"I wouldn't worry about it, Mr. Thomas. I don't think you'll have anymore dreams about Jesse Hamilton."

"Why's that?"

"I just have this feeling, that's all."

"Don't go telling no one about this, Connor. I don't have that many years left and I don't want to spend them in a loony bin," he joked.

"Have no worries, your secret is safe with me."

"Well, I don't know how to thank you for this," he said, holding up the bankbook.

"Don't thank me. In your prayers tonight, thank Jesse," he returned, giving him a wink.

"I might just do that. Come on, let me have the Mrs. get you something to eat," he returned, grabbing his arm and leading him back into the kitchen.

Connor spent the evening enjoying the company of the Thomas clan. All of them had good fortune to celebrate and he reveled in their merriment and optimism. He was sure that even without receiving his financial reprieve, they would have found a way to survive with or without the farm; their patriarch had all his priorities in order. As he took his leave, Jacob and Sarah made him promise to come see them again. He agreed, knowing full well it was an obligation not to be taken lightly.

~ ~ ~

Chapter 63

It was late, almost thirty-six hours later, when Connor finally reached his Madison Avenue home. Pulling up to the curb, he got out, feeling a brisk wind that normally would have chilled him to the bone, instead embraced him, reminding him of the joy of being back. As he walked up the front stairs and looked into the clear night sky, he relished in his new sense of self. His father was right; the experience had changed him, and he felt for the better. In the morning, he decided he would call his Mom and then go down to Pauley's and see if he wanted to take on a partner, maybe he would even buy a piece of Sid. He smiled at the thought of just how much that would tick off Frank Handrahan.

Right now, sleep was the only thing on his agenda. He had called Alex from the road and they decided to get together tomorrow for lunch. He was already talking about going back to the Philippines and helping Lido get the construction project started. Connor felt that maybe a pretty desk clerk at the Pryce Plaza might have something to do with his decision. He also said he'd been talking to George. He had spent some time with his estranged children and was going to take his older boys back to Asia on a visit. Alex said he thought he missed his Filipino girlfriend and kids more than he wanted to let on; he just kept saying that Columbus was too cold for him.

Connor unlocked the front door and flicked on his living room light, stunned and elated by who was there to greet him.

"Where you been, baby?" she asked, cocking her pretty head to one side.

"Chasing ghosts," he answered, his heart fluttering. "How about you, Maggie?"

"I'm not chasing them anymore and they don't seem to be chasing me."

"I'm glad."

"Me, too."

"Do you want to know what happened?"

"You mean about Jesse Hamilton?"

"How did you know?"

"I had a visitor."

"Please Maggie, I don't want to know anymore—not tonight anyway."

"Fair enough, we'll talk about it tomorrow."

"Where did you take off to?"

"Went back to Michigan with my brother for a while. I had to find something out."

"Did you?"

"Yes."

"What was it?'

"Don't you know? I'm here, aren't I?"

"Forever?"

"For now, we'll work on forever."

"Can we start in the morning? I'm pretty tired."

"If you're asking me to bed, we can start right now."

"I guess I'm not that tired."

"I didn't think you would be," she returned, getting up from the couch and running to him. He lifted her in his arms and carried her off to the bedroom. With her, it would always be one day at a time, a small imposition, he thought, to have her back in his life.

~ ~ ~

Epilogue

A few days later and about twenty-five minutes north, Ellen Mason sat on the couch in her Clifton Park home, flipping through the pages of a magazine. The fireplace was starting to go out when she decided against a second cup of coffee. She was feeling a little tired, but not that sleepy, grateful for the safe return of her youngest son. Wes Adams had kept her informed of his whereabouts and she looked forward to seeing him in the morning.

Feeling that she may be able to drift off, she settled in on the leather sofa and closed her eyes, just as one of the dogs barking outside startled her. She stared out the window and noticed them scratching on her husband's office door. She dismissed the commotion and went back to the sofa. The barking persisted and after calling them, she decided to see what was making them carry on.

The sky was clear and the three-quarter moon provided plenty of light for the short walk. The dogs ran to greet her, but then turned their attention back to the office door. She couldn't understand what they were so upset about; the building was locked and no one had been in there in days. She used to check his fax machine daily, but now found it too emotionally painful to do more than once a week. It really hadn't mattered; there had been very few communications since the fax from George Fall. Almost everyone associated with her husband knew he was missing and had stopped trying to reach him.

Taking the key out of her coat pocket, she unlocked the

door and went in. The dogs followed her, wanting to investigate. She turned on the light and found nothing out of order. She thought maybe an animal had gotten on the roof and made the dogs believe Guy was in there. They were used to being with him when he was home. No matter, after finding it empty, they seemed content to follow her back to the house.

Before leaving she decided to check his machine. To her surprise there was a fax, she picked it up and quickly scanned the short message. Suddenly she found it hard to swallow, as a lump developed in her throat and tears started to stream down her face. She couldn't believe what she was seeing as she dropped the message and turned to run back to the house, leaving the office door open and the dogs in hot pursuit. She needed to call her sons right away. They would need to pack. As the paper fell to its resting place on the wooden floor, the letterhead from the Hyatt Hotel, Cayman Islands contained eight words.

"I missed you all.
Come Join the Adventure."

~ ~ ~